*Tactical Exercise
& Other Late Stories*

EVELYN
WAUGH

*Tactical Exercise
& Other Late
Stories*

PENGUIN CLASSICS

Published by the Penguin Group
Penguin Books Ltd, 80 Strand, London WC2R ORL, England
Penguin Group (USA) Inc., 375 Hudson Street, New York, New York 10014, USA
Penguin Group (Canada), 90 Eglinton Avenue East, Suite 700, Toronto, Ontario,
Canada M4P 2Y3 (a division of Pearson Penguin Canada Inc.)
Penguin Ireland, 25 St Stephen's Green, Dublin 2, Ireland (a division of Penguin Books Ltd)
Penguin Group (Australia), 250 Camberwell Road, Camberwell, Victoria 3124, Australia
(a division of Pearson Australia Group Pty Ltd)
Penguin Books India Pvt Ltd, 11 Community Centre, Panchsheel Park,
New Delhi – 110 017, India
Penguin Group (NZ), 67 Apollo Drive, Rosedale, Auckland 0632, New Zealand
(a division of Pearson New Zealand Ltd)
Penguin Books (South Africa) (Pty) Ltd, 24 Sturdee Avenue,
Rosebank, Johannesburg 2196, South Africa

Penguin Books Ltd, Registered Offices: 80 Strand, London WC2R ORL, England

www.penguin.com

This selection published in Penguin Classics 2011

1

Copyright © The Estate of Laura Waugh, 2011
All rights reserved

The first publication details on p. 163 constitute an extension
of this copyright page

Set in 10.5/15pt Joanna MT Pro
Typeset by Jouve (UK), Milton Keynes
Text design by Claire Mason
Printed in Finland by Bookwell Ltd

Without limiting the rights under copyright
reserved above, no part of this publication may be
reproduced, stored in or introduced into a retrieval system,
or transmitted, in any form or by any means (electronic, mechanical,
photocopying, recording or otherwise), without the prior
written permission of both the copyright owner and
the above publisher of this book

A CIP catalogue record for this book is available from the British Library

ISBN: 978-0-141-19357-1

www.greenpenguin.co.uk

Penguin Books is committed to a sustainable
future for our business, our readers and our
planet. This book is made from paper certified
by the Forest Stewardship Council.

Contents

TACTICAL EXERCISE
& OTHER LATE STORIES

Work Suspended (1939)	3
Charles Ryder's Schooldays (1945)	129
Scott-King's Modern Europe (1946)	173
Tactical Exercise (1947)	251
Compassion (1949)	271
Love Among the Ruins: A Romance of the Near Future (1953)	309
Basil Seal Rides Again or The Rake's Regress (1963)	361
Details of First Publication	409

*TACTICAL EXERCISE
& OTHER LATE STORIES*

WORK SUSPENDED

Part One

A Death

I

At the time of my father's death I was in Morocco, at a small French hotel outside the fortifications of Fez. I had been there for six weeks, doing little else but write, and my book, Murder at Mountrichard Castle, was within twenty thousand words of its end. In three weeks I should pack it up for the typist; perhaps sooner, for I had nearly passed that heavy middle period where less conscientious writers introduce their second corpse. I was thirty-four years of age at the time, and a serious writer. I had always been a one-corpse man. I took pains with my work and I found it excellent. Each of my seven books sold better than its predecessor. Moreover, the sale was in their first three months, at seven and sixpence. I did not have to relabel the library edition for the bookstalls. People bought my books and kept them — not in the spare bedrooms but in the library, all seven of them together on a shelf. In six weeks' time, when my manuscript had been typed, revised and delivered, I should receive a cheque for something over nine hundred pounds. Had I wished it, I could have earned considerably more. I never tried to sell my stories as serials; the delicate fibres of a story suffer when it is chopped up into weekly or monthly parts and never completely heal. Often, when I have been reading the work of a competitor, I have said, 'She was writing with an eye on the magazines. She had to close this episode prematurely; she had to introduce that extraneous bit of melodrama, so as to make each instalment a readable unit. Well,' I would reflect, 'she has a husband to support and two sons at school. She must not expect to do two jobs well, to be a good mother and a good novelist.' I chose to live modestly on the royalties of my books.

I have never found economy the least irksome; on the contrary, I take pleasure in it. My friends, I know, considered me parsimonious; it was a joke among them, which I found quite inoffensive. My ambition was to eradicate money as much as I could from my life. I acquired as few possessions as possible. I preferred to pay interest to my bank rather than be bothered by tradesmen's bills. I decided what I wanted to do and then devised ways of doing it cheaply and tidily; money wasted meant more money to be earned. I disliked profusion.

I chose my career deliberately at the age of twenty-one. I had a naturally ingenious and constructive mind and the taste of writing. I was youthfully zealous of good fame. There seemed few ways of which a writer need not be ashamed by which he could make a decent living. To produce something, saleable in large quantities to the public, which had absolutely nothing of myself in it; to sell something for which the kind of people I liked and respected would have a use; that was what I sought, and detective stories fulfilled the purpose. They were an art which admitted of classical canons of technique and taste. It was immune, too, from the obnoxious comment to which lighter work is exposed: 'How you must revel in writing your delicious books, Mr So-and-so.' My friend, Roger Simmonds, who was with me at the University and set up as a professional humorist at the same time as I wrote *Vengeance at the Vatican*, was constantly plagued by that kind of remark. Instead, women said to me, 'How difficult it must be to think of all those complicated clues, Mr Plant.' I agreed. 'It *is*, intolerably difficult.' 'And do you do your writing here in London?' 'No, I find I have to go away to work.' 'Away from telephones and parties and things?' 'Exactly.'

I had tried a dozen or more retreats in England and abroad – country inns, furnished cottages, seaside hotels out of the season – Fez was by far the best of them. It is a splendid, compact city, and in early March, with flowers springing everywhere in the surrounding hills and in the untidy patios of the Arab houses, one of the most beautiful in the world. I liked the little hotel. It was cheap and rather chilly – an indispensable austerity. The food was digestible with, again, that element of sparseness which I find agreeable. I had an intermediate place between the semi-Egyptian splendours of the tourists' palace on the hill, and the bustling commercial hotels of the new town, half an hour's walk away. The clientele was exclusively French; the wives of civil servants and elderly couples of small means wintering in the sun. In the evening Spahi officers came to the bar to play bagatelle. I used to work on the verandah of my room, overlooking a ravine where Senegalese infantrymen were constantly washing their linen. My recreations were few and simple. Once a week after dinner I took the bus to the Moulay Abdullah; once a week I dined at the Consulate. The consul allowed me to come to him for a bath. I used to walk up, under the walls, swinging my sponge-bag through the dusk. He, his wife and their governess were the only English people I met; the only people, indeed, with whom I did more than exchange bare civilities. Sometimes I visited the native cinema where old, silent films were shown in a babel of catcalls. On other evenings I took a dose of Dial and was asleep by half-past nine. In these circumstances the book progressed well. I have since, on occasions, looked back at them with envy.

As an odd survival of the age of capitulations there was at that time a British Post Office at the Consulate, used mainly, the French believed, for treasonable purposes by disaffected Arabs. When there was anything for me the postman used to come down the hill on his bicycle to my hotel. He had a badge in his cap and on his arm a brassard with the royal escutcheon; he invariably honoured me with a stiff, military salute which increased my importance in the hotel at the expense of my reputation as an innocent and unofficial man of letters. It was this postman who brought the news of my father's death in a letter from my Uncle Andrew, his brother.

My father, it appeared, had been knocked down by a motor car more than a week ago and had died without regaining consciousness. I was his only child and, with the exception of my uncle, his only near relative. 'All arrangements' had been made. The funeral was taking place that day. 'In spite of your father's opinions, in the absence of any formal instructions to the contrary [my Uncle Andrew wrote] your Aunt and I thought it best to have a religious ceremony of an unostentatious kind.'

'He might have telegraphed,' I thought; and then, later, 'Why should he have?' There was no question of my having been able to see my father before he died; participation in a 'religious ceremony of an unostentatious kind' was neither in my line nor my father's; nor – to do him justice – in my Uncle Andrew's. It would satisfy the Jellabies.

With regard to the Jellabies my father always avowed a ruthlessness which he was far from practising; he would in fact put himself to considerable inconvenience to accommodate them, but in principle he abhorred any suggestion of discretion or solicitude. It was his belief that no one but himself dealt properly with servants. Two contrasted attitudes drove him to equal fury; what he called the 'pas-devant tomfoolery' of his childhood – the precept that scandal and the mention of exact sums of money should be hushed in their presence – and the more recent idea that their quarters should be prettily decorated and themselves given opportunity for cultural development. 'Jellaby has been with me twenty years,' he would say, 'and is fully cognisant of the facts of life. He and Mrs Jellaby know my income to the nearest shilling, and they know the full history of everyone who comes to this house. I pay them abominably and they supplement their wages by cooking the books. Servants prefer it that way. It preserves their independence and self-respect. The Jellabies eat continually, sleep with the windows shut, go to church every Sunday morning and to chapel in the evening, and entertain surreptitiously at my expense whenever I am out of the house. Jellaby's a teetotaller; Mrs Jellaby takes the port.' He rang the bell whenever he wanted anything fetched and sat as long as he wanted over his wine. 'Poor old Armstrong,' he used to say of a fellow Academician, 'lives like a Hottentot. He keeps a lot of twittering women like waitresses in a railway station buffet. After the first glass of port they open the dining-room door and stick their heads in. After the second glass they do it again. Then instead of throwing something at them, Armstrong says, "I think they want to clear," and we have to move out.'

But he had a warm affection for the Jellabies, and I believe it was largely on Mrs Jellaby's account that he allowed himself to be put up for the Academy. They, in their turn, served him faithfully. It would have been a cruel betrayal to deny them a funeral service, and I am sure my father had them in mind when he omitted any provision against it in his will. He was an exact man who would not have forgotten a point of that kind. On the other hand, he was a dogmatic atheist of the old-fashioned cast and would not have set anything down which might be construed as apostasy. He had left it to my Uncle Andrew's tact. No doubt, too, it was part of my uncle's tact to save me the embarrassment of being present.

II

I sat on my verandah for some time, smoking and considering the situation in its various aspects. There seemed no good reason for a change of plan. My Uncle Andrew would see to everything. The Jellabies would be provided for. Apart from them my father had no obligations. His affairs were always simple and in good order. The counterfoils of his cheques and his own excellent memory were his only account books; he had never owned any investments except the freehold of the house in St John's Wood, which he had bought with the small capital sum left him by his mother.

He lived up to his income and saved nothing. In him the parsimony which I had inherited took the form of a Gallic repugnance to paying direct taxes or, as he preferred it, to subscribing to 'the support of the politicians'. He had, moreover, the conviction that anything he put by would be filched by the Radicals. Lloyd George's ascent to power was the last contemporary event to impress him. Since then he believed, or professed to believe, that public life had become an open conspiracy for the destruction of himself and his class. This class, of which he considered himself the sole survivor, was for him the object of romantic loyalty; he spoke of it as a Jacobite clan proscribed and dispersed after Culloden, in a way which sometimes embarrassed those who did not know him well. 'We have been uprooted and harried,' he would say. 'There are only three classes in England now – politicians, tradesmen and slaves.' Then he would particularize. 'Seventy years ago the politicians and the tradesmen were in alliance; they destroyed the gentry by destroying the value of land; some of the gentry became politicians themselves, others tradesmen; out of what was left they created the new class into which I was born, the moneyless, landless, educated gentry who managed the country for them. My grandfather was a Canon of Christ Church, my father was in the Bengal Civil Service. All the capital they left their sons was education and moral principle. Now the politicians are in alliance with the slaves to destroy the tradesmen. They don't need to bother about us. We are extinct already. I am a Dodo,' he used to say, defiantly staring at his audience. 'You, my poor son, are a petrified egg.' There is a caricature of him by Max Beerbohm, in this posture, saying these words.

My choice of profession confirmed his view. 'Marjorie Steyle's boy works below the streets in a basement, selling haberdashery at four pounds a week. Dick Anderson has married his daughter to a grocer. My son John took a second in Mods and a first in Greats. He writes penny dreadfuls for a living,' he would say.

I always sent him my books, and I think he read them. 'At least your grammar is all right,' he once said. 'Your books will translate, and that's more than can be said for most of these fellows who set up to write Literature.' He had a naturally hierarchic mind, and in his scheme of things, detective stories stood slightly above the librettos of musical comedy and well below political journalism. I once showed him a reference to *Death in the Dukeries* by the Professor of Poetry, in which it was described as 'a work of art'. 'Anyone can buy a don,' was his only comment.

But he was gratified by my prosperity. 'Family love and financial dependence don't go together,' he said. 'My father made me an allowance of thirty shillings a week for the first three years I was in London, and he never forgave it me, *never*. He hadn't cost his father a penny after he took his degree. Nor had *his* father before him. You ran into debt at the University.

That was a thing I never did. It was two years before you were keeping yourself, and you went about as a dandy those two years, which I never did while I was learning to draw. But you've done very well. No nonsense about Literature. You've cut out quite a line for yourself. I saw old Etheridge at the club the other evening. He reads all your books, he told me, and likes 'em. Poor old Etheridge; he brought his boy up to be a barrister and he still has to keep him at the age of thirty-seven.'

My father seldom referred to his contemporaries without the epithet 'old' – usually as 'poor old so-and-so', unless they had prospered conspicuously when they were 'that old humbug'. On the other hand, he spoke of men a few years his juniors as 'whipper-snappers' and 'young puppies'. The truth was that he could not bear to think of anyone as being the same age as himself. It was all part of the aloofness that was his dominant concern in life. It was enough for him to learn that an opinion of his had popular support for him to question and abandon it. His atheism was his response to the simple piety and confused agnosticism of his family circle. He never came to hear much about Marxism; had he done so he would, I am sure, have discovered a number of proofs of the existence of God. In his later years I observed two reversions of opinion in reaction to contemporary fashion. In my boyhood, in the time of their Edwardian popularity, he denounced the Jews roundly on all occasions, and later attributed to them the vogue of post-impressionist painting:

'There was a poor booby called Cézanne, a kind of village idiot who was given a box of paints to keep him quiet. He very properly left his horrible canvases behind him in the hedges. The Jews discovered him and crept round behind him picking them up – just to get something for nothing. Then when he was safely dead and couldn't share in the profits they hired a lot of mercenary lunatics to write him up. They've made thousands out of it.' To the last he maintained that Dreyfus had been guilty, but when, in the early thirties, anti-Semitism showed signs of becoming a popular force, he supported the Jewish cause in many unpublished letters to *The Times*.

Similarly he was used once to profess an esteem for Roman Catholics. 'Their religious opinions are preposterous,' he said. 'But so were those of the ancient Greeks. Think of Socrates spending half his last evening babbling about the topography of the nether world. Grant them their first absurdities and you will find Roman Catholics a reasonable people – and they have civilized habits.' Later, however, when he saw signs of this view gaining acceptance, he became convinced of the existence of a Jesuit conspiracy to embroil the world in war, and wrote several letters to *The Times* on the subject; they, too, were unpublished. But in neither of these periods did his opinions greatly affect his personal relations; Jews and Catholics were among his closest friends all his life.

My father dressed as he thought a painter should, in a

distinct and recognizable garb which made him a familiar and, in his later years, a venerable figure as he took his exercise in the streets round his house. There was no element of ostentation in his poncho capes, check suits, sombrero hats and stock ties. It was rather that he thought it fitting for a man to proclaim unequivocally his station in life, and despised those of his colleagues who seemed to be passing themselves off as guardsmen and stockbrokers. In general he liked his fellow Academicians, though I never heard him express anything but contempt for their work. He regarded the Academy as a club; he enjoyed the dinners and frequently attended the schools, where he was able to state his views on art in Johnsonian terms. He never doubted that the function of painting was representational. He criticized his colleagues for such faults as innocent anatomy, 'triviality' and 'insincerity'. For this he was loosely spoken of as a conservative, but that he never was where his art was concerned. He abominated the standards of his youth. He must have been an intransigently old-fashioned young man, for he was brought up in the hey-day of Whistlerian decorative painting, and his first exhibited work was of a balloon ascent in Manchester — a large canvas crowded with human drama, in the manner of Frith. His practice was chiefly in portraits — many of them posthumous — for presentation to colleges and guildhalls. He seldom succeeded with women, whom he endowed with a statuesque absurdity which was half deliberate, but given the robes of a Doctor of Music or a Knight of Malta he would do something fit to hang with the best panelling in the country; given some whiskers he was a master. 'As a young man I specialized in hair,' he would say, rather as a doctor might say he specialized in noses and throats. 'I paint it incomparably. Nowadays nobody has any to paint,' and it was this aptitude of his which led him to the long, increasingly unsaleable series of historical and scriptural groups, and the scenes of domestic melodrama by which he is known — subjects which had already become slightly ludicrous when he was in his cradle, but which he continued to produce year after year while experimental painters came and went until, right at the end of his life, he suddenly, without realizing it, found himself in the fashion. The first sign of this was in 1935, when his 'Agag before Samuel' was bought at a provincial exhibition for 750 guineas. It was a large canvas at which he had been at work intermittently since 1908. Even he spoke of it, with conscious understatement, as 'something of a white elephant'. White elephants indeed were almost the sole species of four-footed animal that was not somewhere worked into this elaborate composition. When asked why he had introduced such a variety of fauna, he replied, 'I'm sick of Samuel. I've lived with him for twenty years. Every time it comes back from an exhibition I paint out an Israelite and put in an animal. If I live long enough I'll have a Noah's ark in its background.'

The purchaser of this work was Sir Lionel Sterne.

'Honest Sir Lionel,' said my father, as he saw the great canvas packed off to Kensington Palace Gardens, 'I should dearly have liked to shake his hairy paw. I can see him well – a fine, meaty fellow with a great gold watch-chain across his belly, who's been decently employed boiling soap or smelting copper all his life, with no time to read Clive Bell. In every age it has been men like him who kept painting alive.'

I tried to explain that Lionel Sterne was the youthful and elegant millionaire who for ten years had been a leader of aesthetic fashion. 'Nonsense!' said my father. 'Fellows like that collect disjointed Negresses by Gauguin. Only Philistines like my work and, by God, I like only Philistines.'

There was also another, rather less reputable side to my father's business. He received a regular yearly retaining fee from Goodchild and Godley, the Duke Street dealers, for what was called 'restoration'. This sum was a very important part of his income; without it the comfortable little dinners, the trips abroad, the cabs to and fro, between St John's Wood and the Athenaeum, the faithful, predatory Jellabies, the orchid in his buttonhole – all the substantial comforts and refinements which endeared the world and provided him with his air of gentlemanly ease – would have been impossible to him. The truth was that, while excelling at Lely, my father could paint, very passably, in the manner of almost any of the masters of English portraiture, and the private and public collections of the New World were richly representative of his versatility. Very few of his friends knew this traffic; to those who did, he defended it with complete candour. 'Goodchild & Godley buy these pictures for what they are – my own work. They pay me no more than my dexterity merits. What they do with them afterwards is their own business. It would ill become me to go officiously about the markets identifying my own handicraft and upsetting a number of perfectly contented people. It is a great deal better for them to look at beautiful pictures and enjoy them under a misconception about the date, than to make themselves dizzy by goggling at genuine Picassos.'

It was largely on account of his work for Goodchild and Godley that his studio was strictly reserved as a workshop. It was a separate building approached through the garden, and it was excluded from general use. Once a year, when he went abroad, it was 'done out'; once a year, on the Sunday before sending-in day at the Royal Academy, it was open to his friends.

He took a peculiar relish in the gloom of these annual tea-parties, and was at the same pains to make them dismal as he was to enliven his other entertainments. There was a species of dry bright-yellow caraway cake which was known to my childhood as 'Academy cake', and appeared then and only then, from a grocer in Praed Street; there was an enormous Worcester tea service – a wedding present – which was known as 'Academy cups'; there were 'Academy sandwiches' – tiny, triangular and quite tasteless. All these things were part of my earliest memories. I do not know at what date these parties changed from a rather tedious convention to what they certainly were to my father at the end of his life, a huge, grim and solitary jest. If I was in England I was required to attend and to bring a friend or two. It was difficult, until the last two years when, as I have said, my father became the object of fashionable interest, to collect guests. 'When I was a young man,' my father said, sardonically surveying the company, 'there were twenty or more of these parties in St John's Wood alone. People of culture drove round from three in the afternoon to six, from Campden Hill to Hampstead. Today I believe our little gathering is the sole survivor of that deleterious tradition.'

On these occasions his year's work – Goodchild & Godley's items excepted – would be ranged round the studio on mahogany easels; the most important work had a wall to itself against a background of scarlet rep. I had been present at the last of the parties the year before. Lionel Sterne was there with Lady Metroland and a dozen fashionable connoisseurs. My father was at first rather suspicious of his new clients and suspected an impertinent intrusion into his own private joke, a calling of his bluff of seedcake and cress-sandwiches; but their commissions reassured him. People did not carry a joke to such extravagant lengths. Mrs Algernon

Stitch paid 500 guineas for his picture of the year – a tableau of contemporary life conceived and painted with elaborate mastery. My father attached great importance to suitable titles for his work, and after toying with 'The People's Idol', 'Feet of Clay', 'Not on the First Night', 'Their Night of Triumph', 'Success and Failure', 'Not Invited', 'Also Present', he finally called this picture rather enigmatically 'The Neglected Cue'. It represented the dressing room of a leading actress at the close of a triumphant first night. She sat at the dressing-table, her back turned on the company, and her face visible in the mirror, momentarily relaxed in fatigue. Her protector with proprietary swagger was filling the glasses for a circle of admirers. In the background the dresser was in colloquy at the half-open door with an elderly couple of provincial appearance; it is evident from their costume that they have seen the piece from the cheaper seats, and a commissionaire stands behind them uncertain whether he did right in admitting them. He did not do right; they are her old parents arriving most inopportunely. There was no questioning Mrs Stitch's rapturous enjoyment of her acquisition.

I was never to know how my father would react to his vogue. He could paint in any way he chose; perhaps he would have embarked on those vague assemblages of picnic litter which used to cover the walls of the Mansard Gallery in the early twenties; he might have retreated to the standards of the Grosvenor Gallery in the nineties. He might, perhaps, have found popularity less inacceptable than he supposed and allowed himself a luxurious and cosseted old age. He died with his 1939 picture still unfinished. I saw its early stage on my last visit to him; it was to have been called 'Again?' and represented a one-armed veteran of the First World War meditating over a German helmet. My father had given the man a grizzled beard and was revelling in it. That was the last time I saw him.

I had given up living in St John's Wood for four or five years. There was never a definite moment when I 'left home'. For all official purposes the house remained my domicile. There was a bedroom that was known as mine; I kept several trunks full of clothes there and a shelf or two of books. I never set up for myself anywhere else, but during the last five years of my father's life I do not suppose I slept ten nights under his roof. This was not due to any estrangement. I enjoyed his company, and he seemed to enjoy mine, but I was never in London for more than a week or two at a time, and I found that as an occasional visitor I strained and upset my father's household. He and they tried to do too much, and he liked to have his plans clear for some way ahead. 'My dear boy,' he would say on my first evening, 'Please do not misunderstand me. I hope you will stay as long as you possibly can, but I do wish to know whether you will still be here on Thursday the fourteenth, and if so, whether you will be in to dinner.' So I took to staying at my club or with more casual hosts, and to visiting St John's Wood as often as I could, but with formal pre-arrangements.

Nevertheless, I realized, the house had been an important part of my life. It had remained unaltered for as long as I could remember. It was a decent house, built in 1840 or thereabouts, in the contemporary Swiss mode of stucco and ornamental weather boards, one of a street of similar, detached houses when I first saw it. By the time of my father's death the transformation of the district, though not complete, was painfully evident. The skyline of the garden was broken on three sides by blocks of flats. The first of them drove my father into a frenzy of indignation. He wrote to *The Times* about it, addressed a meeting of ratepayers, and for six weeks sported a board advertising the house for sale. At the end of that time he received a liberal offer from the syndicate, who wished to extend their block over the site, and he immediately withdrew it from the market.

This was the period of his lowest professional fortunes, when his subject-pictures remained unsold, the market for dubious old masters was dropping, and public bodies were beginning to look for something 'modern' in their memorial portraits; the period, moreover, when I had finished with the University and was still dependent on my father for pocket money. It was a very unsatisfactory time in his life. I had not then learned to appreciate the massive defences of what people call the 'border line of sanity', and I was at moments genuinely afraid that my father was going out of his mind; there had always seemed an element of persecution-mania about his foibles which might, at a time of great strain, go beyond his control. He used to stand on the opposite pavement watching the new building rise, a conspicuous figure muttering objurgations. I used to imagine scenes in which a policeman would ask him to move on and be met with a wild outburst. I imagined these scenes vividly – my father in swirling cape being hustled off, waving his umbrella. Nothing of the kind occurred. My father, for all his oddity, was a man of indestructible sanity, and in his later years he found a keen pleasure in contemplating the rapid deterioration of the hated buildings. 'Very good news of Hill Crest Court,' he announced one day. 'Typhoid and rats.' And on another occasion. 'Jellaby reports the presence of prostitutes at St Eustace's. They'll have a suicide there soon, you'll see.' There was a suicide, and for two rapturous days my father watched the coming and going of police and journalists. After that fewer chintz curtains were visible in the windows, rents began to fall and the lift-man smoked on duty. My father observed and gleefully noted all these signs. Hill Crest Court changed hands; decorators', plumbers' and electricians' boards appeared all round it; a commissionaire with a new uniform stood at the doors. On the last evening I dined with my father he told me about a visit he had made there, posing as a potential tenant. 'The place is a deserted slum,' he said. 'A miserable, down-at-heel kind of secretary took me round flat after flat — all empty. There were great cracks in the concrete stuffed up with putty. The hot pipes were cold. The doors jammed. He started asking three hundred pounds a year for the best of them, and dropped to one hundred and seventy-five pounds before I saw the kitchen. Then he made it one hundred and fifty pounds. In the end he proposed what he called a "special form of tenancy for people of good social position" — offered to let me live there for a pound a week on condition I turned out if he found someone who was willing to pay the real rent. "Strictly between ourselves," he said, "I can promise you will not be disturbed." Poor beast, I nearly took his flat, he was so paintable.'

Now, I supposed, the house would be sold; another speculator would pull it to pieces; another great, uninhabitable barrack would appear, like a refugee ship in harbour; it would be filled, sold, emptied, resold, refilled, re-emptied, while the concrete got discoloured and the green wood shrank, and the rats crept up in their thousands out of the Metropolitan Railway tunnel: and the trees and gardens all round it disappeared one by one until the place became a working-class district and at last took on a gaiety and life of some sort; until it was condemned by government inspectors and its inhabitants driven further into the country and the process began all over again. I thought of all this, sadly, as I looked out at the fine masonry of Fez, cut four hundred years back by Portuguese prisoners ... I must go back to England soon to arrange for the destruction of my father's house. Meanwhile there seemed no reason for an immediate change of plan.

III

It was the evening when I usually visited the Moulay Abdullah — the walled *quartier toléré* between the old city and the ghetto. I had gone there first with a sense of adventure; now it had become part of my routine, a regular resort, like the cinema and the Consulate, one of the recreations which gave incident to my week and helped clear my mind of the elaborate villainies of Lady Mountrichard.

I dined at seven and soon afterwards caught my bus at the new gate. Before starting I removed my watch and emptied my pockets of all except the few francs which I proposed to spend — a superstitious precaution which still survived from the first evening, when memories of Marseilles and Naples had even moved me to carry a life-preserver. The Moulay Abdullah was an orderly place, particularly in the early evening when I frequented it. I had formed an attachment for this sole place of its kind which endowed its trade with something approaching glamour. There really was a memory of 'the East', as adolescents imagine it, in that silent courtyard with its single light, the Negro sentries on either side of the lofty Moorish arch, the black lane beyond, between the walls and the water-wheel, full of the thump and stumble of French military boots and the soft pad and rustle of the natives, the second arch into the lighted bazaar, the bright open doors and the tiled patios, the little one-roomed huts where the women stood against the lamplight – shadows without race or age – the larger houses with their bars and gramophones.

I always visited the same house and the same girl – a chubby little Berber with the scarred cheeks of her people and tattooed ornaments, blue on brown, at her forehead and throat. She spoke the peculiar French which she had picked up from the soldiers, and she went by the unassuming, professional name of Fatima. Other girls of the place called themselves 'Lola' and 'Fifi'; there was even an arrogant, coal-black Sudanese named 'Whiskey-soda'. But Fatima had none of these airs; she was a cheerful, affectionate girl working hard to collect her marriage dot; she professed to like everyone in the house, even the proprietress, a forbidding Levantine from Tetuan, and the proprietress's Algerian husband, who wore a European suit, carried round the mint tea, put records on the gramophone and collected the money. (The Moors are a strict people and take no share in the profits of the Moulay Abdullah.)

To regular and serious customers it was an inexpensive place – fifteen francs to the house, ten to Fatima, five for the mint tea, a few sous to the old fellow who tidied Fatima's alcove and blew up the brazier of sweet gum. Soldiers paid less, but they had to make way for more important customers; often they were penniless men from the Foreign Legion who dropped in merely to hear the music and left nothing behind them but cigarette ends. Now and then tourists appeared with a guide from the big hotel, and the girls were made to line up and give a performance of shuffling and hand clapping which was called a native dance. Women tourists particularly seemed to like these expeditions and paid heavily for them – a hundred francs or more. But they were unpopular with everyone, particularly with the girls, who regarded it as an unseemly proceeding. Once I came in when Fatima was taking part in one of these dances and saw her genuinely and deeply abashed.

On my visit I told Fatima that I had a wife and six children in England; this greatly enhanced my importance in her eyes and she always asked after them.

'You have had a letter from England? The little ones are well?'

'They are very well.'

'And your father and mother?'

'They, too.'

We sat in a tiled hall, two steps below street level, drinking our mint tea – or, rather, Fatima drank hers while I let mine cool in the glass. It was a noisome beverage.

'Whiskey-soda lent me some cigarettes yesterday. Will you give her them?'

I ordered a packet from the bar.

'Yesterday I had a stomach-ache and stayed in my room. That is why Whiskey-soda gave me her cigarettes.'

She asked about my business.

I had told her I exported dates.

The date market was steady, I assured her.

When I was in the Moulay Abdullah I almost believed in this aspect of myself as a philoprogenitive fruiterer; St John's Wood and Mountrichard Castle seemed equally remote. That was the charm of the quarter for me – not its simple pleasures but its privacy and anonymity, the hide-and-seek with one's own personality which redeems vice of its tedium.

That night there was a rude interruption. The gramophone suddenly stopped playing; there was a scuttling among the alcoves; two seedy figures in raincoats strode across the room and began questioning the proprietress; a guard of military police stood at the street door.

Raids of this kind, to round up bad characters, are common enough in French Protectorates. It was the first time I had been caught in one. The girls were made to stand along one wall while the detectives checked their medical certificates. Then two or three soldiers stood to attention and gave a satisfactory account of themselves. Then I was asked for my *carte d'identité*. By the capitulations the French police had little authority over British subjects, and since the criminal class of Morocco mostly possessed Maltese papers, this immunity was good ground for vexation. The detectives were surly fellows, African born. Even the sacred word 'tourist' failed to soften them. Where was my guide? Tourists did not visit the Moulay Abdullah alone. Where was my passport? At my hotel. The Jamai Palace No? Tourists did not stay at the hotel I mentioned. Was I registered at the police headquarters? Yes. Very well, I must come with them. In the morning I should have the opportunity to identify myself. A hundred francs, no doubt, would have established my respectability, but my money lay with my passport in the hotel. I did not relish a night in gaol in company with the paperless characters of the Moulay Abdullah. I told them I was a friend of the British Consul. He would vouch for me. They grumbled that they had no time for special inquiries of that kind. The Chief would see about it next morning. Then when I had despaired, they despaired too. There was clearly no money coming for them. They had been in the profession long enough to know that no lasting satisfaction results from vexing British subjects. There was a police post in the quarter and they consented to telephone from it. A few minutes later I was set at liberty with a curt reminder that it was advisable to keep my passport accessible if I wanted to wander about the town at night.

I did not return to Fatima. Instead I set off for the bus stop, but the annoyances of the night were not yet over. I was halted again at the gates and the interrogation was repeated. I explained that I had already satisfied their colleagues and had been discharged. We re-enacted the scene, with the fading hope of a tip as the recurring motive. Finally they, too, telephoned to the Consulate, and I was free to take my bus home.

They were still serving dinner at the hotel; the same game of billiards was in progress in the bar; it was less than an hour since I went out. But that hour had been decisive; I was finished with Fez; its privacy had been violated. My weekly visit to the Consulate could never be repeated on the same terms. Twice in twenty minutes the Consul had been called to the telephone to learn that I was in the hands of the police in the Moulay Abdullah; he would not, I thought, be censorious or resentful; the vexation had been mild and the situation slightly absurd — nothing more; but when we next met our relations would be changed. Till then they had been serenely remote; we had talked of the news from England and the Moorish antiquities. We had exposed the bare minimum of ourselves; now a sudden, mutually unwelcome confidence had been forced. The bitterness lay, not in the Consul's knowing the fact of my private recreations, but in his knowing that I knew he knew. It was a salient in the defensive line between us that could only be made safe by a wide rectification of frontier or by a complete evacuation. I had no friendly territory into which to withdraw. I was deployed on the dunes between the sea and the foothills. The transports riding at anchor were my sole lines of support.

In the matter of Good Conscience, I was a man of few possessions, and held them at a corresponding value. As a spinster in mean lodgings fusses over her fragments of gentility – a rosewood work-box, a Spode plate, a crested tea-kettle – which in a house of abundance would be risked in the rough and tumble of general use, I set a price on Modesty which those of ampler virtues might justly regard as fanciful.

Next day I set off for London with my book unfinished.

IV

I travelled from spring into winter; sunlit spray in the Straits of Gibraltar changed to dark, heavy seas in the Bay of Biscay; fog off Finisterre, fog in the Channel, clear grey weather in the Thames estuary and a horizon of factories and naked trees. We berthed in London and I drove through cold and dirty streets to meet my Uncle Andrew.

He told me the full circumstances of my father's death; the commercial traveller, against whom a case was being brought for reckless driving, had outraged my uncle by sending a wreath of flowers to the funeral; apart from this everything had been satisfactory. My uncle passed over to me the undertaker's receipted account; he had questioned one or two of the items and obtained an inconsiderable reduction. 'I am convinced,' my uncle said, 'that there is a great deal of sharp practice among these people. They trade upon the popular conception of delicacy. In fact they are the only profession who literally rob the widow and the orphan.' I thanked my uncle for having saved me £3 18s. It was a matter of principle, he said.

As I expected, I was my father's sole heir. Besides the house and its contents I inherited £2,000 in an insurance policy which my father had taken out at the time of his marriage and, without my knowledge, kept up ever since. An injunction, in the brief will, to 'provide suitably' for the servants in my father's employment, had already been obeyed. The Jellabies had been given £250. It was clear from my father's words that he had no conception of what a suitable provision should be. Neither had I, and I was grateful to my uncle for taking responsibility in the matter. For their part the Jellabies had expected nothing. My father, as long ago as I could remember him, was accustomed to talk with relish of his approaching death. I had heard him often admonish Jellaby: 'You have joined fortune with a poor man. Make what you can while I still have my faculties. My death will be an occasion for unrelieved lamentation,' and the Jellabies, in the manner of their kind, took his words literally, kept a keen watch on all sources of perquisite, and expected nothing.

Jellaby took his cheque, my uncle said, without any demonstration of gratitude or disappointment, murmuring ungraciously that it would come in quite useful. No doubt he thought no thanks were due to my uncle, for it was not his money; nor to my father, for it was no intention of his to give it. It was a last, substantial perquisite.

The Jellabies had been much in my mind, off and on, during the journey from Fez. I had fretted, in a way I have, imagining our meeting and a scene of embarrassing condolence and reminiscence, questioning the propriety of removing them immediately, if ever, from the place where they had spent so much of their lives; I even saw myself, on the Jellabies' account, assuming my father's way of life, settling in St John's Wood, entertaining small dinner parties, lunching regularly at my club and taking three weeks' holiday abroad in the early summer. As things turned out, however, I never saw the Jellabies again. They had done their packing before the funeral, and went straight to the railway station in their black clothes. Their plans had been laid years in advance. They had put away a fair sum and invested it in Portsmouth, not, as would have been conventional, in a lodging-house, but in a shop in a poor quarter of the town which enjoyed a trade in second-hand wireless apparatus. Mrs Jellaby's stepbrother had been keeping the business warm for them, and there they retired with an alacrity which was slightly shocking but highly convenient. I wrote to them some time later when I was going through my father's possessions, to ask if they would like to have some small personal memento of him; they might value one of his sketches, I suggested, for the walls of their new home. The answer took some time in coming. When it came it was on a sheet of trade-paper with a printed heading: '*T. Jellaby. Every Radio want promptly supplied for cash.*' Mrs Jellaby wrote the letter. They had not much room for pictures, she said, but would greatly appreciate some blankets, as it was chilly at nights in Portsmouth; she specified a particular pair which my father had bought shortly before his death; they were lying, folded, in the hot cupboard . . .

Uncle Andrew gave me the keys of my father's house. I went straight there from lunching with him. The shutters were up and the curtains drawn; the water and electric light were already cut off; all this my uncle had accomplished in a few days. I stumbled among sheeted furniture to the windows and let in the daylight. I went from room to room in this way. The place still retained its own smell – an agreeable, rather stuffy atmosphere of cigar smoke and cantaloup; a masculine smell – women had always seemed a little out of place there, as in a London club on Coronation Day.

The house was sombre, but never positively shabby, so that, I suppose, various imperceptible renovations and replacements must have occurred from time to time. It looked what it was, the house of an unfashionable artist of the 1880s. The curtains and chair-covers were of indestructible Morris tapestry; there were Dutch tiles round the fireplaces; Levantine rugs on the floors; on the walls Arundel prints, photographs from the old masters, and majolica dishes. The furniture, now shrouded, had the inimitable air of having been in the same place for a generation; it was a harmonious, unobstructive jumble of inherited rosewood and mahogany, and of inexpensive collected pieces of carved German oak, Spanish walnut, English chests and dressers, copper ewers and brass candlesticks. Every object was familiar and yet so much a part of its surroundings that later, when they came to be moved, I found a number of things which I barely recognized. Books of an antiquated sort were all over the house in a variety of hanging, standing and revolving shelves.

I opened the french windows in my father's study and stepped down into the garden. There was little of spring to be seen here. The two plane trees were bare; under the sooty laurels last year's leaves lay rotting. It was never a garden of any character. Once, before the flats came, we used to dine there sometimes, in extreme discomfort under the catalpa tree; for years now it had been a no-man's land, isolating the studio at the farther end; on one side, behind a trellis, were some neglected frames and beds where my father had once tried to raise French vegetables. The mottled concrete of the flats, with its soil-pipes and fire-escapes and its rash of ironframed casement windows, shut out half the sky. The tenants of these flats were forbidden, in their leases, to do their laundry, but the owners had long since despaired of a genteel appearance, and you could tell which of the rooms were occupied by the stockings hanging to dry along the windowsills.

In his death my father's privacy was still respected, and no one had laid dust-sheets in the studio. 'Again?' stood as he had left it on the easel. More than half was finished. My father made copious and elaborate studies for his pictures and worked quickly when he came to their final stage, painting over a monochrome sketch, methodically, in fine detail, left to right across the canvas as though he were lifting the backing of a child's 'transfer'. 'Do your thinking first,' he used to tell the Academy students. 'Don't muddle it out on the canvas. Have the whole composition clear in your head before you start,' and if anyone objected that this was seldom the method of the greatest masters, he would say, 'You're here to become Royal Academicians, not great masters. If you want to write books on Art, trot round Europe studying the Rubenses. If you want to learn to paint, watch me.' The four or five square feet of finished painting were a monument of my father's art. There had been a time when I had scant respect for it. Lately I had come to see that it was more than a mere matter of dexterity and resolution. He had an historic position, for he completed a period of English painting that through other circumstances had never, until him, come to maturity. Phrases, as though for an obituary article, came to my mind: '... fulfilling the broken promise of the young Millais...Winterhalter suffused with the spirit of Dickens... English painting as it might have been, had there not been any Aesthetic Movement...' and with the phrases my esteem for my father took form and my sense of loss became tangible and permanent.

No good comes of this dependence on verbal forms. It saves nothing in the end. Suffering is none the less acute and much more lasting when it is put into words. In the house my memories had been all of myself – of the countless home-comings and departures of thirty-three years, of adolescence like a stained tablecloth – but in the studio my thoughts were of my father and grief, nearly a week delayed, overtook and overwhelmed me. It had been delayed somewhat by the strangeness of my surroundings and the business of travel, but most by this literary habit; it had lacked words. Now the words came; I began, in my mind, to lament my father, addressing, as it were, funeral orations to my own literary memories, and sorrow, dammed and canalized, flowed fast.

For the civilized man there are none of those swift transitions of joy and pain which possess the savage; words form slowly like pus about his hurts; there are no clean wounds for him; first a numbness, then a long festering, then a scar ever ready to re-open. Not until they have assumed the livery of the defence can his emotions pass through the lines; sometimes they come massed in a wooden horse, sometimes as single spies, but there is always a Fifth Column among the garrison ready to receive them. Sabotage behind the lines, a blind raised and lowered at a lighted window, a wire cut, a bolt loosened, a file disordered – that is how the civilized man is undone.

I returned to the house and darkened the rooms once more, relaid the dust-sheets I had lifted, and left everything as it had been.

V

The manuscript of *Murder at Mountrichard Castle* lay on the chest of drawers in my club bedroom, reproaching me morning, evening and night. It was promised for publication in June, and I had never before disappointed my publishers. This year, however, I should have to ask grace for a postponement. I made two attemps at it, bearing the pile of foolscap to an upper room of the club which was known as the library and used by the older members for sleeping between luncheon and tea. But I found it impossible to take up the story with any interest; so I went to my publishers and tried to explain.

'I have been writing for over eight years,' I said, 'and am nearing a climacteric.'

'I don't quite follow,' said Mr Benwell anxiously.

'I mean a turning point in my career.'

'Oh, dear, I hope you're not thinking of making a contract elsewhere?'

'No, no. I mean that I feel in danger of turning into a stock best-seller.'

'If I may say so, in very imminent danger,' said Benwell, and he made a kind of little bow from the seat of his swivel chair and smirked in the wry fashion people sometimes assume when they feel they have said something elaborately polite; a smile normally kept for his women writers; the word 'climacteric' had clearly upset him.

'I mean, I am in danger of becoming purely a technical expert. Take my father . . .' Mr Benwell gave a deferential grunt and quickly changed his expression to one of gravity suitable to the mention of someone recently dead. 'He spent his whole life perfecting his technique. It seems to me I am in danger of becoming mechanical, turning out year after year the kind of book I know I can write well. I feel I have got as good as I ever can be at this particular sort of writing. I need new worlds to conquer.' I added this last remark in compassion for Mr Benwell, whose gravity had deepened to genuine concern. I believed he would feel the easier for a little facetiousness — erroneously, for Mr Benwell had suffered similar, too serious conversations with other writers than me.

'You've not been writing *poetry* in Morocco?'

'No, no.'

'Sooner or later almost all my novelists come to me and say they have written poetry. I can't think why. It does them infinite harm. Only last week Roger Simmonds was here with a kind of play. You never saw such a thing. All the characters were parts of a motor-car – not in the least funny.'

'Oh, it won't be anything like that,' I said. 'Just some new technical experiments. I don't suppose the average reader will notice them at all.'

'I hope not,' said Mr Benwell. 'I mean, now you've found your public . . . well, look at Simmonds.'

I knew what he was thinking: 'The trouble about Plant is, he's come in for money.'

In a way he was right. The money my father had left me, and the proceeds which I expected from the sale of the house, relieved me of the need to work for two or three years; it was a matter of pure athletics to go on doing something merely because one did it well. The heap of foolscap began to disgust me. Twice I hid it under my shirts, twice the club valet unearthed it and laid it in the open. I had nowhere to keep things, except in this little hired room above the traffic.

This sense of homelessness was new to me. Before I had moved constantly from one place to another; every few weeks I would descend upon St John's Wood with a trunk, leave some books, collect others, put away summer clothes for the winter; seldom as I slept there, the house in St John's Wood had been my headquarters and my home; that earth had now been stopped, and I thought, not far away, I could hear the hounds.

My worries at this period became symbolized in a single problem; what to do with my hats. I owned what now seemed a multitude of them, of one sort and another; two of them of silk – the tall hat I took to weddings and a second I had bought some years earlier when I thought for a time that I was going to take to fox-hunting; there were a bowler, a panama, a black, a brown and a grey soft hat, a green hat from Salzburg, a sombrero, some tweed caps for use on board ship and in trains – all these had accumulated from time to time and all, with the possible exception of the sombrero, were more or less indispensable. Was I doomed for the rest of my life to travel everywhere with this preposterous collection? At the moment they were, most of them, in St John's Wood, but, any day now, the negotiations for the sale might be finished and the furniture removed, sold or sent to store.

Somewhere to hang up my hat, that was what I needed.

I consulted Roger Simmonds, who was lunching with me. I felt as though I had known Roger all my life; actually I had first met him in our second year at Oxford; we edited an undergraduate weekly together, and had been close associates ever since. He was one of the very few people I corresponded with when I was away; we met often when I was in London. Sometimes I even stayed with him, for he and half a dozen others constituted a kind of set. We had all known each other intimately over a number of years, had from time to time passed on girls from one to the other, borrowed and lent freely. When we were together we drank more and talked more boastfully than we normally did. We had grown rather to dislike one another; certainly when any two or three of us were alone we blackguarded the rest, and if asked about them on neutral ground I denied their friendship. About Roger I used to say, 'I don't think he's interested in anything except politics now.'

This was more or less true. In the late twenties he set up as a writer and published some genuinely funny novels on the strength of which he filled a succession of jobs with newspapers and film companies, but lately he had married an unknown heiress, joined the Socialist Party, and become generally conventional.

'I never wear a hat now I am married,' said Roger virtuously. 'Lucy says they're *kulak*. Besides, I was beginning to lose my hair.'

'My dear Roger, you've been bald as a coot for ten years. But it isn't only a question of hats. There are overcoats.'

'Only in front. It's as thick as anything at the back. How many overcoats have you got?'

'Four, I think.'

'Too many.'

We discussed it at length and decided it was possible to manage with three.

'Workers pawn their overcoats in June and take them out again in October,' Roger said. He wanted to talk about his play, *Internal Combustion*. 'The usual trouble with ideological drama,' he said, 'is that they're too mechanical. I mean the characters are economic types, not individuals, and as long as they look and speak like individuals it's bad art. D'you see what I mean?'

'I do, indeed.'

'Human beings without human interest.'

'Very true. I . . .'

'Well, I've cut human beings out altogether.'

'Sounds rather like an old-fashioned ballet.'

'*Exactly*,' Roger said with great pleasure. 'It *is* an old-fashioned ballet. I knew you'd understand. Poor old Benwell couldn't. The Finsbury International Theatre are sitting on it now, and if it's orthodox – and I *think* it is – they may put it on this summer if Lucy finds the money.'

'Is she keen, too?'

'Well, not very, as a matter of fact. You see, she's having a baby, and that seems to keep her interested at the moment.'

'But to return to the question of my hats . . .'

'I tell you what. Why don't you buy a nice quiet house in

the country? I shall want somewhere to stay while this baby is born.'

There was the rub. It was precisely this fear that had been working in my mind for days, the fear of making myself a sitting shot to the world. It lay at the root of the problem of privacy; the choice which torments to the verge of mania, between perpetual flight and perpetual siege; and the unresolved universal paradox of losing things in order to find them.

'Surely that is odd advice from a Socialist?'

Roger became suddenly wary; he had been caught and challenged in loose talk. 'Ideally, of course, it would be,' he said. 'But I dare say that in practice, for the first generation, we shall allow a certain amount of private property where its value is purely sentimental. Anyway, any investment you make now is bound to be temporary. That's why I feel no repugnance about living on Lucy's money . . .' Marxist ethics kept him talking until we had finished luncheon. Over the coffee he referred to Ingres as a 'bourgeois' painter. When he left me I sat for some time in the leather armchair finishing my cigar. The club was emptying as the younger members went back to their work and their elders padded off to the library for the afternoon nap. I belonged to neither world. I had nothing whatever to do. At three in the afternoon my friends would all be busy and, in any case, I did not want to see them. I was ready for a new deal. I climbed to my room, began re-reading the early chapters of *Murder at*

Mountrichard Castle, put it from me and faced the boredom of an afternoon in London. Then the telephone rang and the porter said, 'Mr Thurston is downstairs to see you.'

'Who?'

'Mr Thurston. He says he has an appointment.'

'I don't know anything about him. Will you ask what he wants?'

A pause: 'Mr Thurston says will you see him very particular.'

'Very well, I'll come down.'

A tall young man in a raincoat was standing in the hall. He had reddish hair and an unusually low, concave forehead. He looked as though he had come to sell some hopelessly unsuitable commodity and had already despaired of success.

'Mr Thurston?' He took my hand in a savage grip. 'You say you have an appointment with me. I am afraid I don't remember it.'

'No, well, you see, I thought we ought to have a yarn, and you know how suspicious these porter fellows are at clubs. I knew you wouldn't mind my stretching a point.' He spoke with a kind of fierce jauntiness. 'I had to give up my club. Couldn't run to it.'

'Perhaps you will tell me what I can do for you.'

'I used to belong to the Wimpole. I expect you know it?'

'I'm not sure that I do.'

'No. You would have liked it. I could have taken you there and introduced you to some of the chaps.'

'That, I gather, is now impossible.'

'Yes. It's a pity. There are some good scouts there. I dare say you know the Bachelors?'

'Yes. Were you a member there, too?'

'Yes – at least, not exactly, but a great pal of mine was – Jimmie Grainger. I expect you've often run across Jimmie?'

'No, I don't think I have.'

'Funny. Jimmie knows almost everyone. You'd like him. I must bring you together.' Having failed to establish contact, Thurston seemed now to think that responsibility for the conversation devolved on me.

'Mr Thurston,' I said, 'is there anything particular you wished to say to me? Because otherwise . . .'

'I was coming to that,' said Thurston. 'Isn't there somewhere more private where we could go and talk?'

It was a reasonable suggestion. Two page boys sat on a bench beside us, the hall porter watched us curiously from behind his glass screen, two or three members passing through paused by the tape machine to take a closer look at my odd visitor. I was tolerably certain that he was not one of the enthusiasts for my work who occasionally beset me, but was either a beggar or a madman or both; at another time I should have sent him away, but that afternoon, with no prospect of other interest, I hesitated. 'Be a good scout,' he urged.

There is at my club a nondescript little room of depressing aspect where members give interviews to the press, go through figures with their accountants, and in general transact business which they think would be conspicuous in the more public rooms. I took Thurston there.

'Snug little place,' he said. 'O.K. if I smoke?'

'Perfectly.'

'Have one?'

'No, thank you.'

He lit a cigarette, drew a deep breath of smoke, gazed at the ceiling and, as though coming to the point, said, 'Quite like the old Wimpole.'

My heart sank. 'Mr Thurston,' I said, 'you have surely not troubled to come here simply to talk to me about the Wimpole Club?'

'No. But, you see, it's rather awkward. Don't exactly know how to begin. I thought I might lead up to it naturally. But I realize that your time's valuable, Mr Plant, so I may as well admit right out that I owe you an apology.'

'Yes?'

'Yes. I'm here under false pretences. My name isn't Thurston.'

'No?'

'No. I'd better tell you who I am, hadn't I?'

'If you wish to.'

'Well, here goes. I'm Arthur Atwater.' The name was spoken with such an air of bravado, with such confidence of its making a stir, that I felt bewildered. It meant absolutely nothing to me. Where and how should I have heard it? Was this a fellow-writer, a distant cousin, a popular athlete? Atwater? Atwater? I repeated it to myself. No association came. My visitor meanwhile seemed unconscious of how flat his revelation had fallen, and was talking away vehemently:

'Now you see why I couldn't give my name. It's awfully decent of you to take it like this. I might have known you were a good scout. I've been through hell, I can tell you, ever since it happened. I haven't slept a wink. It's been terrible. You know how it is when one's nerve's gone. I shouldn't be fit for work now even if they'd kept me on in the job. Not that I care about that. Let them keep their lousy job. I told the manager that to his face. I wasn't brought up and educated to sell stockings. I ought to have gone abroad long ago. There's no opportunity in England now, unless you've got influence or are willing to suck up to a lot of snobs. You get a fair chance out there in the colonies where one man's as good as another and no questions asked.'

I can seldom bear to let a misstatement pass uncorrected. 'Believe me, Mr Atwater,' I said, 'you have a totally mistaken view of colonial life. You will find people just as discriminating and inquisitive there as they are here.'

'Not where I'm going,' he said. 'I'm clearing right out. I'm fed up. This case hanging over me and nothing to do all day except think about the accident. It *was* an accident, too. No one can try and hang the blame on me and get away with it.

I was on my proper side of the road and hooted twice. It wasn't a Belisha crossing. It was my road. The old man just wouldn't budge. He saw me coming, looked straight at me, as if he was daring me to drive into him. Well, I thought I'd give him a fright. You know how it is when you're driving all day. You get fed to the teeth with people making one get out of their way all the time. I like to wake them up now and then when there's no copper near, and make them jump for it. It seems like an hour now, but it all happened in two seconds. I kept on, waiting for him to skip, and he kept on, strolling across the road as if he'd bought it. It wasn't till I was right on top of him I realized he didn't intend to move. Then it was too late to stop. I put on my brakes and tried to swerve. Even then I might have missed him if he'd stopped, but he just kept on walking right into me and the mudguard got him. That's how it was. No one can blame it on me.'

It was just as my uncle Andrew had described it.

'Mr Atwater,' I said, 'do I understand that you are the man who killed my father?'

'Don't put it that way, Mr Plant. I feel sore enough about it. He was a great artist. I read about him in the papers. It makes it worse, his having been a great artist. There's too little beauty in the world as it is. I should have liked to be an artist myself, only the family went broke. Father took me away from school young, just when I might have got into the eleven. Since then I've had nothing but odd jobs. I've never had a real chance. I want to start again, somewhere else.'

I interrupted him, frigidly I thought. 'And why, precisely, have you come to me?'

But nothing could disabuse him of the idea that I was well disposed. 'I knew I could rely on you,' he said. 'And I'll never forget it, not as long as I live. I've thought everything out. I've a pal who went out to Rhodesia; I think it was Rhodesia. Somewhere in Africa, anyway. He'll give me a shakedown till I get on my feet. He's a great fellow. Won't he be surprised when I walk in on him! All I need is my passage money — third class, I don't care. I'm used to roughing it these days — and something to make a start with. I could do it on fifty pounds.'

'Mr Atwater,' I said, 'have I misunderstood you, or are you asking me to break the law by helping you to evade your trial and also give you a large sum of money?'

'You'll get it back, every penny of it.'

'And our sole connexion is the fact that, through pure insolence, you killed my father.'

'Oh, well, if you feel like that about it . . .'

'I am afraid you greatly overrate my good nature.'

'Tell you what. I'll make you a sporting offer. You give me fifty pounds now and I'll pay it back in a year plus another fifty pounds to any charity you care to name. How's that?'

'Will you please go?'

'Certainly I'll go. If that's how you take it. I'm sorry I ever came. It's typical of the world,' he said, rising huffily. 'Everyone's all over you till you get into a spot of trouble. It's "good old Arthur" while you're in funds. Then, when you need a pal it's "you overrate my good nature, Mr Atwater".'

I followed him across the room, but before we reached the door his mood had changed. 'You don't understand,' he said. 'They may send me to prison for this. That's what happens in this country to a man earning his living. If I'd been driving my own Rolls Royce they'd all be touching their caps. "Very regrettable accident," they'd be saying. "Hope your nerves have not been shocked, Mr Atwater" – but to a poor man driving a two-seater . . . Mr Plant, your father wouldn't have wanted me sent to prison.'

'He often expressed the view that all motorists of all classes should be kept permanently in prison.'

Atwater received this with disconcerting enthusiasm. 'And he was quite right,' he cried in louder tones than can ever have been used in that room except perhaps during spring cleaning. 'I'm fed to the teeth with motor-cars. I'm fed to the teeth with civilization. I want to farm. That's a man's life.'

'Mr Atwater, will nothing I say persuade you that your aspirations are no concern of mine?'

'There's no call to be sarcastic. If I'm not wanted, you've only to say so straight.'

'You are not wanted.'

'Thank you,' he said. 'That's all I wanted to know.'

I got him through the door, but half-way across the front hall he paused again. 'I spent my last ten bob on a wreath.'

'I'm sorry you did that. I'll refund it.'

He turned on me with a look of scorn. 'Plant,' he said, 'I didn't think it was in you to say a thing like that. Those flowers were a sacred thing. You wouldn't understand that, would you? I'd have starved to send them. I may have sunk pretty low, but I have some decency left, and that's more than some people can say even if they belong to posh clubs and look down on fellows who earn a decent living. Goodbye, Plant. We shall not meet again. D'you mind if I don't shake hands?'

That was how he left me, but it was not the last of him. That evening I was called to the telephone to speak to a Mr Long. Familiar tones, jaunty once more, greeted me. 'That you, Plant? Atwater here. Excuse the alias, won't you? I say, I hope you didn't take offence at the way I went off today. I've been thinking, and I see you were perfectly right. May I come round for another yarn?'

'No.'

'Tomorrow, then?'

'No.'

'Well, when shall I come?'

'Never.'

'No, I quite understand, old man. I'd feel the same myself.

It's only this. In the circumstances I'd like to accept your very sporting offer to pay for those flowers. I'll call round for the money if you like, or will you send it?'

'I'll send it.'

'Care of the Holborn Post Office finds me. Fifteen bob they cost.'

'You said ten this afternoon.'

'Did I? I meant fifteen.'

'I will send you ten shillings. Good-bye.'

'Good scout,' said Atwater.

So I put a note in an envelope and sent it to the man who killed my father.

VI

Time dragged.

The sale of the house in St John's Wood proved more irksome than I had expected. Ten years before the St John's Wood Residential Amenities Company, who built the neighbouring flats, had offered my father £6,000 for his freehold; he had preserved the letter, which was signed 'Alfred Hardcastle, Chairman'. Their successors, the Hill Crest Court Exploitation Co., now offered me £2,500; their letter was also signed Mr Hardcastle. I refused, and put the house into an agent's hands; after two months they reported one offer – of

£2,500 from a Mr Hardcastle, the managing director of St John's Wood Residential Estates Ltd. 'In the circumstances,' they wrote, 'we consider this a satisfactory price.' The circumstances were that no one who liked that kind of house would tolerate its surroundings; having dominated the district, the flats could make their own price. I accepted it and went to sign the final papers at Mr Hardcastle's office, expecting an atmosphere of opulence and bluster; instead, I found a modest pair of rooms, one of the unlet flats at the top of the building. On the door were painted the names of half a dozen real estate companies, and the woodwork bore traces of other names which had stood there and been obliterated; the chairman opened the door himself and let me in. He was a large, neat, middle-aged, melancholy, likeable fellow, who before coming to business praised my father's painting with what I believe was complete sincerity.

There was no other visible staff; just Mr Hardcastle sitting among his folders and filing cabinets, telling me how he had felt when he lost his own father. Throughout all the vicissitudes of the flats this man had controlled them and lived for them; little companies had gone into liquidation; little, allied companies had been floated; the names of nephews and brothers-in-law had come and gone at the head of the notepaper; stocks had been written down and up, new shares had been issued, bonuses and dividends declared, mortgages transferred and foreclosed, little blocks of figures moved from one balance sheet to another, all in this single room. For the last ten years a few thousand pounds capital had been borrowed and lent backwards and forwards from one account to another and somehow, working sixteen hours a day, doing his own typing and accountancy, Mr Hardcastle had sustained life, kept his shoes polished and his trousers creased, had his hair cut regularly and often, bought occasional concert tickets on family anniversaries and educated, he told me, a son in the United States and a daughter in Belgium. The company to which I finally conveyed my freehold was a brand new one, registered for the occasion and soon, no doubt, doomed to lose its identity in the kaleidoscopic changes of small finance. The cheque, signed by Mr Hardcastle, was duly honoured, and when the sum, largely depleted by my solicitor, was paid into my account, I found that with the insurance money added and my overdraft taken away, I had a credit balance for the first time in my life, of rather more than £3,500. With this I set about planning a new life.

Mr Hardcastle had been willing to wait a long time to make his purchase; once it was done, however, his plans developed with surprising speed. Workmen were cutting the trees and erecting a screen of hoarding while the vans were removing the furniture to store; a week later I came to visit the house; it was a ruin; it might have been mined. Presumably there is some method in the business of demolition;

none was apparent to a layman, the roof was off, the front was down, and on one side the basement lay open; on the other the walls still stood their full height, and the rooms, three-sided like stage settings, exposed their Morris papers, flapping loose in the wind where the fireplaces and window-frames had been torn out. The studio had disappeared, leaving a square of rubble to mark its site; new shoots appeared here and there in the trampled mess of the garden. A dozen or more workmen were there, two or three of them delving away in a leisurely fashion, the rest leaning on their tools and talking; it seemed inconceivable that in this fashion they could have done so much in such little time. The air was full of flying grit. It was no place to linger. When next I passed that way, a great concrete wing covered the site; it was cleaner than the rest of the block and, by a miscalculation of the architects, the windows were each a foot or two below the general line; but, like them, were devoid of curtains.

Part Two

A Birth

I

My project of settling in the country was well received by my friends.

Each saw in it a likely convenience for himself. I understood their attitude well. Country houses meant something particular and important in their lives, a system of permanent boltholes. They had, most of them, gradually dropped out of the round of formal entertaining; country life for them meant not a series of invitations, but of successful, predatory raids. Their lives were liable to sharp reverses; their quarters in London were camps which could be struck at an hour's notice, as soon as the telephone was cut off. Country houses were permanent; even when the owner was abroad, the house was there, with a couple of servants or, at the worst, someone at a cottage who came in to light fires and open windows, someone who, at a pinch, could be persuaded also to make the bed and wash up. They were places where wives and children could be left for long periods, where one retired to write a book, where one could be ill, where, in the course of a love affair, one could take a girl and, by being her guide and sponsor in strange surroundings, establish a degree of proprietorship impossible on the neutral ground of London. The owners of these places were, by their nature, a patient race, but repeated abuse was apt to sour them; new blood in their ranks was highly welcome. I detected this greeting in every eye.

There was also another, more amiable, reason for their interest. Nearly all of them – and, for that matter, myself as well – professed a specialized enthusiasm for domestic architecture. It was one of the peculiarities of my generation, and there is no accounting for it. In youth we had pruned our aesthetic emotions hard back so that in many cases they had reverted to briar stock; we none of us wrote or read poetry, or, if we did, it was of a kind which left unsatisfied those wistful, half-romantic, half-aesthetic, peculiarly British longings which, in the past, used to find expression in so many slim lambskin volumes. When the poetic mood was on us, we turned to buildings, and gave them the place which our fathers accorded to Nature – to almost any buildings, but particularly those in the classical tradition, and, more particularly, in its decay. It was a kind of nostalgia for the style of living which we emphatically rejected in practical affairs. The nobilities of Whig society became, for us, what the Arthurian paladins were in the time of Tennyson. There was never a time when so many landless men could talk at length about landscape gardening. Even Roger compromised with his Marxist austerities so far as to keep up his collection of the works of Batty Langley and William Halfpenny. 'The nucleus of my museum,' he explained. 'When the revolution comes, I've no ambitions to be a commissar or a secret policeman. I want to be director of the Museum of Bourgeois Art.'

He was overworking the Marxist vocabulary. That was always Roger's way, to become obsessed with a new set of words and to extend them, deliberately, beyond the limits of sense; it corresponded to some sombre, interior need of his to parody whatever, for the moment, he found venerable; when he indulged it I was reminded of the ecclesiastical jokes of those on the verge of religious melancholy. Roger had been in that phase himself when I first met him.

One evening, at his house, the talk was all about the kind of house I should buy. It was clear that my friends had very much more elaborate plans for me than I had for myself. After dinner Roger produced a copper engraving of 1767 of *A Composed Hermitage in the Chinese Taste*. It was a preposterous design. 'He actually built it,' Roger said, 'and it's still standing a mile or two out of Bath. We went to see it the other day. It only wants putting into repair. Just the house for you.'

Everyone seemed to agree.

I knew exactly what he meant. It *was* just the house one would want someone else to have. I was graduating from the exploiting to the exploited class.

But Lucy said: 'I can't think why John should want to have a house like that.'

When she said that I had a sudden sense of keen pleasure. She and I were on the same side.

Roger and Lucy had become my main interest during the months while I was waiting to settle up in St John's Wood. They lived in Victoria Square, where they had taken a three years' lease of a furnished house. 'Bourgeois furniture,' Roger complained, rather more accurately than usual. They shut away the model ships and fire-bucket wastepaper baskets in a store cupboard and introduced a prodigious radio-gramophone; they hung their own pictures in place of the Bartolozzi prints, but the house retained its character, and Roger and Lucy, each in a different way, looked out of place there. It was here that Roger had written his ideological play.

They had been married in November. I had spent all the previous autumn abroad on a leisurely, aimless trip before settling at Fez for the winter's work. My mail at Malta, in September, told me that Roger had taken up with a rich girl and was having difficulty with her family; at Tetuan I learned that he was married. Apparently he had been in pursuit of her all the summer, unknown to us. It was not until I reached London that I heard the full story. Basil Seal told me, rather resentfully, because for many years now he had himself been in search of an heiress and had evolved theories on the subject of how and where they might be taken. 'You must go to the provinces,' he used to say. 'The competition in London is far too hot for chaps like us. Americans and Colonials want value for money. The trouble is that the very rich have a natural affinity for one another. You can see it happening all the time — stinking rich people getting fixed up. And what happens? They simply double their supertax and no one is the better off. But they respect brains in the provinces. They like a man to be ambitious there, with his way to make in the world, and there are plenty of solid, mercantile families who can settle a hundred thousand on a daughter without turning a hair, who don't care a hoot about polo, but think a Member of Parliament very fine. That's the way to get in with them. Stand for Parliament.'

In accordance with this plan Basil had stood three times — or rather had three times been adopted as candidate; on two occasions he fell out with his committee before the election. At least that was his excuse to his friends for not standing; in fact he, too, thought it a fine thing to be a Member of Parliament. He never got in, and he was still unmarried. A kind of truculent honesty which he could never dissemble for long always stood in his way. It was bitter for him to be still living at home, dependent on his mother for pocket money, liable to be impelled by her into unwelcome jobs two or three times a year while Roger had established himself almost effortlessly and was sitting back in comfort to await the World Revolution.

Not that Lucy was really rich, Basil hastened to assure me, but she had been left an orphan at an early age, and her originally modest fortune had doubled itself. 'Fifty-eight thousand in trustee stock, old boy. I wanted Lucy to take it out and let me handle it for her. I could have fixed her up very nicely. But Roger wasn't playing. He's always groaning about things being bourgeois. I can't think of anything more bourgeois than three and a half per cent.'

'Is she hideous?' I asked.

'No, that's the worst part about it. She's a grand girl. She's all right for a chap.'

'What like?'

'Remember Trixie?'

'Vaguely.'

'Well, not at all like her.'

Trixie had been Roger's last girl. Basil had passed her on to him, resumed the use of her for a week or two, then passed her back. None of us had liked Trixie. She always gave the impression that she was not being treated with the respect she was used to.

'How did he come by her?'

Basil told me at length, unable to hide his admiration for Roger's duplicity in the matter. All the previous summer, during the second Trixie period, Roger had been at work, without a word to any of us. I remembered, now, that he had suddenly become rather conspicuous in his clothes, affecting dark shirts and light ties, and a generally artistic appearance which, had he not been so bald, would have gone with long, untidy hair. It had embarrassed Trixie, she said, when at a bar they saw cousins of hers who were in the Air Force. 'They'll tell everyone I'm going about with a pansy.' So that was the explanation. It was greatly to Roger's credit, we agreed.

Improbable as it sounded, the truth was that they had met at a ball in Pont Street, given by a relative of Roger's. He had gone, under protest, to make up the table at dinner in answer to an SOS half an hour before the time. Someone had fallen out. It was five or six years since he had been in a London ballroom and, he explained afterwards, the spectacle of his pimply and inept juniors had inflated him with a self-esteem which must, he said, have been infectious. He had sat next to Lucy at dinner. She was, for our world, very young but, for her own, of a hoary age; that is to say, she was twenty-four. For six years she had been sent to dances by her aunt, keeping up an unfashionable, middle stratum of life in which her contemporaries had either married or taken to other occupations. This aunt occupied a peculiar position with regard to Lucy; she had brought her up and now did what she described as 'making a home' for her, which meant that she subsisted largely upon Lucy's income. She had two other nieces younger than Lucy, and it was greatly to their interest that they should move to London annually for the season. The aunt was a lady of delicate conscience where the issues of Lucy's marriage were involved. Once or twice before she had been apprehensive – without cause as it happened – that Lucy was preparing to 'throw herself away'. Roger, however, was a case that admitted of no doubt. Everything she learned about him was reprehensible; she fought him in the full confidence of a just cause, but she had no serviceable weapon. In six years of social life Lucy had never met anyone the least like Roger.

'And he took care she shouldn't meet us,' said Basil. 'What's more, she thinks him a great writer.'

This was true. I did not believe Basil, but after I had seen her and Roger together I was forced to accept it. It was one of the most disconcerting features of the marriage for all of us. It is hard to explain exactly why I found it so shocking. Roger was a very good novelist – every bit as good in his own way as I in mine; when one came to think of it, it was impossible to name anyone else, alive, who could do what he did; there was no good reason why his books should not be compared with those of prominent writers of the past, nor why we should not speculate about their ultimate fame. But to do so struck us all as the worst of taste. Whatever, secretly, we thought about our own work, we professed, in public, to regard it as drudgery and our triumphs as successful impostures on the world at large. To speak otherwise would be to suggest that we were concerned with anyone else's interest but our own; it would be a denial of the *sauve qui peut* principle which we had all adopted. But Lucy, I soon realized, found this attitude unintelligible. She was a serious girl. When we talked cynically about our own work she simply thought less of it and of us; if we treated Roger in the same way, she resented it as bad manners. It was greatly to Roger's credit that he had spotted this idiosyncrasy of hers at once and played his game accordingly. Hence the undergraduate costume and the talk about the Art of the Transition. Lucy had not abandoned her young cousins without grave thought. She perfectly understood that, for them, happiness of a particular kind depended on her continued support; but she also thought it a great wrong that a man of Roger's genius should waste his talents on film scenarios and advertisements. Roger convinced her that a succession of London seasons and marriage to a well-born chartered accountant were not really the highest possible good. Moreover, she was in love with Roger.

'So the poor fellow has had to become a highbrow again,' said Basil. 'Back exactly where he started in the New College Essay Society.'

'She doesn't sound too keen on this play of his.'

'She isn't. She's a critical girl. That's going to be Roger's headache.'

This was Basil's version of the marriage and it was substantially accurate. It omits, however, as any narrative of Basil's was bound to, the consideration that Roger was, in his way, in love with Lucy. Her fortune was a secondary attraction; he lacked the Mediterranean mentality that can regard marriage as an honourable profession, perhaps because he lacked Mediterranean respect for the permanence of the arrangement. At the time when he met Lucy he was earning an ample income without undue exertion; money alone would not have been worth the pains he had taken for her; the artistic clothes and the intellectual talk were measures of the respect in which he held Lucy. Her fifty-eight thousand in trustee stock was, no doubt, what made him push his suit to the extreme of marriage, but the prime motive and zest of the campaign was Lucy herself.

To write of someone loved, of oneself loving, above all of oneself being loved – how can these things be done with propriety? How can they be done at all? I have treated of love in my published work; I have used it – with avarice, envy, revenge – as one of the compelling motives of conduct. I have written it up as something prolonged and passionate and tragic; I have written it down as a modest but sufficient annuity with which to reward the just; I have spoken of it continually as a game of profit and loss. How does any of this avail for the simple task of describing, so that others may see her, the woman one loves? How can others see her except through one's own eyes, and how, so seeing her, can they turn the pages and close the book and live on as they have lived before, without becoming themselves the author and themselves the lover? The catalogues of excellencies of the Renaissance poets, those competitive advertisements, each man outdoing the next in metaphor, that great blurb – like a publisher's list in the Sunday newspapers – the Song of Solomon, how do these accord with the voice of love – love that delights in weakness, seeks out and fills the empty places and completes itself in its work of completion; how can one transcribe those accents? Love, which has its own life, its hours of sleep and waking, its health and sickness, growth, death and immortality, its ignorance and knowledge, experiment and mastery – how can one relate this hooded stranger to the men and women with whom he keeps pace? It is a problem beyond the proper scope of letters.

I first met Lucy after I had been some weeks in London; I had seen Roger several times; he always said, 'You must come and meet Lucy,' but nothing came of these vague proposals until finally, full of curiosity, I went with Basil uninvited.

I met him in the London Library, late one afternoon.

'Are you going to the young Simmondses?' he said.

'Not so far as I know.'

'They've a party today.'

'Roger never said anything to me about it.'

'He told me to tell everyone. I'm just on my way there now. Why don't you come along?'

So we took a taxi to Victoria Square, for which I paid.

As it turned out, Roger and Lucy were not expecting anyone. He went to work now, in the afternoons, with a committee for the relief of Spanish refugees; he had only just come in and was in his bath. Lucy was listening to the six o'clock news on the wireless. She said, 'D'you mind if I keep it on for a minute? There may be something about the dock strike in Madras. Roger will be down in a minute.'

She did not say anything about a drink, so Basil said, 'May I go and look for the whisky?'

'Yes, of course. How stupid of me. I always forget. There's probably some in the dining-room.'

He went out and I stayed with Lucy in her hired drawing-room. She sat quite still listening to the announcer's voice. She was five months gone with child – 'Even Roger has to admit that it's proletarian action,' she said later – but as yet scarcely showed it in body; but she was pale, paler, I guessed, than normal, and she wore that incurious, self-regarding expression which sometimes goes with a first pregnancy. Above the sound of the wireless I heard Basil outside, calling upstairs, 'Roger. Where do you keep the corkscrew?' When they got back to the stock prices, Lucy switched off. 'Nothing from Madras,' she said. 'But perhaps you aren't interested in politics.'

'Not much,' I said.

'Very few of Roger's friends seem to be.'

'It's rather a new thing with him,' I said.

'I expect he doesn't talk about it unless he thinks people are interested.'

That was outrageous, first because it amounted to the claim to know Roger better than I did and, secondly, because I was still smarting with the ruthless boredom of my last two or three meetings with him.

'You'd be doing us all a great service if you could keep him to that,' I said.

It is a most painful experience to find, when one has been rude, that one has caused no surprise. That is how Lucy received my remark. She merely said, 'We've got to go out almost at once. We're going to the theatre in Finsbury and it starts at seven.'

'Very inconvenient.'

'It suits the workers,' she said. 'They have to get up earlier than we do, you see.'

Then Roger and Basil came in with the drinks. Roger said, 'We're just going out. They're doing the Tractor Trilogy at Finsbury. Why don't you come too? We could probably get another seat, couldn't we, Lucy?'

'I doubt it,' said Lucy. 'They're tremendously booked up.'

'I don't think I will,' I said.

'Anyway, join us afterwards at the Café Royal.'

'I might,' I said.

'What have you and Lucy been talking about?'

'We listened to the news,' said Lucy. 'Nothing from Madras.'

'They've probably got orders to shut down on it. I.D.C. have got the B.B.C. in their pocket.'

'I.D.C.?' I asked.

'Imperial Defence College. They're the new hush-hush crypto-fascist department. They're in up to the neck with I.C.I. and the oil companies.'

'I.C.I.?'

'Imperial Chemicals.'

'Roger,' said Lucy, 'we really must go if we're to get anything to eat.'

'All right,' he said. 'See you later at the Café.'

I waited for Lucy to say something encouraging. She said. 'We shall be there by eleven,' and began looking for her bag among the chintz cushions.

I said, 'I doubt if I can manage it.'

'Are we taking the car?' Roger asked.

'No, I sent it away. I've had him out all day.'

'I'll order some taxis.'

'We could drop Basil and John somewhere,' said Lucy.

'No,' I said, 'get two.'

'We're going by way of Appenrodts,' said Lucy.

'No good for me,' I said, although, in fact, they would pass the corner of St James's, where I was bound.

'I'll come and watch you eat your sandwiches,' said Basil.

That was the end of our first meeting. I came away feeling badly about it, particularly the way in which she had used my Christian name and acquiesced in my joining them later. A commonplace girl who wanted to be snubbing would have been conspicuously aloof and have said 'Mr Plant', and I should have recovered some of the lost ground. But Lucy was faultless.

I have seen so many young wives go wrong on this point. They have either tried to force an intimacy with their husband's friends, claiming, as it were, continuity and identity with the powers of the invaded territory, or they have cancelled the passports of the old régime and proclaimed that fresh application must be made to the new authorities and applicants be treated strictly on their merits. Lucy seemed serenely unaware of either danger. I had come inopportunely and been rather rude, but I was one of Roger's friends; they were like his family to her, or hers to him; we had manifest defects which it was none of her business to reform; we had the right to come to her house unexpectedly, to shout upstairs for the corkscrew, to join her table at supper. The question of intrusion did not arise. It was simply that as far as she was concerned we had no separate or individual existence. It was, as I say, a faultless and highly provocative attitude. I found that in the next few days a surprising amount of my time, which, anyway, was lying heavy on me, was occupied on considering how this attitude, with regard to myself, could be altered.

My first move was to ask her and Roger to luncheon. I was confident that none of their other friends – none of those, that is to say, from whom I wished to dissociate myself – would have done such a thing. I did it formally, some days ahead, by letter to Lucy. All this, I knew, would come as a surprise to Roger. He telephoned me to ask, 'What's all this Lucy tells me about you asking us to luncheon?'

'Can you come?'

'Yes, I suppose so. But what's it all about?'

'It's not "about" anything. I just want you to lunch with me.'

'Why?'

'It's quite usual, you know, when one's friends marry. Just politeness.'

'You haven't got some ghastly foreigners you stayed with abroad?'

'No, nothing like that.'

'Well, it all seems very odd to me. Writing a letter, I mean, and everything . . .'

I rang off.

Lucy answered with a formal acceptance. I studied her writing; she wrote like a man.

Dear John,

Roger and I shall be delighted to lunch with you at the Ritz on Thursday week at 1.30.

Yours sincerely,
Lucy Simmonds.

Should it not have been 'Yours ever' after the 'Dear John'? I wondered whether she had wondered what to put. Another girl might have written 'Yours' with a non-committal squiggle, but her writing did not lend itself to that kind of evasion. I had ended my note, 'Love to Roger.'

Was she not a little over-formal in repeating the place and time? Had she written straight off, without thinking, or had she sucked the top of her pen a little?

The paper was presumably the choice of their landlord, in unobtrusive good taste. I smelled it and thought I detected a whiff of soap.

At this point I lost patience with myself; it was ludicrous to sit brooding over a note of this kind. I began, instead, to wonder whom I should ask to meet her — certainly none of the gang she had learned to look on as 'Roger's friends'. On the other hand, it must be clear that the party was for her. Roger would be the first to impute that they were being made use of. In the end, after due thought and one or two failures, I secured a middle-aged, highly reputable woman-novelist and Andrew Desert and his wife – an eminently sociable couple. When Roger saw his fellow guests he was more puzzled than ever. I could see him all through luncheon trying to work it out, why I should have spent five pounds in this peculiar fashion.

I enjoyed my party. Lucy began by talking about my father's painting.

'Yes,' I said, 'it's very fashionable at the moment.'

'Oh, I don't mean that,' she said in frank surprise and went on to tell me how she had stopped before a shop window in Duke Street where a battle picture of my father's was on view; there had been two private soldiers construing it together, point by point. 'I think that's worth a dozen columns of praise in the weekly papers,' she said.

'Just like Kipling's *Light That Failed*,' said the woman-novelist.

'Is it? I didn't know.' She told us she had never read any Kipling.

'That shows the ten years between us,' I said, and so the conversation became a little more personal as we discussed the differences between those who were born before the First World War and those born after it; in fact, so far as it could be worked, the differences between Lucy and myself.

Roger always showed signs of persecution-mania in the Ritz. He did not like it when we knew people at other tables whom he didn't know and, when the waiter brought him the wrong dish, he began on a set-piece which I had heard him use before in this same place. 'Fashionable restaurants are the same all over the world,' he said. 'There are always exactly twenty per cent more tables than the waiters can manage. It's a very good thing for the workers' cause that no one except the rich know the deficiencies of the luxury world. Think of the idea Hollywood gives of a place like this,' he said, warming to his subject. 'A *maître d'hôtel* like an ambassador, bowing famous beauties across acres of unencumbered carpet – and look at poor Lorenzo there, sweating under his collar, jostling a way through for dowdy Middle West Americans . . .' But it was not a success. Lucy, I could see, thought it odd of him to complain when he was a guest. I pointed out that the couple Roger condemned as Middle West Americans were in fact called Lord and Lady Settringham, and Andrew led the conversation, where Roger could not follow it, to the topic of which ambassadors looked like *maîtres d'hôtel*. The woman-novelist began a eulogy of the Middle West which she knew and Roger did not. So he was left with his theme undeveloped. All this was worth five pounds to me, and more.

I thought it typical of the way Lucy had been brought up that she returned my invitation in a day or two.

Roger got in first on the telephone. 'I say, are you free on Wednesday evening?'

'I'm not sure. Why?'

'I wondered if you'd dine with us.'

'Not at half-past six for the Finsbury Theatre?'

'No. I work late these days at the Relief Committee.'

'What time then?'

'Oh, any time after eight. Dress or not, just as you feel like it.'

'What will you and Lucy be doing?'

'Well, I suppose we shall dress. In case anyone wants to go on anywhere.'

'In fact, it's a dinner party?'

'Well, yes, in a kind of way.'

It was plain that poor Roger was dismayed at this social mushroom which had sprung up under his nose. As a face-saver the telephone call was misconceived, for a little note from Lucy was already in the post for me. It was not for me to mock these little notes; I had begun it. But an end had to be made to them, so I decided to answer this by telephone, choosing the early afternoon when I assumed Roger would be out. He was in, and answered me. 'I wanted to speak to Lucy.'

'Yes?'

'Just to accept her invitation to dinner.'

'But you've already accepted.'

'Yes, but I thought I'd better just tell her.'

'I told her. What d'you think?'

'Ah, good, I was afraid you might have forgotten.'

I had come badly out of that.

From first to last the whole episode of the dinner was calamitous. It was a party of ten, and one glance round the room showed me that this was an occasion of what Lucy had been brought up to call 'duty'. That is to say, we were all people whom for one reason or another she had felt obliged to ask. She was offering us all up together in a single propitiatory holocaust to the gods of the schoolroom. Even Mr Benwell was there. He did not realize that Lucy had taken the house furnished, and was congratulating her upon the decorations; 'I like a London house to look like a London house,' he was saying.

Roger was carrying things off rather splendidly with a kind of sardonic gusto which he could often assume in times of stress. I knew him in that mood and respected it. I knew, too, that my presence added a particular zest to his performance. Throughout the evening I caught him in constant inquiry of me: was I attending to this parody of himself? I was his audience, not Lucy.

The fate in store for myself was manifest as soon as I came into the room. It was Lucy's cousin Julia, the younger of the two girls Basil had told me of, the one whose début had been so disturbed by Lucy's marriage. It would not, I felt, be a grave setback. Julia had that particular kind of succulent charm — bright, dotty, soft, eager, acquiescent, flattering, impudent — that is specially, it seems, produced for the delight of Anglo-Saxon manhood. She had no need of a London season to find a happy future. 'Julia is staying with us. She is a great fan of yours,' said Lucy in her Pont Street manner; a manner which, like Roger's but much more subtly, had an element of dumb crambo in it. What she said turned out to be true.

'My word, this *is* exciting,' said Julia, and settled down to enjoy me as though I were a box of chocolates open on her knees.

'What a lot of people Lucy's got here tonight.'

'Yes, it's her first real dinner party, and she says it will be her last. She says she doesn't like parties any more.'

'Did she ever?' I was ready to talk about Lucy at length, but this was not Julia's plan.

'Everyone does at first,' she said briefly, and then began the conversation as she had rehearsed it, I am sure, in her bath. 'I knew you the moment you came into the room. Guess how.'

'You heard my name announced.'

'Oh, no. Guess again.'

An American hero would have said, 'For Christ's sake,' but I said, 'Really, I've no idea, unless perhaps you knew everyone else already.'

'Oh, no. Shall I tell you? I saw you in the Ritz the day Lucy lunched with you.'

'Why didn't you come and talk to us?'

'Lucy wouldn't let me. She said she'd ask you to dinner instead.'

'Ah.'

'You see, for years and years the one thing in the world I've wanted most – or nearly most – was to meet you, and when Lucy calmly said she was going to lunch with you I cried with envy – literally, so I had to put a cold sponge on my eyes before going out.'

Talking to this delicious girl about Lucy, I thought, was like sitting in the dentist's chair with one's mouth full of instruments and the certainty that, all in good time, he would begin to hurt.

'Did she talk about it much before she came to lunch?'

'Oh no, she just said "I'm afraid I've got to leave you today as Roger wants me to lunch with one of his old friends." So I said, "How rotten, who?" and she said, "John Plant," just like that, and I said, "*John Plant*," and she said, "Oh, I forgot you were keen on thrillers." *Thrillers*, as though you were just anybody. And I said, "Couldn't I possibly come?" and she said, "Not possibly," and then when I was crying she said I might come with her to the lounge and sit behind a pillar and see you come in.'

'How did she describe me?'

'She just said you'd be the one who paid for the cocktails. Isn't that just like Lucy, or don't you know her well enough to tell?'

'What did she say about the lunch afterwards?'

'She said everyone talked about Kipling.'

'Was that all?'

'And she thought Roger had behaved badly because he doesn't like smart restaurants, and she said neither did she, but it had cost you a lot of money, so it was nasty to complain. Of course, I wanted to hear all about *you* and what *you* said, and she couldn't remember anything. She just said you seemed very clever.'

'Oh, she said that.'

'She says that about all Roger's friends. But, anyway, it's my turn now. I've got you to myself for the evening.'

She had. We were sitting at dinner now. Lucy was still talking to Mr Benwell. On my other side there was some kind of relative of Roger's. She talked to me for a bit about how Roger had settled down since marriage. 'I don't take those political opinions of his seriously,' she said, 'and, anyway, it's all right to be a communist nowadays. Everyone is.'

'I'm not,' I said.

'Well, I mean all the clever young people.'

So I turned back to Julia. She was waiting for me.

'D'you know you once wrote me a letter?'

'Good gracious. Why?'

'Dear Madam, – Thank you for your letter. If you will read the passage in question more attentively you will note that the down train was four minutes late at Frasham. There was thus ample time for the disposal of the bicycle bell. Yours faithfully, John Plant,' she quoted.

'Did I write that?'

'Don't you remember?'

'Vaguely. It was about *The Frightened Footman*, wasn't it?'

'Mm. Of course I knew perfectly well about the train. I just wrote in the hope of getting an answer, and it worked. I liked you for being so severe. There was another girl at school who was literary, too, and she had a crush on Gilbert Warwick. He wrote her three pages beginning, My Dear Anthea, all about his house and the tithe barn he's turned into his work-room, and ending, Write to me again; I hope you like Sylvia as much as Heather – those were two of his heroines – and she thought it showed what a better writer he was than you, but I knew just the opposite. And later Anthea did write again, and she had another long letter just like the first all about his tithe barn, and that made her very cynical. So I wrote to you again to show how different you were.'

'Did I answer?'

'No. So then all the Literary Club took to admiring you instead of Gilbert Warwick.'

'Because I didn't answer letters?'

'Yes. You see, it showed you were a real artist and didn't care a bit for your public, and just lived for your work.'

'I see.'

After dinner Roger said, 'Has little Julia been boring you frightfully?'

'Yes.'

'I thought she was. She's very pretty. It's a great evening for her.'

Eventually we returned to the drawing-room and sat about. Roger did not know how to manage this stage of his party. He talked vaguely of going on somewhere to dance and of playing a new parlour game that had lately arrived from New York. No one encouraged him. I did not speak to Lucy until I came to say good-bye, which was very early, as soon as the first guest moved and everyone, on the instant, rose too. When I said good-bye to her, Julia said, 'Please, I must tell you. You're a thousand times grander than I ever imagined. It was half a game before – now it's serious.'

I could imagine the relief in the house as the last of us left, Roger and Lucy emerging into one another's arms as though from shelter after a storm . . . 'So that's over. Was it as bad as you expected?' 'Worse, worse. You were splendid.' . . . perhaps they – and Julia, too? – were cutting a caper on the drawing-room carpet in an ecstasy of liberation.

'That,' I said to myself, 'is what you have bought with your five pounds.'

That evening, next day and for several days, I disliked Lucy. I made a story for all who knew him, of Roger's dinner party, leaving the impression that this was the kind of life Lucy enjoyed and that she was driving Roger into it. But for all that I did not abate my resolve to force my friendship upon her. I sought recognition. I wanted to assert the simple fact of my separate and individual existence. I could not by any effort of will regard her as being, like Trixie, 'one of Roger's girls', and I demanded reciprocation; I would not be regarded as, like Basil, 'one of Roger's friends'; still less, like Mr Benwell, as someone who had to be asked to dinner every now and then. I had little else to think about at the time, and the thing became an itch with me. I felt about her, I suppose, as old men feel who are impelled by habit to touch every third lamp-post on their walks; occasionally something happens to distract them, they see a friend or a street accident and they pass a lamp-post by; then all day they fret and fidget until, after tea, they set out shamefacedly to put the matter right. That was how I felt about Lucy; our relationship constituted a tiny disorder in my life that had to be adjusted.

That at least is how, in those earliest days, I explained my obsession to myself, but looking at it now, down the mirrored corridor of cumulative emotion, I see no beginning to the perspective. There is in the apprehension of woman's beauty an exquisite, early intimation of loveliness when, seeing some face, strange or familiar, one gains, suddenly, a further glimpse and foresees, out of a thousand possible futures, how it might be transfigured by love. With Lucy – her grace daily more encumbered by her pregnancy; deprived of sex, as women are, by its fulfilment – the vision was extended and clarified until, with no perceptible transition, it became the reality. But I cannot say when it first appeared. Perhaps, that evening when she said, about the *Composed Hermitage in the Chinese Taste*, 'I can't think why John should want to have a house like that,' but it came without surprise; I had sensed it on its way, as an animal, still in profound darkness and surrounded by all the sounds of night, will lift its head, sniff, and know, inwardly, that dawn is near. Meanwhile, I moved for advantage as in a parlour game.

Julia brought me success. Our meeting, so far from disillusioning her, made her cult of me keener and more direct. It was no fault of mine, I assured Roger, when he came to grumble about it; I had not been in the least agreeable to her; indeed, towards the end of the evening I had been openly savage.

'The girl's a masochist,' he said, adding with deeper gloom, 'and Lucy says she's a virgin.'

'There's plenty of time for her. The two troubles are often cured simultaneously.'

'That's all very well, but she's staying another ten days. She never stops talking about you.'

'Does Lucy mind?'

'Of course she minds. It's driving us both nuts. Does she write you a lot of letters?'

'Yes.'

'What does she say?'

'I don't read them. I feel as though they were meant for somebody else. Besides, they're in pencil.'

'I expect she writes them in bed. No one's ever gone for me like that.'

'Nor for me,' I said. 'It's not really at all disagreeable.'

'I daresay not,' said Roger. 'I thought only actors and sex-novelists and clergymen came in for it.'

'No, no, anybody may – scientists, politicians, professional cyclists – anyone whose name gets into the papers. It's just that young girls are naturally religious.'

'Julia's eighteen.'

'She'll get over it soon. She's been stirred up by suddenly meeting me in the flesh after two or three years' distant devotion. She's a nice child.'

'That's all very well,' said Roger, returning sulkily to his original point. 'It isn't Julia I'm worried about, it's ourselves, Lucy and me – she's staying another ten days. Lucy says you've got to be nice about it, and come out this evening, the four of us. I'm sorry, but there it is.'

So for a week I went often to Victoria Square, and there was the beginning of a half-secret joke between Lucy and me in Julia's devotion. While I was there Julia sat smug and gay, she was a child of enchanting prettiness. When I was absent, Roger told me, she moped a good deal and spent much time in her bedroom writing and destroying letters to me. She talked about herself, mostly, and her sister and family. Her father was a major and they lived at Aldershot; they would have to stay there all the year round now that Lucy no longer needed their company in London. She did not like Roger. 'He's not very nice about you,' she said.

'Roger and I are like that,' I explained. 'We're always foul about each other. It's our fun. Is Lucy nice about me?'

'Lucy's an angel,' said Julia, 'that's why we hate Roger so.'

Finally there was the evening of Julia's last party. Eight of us went to dance at a restaurant. Julia was at first very gay, but her spirits dropped towards the end of the evening. I was living in Ebury Street; it was easy for me to walk home from Victoria Square, so I went back with them and had a last drink. 'Lucy's promised to leave us alone, just for a minute, to say good-bye,' Julia whispered.

When we were alone, she said, 'It's been absolutely wonderful the last two weeks. I didn't know it was possible to be so happy. I wish you'd give me something as a kind of souvenir.'

'Of course. I'll send you one of my books, shall I?'

'No,' she said, 'I'm not interested in your books any more. At least, of course, I am, terribly, but I mean it's *you* I love.'

'Nonsense,' I said.

'Will you kiss me, once, just to say good-bye.'

I kissed her paternally on the cheek.

Then she said suddenly, 'You're in love with Lucy, aren't you?'

'Good heavens, no. What on earth put that into your head?'

'I can tell. Through loving you so much, I expect. You may not know it, but you are. And it's no good. She loves that horrid Roger. Oh, dear, they're coming back. I'll come and say good-bye to you tomorrow, may I?'

'No.'

'*Please*. This hasn't been how I planned it at all.'

Then Roger and Lucy came into the room with a sly look as though they had been discussing what was going on and how long they should give us. So I shook hands with Julia and went home.

She came to my rooms at ten next morning. Mrs Legge, the landlady, showed her up. She stood in the door, swinging a small parcel. 'I've got five minutes,' she said, 'the taxi's waiting. I told Lucy I had some last-minute shopping.'

'You know you oughtn't to do this sort of thing.'

'I've been here before. When I knew you were out. I pretended I was your sister and had come to fetch something for you.'

'Mrs Legge never said anything to me about it.'

'No. I asked her not to. In fact, I gave her ten shillings. You see, she caught me at it.'

'At what?'

'Well, it sounds rather silly. I was in your bedroom, kissing things – you know, pillows, pyjamas, hair brushes. I'd just got to the washstand and was kissing your razor when I looked up and found Mrs Whatever-she's-called standing in the door.'

'Good God, I shall never be able to look her in the face again.'

'Oh, she was quite sympathetic. I suppose I must have looked funny, like a goose grazing.' She gave a little, rather hysterical giggle, and added, 'Oh, John, I do love you so.'

'Nonsense. I shall turn you out if you talk like that.'

'Well, I do. And I've got you a present.' She gave me the square parcel. 'Open it.'

'I shan't accept it,' I said, unwrapping a box of cigars.

'But you must. You see, they'd be no good to me, would they? Are they good ones?'

'Yes,' I said, looking at the box. 'Very good ones indeed.'

'The best.'

'Quite the best, but . . .'

'That's what the man in the shop said. Smoke one now.'

'Julia, dear, I couldn't. I've only just finished breakfast.'

She saw the point of that. 'When will you smoke the first one? After luncheon? I'd like to think of you smoking the first one.'

'Julia, dear, it's perfectly sweet of you, but I can't honestly . . .'

'I know what you're thinking, that I can't afford it. Well, that's all right. You see, Lucy gave me five pounds yesterday to buy a hat. I thought she would – she often does. But I had to wait and be sure. I'd got them ready, hidden yesterday evening. I meant to give you them then. But I never got a proper chance. So here they are.' And then, as I hesitated, with rising voice, 'Don't you see I'd much rather give you cigars than have a new hat? Don't you see I shall go back to Aldershot absolutely miserable, the whole time in London quite spoilt, if you won't take them?'

She had clearly been crying that morning and was near tears again.

'Of course I'll take them,' I said. 'I think it's perfectly sweet of you.'

Her face cleared in sudden, infectious joy.

'There. Now we can say good-bye.'

She stood waiting for me, not petitioning this time, but claiming her right. I put my hands on her shoulders and gave her a single, warm kiss on the lips. She shut her eyes and sighed. 'Thank you,' she said in a small voice, and hurried out to her waiting taxi, leaving the box of cigars on my table.

Sweet Julia! I thought. It was a supremely unselfish present; something quite impersonal and unsentimental – no keepsake – something which would be gone, literally in smoke, in less than six weeks; a thing she had not even the fun of choosing for herself; she had gone to the counter and left it to the shopman – 'I want a box of the best cigars you keep, please – as many as I can get for five pounds.' She just wanted something which she could be sure would give pleasure.

And chiefly because she thought I had been kind to her cousin, Lucy took me into her friendship.

Roger's engraving showed a pavilion, still rigidly orthodox in plan, but, in elevation decked with ornament conceived in a wild ignorance of oriental forms; there were balconies and balustrades of geometric patterns; the cornices swerved upwards at the corners in the lines of a pagoda; the roof was crowned with an onion cupola which might have been Russian, bells hung from the capitals of barley-sugar columns; the windows were freely derived from the Alhambra; there was a minaret. To complete the atmosphere the engraver had added a little group of Turkish military performing the bastinado upon a curiously complacent malefactor, an Arabian camel and a mandarin carrying a bird in a cage.

'My word, what a gem,' they said. 'It is really all there?'

'The minaret's down and it's all rather overgrown.'

'What a chance. John must get it.'

'It will be fun to furnish. I know just the chairs for it.'

This was the first time I had been to Victoria Square since Julia left.

And Lucy said, 'I can't think why John should want to have a house like that.'

II

Lucy was a girl of few friends; she had, in fact, at the time I was admitted to their number, only two: a man named Peter Baverstock, in the Malay States, whom I never saw, and a Miss Muriel Meikeljohn, whom I saw all too often. Peter Baverstock had wanted to marry Lucy since she was seven, and proposed to her whenever he came home on leave, every eighteen months, until she married Roger, when he sent her a very elaborate wedding present, an immense thing in carved wood, ivory and gilt which caused much speculation with regard to its purpose; later he wrote and explained. I forget the explanation. I think it was the gift which, by local usage, men of high birth gave to their granddaughters when they were delivered of male twins; it was, anyway, connected with twins and grandparents, of great rarity, and a token of high esteem in the parts it came from. Lucy wrote long letters to Baverstock every fortnight. I often watched her at work on those letters, sitting square to her table, head bowed, hand travelling evenly across the page, as, I remembered reading in some book of memoirs, Sir Walter Scott's had been seen at a lighted window, writing the Waverley novels. It was a tradition of her upbringing that letters for the East must always be written on very thin, lined paper. 'I'm just telling Peter about your house,' she would say.

'How can that possibly interest him?'

'Oh, he's interested in everything. He's so far away.'

It seemed an odd reason.

Miss Meikeljohn was a pale, possessive girl, who had been a fellow boarder with Lucy in the house of a distressed gentlewoman in Vienna where they had both been sent to learn singing. They had shared a passion for a leading tenor, and had once got into his dressing-room at the Opera House by wearing mackintoshes and pretending to be reporters sent to interview him. Lucy still kept a photograph of this tenor, in costume, on her dressing-table, but she had shed her musical aspirations with the rest of her Pont Street life. Miss Meikeljohn still sang, once a week, to a tutor. It was after these lessons that she came to luncheon with Lucy, and the afternoon was hers by prescriptive right for shopping, or for a cinema, or for what she liked best, a 'good talk'. These Tuesdays were 'Muriel's days', and no one might interfere with them.

'They are the only times she comes into London. Her parents are separated and terrible poor,' Lucy said, as though in complete explanation.

When they went to the cinema or play together they went in the cheap seats because Miss Meikeljohn insisted on paying her share. Lucy thought this evidence of Miss Meikeljohn's integrity of character; she often came back from these entertainments with a headache from having had to sit so close to the screen.

The friendship was odd in many ways, notably because Miss Meikeljohn luxuriated in heart-to-heart confidences — in what my father's generation coarsely called 'taking down her back hair', an exhibition that was abhorrent to Lucy, who in friendship had all the modesty of the naked savage.

I must accept the modesty of the naked savage on trust, on the authority of numerous travel books. The savages I have met on my travels have all been formidably overdressed. But if there existed nowhere else on the globe that lithe, chaste and unstudied nudity of which I have so often read, it was there, dazzlingly, in the mind of Lucy. There were no reservations in her friendship, and it was an experience for which I was little qualified, to be admitted, as it were, through a door in the wall to wander at will over that rich estate. The idea of an occasional opening to the public in aid of the cottage hospital, of extra gardeners working a week beforehand to tidy the walks, of an upper housemaid to act as guide, of red cord looped across the arms of the chairs, of special objects of value to be noted, of 'that door leads to the family's private apartments. They are never shown', of vigilance at the hot-house for fear of a nectarine being pocketed, of 'now you have seen *everything*: please make way for the next party', and of the open palm — of all, in fact, which constituted Miss Meikeljohn's, and most people's, habit of intimacy, was inconceivable to Lucy.

When I began to realize the spaces and treasures of which

I had been made free, I was like a slum child alternately afraid to touch or impudently curious. Or, rather, I felt too old. Years earlier when Lucy was in her cradle, I had known this kind of friendship. There was a boy at my private school with whom I enjoyed a week of unrestrained confidence; one afternoon, sitting with him in a kind of nest, itself a secret, which we had devised for ourselves from a gym mat and piled benches in a corner of the place where we played on wet afternoons, I revealed my greatest secret, that my father was an artist and not, as I had given it out, an officer in the Navy; by tea-time the story was all over the school, that Plant's pater had long hair and did not wash. (Revenge came sooner than I could have hoped, for this was the summer term, 1914, and my betrayer had an aunt married to an Austrian nobleman; he had boasted at length of staying in their castle; when school reassembled in September I was at the head of the mob which hounded him in tears to the matron's room with cries of 'German spy'.) It was the first and, to my mind, most dramatic of the normal betrayals of adolescence. With the years I had grown cautious. There was little love and no trust at all between any of my friends. Moreover, we were bored; each knew the other so well that it was only by making our relationship into a kind of competitive parlour game that we kept it alive at all. We had all from time to time cut out divergent trails and camped in new ground, but we always, as it were, returned to the same base for supplies, and swapped yarns of our exploration. That was what I meant by friendship at the age of thirty-four, and Lucy, finding herself without preparation among people like myself, had been disconcerted. That was the origin of what, at first, I took for priggishness in her. Her lack of shyness cut her off from us. She could not cope with the attack and defence, deception and exposure, which was our habitual intercourse. Anything less than absolute intimacy embarrassed her, so she fell back upon her good upbringing, that armoury of schoolroom virtues and graces with which she had been equipped, and lived, as best she could, independently, rather as, it is said, Chinese gentlemen of the old school can pursue interminable, courteous, traditionally prescribed conversations with their minds abstracted in realms of distant beauty.

But it was not enough. She was lonely. In particular she was cut off by her pregnancy from Roger. For a term of months she was unsexed, the roots of her love for Roger wintering, out of sight in the ground, without leaf. So she looked for a friend and, because she thought I had been kind to Julia, and because, in a way, I had responded to her in her schoolroom mood, she chose me. I had not misinterpreted her change of manner. She had made up her mind that I was to be a friend. I began, almost at once, to spend the greater part of the day in her company, and as my pre-occupation at the time was in finding a house that quest became the structure of our friendship. Together we went over the sheaves of house agents' notices, and several times we went on long expeditions together to look at houses in the country. We talked of everything except the single topic of politics. The attraction of Socialism for Lucy was double. It was a part of the break she had made with Aldershot and Pont Street, and it relieved her of the responsibility she felt for her own private fortune. Money, her money, was of great importance to her. If she had lived among the rich it would have been different; she would then have thought it normal to be assured, for life, of the possessions for which others toiled, she would, indeed, have thought herself rather meagrely provided. But she had been brought up among people poorer than herself to regard herself as somebody quite singular. When the age came of her going to dances, her aunt had impressed on her the danger she ran of fortune-hunters and, indeed, nearly all the young men with whom she consorted, and their mothers, regarded £58,000 as a notable prize. 'Sometimes by the way that girl talks,' Basil had said, 'you'd think she was the Woolworth heiress.' It was quite true. She did think herself extremely rich and responsible. One of the advantages to her of marrying Roger was the belief that her money was being put to good use in rescuing a literary genius from wage-slavery. She was much more afraid of misusing her money than of losing it. Thus when she was convinced that all private fortunes like her own were very shortly to be abolished and all undeserved prominence levelled, she was delighted. Moreover, her conversion had coincided with her falling in love. She and Roger had been to meetings together, and together read epitomes of Marxist philosophy. Her faith, like a Christian's, was essential to her marriage, so, knowing that I was hostile, she sequestered it from me.

It was convenient for Roger to have me in attendance. He was not domestic by nature. He did not, as some husbands do, resent his wife's pregnancy. It was as though he had bought a hunter at the end of the season and turned him out; discerning friends, he knew, would appreciate the fine lines under the rough coat, but he would sooner have shown something glossy in the stable. He had summer business to do, moreover; the horse must wait till the late autumn. That, at least, was one way in which he saw the situation, but the analogy was incomplete. It was rather *he* that had been acquired and put to grass, and he was conscious of that aspect, too. Roger was hobbled and prevented from taking the full stride required of him, by the habit, long settled, of regarding sex relationships in terms of ownership and use. Confronted with the new fact of pregnancy, of joint ownership, his terms failed him. As a result he was restless and no longer master of the situation; the practical business of getting through the day was becoming onerous, so that my adhesion was agreeable to him. Grossly, it confirmed his opinion of Lucy's value and at the same time took her off his hands. Then one morning, when I made my now habitual call at Victoria Square, Lucy, not yet up but lying in bed in a chaos of newspapers, letters and manicure tools, greeted me by saying, 'Roger's writing.'

Couched as she was, amid quilted bed-jacket and tumbled sheets — one arm bare to the elbow where the wide sleeve fell back and showed the tender places of wrist and forearm, the other lost in the warm depths of the bed, with her pale skin taking colour against the dead white linen, and her smile of confident, morning welcome; as I had greeted her countless times and always with a keener joy, until that morning I seemed to have come to the end of an investigation and held as a certainty what before I had roughly surmised — her beauty rang through the room like a peal of bells; thus I have stood, stunned, in a Somerset garden, with the close turf wet and glittering underfoot in the dew, when, from beyond the walls of box, the grey church tower had suddenly scattered the heavens in tumult.

'Poor fellow,' I said. 'What about?'

'It's my fault,' she said, 'a detective story,' and she went on to explain that since I had talked to her about my books, she had read them — 'You were perfectly right. They *are* works of art. I had no idea' — and talked of them to Roger until he had suddenly said, 'Oh, God, another Julia.' Then he had told her that for many years he had kept a plot in his mind, waiting for a suitable time to put it into writing.

'He'll do it very well,' I said. 'Roger can write anything.'
'Yes.'

But while she was telling me this and I was answering, I thought only of Lucy's new beauty. I knew that beauty of that kind did not come from a suitable light or a lucky way with the hair or a sound eight hours' sleep, but from an inner secret; and I knew this morning that the secret was the fact of Roger's jealousy. So another stage was reached in my falling in love with Lucy, while each week she grew heavier and slower and less apt for love, so that I accepted the joy of her companionship without reasoning. Lucy and I were like characters in the stock intrigue of Renaissance comedy, where the heroine follows the hero in male attire and is wooed by him, unknowing, in the terms of rough friendship.

In these weeks Lucy and I grew adept in construing the jargon of the estate agents. I had a clear idea of what I required. In the first place, it must not cost, all told, when the decorators and plumbers had moved out and the lawyers been paid for the conveyance, more than £3,000; it must be in agricultural country, preferably within five miles of an antiquated market town, it must be at least a hundred years old, and it must be a *house*, no matter how dingy, rather than a cottage, however luxurious; there must be a cellar, two staircases, high ceilings, a marble chimney-piece in the drawing-room, room to turn a car at the front door, a coach-house and stable yard, a walled kitchen garden, a paddock and one or two substantial trees – these seemed to me the minimum requisites of the standard of gentility at which I aimed, something between the squire's and the retired admiral's. Lucy had a womanly love of sunlight and a Marxist faith in the superior beauties of concrete and steel. She had, moreover, a horror, born of long association, of the rural bourgeois with whom I was determined to enrol myself. I was able to excuse my predilection to others by describing it as Gallic; French writers, I explained, owed their great strength, as had the writers of nineteenth-century England, to their middle-class status; the best of them all owned square white houses, saved their money, dined with the mayor and had their eyes closed for them at death by faithful, repellent house-keepers; English and American writers squandered their energy in being fashionable or bohemian or, worst of all, in an unhappy alternation between the two. This theme went down well with Mr Benwell, who, in the week or two after I expounded it to him, gave deathless offence to several of his authors by exhorting them to be middle-class, too, but it left Lucy unimpressed. She thought the object of my search grotesque, but followed in a cheerful and purely sporting spirit as one may hunt a fox which one has no taste to eat.

The last occasion of her leaving London before her confinement was to look at a house with me, below the Berkshire downs. It was too far to travel comfortably in a day, and we spent the night with relatives of hers near Abingdon. We had by now grown so accustomed to one another's company that there seemed nothing odd to us in Lucy proposing me as a guest. Our host and hostess, however, thought it most irregular, and their manifest surprise was a further bond between us. Lucy was by now eight months with child, and at the back of her relatives' concern was the fear that she might be delivered prematurely in their house. They treated her with a solicitude that all too clearly was a rebuke to my own easy-going acceptance of the situation. Try how I might to realize the dangers she ran, I could never feel protective towards Lucy. She looked, we agreed, like Tweedledum armed for battle, and I saw her at this time as preternaturally solid, with an armour of new life defending her from the world. Biologically, no doubt, this was a fallacy, but it was the attitude we jointly accepted, so that we made an immediate bad impression by being struck with fou rire in the first five minutes of our visit, when our hostess whispered that she had fitted up a bedroom for Lucy on the ground floor so that she should not be troubled by stairs.

The house we had come to see proved, like so many others, to be quite uninhabitable. Its owner, in fact, was living in his lodge. 'Too big for me these days,' he said of the house which, when he opened it to us, gave the impression of having been designed as a small villa and wantonly extended, as though no one had remembered to tell the workmen when to stop and they had gone on adding room to room like cells in a wasp-nest. 'I never had the money to spend on it,' the owner said gloomily; 'you could make something of it with a little money.'

We went upstairs and along a lightless passage. He had been showing people over this house since 1902, he said, and with the years he had adopted a regular patter. 'Nice little room this, very warm in the winter . . . You get a good view of the downs here, if you stand in the corner . . . It's a dry house. You can see that. I've never had any trouble with damp . . . These used to be the nurseries. They'd make a nice suite of spare bedroom, dressing-room and bath if you didn't . . .' and at that point, remembering Lucy, he stopped abruptly and in such embarrassment that he scarcely spoke until we left him.

'I'll write to you,' I said.

'Yes,' he said with great gloom, knowing what I meant. 'I sometimes think the place might do as a school. It's very healthy.'

So we drove back to Lucy's relatives. They wanted her to dine in bed or, anyway, to go to her room and lie down until dinner. Instead she came out with me into the evening sunlight, and we sat in what Lucy's relatives called their 'blue garden', reconstructing a life story of the sad little man who had shown us his house. Lucy's relatives thought us and our presence there and our whole expedition extremely odd.

There was something going on, they felt, which they did not understand, and Lucy and I, infected by the atmosphere, became, as it were, confederates in this house which she had known all her life; in the garden where, as a little girl, she had once, she told me, buried a dead starling, with tears.

After this expedition Lucy remained in London, spending more and more of her time indoors. When I finally found a house to suit me, I was alone.

'You might have waited,' said Lucy. It seemed quite natural that she should reproach me. She had a share in my house. 'Damn this baby,' she added.

III

In the last week before the birth of her child Lucy began for the first time to betray impatience; she was never, at any time, at all apprehensive — merely bored and weary and vexed past bearing by the nurse who had now taken up residence in the house. Roger and Miss Meikeljohn had made up their minds that she was going to die. 'It's all this damned pre-natal care,' said Roger. 'Do you realize that maternal mortality is higher in this country than it's ever been? D'you know there are cases of women going completely bald after childbirth? And permanently insane? It's worse among the rich than the poor, too.'

Miss Meikeljohn said: 'Lucy's being so wonderful. She doesn't *realize*.'

The nurse occupied herself with extravagant shopping lists. 'Does *everyone* have to have all these things?' Lucy asked, aghast at the multitude of medical and nursery supplies which began to pour into the house. 'Everyone who can afford them,' said Sister Kemp briskly, unconscious of irony. Roger found some comfort in generalizing. 'It's anthropologically very interesting,' he said, 'all this purely ceremonial accumulation of rubbish – like turtle doves brought to the gates of a temple. Everyone according to his means sacrificing to the racial god of hygiene.'

He showed remarkable forbearance to Sister Kemp, who brought with her an atmosphere of impending doom and accepted a cocktail every evening, saying, 'I'm not really on duty *yet*,' or 'No time for this *after the day*.'

She watched confidently for The Day, her apotheosis, when Lucy would have no need for Roger or me or Miss Meikeljohn, only for herself.

'I shall call you Mrs Simmonds until The Day,' she said. 'After that you will be my Lucy.' She sat about with us in the drawing-room, and in Lucy's bedroom where we spent most of the day, now; like an alien, sitting at a café; an alien anarchist, with a bomb beside him, watching the passing life of a foreign city, waiting for his signal from the higher powers, the password which might come at once or in a very few days, whispered in his ear, perhaps, by the waiter, or scrawled on the corner of his evening newspaper – the signal that the hour of liberation had come when he would take possession of all he beheld. 'The fathers need nearly as much care as the mothers,' said Sister Kemp. 'No, not another, thank you, Mr Simmonds. I've got to keep in readiness, you know. It would never do if baby came knocking at the door and found Sister unable to lift the latch.'

'No,' said Roger. 'No, I suppose it wouldn't.'

Sister Kemp belonged to a particularly select and highly paid corps of nurses. A baby wheeled out by her, as it would be daily for the first month, would have access to certain paths in the Park where inferior nurses trespassed at the risk of cold looks. Lucy's perambulator would thus be socially established, and the regular nurse, when she took over, would find her charge already well known and respected. Sister Kemp explained this, adding as a concession to Lucy's political opinions, 'The snobbery among nurses is terrible. I've seen many a girl go home from Stanhope Gate in tears.' And then, *esprit de corps* asserting itself, 'Of course, they ought to have known. There's always Kensington Gardens for them.'

Once Sister Kemp had attended a house in Seamore Place, in nodding distance of Royalty, but the gardens there, though supremely grand, had been, she said, 'dull', by which we understood that even for her there were close circles. Roger was delighted with this. 'It's like something out of

Thackeray,' he said and pressed for further details, but Lucy was past taking relish in social survivals; she was concerned only with the single, physical fact of her own exhaustion. 'I hate this baby already,' she said. 'I'm going to hate it all my life.'

Roger worked hard at this time, in the mornings at his detective story, in the afternoons at his committee for Spanish aid. Miss Meikeljohn and I tried to keep Lucy amused with increasingly little success. Miss Meikeljohn took her to concerts and cinemas where, now, she allowed Lucy to buy the seats, as extreme comfort was clearly necessary for her. I took her to the Zoo, every morning at twelve o'clock. There was a sooty, devilish creature in the monkey house named Humboldt's Gibbon which we would watch morosely for half an hour at a time; he seemed to exercise some kind of hypnotic fascination over Lucy; she could not be got to other cages. 'If I have a boy I'll call him Humboldt,' she said. 'D'you know that before I was born, so Aunt Maureen says, my mother used to sit in front of a Flaxman bas-relief so as to give me ideal beauty. Poor mother, she died when I was born.' Lucy could say that without embarrasment because she felt no danger in her own future. 'I don't care how disagreeable it's going to be,' she said. 'I only want it soon.'

Because of my confidence in her, and my resentment of the proprietary qualms of Roger and Miss Meikeljohn, I accepted her attitude; and was correspondingly shocked when the actual day came.

Roger telephoned to me at breakfast time. 'The baby's begun.'

'Good,' I said.

'What d'you mean, good?'

'Well, it is good, isn't it? When did it start?'

'Last night, about an hour after you left.'

'It ought to be over soon.'

'I suppose so. Shall I come round?'

He came, yawning a great deal from having been up all night. 'I was with her for an hour or two. I always imagined people stayed in bed when they were having babies. Lucy's up, going about the house. It was horrible. Now she doesn't want me.'

'What happened exactly?'

He began to tell me and then I was sorry I had asked. 'That nurse seems very good,' he said at the end. 'The doctor didn't come until half an hour ago. He went away again right away. They haven't given her any chloroform yet. They say they are keeping that until the pains get worse. I don't see how they could be. You've no conception what it was like.' He stayed with me for half an hour and read my newspapers. Then he went home. 'I'll telephone you when there's any news,' he said.

Two hours later I rang up. 'No,' he said, 'there's no news. I said I'd telephone you if there was.'

'But what's happening?'

'I don't know. Some kind of lull.'

'But she's all right, isn't she? I mean they're not anxious.'

'I don't know. The doctor's coming again. I went in to see her, but she didn't say anything. She was just crying quietly.'

'Nothing I can do, is there?'

'No, how could there be?'

'I mean about lunch or anything. You don't feel like coming out?'

'No, I ought to stay around here.'

The thought of the lull, of Lucy not speaking, but lying there in tears, waiting for her labour to start again, pierced me as no tale could have done of cumulative pain; but beyond my sense of compassion I was not scared. I had been smoking a pipe; my mouth had gone dry, and when I knocked out the smouldering tobacco the smell of it sickened me. I went out into Ebury Street as though to the deck of a ship, breathing hard against nausea, and, from habit more than sentiment, took a cab to the Zoo.

The man at the turnstile knew me as a familiar figure. 'Your lady not with you today, sir?'

'No, not today.'

'I've got five myself,' he said.

I did not understand him and repeated foolishly, 'Five?'

'Being a married man,' he added.

Humboldt's Gibbon seemed disinclined for company. He sat hunched up at the back of his cage, fixing on me a steady and rather bilious stare. He was never, at the best of times, an animal who courted popularity. In the cage on his left lived a sycophantic, shrivelled, grey monkey from India who salaamed for titbits of food; on his right were a troupe of patchy buffoons who swung and tumbled about their cage to attract attention. Not so Humboldt's Gibbon; visitors passed him by — often with almost superstitious aversion and some such comment as 'Nasty things'; he had no tricks, or, if he had, he performed them alone, for his own satisfaction, after dark, ritualistically, when, in that exotic enclave among the stucco terraces, the prisoners awake and commemorate the jungles where they had their birth, as exiled darkies, when their work is done, will tread out the music of Africa in a vacant lot behind the drug-store.

Lucy used always to bring fruit to the ape; I had nothing, but, to deceive him, I rattled the wire and held out my empty fingers as though they held a gift. He unrolled himself, revealing an extraordinary length of black limb, and came delicately towards me on toes and finger-tips; his body was slightly pigeon-chested and his fur dense and short, his head spherical, without the poodle-snout of his neighbours — merely two eyes and a line of yellow teeth set in leather, like a bare patch worn in a rug. He was less like a man than any of his kind, and he lacked their human vulgarity. When, at short range, he realized that I held nothing for him he leapt suddenly at the bars and hung there, spread out to his full span, spiderish, snarling with contempt; then dropped to the floor and, turning about, walked delicately back to the corner from which I had lured him. So I looked at him and thought of Lucy, and the minutes passed.

Presently I was aware of someone passing behind me from the salaaming monkey to the troupe of tumblers, and back again, and at either side peering not at the animals but at me. I gazed fixedly at the ape, hoping that this nuisance would pass. Finally a voice said, 'I say.'

I turned and found Arthur Atwater. He was dressed as I had seen him before, in his raincoat, though it was a fine, warm day, and his soft grey hat, worn at what should have been a raffish angle but which, in effect, looked merely lopsided. (He explained the raincoat in the course of our conversation, saying, 'You know how it is in digs. If you leave anything behind when you go out for the day, someone's sure to take a fancy to it.') 'It is Plant, isn't it?' he said.

'Yes.'

'Thought so. I never forget a face. They call it the royal gift, don't they?'

'Do they?'

'Yes, that and punctuality. I'm punctual, too. It's a curious thing because you see, actually, though I don't make any fuss about it in the position I'm in, I'm descended from Henry seven.' There seemed no suitable answer to this piece of information so, since I was silent, he added suddenly, 'I say, you do remember me, don't you?'

'Vividly.'

He came closer and leant beside me on the rail which separated us from the cage. It was as though we stood on board ship and were looking out to sea, only instead of the passing waters we saw the solitary, still person of Humboldt's Gibbon. 'I don't mind telling you,' said Atwater, 'I've had a pretty thin time of it since we last met.'

'I saw you were acquitted at the trial. I thought you were very fortunate.'

'Fortunate! You should have heard the things the beak said. Things he had no right to say and wouldn't have dared say to a rich man, and said in a very nasty way, too — things I shan't forget in a hurry. Mr Justice Longworth — *Justice*, that's funny. Acquitted without a stain! — innocent! Does that give me back my job?'

'But I understood from the evidence at the trial that you were under notice to go anyway.'

'Yes. And why? Because sales were dropping. Why should I sell their beastly stockings for them anyway? Money — that's all anyone cares about now. And I'm beginning to feel the same way. When do you suppose I had my last meal — my last square meal?'

'I've really no idea, I'm afraid.'

'Tuesday. I'm hungry, Plant — literally hungry.'

'You could have saved yourself the sixpence admission here, couldn't you?'

'I'm a Fellow,' said Atwater with surprising readiness.

'Oh.'

'You don't believe that, do you?'

'I have no reason not to.'

'I can prove it; look here – Fellow's tickets, two of them.' He produced and pressed on my attention two tickets of admission signed in a thin, feminine hand. 'My dear Atwater,' I said, 'these don't make you a Fellow; they've merely been given you by someone who is – not that it matters.'

'Not that it matters! Let me tell you this. D'you know who gave me these? – the mother of a chap I know; chap I know well. I dropped round to see him the other evening, at the address I found in the telephone book. It was his mother's house as it happened. My pal was abroad. But, anyway, I got talking to the mother and told her about how I was placed and what pals her son and I had been. She seemed a decent old bird. At the end she said, "How very sad. Do let me give you something," and began fumbling in her bag. I thought at least a quid was coming, and what did she give me? These tickets for the Zoo. I ask you!'

'Well,' I said, with a tone as encouraging as I could manage, for it did seem to me that in this instance he had been unfairly disappointed, 'the Zoo is a very pleasant place.'

At this suggestion Atwater showed a mercurial change of

mood from resentment to simple enthusiasm. 'It's wonderful,' he said, 'there's nothing like it. All these animals from all over the world. Think what they've seen — forests and rivers, places probably where no white man's ever been. It makes you long to get away, doesn't it? Think of paddling your canoe upstream in undiscovered country, with strings of orchids overhead and parrots in the trees and great butterflies, and native servants, and hanging your hammock in the open at night and starting off in the morning with no one to worry you, living on fish and fruit — that's life,' said Atwater.

Once again I felt impelled to correct his misconceptions of colonial life. 'If you are still thinking of settling in Rhodesia,' I said, 'I must warn you you will find conditions very different from those you describe.'

'Rhodesia's off,' said Atwater. 'I've other plans.'

He told me of them at length, and because they distracted me from thinking of Lucy, I listened gratefully. They depended, primarily, on his finding a man of his acquaintance — a good scout named Appleby — who had lately disappeared as so many of Atwater's associates seemed to have done, leaving no indication of his whereabouts. Appleby knew of a cave in Bolivia where the Jesuits, in bygone years, had stored their treasure. When they were driven out, they put a curse on the place, so that the superstitious natives left the hoard inviolate. Appleby had old parchments which made the matter clear. More than this, Appleby had an aerial photograph of the locality, and by a special process known to himself, was able to treat the plate so that auriferous ground came out dark; the hill where the Jesuits had left their treasure was almost solid black; the few white spots indicated chests of jewels and, possibly, bar platinum. 'Appleby's idea was to collect ten stout fellows who would put up a hundred quid each for our fares and digging expenses. I'd have gone like a shot. Had it all fixed up. The only snag was that just at that time I couldn't put my hands on a hundred quid.'

'Did the expedition ever start?'

'I don't think so. You see a lot of the chaps were in the same position. Besides old Appleby would never start without me. He's a good scout. If I only knew where he hung out I should be all right.'

'Where used he to hang out?'

'You could always find him at the old Wimpole. He was what our barman called one of the regulars.'

'Surely they would know his address there?' I kept talking. As long as I was learning about old Appleby I had only half my mind for Lucy.

'Well, you see, the Wimpole's rather free and easy in some ways. As long as you're a good chap you're taken as you come and no questions asked. Subs are paid by the month; you know the kind of place. If you're shy of the ante, as we used to call it, the doorman doesn't let you in.'

'And old Appleby was shy of the ante?'

'That's it. It wasn't a thing to worry about. Most of the chaps one time or another had been shown the door. I expect it's the same at your club. No disgrace attached. But old Appleby's a bit touchy and began telling off the doorman good and proper, and then the secretary butted in and, to cut a long story short, there was something of a schmozzle.'

'Yes,' I said, 'I see.' And even as I spoke all interest in Appleby's schmozzle faded completely away and I thought of Lucy, lying at home in tears, waiting for her pain. 'For God's sake, tell me some more.' I said.

'More about Appleby?'

'More about anything. Tell me about all the chaps in the Wimpole. Tell me their names one by one and exactly what they look like. Tell me your family history. Tell me the full details of every job you have ever lost. Tell me all the funny stories you have ever heard. Tell my fortune. Don't you see, I want to be *told*?'

'I don't quite twig,' said Atwater. 'But if you are trying to hint that I'm boring you . . .'

'Atwater,' I said earnestly, 'I will pay you just to talk to me. Here is a pound, look, take it. There. Does that look as though I was bored?'

'It looks to me as though you were barmy,' said Atwater, pocketing the note. 'Much obliged all the same. It'll come in handy just at the moment, only as a loan, mind.'

'Only as a loan,' I said, and we both of us lapsed into silence, he, no doubt, thinking of my barminess, I of Lucy. The black ape walked slowly round his cage raking the sawdust and nut shells with the back of his hand, looking vainly for some neglected morsel of food. Presently there was an excited scurry in the cage next to us; two women had appeared with a bunch of bananas. 'Excuse me, please,' they said and pushed in front of us to feed Humboldt's Gibbon; then they passed on to the grey sycophant beyond, and so down all the cages until their bag was empty. 'Where shall we go now?' one of them said. 'I don't see the point of animals you aren't allowed to feed.'

Atwater overheard this remark; it worked in his mind so that by the time they had left the monkey house, he was in another mood. Atwater the dreamer, Atwater the good scout, and Atwater the underdog seemed to appear in more or less regular sequence. It was Atwater the good scout I liked best, but one clearly had to take him as he came. 'Feeding animals while men and women starve,' he said bitterly.

It was a topic; a topic dry, scentless and colourless as a pressed flower; a topic on which in the school debating society one had despaired of finding anything new to say – 'The motion before the House is that too much kindness is shown to animals, proposed by Mr John Plant, Headmaster's House' – nevertheless, it was something to talk about.

'The animals are paid for their entertainment value,'

I said. 'We don't send out hampers to monkeys in their own forests' — Or did we? There was no knowing what humane ladies in England would not do — 'We bring the monkeys here to amuse us.'

'What's amusing about that black creature there?'

'Well, he's very beautiful.'

'Beautiful?' Atwater stared into the hostile little face beyond the bars. 'Can't see it myself.' Then rather truculently, 'I suppose you'd say he was more beautiful than me.'

'Well, as a matter of fact, since you raise the point . . .'

'You think that thing beautiful and feed it and shelter it, while you leave me to starve.'

This seemed unfair. I had just given Atwater a pound; moreover, it was not I who had fed the ape. I pointed this out.

'I see,' said Atwater. 'You're paying me for my entertainment value. You think I'm a kind of monkey.'

This was uncomfortably near the truth. 'You misunderstand me,' I said.

'I hope I do. A remark like that would start a rough-house at the Wimpole.'

A new and glorious idea came to me. 'Atwater,' I said, cautiously, for his oppressed mood was still on him. 'Please do not take offence at my suggestion but, supposing I were to pay — as a loan, of course — would it be possible for us, do you think, to lunch at the Wimpole?'

He took the suggestion quite well. 'I'll be frank with you,' he said. 'I haven't paid this month's sub. yet. It's seven and sixpence.'

'We'll include that in the loan.'

'Good scout. I know you'll like the place.'

The taxi driver, to whom I gave the address 'Wimpole Club', was nonplussed. 'Now you've got me,' he said. 'I thought I knew them all. It's not what used to be called the "Palm Beach"?'

'No,' said Atwater, and gave more exact directions.

We drove to a mews off Wimpole Street ('It's handy for chaps in the motor business Great Portland Street way,' said Atwater). 'By the way, I may as well explain, I'm known as Norton at the club.'

'Why?'

'Lots of the chaps there use a different name. I expect it's the same at your club.'

'I shouldn't be surprised,' I said.

I paid the taxi. Atwater kicked open a green door and led me into the hall where a porter, behind the counter, was lunching off tea and sandwiches.

'I've been out of town,' said Atwater. 'Just dropped in to pay my subscription. Anyone about?'

'Very quiet,' said the porter.

The room into which he led me was entirely empty. It was at once bar, lounge and dining-room, but mostly bar, for which a kind of film-set had been erected, built far into the room, with oak rafters, a thatched roof, a wrought-iron lantern and an inn-sign painted in mock heraldry with quartered bottles and tankards.

'Jim!' cried Atwater.

'Sir.' A head appeared above the bar. 'Well, Mr Norton, we haven't seen you for a long time. I was just having my bit of dinner.'

'May I interrupt that important function and give my friend here something in the nature of a snorter' – this was a new and greatly expanded version of Atwater the good scout. 'Two of your specials, please, Jim.' To me, 'Jim's specials are famous.' To Jim, 'This is one of my best pals, Mr Plant.' To me, 'There's not much Jim doesn't know about me.' To Jim, 'Where's the gang?'

'They don't seem to come here like they did, Mr Norton. There's not the money about.'

'You've said it.' Jim put two cocktails on the bar before us. 'I presume, Jim, that since this is Mr Plant's first time among us, in pursuance of the old Wimpole custom, these are on the house?'

Jim laughed rather anxiously. 'Mr Norton likes his joke.'

'Joke? Jim, you shame me before my friends. But never fear. I have found a rich backer; if we aren't having this with you, you must have one with us.'

The barman poured himself out something from a bottle

which he kept for the purpose on a shelf below the bar, and said, 'First today,' as we toasted one another. Atwater said, 'It's one of the mysteries of the club what Jim keeps in that bottle of his.' I knew; it was what every barman kept, cold tea, but I thought it would spoil Atwater's treat if I told him.

Jim's 'special' was strong and agreeable.

'Is it all right for me to order a round?' I asked.

'It's more than all right. It's perfect.'

Jim shook up another cocktail and refilled his own glass.

'D'you remember the time I drank twelve of your specials before dinner with Mr Appleby?'

'I do, sir.'

'A tiny bit spifflicated that night, eh, Jim?'

'A tiny bit, sir.'

We had further rounds; Jim took cash for the drinks — three shillings a round. After the first round, when Atwater broke into his pound note, I paid. Every other time he said, 'Chalk it up to the national debt,' or similar reference to the fiction of our loan. Soon Jim and Atwater were deep in reminiscence of Atwater's past.

After a time I found my thoughts wandering and went to telephone to Victoria Square. Roger answered. 'It seems things are coming more or less normally,' he said.

'How is she?'

'I haven't been in. The doctor's here now, in a white coat like an umpire. He keeps saying I'm not to worry.'

'But is she in danger?'

'Of course she is, it's a dangerous business.'

'But I mean, more than most people?'

'Yes. No. I don't know. They said everything was quite normal, whatever that means.'

'I suppose it means she's not in more danger than most people.'

'I suppose so.'

'Does it bore you my ringing up to ask?'

'No, not really. Where are you?'

'At a club called the Wimpole.'

'Never heard of it.'

'No. I'll tell you about it later. Very interesting.'

'Good. Do tell me later.'

I returned to the bar. 'I thought our old comrade had passed out on us,' said Atwater. 'Been sick?'

'Good heavens, no.'

'You look a terrible colour, doesn't he, Jim? Perhaps a special is what he needs. I was sick that night old Grainger sold his Bentley, sick as a dog . . .'

When I had spent about thirty shillings Jim began to tire of his cold tea. 'Why don't you gentlemen sit down at a table and let me order you a nice grill?' he asked.

'All in good time, Jim, all in good time. Mr Plant here would like one of your specials first just to give him an appetite, and I think rather than see an old pal drink alone, I'll join him.'

Later, when we were very drunk, steaks appeared which neither of us remembered ordering. We ate them at the bar with, at Jim's advice, great quantities of Worcester sauce. Our conversation, I think, was mainly about Appleby and the need of finding him. We rang up one or two people of that name, whom we found in the telephone book, but they disclaimed all knowledge of Jesuit treasure.

It must have been four o'clock in the afternoon when we left the Wimpole. Atwater was more drunk than I. Next day I remembered most of our conversation verbatim. In the mews I asked him: 'Where are you living?'

'Digs. Awful hole. But it's all right now I've got money – I can sleep on the Embankment. Police won't let you sleep on the Embankment unless you've got money. Vagrancy. One law for the rich, one for the poor. Iniquitous system.'

'Why don't you come and live with me. I've got a house in the country, plenty of room. Stay as long as you like. Die there.'

'Thanks, I will. Must go the Embankment first and pack.'

And we separated, for the time, he sauntering unsteadily along Wimpole Street, past the rows of brass plates, I driving in a taxi to my rooms in Ebury Street, where I undressed, folded my clothes, and went quietly to bed. I awoke, in the dark, hours later, in confusion as to where I was and how I had got there.

The telephone was ringing next door in the sitting-room. It was Roger. He said that Lucy had had a son two hours ago; he had been ringing up relatives ever since. She was perfectly well; the first thing she had asked for when she came round from the chloroform was a cigarette. 'I feel like going out and getting drunk,' said Roger. 'Don't you?'

'No,' I said. 'No, I'm afraid not,' and returned to bed.

IV

When I got drunk I could sleep it off and wake in tolerable health; Roger could not; in the past we had often discussed this alcoholic insomnia of his and found no remedy for it except temperance. After telephoning to me he had gone out with Basil; he looked a wreck next morning.

'It's extraordinary,' he said. 'I've got absolutely no feeling about this baby at all. I kept telling myself all these last months that when I actually saw it, all manner of deep-rooted, atavistic emotions would come surging up. I was all set for a deep spiritual experience. They brought the thing in and showed it to me. I looked at it and waited — and nothing at all happened. It was just like the first time one takes hashish — or being "confirmed" at school.'

'I knew a man who had five children,' I said. 'He felt just as you did until the fifth. Then he was suddenly overcome with love; he bought a thermometer and kept taking its temperature when the nurse was out of the room. I daresay it's a habit, like hashish.'

'I don't feel as if I had anything to do with it. It's as though they showed me Lucy's appendix or a tooth they'd pulled out of her.'

'What's it like? I mean, it isn't a freak or anything?'

'No, I've been into that; two arms, two legs, one head, white — just a baby. Of course, you can't tell for some time if it's sane or not. I believe the first sign is that it can't take hold of things with its hands. Did you know that Lucy's grandmother was shut up?'

'I had no idea.'

'Yes. Lucy never saw her, of course. It's why she's anxious about Julia.'

'Is she anxious about Julia?'

'Who wouldn't be?'

'How soon can you tell if they're blind?'

'Not for weeks, I believe. I asked Sister Kemp. She said "The very idea" and whisked the baby off as if I wanted to injure it, poor little brute. D'you know what Lucy calls Sister Kemp now? — Kempy.'

'It's not possible.'

It was true. I went in to see her for five minutes and twice during that time she said 'Kempy.' When we were alone for a minute I asked her why. 'She asked me to,' said Lucy, 'and she's really very sweet.'

'Sweet?'

'She was absolutely sweet to me yesterday.'

I had brought some flowers, but the room was full of them. Lucy lay in bed; slack and smiling. I sat down by her and held her hand. 'Everyone's been so sweet,' she said. 'Have you seen my baby?'

'No.'

'He's in the dressing-room. Ask Kempy to show you.'

'Are you pleased with him?'

'I love him. I do really. I never thought I should. He's such a *person*.'

This was incomprehensible.

'You haven't gone bald?' I said.

'No, but my hair's terrible. What did you do yesterday?'

'I got drunk.'

'So did poor Roger. Were you with him?'

'No,' I said, 'it was really very amusing.' I began to tell her about Atwater, but she was not listening.

Then Sister Kemp came in with more flowers – from Mr Benwell.

'How sweet he is,' said Lucy.

This was past bearing – first Sister Kemp, now Mr Benwell. I felt stifled in this pastry-cook's atmosphere. 'I've come to say good-bye,' I said. 'I'm going back to the country to see about my house.'

'I'm so glad. It's lovely for you. I'm coming to see it as soon as I'm better.'

She did not want me, I thought; Humboldt's Gibbon and I had done our part. 'You'll be my first guest,' I said.

'Yes. Quite soon.'

Sister Kemp went with me to the landing. 'Now,' she said, 'come and see something very precious.'

There was a cradle in Roger's dressing-room, made of white stuff and ribbons, and a baby in it.

'Isn't he a fine big man?'

'Magnificent,' I said, 'and very sweet . . . Kempy.'

POSTSCRIPT

The date of the child's birth was 25 August, 1939, and while Lucy was still in bed the air-raid sirens sounded the first false alarm of the second World War. And so an epoch, my epoch, came to an end. Intellectually we had foreseen the event, and had calmly discussed it, but our inherited habits continued to the last moment.

Beavers bred in captivity, inhabiting a concrete pool, will, if given the timber, fatuously go through all the motions of damming an ancestral stream. So I and my friends busied ourselves with our privacies and intimacies. My father's death, the abandonment of my home, my quickening love of Lucy, my literary innovations, my house in the country – all these had seemed to presage a new life. The new life came, not by my contrivance.

Neither book – the last of my old life, the first of my new – was ever finished. As for my house, I never spent a night there. It was requisitioned, filled with pregnant women, and through five years bit by bit befouled and dismembered. My friends were dispersed. Lucy and her baby moved back to her aunt's. Roger rose from department to department in the office of Political Warfare. Basil sought and found a series of irregular adventures. For myself plain regimental soldiering proved an orderly and not disagreeable way of life.

I met Atwater several times in the course of the war – the Good-scout of the officer's club, the Under-dog in the transit-camp, the Dreamer lecturing troops about post-war conditions. He was reunited, it seemed, with all his legendary lost friends, he prospered and the Good-scout predominated. Today, I believe, he holds sway over a large area of Germany. No one of my close acquaintance was killed, but all our lives, as we had constructed them, quietly came to an end. Our story, like my novel, remained unfinished – a heap of neglected foolscap at the back of a drawer.

Charles Ryder's Schooldays

I

There was a scent of dust in the air; a thin vestige surviving in the twilight from the golden clouds with which before chapel the House Room fags had filled the evening sunshine. Light was failing. Beyond the trefoils and branched mullions of the windows the towering autumnal leaf was now flat and colourless. All the eastward slope of Spierpoint Down, where the College buildings stood, lay lost in shadow; above and behind, on the high lines of Chanctonbury and Spierpoint Ring, the first day of term was gently dying.

In the House Room thirty heads were bent over their books. Few form-masters had set any preparation that day. The Classical Upper Fifth, Charles Ryder's new form, were 'revising last term's work' and Charles was writing his diary under cover of Hassall's *History*. He looked up from the page to the darkling texts which ran in Gothic script around the frieze. '*Qui diligit Deum diligit et fratrem suum.*'

'Get on with your work, Ryder,' said Apthorpe.

Apthorpe has greased into being a house-captain this term, Charles wrote. *This is his first Evening School. He is being thoroughly officious and on his dignity.*

'Can we have the light on, please?'

'All right. Wykham-Blake, put it on.' A small boy rose from the under-school table. 'Wykham-Blake, I said. There's no need for everyone to move.'

A rattle of the chain, a hiss of gas, a brilliant white light over half the room. The other light hung over the new boys' table.

'Put the light on, one of you, whatever your names are.'

Six startled little boys looked at Apthorpe and at one another, all began to rise together, all sat down, all looked at Apthorpe in consternation.

'Oh, for heaven's sake.'

Apthorpe leaned over their heads and pulled the chain; there was a hiss of gas but no light. 'The bye-pass is out. Light it, you.' He threw a box of matches to one of the new boys who dropped it, picked it up, climbed on the table and looked miserably at the white glass shade, the three hissing mantles and at Apthorpe. He had never seen a lamp of this kind before; at home and at his private school there was electricity. He lit a match and poked at the lamp, at first without effect; then there was a loud explosion; he stepped back, stumbled and nearly lost his footing among the books and ink-pots, blushed hotly and regained the bench. The matches remained in his hand and he stared at them, lost in an agony of indecision. How should he dispose of them? No head was raised but everyone in the House Room exulted in the drama. From the other side of the room Apthorpe held out his hand invitingly.

'When you have quite finished with my matches perhaps you'll be so kind as to give them back.'

In despair the new boy threw them towards the house-captain; in despair he threw slightly wide. Apthorpe made no attempt to catch them, but watched them curiously as they fell to the floor. 'How very extraordinary,' he said. The new boy looked at the match-box; Apthorpe looked at the new boy. 'Would it be troubling you too much if I asked you to give me my matches?' he said.

The new boy rose to his feet, walked the few steps, picked up the match-box and gave it to the house-captain, with the ghastly semblance of a smile.

'Extraordinary crew of new men we have this term,' said Apthorpe. 'They seem to be entirely half-witted. Has anyone been turned on to look after this man?'

'Please, I have,' said Wykham-Blake.

'A grave responsibility for one so young. Try and convey to his limited intelligence that it may prove a painful practice here to throw match-boxes about in Evening School, and laugh at house officials. By the way, is that a work-book you're reading?'

'Oh, yes, Apthorpe.' Wykham-Blake raised a face of cherubic innocence and presented the back of the *Golden Treasury*.

'Who's it for?'

'Mr Graves. We're to learn any poem we like.'

'And what have you chosen?'

'Milton-on-his-blindness.'

'How, may one ask, did that take your fancy?'

'I learned it once before,' said Wykham-Blake and Apthorpe laughed indulgently.

'Young blighter,' he said.

Charles wrote:

Now he is snooping round seeing what books men are reading. It would be typical if he got someone beaten his first Evening School. The day before yesterday this time I was in my dinner-jacket just setting out for dinner at the d'Italie with Aunt Philippa before going to The Choice *at Wyndhams.* Quantum mutatus ab illo Hectore. *We live in water-tight compartments. Now I am absorbed in the trivial round of House politics. Graves has played hell with the house. Apthorpe a house-captain and O'Malley on the Settle. The only consolation was seeing the woe on Wheatley's fat face when the locker list went up. He thought he was a cert for the Settle this term. Bad luck on Tamplin though. I never expected to get on but I ought by all rights to have been above O'Malley. What a tick Graves is. It all comes of this rotten system of switching round house-tutors. We ought to have the best of Heads instead of which they try out ticks like Graves on us before giving them a house. If only we still had Frank.*

Charles's handwriting had lately begun to develop certain ornamental features – Greek E's and flourished crossings. He wrote with conscious style. Whenever Apthorpe came past he would turn a page in the history book, hesitate and then write as though making a note from the text. The hands of the clock crept on to half past seven when the porter's hand-bell began to sound in the cloisters on the far side of Lower Quad. This was the signal of release. Throughout the House Room heads were raised, pages blotted, books closed, fountain-pens screwed up. 'Get on with your work,' said Apthorpe; 'I haven't said anything about moving.' The porter and his bell passed up the cloisters, grew faint under the arch by the library steps, were barely audible in the Upper Quad, grew louder on the steps of Old's House and very loud in the cloister outside Head's. At last Apthorpe tossed the *Bystander* on the table and said 'All right.'

The House Room rose noisily. Charles underlined the date at the head of his page – *Wednesday Sept. 24th, 1919* – blotted it and put the note-book in his locker. Then with his hands in his pockets he followed the crowd into the dusk.

To keep his hands in his pockets thus – with his coat back and the middle button alone fastened – was now his privilege, for he was in his third year. He could also wear coloured socks and was indeed at the moment wearing a pair of heliotrope silk with white clocks, purchased the day before in Jermyn Street. There were several things, formerly forbidden, which were now his right. He could link his arm in a friend's and he did so now, strolling across to Hall arm-in-arm with Tamplin.

They paused at the top of the steps and stared out in the gloaming. To their left the great bulk of the chapel loomed immensely; below them the land fell away in terraces to the playing-fields with their dark fringe of elm; headlights moved continuously up and down the coast road; the estuary was just traceable, a lighter streak across the grey lowland, before it merged into the calm and invisible sea.

'Same old view,' said Tamplin.

'Give me the lights of London,' said Charles. 'I say, it's rotten luck for you about the Settle.'

'Oh, I never had a chance. It's rotten luck on *you*.'

'Oh, I never had a chance. But O'*Malley*.'

'It all comes of having that tick Graves instead of Frank.'

'The buxom Wheatley looked jolly bored. Anyway, I don't envy O'Malley's job as head of the dormitory.'

'That's how he got on the Settle. Tell you later.'

From the moment they reached the Hall steps they had to unlink their arms, take their hands out of their pockets and stop talking. When Grace had been said Tamplin took up the story.

'Graves had him in at the end of last term and said he was making him head of the dormitory. The head of Upper Dormitory never has been on the Settle before last term when they moved Easton up from Lower Anteroom after we ragged Fletcher. O'Malley told Graves he couldn't take it unless he had an official position.'

'How d'you know?'

'O'Malley told me. He thought he'd been rather fly.'

'Typical of Graves to fall for a tick like that.'

'It's all very well,' said Wheatley, plaintively, from across the table; 'I don't think they've any right to put Graves in like this. I only came to Spierpoint because my father knew Frank's brother in the Guards. I was jolly bored, I can tell you, when they moved Frank. I think he wrote to the Head about it. We pay more in Head's and get the worst of everything.'

'Tea, please.'

'Same old College tea.'

'Same old College eggs.'

'It always takes a week before one gets used to College food.'

'I never get used to it.'

'Did you go to many London restaurants in the holidays?'

'I was only in London a week. My brother took me to lunch at the Berkeley. Wish I was there now. I had two glasses of port.'

'The Berkeley's all right in the evening,' said Charles, 'if you want to dance.'

'It's jolly well all right for luncheon. You should see their hors d'oeuvres. I reckon there were twenty or thirty things to choose from. After that we had grouse and meringues with ices in them.'

'I went to dinner at the d'Italie.'

'Oh, where's that?'

'It's a little place in Soho not many people know about. My aunt speaks Italian like a native so she knows all those places. Of course, there's no marble or music. It just exists for the cooking. Literary people and artists go there. My aunt knows lots of them.'

'My brother says all the men from Sandhurst go to the Berkeley. Of course, they fairly rook you.'

'I always think the Berkeley's rather rowdy,' said Wheatley. 'We stayed at Claridges after we came back from Scotland because our flat was still being done up.'

'My brother says Claridges is a deadly hole.'

'Of course, it isn't everyone's taste. It's rather exclusive.'

'Then how did our buxom Wheatley come to be staying there, I wonder?'

'There's no need to be cheap, Tamplin.'

'I always say,' suddenly said a boy named Jorkins, 'that you get the best meal in London at the Holborn Grill.'

Charles, Tamplin and Wheatley turned with cold curiosity on the interrupter, united at last in their disdain. 'Do you, Jorkins? How very original of you.'

'Do you *always* say that, Jorkins? Don't you sometimes get tired of *always* saying the same thing?'

'There's a four-and-sixpenny table d'hôte.'

'Please, Jorkins, spare us the hideous details of your gormandizing.'

'Oh, all right. I thought you were interested, that's all.'

'Do you think,' said Tamplin, confining himself ostentatiously to Charles and Wheatley, 'that Apthorpe is keen on Wykham-Blake?'

'No, is he?'

'Well, he couldn't keep away from him in Evening School.'

'I suppose the boy had to find consolation now his case Sugdon's left. He hasn't a friend among the under-schools.'

'What d'you make of the man Peacock?' (Charles, Tamplin and Wheatley were all in the Classical Upper Fifth under Mr Peacock.)

'He's started decently. No work tonight.'

'Raggable?'

'I doubt it. But slack.'

'I'd sooner a master were slack than raggable. I got quite exhausted last term ragging the Tea-cake.'

'It was witty, though.'

'I hope he's not so slack that we shan't get our Certificates next summer.'

'One can always sweat the last term. At the University no one ever does any work until just before the exams. Then they sit up all night with black coffee and strychnine.'

'It would be jolly witty if no one passed his Certificate.'

'I wonder what they'd do.'

'Give Peacock the push, I should think.'

Presently Grace was said and the school streamed out into the cloisters. It was now dark. The cloisters were lit at intervals by gas-lamps. As one walked, one's shadow lengthened and grew fainter before one until, approaching the next source of light, it disappeared, fell behind, followed one's heels, shortened, deepened, disappeared and started again at one's toes. The quarter of an hour between Hall and Second Evening was mainly spent in walking the cloisters in pairs or in threes; to walk four abreast was the privilege of school prefects. On the steps of Hall, Charles was approached by O'Malley. He was an ungainly boy, an upstart who had come to Spierpoint late, in a bye-term. He was in Army Class B and his sole distinction was staying-power in cross-country running.

'Coming to the Graves?'

'No.'

'D'you mind if I hitch on to you for a minute?'

'Not particularly.'

They joined the conventional, perambulating couples, their shadows, lengthened before them, apart. Charles did not take O'Malley's arm. O'Malley might not take Charles's. The Settle was purely a House Dignity. In the cloisters Charles was senior by right of his two years at Spierpoint.

'I'm awfully sorry about the Settle,' said O'Malley.

'I should have thought you'd be pleased.'

'I'm not, honestly. It's the last thing I wanted. Graves sent me a postcard a week ago. It spoiled the end of the holidays. I'll tell you what happened. Graves had me in on the last day last term. You know the way he has. He said, "I've some unpleasant news for you, O'Malley. I'm putting you head of the Upper Dormitory." I said, "It ought to be someone on the Settle. No one else could keep order." I thought he'd keep Easton up there. He said, "These things are a matter of personality, not of official position." I said, "It's been proved you have an official. You know how bolshie we were with Fletcher." He said, "Fletcher wasn't the man for the job. He wasn't my appointment."'

'Typical of his lip. Fletcher was Frank's appointment.'

'I wish we had Frank still.'

'So does everyone. Anyway, why are you telling me all this?'

'I didn't want you to think I'd been greasing. I heard Tamplin say I had.'

'Well, you are on the Settle and you are head of the dormitory, so what's the trouble?'

'Will you back me up, Ryder?'

'Have you ever known me back anyone up, as you call it?'

'No,' said O'Malley miserably, 'that's just it.'

'Well, why d'you suppose I should start with you?'

'I just thought you might.'

'Well, think again.'

They had walked three sides of the square and were now at the door of Head's House. Mr Graves was standing outside his own room talking to Mr Peacock.

'Charles,' he said, 'come here a minute. Have you met this young man yet, Peacock? He's one of yours.'

'Yes, I think so,' said Mr Peacock doubtfully.

'He's one of my problem children. Come in here, Charles. I want to have a chat to you.'

Mr Graves took him by the elbow and led him into his room.

There were no fires yet and the two armchairs stood before an empty grate; everything was unnaturally bare and neat after the holiday cleaning.

'Sit you down.'

Mr Graves filled his pipe and gave Charles a long, soft and quizzical stare. He was a man still under thirty, dressed in Lovat tweed with an Old Rugbeian tie. He had been at Spierpoint during Charles's first term and they had met once on the miniature range; in that bleak, untouchable epoch Charles had been warmed by his affability. Then Mr Graves was called up for the army and now had returned, the term before, as House Tutor of Head's. Charles had grown confident in the meantime and felt no need of affable masters; only for Frank whom Mr Graves had supplanted. The ghost of Frank filled the room. Mr Graves had hung some Medici prints in the place of Frank's football groups. The set of

Georgian Poetry in the bookcase was his, not Frank's. His college arms embellished the tobacco jar on the chimney-piece.

'Well, Charles Ryder,' said Mr Graves at length, 'are you feeling sore with me?'

'Sir?'

Mr Graves became suddenly snappish. 'If you choose to sit there like a stone image, I can't help you.'

Still Charles said nothing.

'I have a friend,' said Mr Graves, 'who goes in for illumination. I thought you might like me to show him the work you sent in to the Art Competition last term.'

'I'm afraid I left it at home, sir.'

'Did you do any during the holidays?'

'One or two things, sir.'

'You never try painting from nature?'

'Never, sir.'

'It seems rather a crabbed, shut-in sort of pursuit for a boy of your age. Still, that's your own business.'

'Yes, sir.'

'Difficult chap to talk to, aren't you, Charles?'

'Not with everyone. Not with Frank,' Charles wished to say; 'I could talk to Frank by the hour.' Instead he said, 'I suppose I am, sir.'

'Well, I want to talk to you. I dare say you feel you have been a little ill-used this term. Of course, all your year are in rather a difficult position. Normally there would have been seven or eight people leaving at the end of last term but with the war coming to an end they are staying on an extra year, trying for University scholarships and so on. Only Sugdon left, so instead of a general move there was only one vacancy at the top. That meant only one vacancy on the Settle. I dare say you think you ought to have had it.'

'No, sir. There were two people ahead of me.'

'But not O'Malley. I wonder if I can make you understand why I put him over you. You were the obvious man in many ways. The thing is, some people *need* authority, others don't. You've got plenty of personality. O'Malley isn't at all sure of himself. He might easily develop into rather a second-rater. You're in no danger of that. What's more, there's the dormitory to consider. I think I can trust you to work loyally under O'Malley. I'm not so sure I could trust him to work under you. See? It's always been a difficult dormitory. I don't want a repetition of what happened with Fletcher. Do you understand?'

'I understand what you mean, sir.'

'Grim young devil, aren't you?'

'Sir?'

'Oh, all right, go away. I shan't waste any more time with you.'

'Thank you, sir.'

Charles rose to go.

'I'm getting a small hand printing-press this term,' said Mr Graves. 'I thought it might interest you.'

It did interest Charles intensely. It was one of the large features of his day-dreams; in chapel, in school, in bed, in all the rare periods of abstraction, when others thought of racing motor-cars and hunters and speed-boats, Charles thought long and often of a private press. But he would not betray to Mr Graves the intense surge of images that rose in his mind.

'I think the invention of movable type was a disaster, sir. It destroyed calligraphy.'

'You're a prig, Charles,' said Mr Graves. 'I'm sick of you. Go away. Tell Wheatley I want him. And try not to dislike me so much. It wastes both our time.'

Second Evening had begun when Charles returned to the House Room; he reported to the house-captain in charge, despatched Wheatley to Mr Graves and settled down over his Hassall to half an hour's day-dream, imagining the tall folios, the wide margins, the deckle-edged mould-made paper, the engraved initials, the rubrics and colophons of his private press. In Third Evening one could 'read'; Charles read Hugh Walpole's *Fortitude*.

Wheatley did not return until the bell was ringing for the end of Evening School.

Tamplin greeted him with 'Bad luck, Wheatley. How many did you get? Was he tight?'; Charles with 'Well, you've had a long hot-air with Graves. What on earth did he talk about?'

'It was all rather confidential,' said Wheatley solemnly.

'Oh, sorry.'

'No, I'll tell you sometime if you promise to keep it to yourself.' Together they ascended the turret stair to their dormitory. 'I say, have you noticed something? Apthorpe is in the Upper Anteroom this term. Have you ever known the junior house-captain anywhere except in the Lower Anteroom? I wonder how he worked it.'

'Why should he want to?'

'Because, my innocent, Wykham-Blake has been moved into the Upper Anteroom.'

'Tactful of Graves.'

'You know, I sometimes think perhaps we've rather misjudged Graves.'

'You didn't think so in Hall.'

'No, but I've been thinking since.'

'You mean he's been greasing up to you.'

'Well, all I can say is, when he wants to be decent, he *is* decent. I find we know quite a lot of the same people in the holidays. He once stayed on the moor next to ours.'

'I don't see anything particularly decent in that.'

'Well, it makes a sort of link. He explained why he put O'Malley on the Settle. He's a student of character, you know.'

'Who? O'Malley?'

'No, Graves. He said that's the only reason he is a school master.'

'I expect he's a schoolmaster because it's so jolly slack.'

'Not at all. As a matter of fact, he was going into the Diplomatic, just as I am.'

'I don't expect he could pass the exam. It's frightfully stiff. Graves only takes the Middle Fourth.'

'The exam is only to keep out undesirable types.'

'Then it would floor Graves.'

'He says schoolmastering is the most *human* calling in the world. Spierpoint is not an arena for competition. We have to stop the weakest going to the wall.'

'Did Graves say that?'

'Yes.'

'I must remember that if there's any unpleasantness with Peacock. What else did he say?'

'Oh, we talked about people, you know, and their characters. Would you say O'Malley had poise?'

'Good God, no.'

'That's just what Graves thinks. He says some people have it naturally and they can look after themselves. Others, like O'Malley, need bringing on. He thinks authority will give O'Malley poise.'

'Well, it doesn't seem to have worked yet,' said Charles, as O'Malley loped past their beds to his corner.

'Welcome to the head of the dormitory,' said Tamplin. 'Are we all late? Are you going to report us?'

O'Malley looked at his watch. 'As a matter of fact, you have exactly seven minutes.'

'Not by my watch.'

'We go by mine.'

'Really,' said Tamplin. 'Has your watch been put on the Settle, too? It looks a cheap kind of instrument to me.'

'When I am speaking officially I don't want any impertinence, Tamplin.'

'His watch *has* been put on the Settle. It's the first time I ever heard one could be impertinent to a watch.'

They undressed and washed their teeth. O'Malley looked repeatedly at his watch and at last said, 'Say your dibs.'

Everyone knelt at his bedside and buried his face in the bedclothes. After a minute, in quick succession, they rose and got into bed; all save Tamplin who remained kneeling. O'Malley stood in the middle of the dormitory, irresolute, his hand on the chain of the gas-lamp. Three minutes passed; it was the convention that no one spoke while anyone was still saying his prayers; several boys began to giggle. 'Hurry up,' said O'Malley.

Tamplin raised a face of pained rebuke. '*Please*, O'Malley. I'm saying my dibs.'

'Well, you're late.'

Tamplin remained with his face buried in the blanket. O'Malley pulled the chain and extinguished the light, all save the pale glow of the bye-pass under the white enamel shade. It was the custom, when doing this, to say 'Goodnight'; but Tamplin was still ostensibly in prayer; in this black predicament O'Malley stalked to his bed in silence.

'Aren't you going to say "Goodnight" to us?' asked Charles.

'Goodnight.'

A dozen voices irregularly took up the cry. 'Goodnight, O'Malley . . . I hope the official watch doesn't stop in the night . . . happy dreams, O'Malley.'

'Really, you know,' said Wheatley, 'there's a man still saying his prayers.'

'Stop talking.'

'*Please*,' said Tamplin, on his knees. He remained there for half a minute more, then rose and got into bed.

'You understand, Tamplin? You're late.'

'Oh, but I don't think I can be, even by your watch. I was perfectly ready when you said "Say your dibs."'

'If you want to take as long as that you must start sooner.'

'But I couldn't with all that noise going on, could I, O'Malley? All that wrangling about watches?'

'We'll talk about it in the morning.'

'Goodnight, O'Malley.'

At this moment the door opened and the house-captain in charge of the dormitory came in. 'What the devil's all this talking about?' he asked.

Now, O'Malley had not the smallest intention of giving Tamplin a 'late'. It was a delicate legal point, of the kind that was debated endlessly at Spierpoint, whether in the circumstances he could properly do so. It had been in O'Malley's mind to appeal to Tamplin's better nature in the morning, to say that he could take a joke as well as the next man, that his official position was repugnant to him, that the last thing he wished to do was start the term by using his new authority on his former associates; he would say all this and ask Tamplin to 'back him up'. But now, suddenly challenged out of the darkness, he lost his head and said, 'I was giving Tamplin a "late", Anderson.'

'Well, remind me in the morning and for Christ's sake don't make such a racket over it.'

'Please, Anderson, I don't think I was late,' said Tamplin; 'it's just that I took longer than the others over my prayers. I was perfectly ready when we were told to say them.'

'But he was still out of bed when I put the light out,' said O'Malley.

'Well, it's usual to wait until everyone's ready, isn't it?'

'Yes, Anderson. I did wait about five minutes.'

'I see. Anyhow, lates count from the time you start saying your dibs. You know that. Better wash the whole thing out.'

'Thank you, Anderson,' said Tamplin.

The house-captain lit the candle which stood in a biscuit-box shade on the press by his bed. He undressed slowly, washed and, without saying prayers, got into bed. Then he lay there reading. The tin hid the light from the dormitory and cast a small, yellow patch over his book and pillow; that and the faint circle of the gas-lamp were the only lights; gradually in the darkness the lancet windows became dimly visible. Charles lay on his back thinking; O'Malley had made a fiasco of his first evening; first and last he could not have done things worse; it seemed a rough and tortuous road on which Mr Graves had set his feet, to self-confidence and poise.

Then, as he grew sleepier, Charles's thoughts, like a roulette ball when the wheel runs slow, sought their lodging and came at last firmly to rest on that day, never far distant, at the end of his second term; the raw and gusty day of the junior steeplechase when, shivering and half-changed, queasy with apprehension of the trial ahead, he had been summoned by Frank, had shuffled into his clothes, run headlong down the turret stairs and with a new and deeper alarm knocked at the door.

'Charles, I have just had a telegram from your father which you must read. I'll leave you alone with it.'

He shed no tear, then or later; he did not remember what was said when two minutes later Frank returned; there was a numb, anaesthetized patch at the heart of his sorrow; he remembered, rather, the order of the day. Instead of running he had gone down in his overcoat with Frank to watch the finish of the race; word had gone round the house and no questions were asked; he had tea with the matron, spent the evening in her room and slept that night in a room in the Headmaster's private house; next morning his Aunt Philippa came and took him home. He remembered all that went on outside himself, the sight and sound and smell of the place, so that, on his return to them, they all spoke of his loss, of the sharp severance of all the bonds of childhood, and it seemed to him that it was not in the uplands of Bosnia but here at Spierpoint, on the turret stairs, in the unlighted box-room passage, in the windy cloisters, that his mother had fallen, killed not by a German shell but by the shrill voice sounding across the changing room, 'Ryder here? Ryder? Frank wants him at the double.'

II

Thursday, September 25th, 1919. Peacock began well by not turning up for early school so at five past we walked out and went back to our House Rooms and I read Fortitude by Walpole; it is strong meat but rather unnecessary in places. After breakfast O'Malley came greasing up to Tamplin and apologized. Everyone is against him. I maintain he was in the right until he reported him late to Anderson. No possible defence for that — sheer windiness. Peacock deigned to turn up for Double Greek. We mocked him somewhat. He is trying to make us use the new pronunciation; when he said o'ú there was a wail of 'ooh' and Tamplin pronounced subjunctive soobyoongteewny — very witty. Peacock got bored and said he'd report him to Graves but relented. Library was open 5–6 tonight. I went meaning to put in some time on Walter Crane's Bases of

Design but Mercer came up with that weird man in Brent's called Curtis-Dunne. I envy them having Frank as house-master. He is talking of starting a literary and artistic society for men not in the Sixth. Curtis-Dunne wants to start a political group. Pretty good lift considering this is his second term although he is sixteen and has been at Dartmouth. Mercer gave me a poem to read — very sloppy. Before this there was a House Game. Everyone puffing and blowing after the holidays. Anderson said I shall probably be centre-half in the Under Sixteens — the sweatiest place in the field. I must get into training quickly.

Friday 26th. Corps day but quite slack. Reorganization. I am in A Company at last. A tick in Boucher's called Spratt is platoon commander. We ragged him a bit. Wheatley is a section commander! Peacock sent Bankes out of the room in Greek Testament for saying 'Who will rid me of this turbulent priest' when put on to translate. Jolly witty. He began to argue. Peacock said, 'Must I throw you out by force?' Bankes began to go but muttered 'Muscular Christianity.' Peacock: 'What did you say?'; 'Nothing, sir'; 'Get out before I kick you.' Things got a bit duller after that. Uncle George gave Bankes three.

Saturday 27th. Things very dull in school. Luckily Peacock forgot to set any preparation. Pop. Sci. in last period. Tamplin and Mercer got some of the weights that are so precious they are kept in a glass case and picked up with tweezers, made them red hot on a bunsen burner and dropped them in cold water. A witty thing to do. House Game — Under Sixteen team against a mixed side. They have put Wykham-Blake centre-half and me in goal; a godless place. Library again. Curtis-Dunne buttonholed me again. He drawled 'My father is in parliament but he is a very unenlightened conservative. I of course am a socialist. That's the reason I chucked the Navy.' I said, 'Or did they chuck you?' 'The pangs of parting were endured by both sides with mutual stoicism'. He spoke of Frank as 'essentially a well-intentioned fellow'. Sunday tomorrow thank God. I may be able to get on with illuminating 'The Bells of Heaven'.

III

Normally on Sundays there was a choice of service. Matins at a quarter to eight or Communion at quarter past. On the first Sunday of term there was Choral Communion for all at eight o'clock.

The chapel was huge, bare, and still unfinished, one of the great monuments of the Oxford Movement and the Gothic revival. Like an iceberg it revealed only a small part of its bulk above the surface of the terraced down; below lay a crypt and below that foundations of great depth. The Founder had chosen the site and stubbornly refused to change it so that the original estimates had been exceeded before the upper chapel was begun. Visiting preachers frequently drew a lesson from the disappointments, uncertainties and final achievement of the Founder's 'vision'. Now the whole nave rose triumphantly over the surrounding landscape, immense, clustered shafts supporting the groined roof; at the west it ended abruptly in concrete and timber and corrugated iron, while behind, in a waste land near the kitchens, where the Corps band practised their bugles in the early morning, lay a nettle-and-bramble-grown ruin, the base of a tower, twice as high as the chapel, which one day was to rise so that on stormy nights, the Founder had decreed, prayers might be sung at its summit for sailors in peril on the sea.

From outside the windows had a deep, submarine tinge, but from inside they were clear white, and the morning sun streamed in over the altar and the assembled school. The prefect in Charles's row was Symonds, editor of the Magazine, president of the Debating Society, the leading intellectual. Symonds was in Head's; he pursued a course of lonely study, seldom taking Evening School, never playing any game except, late in the evenings of the summer term, an occasional single of lawn tennis, appearing rarely even in the Sixth Form, but working in private under Mr A. A. Carmichael for the Balliol scholarship. Symonds kept a leather-bound copy of the *Greek Anthology* in his place in chapel and read it throughout the services with a finely negligent air.

The masters sat in stalls orientated between the columns, the clergy in surplices, laymen in gowns. Some of the masters who taught the Modern Side wore hoods of the newer universities; Major Stebbing, the adjutant of the O.T.C., had no gown at all; Mr A. A. Carmichael – awfully known at Spierpoint as 'A.A.', the splendid dandy and wit, fine flower of the Oxford Union and the New College Essay Society, the reviewer of works of classical scholarship for the *New Statesman*, to whom Charles had never yet spoken; whom Charles had never yet heard speak directly, but only at third hand as his *mots*, in their idiosyncratic modulations, passed from mouth to mouth from the Sixth in sanctuary to the catechumens in the porch; whom Charles worshipped from afar – Mr Carmichael, from a variety of academic costume, was this morning robed as a baccalaureate of Salamanca. He looked, as he stooped over his desk, like the prosecuting counsel in a cartoon by Daumier.

Nearly opposite him across the chapel stood Frank Bates; an unbridged gulf of boys separated these rival and contrasted deities, that one the ineffable dweller on cloud-capped Olympus, this the homely clay image, the intimate of hearth and household, the patron of threshing-floor and olive-press. Frank wore only an ermine hood, a B. A.'s gown, and loose, unremarkable clothes, subfusc today, with the Corinthian tie which alternated with the Carthusian, week in, week out. He was a clean, curly, spare fellow; a little wan for he was in constant pain from an injury on the football field which had left him lame and kept him at Spierpoint throughout the war. This pain of his redeemed him from heartiness. In chapel his innocent, blue eyes assumed a puzzled, rather glum expression like those of an old-fashioned child in a room full of grown-ups. Frank was a bishop's son.

Behind the masters, out of sight in the side aisles, was a dowdy huddle of matrons and wives.

The service began with a procession of the choir: 'Hail Festal Day', with Wykham-Blake as the treble cantor. At the rear of the procession came Mr Peacock, the Chaplain and the Headmaster. A week ago Charles had gone to church in London with Aunt Philippa. He did not as a rule go to church in the holidays, but being in London for the last week Aunt Philippa had said, 'There's nothing much we can do today. Let's see what entertainment the Church can offer. I'm told there is a very remarkable freak named Father Wimperis.' So, together, they had gone on the top of a bus to a northern suburb where Mr Wimperis was at the time drawing great congregations. His preaching was not theatrical by Neapolitan standards, Aunt Philippa said afterwards; 'However, I enjoyed him hugely. He is irresistibly common.' For twenty minutes Mr Wimperis alternately fluted and boomed from the pulpit, wrestled with the reading-stand and summoned the country to industrial peace. At the end he performed a little ceremony of his own invention, advancing to the church steps in cope and biretta with what proved to be a large silver salt cellar in his hands. 'My people,' he said simply, scattering salt before him, 'you are the salt of the earth.'

'I believe he has something new like that every week,' said Aunt Philippa. 'It must be lovely to live in his neighbourhood.'

Charles's was not a God-fearing home. Until August 1914 his father had been accustomed to read family prayers every morning; on the outbreak of war he abruptly stopped the practice, explaining, when asked, that there was now nothing left to pray for. When Charles's mother was killed there was a memorial service for her at Boughton, his home village, but Charles's father did not go with him and Aunt Philippa. 'It was all her confounded patriotism,' he said, not to Charles but to Aunt Philippa, who did not repeat the remark until many years later. 'She had no business to go off to Serbia like that. Do you think it my duty to marry again?'

'No,' said Aunt Philippa.

'Nothing would induce me to – least of all my duty.'

The service followed its course. As often happened, two small boys fainted and were carried out by house-captains; a third left bleeding at the nose. Mr Peacock sang the Gospel over-loudly. It was his first public appearance. Symonds looked up from his Greek, frowned and continued reading. Presently it was time for Communion; most of the boys who had been confirmed went up to the chancel rails, Charles with them. Symonds sat back, twisted his long legs into the aisle to allow his row to pass, and remained in his place. Charles took Communion and returned to his row. He had been confirmed the term before, incuriously, without expectation or disappointment. When, later in life, he read accounts of the emotional disturbances caused in other boys by the ceremony he found them unintelligible; to Charles it was one of the rites of adolescence, like being made, when a new boy, to stand on the table and sing. The Chaplain had 'prepared' him and had confined his conferences to theology. There had been no probing of his sexual life; he had no sexual life to probe. Instead they had talked of prayer and the sacraments.

Spierpoint was a product of the Oxford Movement, founded with definite religious aims; in eighty years it had grown more and more to resemble the older Public Schools, but there was still a strong ecclesiastical flavour in the place. Some boys were genuinely devout and their peculiarity was respected; in general profanity was rare and ill-looked-on. Most of the Sixth professed themselves agnostic or atheist.

The school had been chosen for Charles because, at the age of eleven, he had had a 'religious phase' and told his father that he wished to become a priest.

'Good heavens,' his father said; 'or do you mean a parson?'

'A priest of the Anglican Church,' said Charles precisely.

'That's better. I thought you meant a Roman Catholic. Well, a parson's is not at all a bad life for a man with a little money of his own. They can't remove you except for flagrant immorality. Your uncle has been trying to get rid of his fellow at Boughton for ten years – a most offensive fellow but perfectly chaste. He won't budge. It's a great thing in life to have a place you can't be removed from – too few of them.'

But the 'phase' had passed and lingered now only in Charles's love of Gothic architecture and breviaries.

After Communion Charles sat back in his chair thinking about the secular, indeed slightly anti-clerical, lyric which, already inscribed, he was about to illuminate, while the masters and, after them, the women from the side aisles, went up to the rails.

The food on Sundays was always appreciably worse than on other days; breakfast invariably consisted of boiled eggs, over-boiled and lukewarm.

Wheatley said, 'How many ties do you suppose A. A.'s got?'

'I began counting last term,' said Tamplin, 'and got to thirty.'

'Including bows?'

'Yes.'

'Of course, he's jolly rich.'

'Why doesn't he keep a car, then?' asked Jorkins.

The hour after breakfast was normally devoted to letter-writing, but today a railway strike had been called and there were no posts. Moreover, since it was the start of term, there was no Sunday Lesson. The whole morning was therefore free and Charles had extracted permission to spend it in the Drawing School. He collected his materials and was soon happily at work.

The poem – Ralph Hodgson's ''Twould ring the bells of Heaven The wildest peal for years, If Parson lost his senses And people came to theirs . . .' – was one of Frank's favourites. In the happy days when he had been House Tutor of Head's, Frank had read poetry aloud on Sunday evenings to any in Head's who cared to come, which was mostly the lower half of the House. He read 'There swimmeth One Who swam e'er rivers were begun, And under that Almighty Fin the littlest fish may enter in' and 'Abou Ben Adhem, may his tribe increase' and 'Under the wide and starry sky' and 'What have I done for you, England, my England . . . ?' and many others of the same comfortable kind; but always before the end of the evening someone would say 'Please, sir, can we have "The Bells of Heaven"?' Now he read only to his own house but the poems, Frank's pleasant voices, his nightingales, were awake still, warm and bright with remembered firelight.

Charles did not question whether the poem was not perfectly suited to the compressed thirteenth-century script in which he had written it. His method of writing was first to draw the letters faintly, free-hand in pencil; then with a ruler and ruling-pen to ink in the uprights firmly in Indian ink until the page consisted of lines of short and long black perpendiculars; then with a mapping-pen he joined them with hair strokes and completed their lozenge-shaped terminals. It was a method he had evolved for himself by trial and error. The initial letters of each line were left blank and these, during the last week of the holidays, he had filled with vermilion, carefully drawn, 'Old English' capitals. The T alone remained to do and for this he had selected a model from Shaw's *Alphabets*, now open before him on the table. It was a florid fifteenth-century letter which needed considerable ingenuity of adaption, for he had decided to attach to it the decorative tail of the J. He worked happily, entirely absorbed, drawing in pencil, then tensely, with breath held, inking the outline with a mapping-pen; then, when it was dry – how often, in his impatience, he had ruined his work by attempting this too soon – rubbing away the pencil lines. Finally he got out his water colours and his red sable brushes. At heart he knew he was going too fast – a monk would take a week over a single letter – but he worked with intensity and in less than two hours the initial with its pendant, convoluted border was finished. Then, as he put away his brushes, the exhilaration left him. It was no good; it was botched; the ink outline varied in thickness, the curves seemed to feel their way cautiously where they should have been bold; in places the colour overran the line and everywhere in contrast to the opaque lithographic ink it was watery and transparent. It was no good.

Despondently Charles shut his drawing book and put his things together. Outside the Drawing School, steps led down to the Upper Quad past the doors of Brent's House – Frank's. Here he met Mercer.

'Hullo, been painting?'

'Yes, if you can call it that.'

'Let me see.'

'No.'

'Please.'

'It's absolutely beastly. I hate it, I tell you. I'd have torn it up if I wasn't going to keep it as a humiliation to look at in case I ever begin to feel I know anything about art.'

'You're always dissatisfied, Ryder. It's the mark of a true artist, I suppose.'

'If I was an artist I shouldn't do things I'd be dissatisfied with. Here, look at it, if you must.'

Mercer gazed at the open page. 'What don't you like about it?'

'The whole thing's nauseating.'

'I suppose it is a bit ornate.'

'There, my dear Mercer, with your usual unerring discernment you have hit upon the one quality that is at all tolerable.'

'Oh, sorry. Anyway, I think the whole thing absolutely first-class.'

'Do you, Mercer. I'm greatly encouraged.'

'You know you're a frightfully difficult man. I don't know why I like you.'

'I know why I like you. Because you are so extremely easy.'

'Coming to the library?'

'I suppose so.'

When the library was open a prefect sat there entering in a ledger the books which boys took out. Charles as usual made his way to the case where the Art books were kept but before he had time to settle down, as he liked to do, he was accosted by Curtis-Dunne, the old new boy of last term in Brent's. 'Don't you think it scandalous,' he said, 'that on one of the few days of the week when we have the chance to use the library, we should have to kick our heels waiting until some semi-literate prefect chooses to turn up and take us in? I've taken the matter up with the good Frank.'

'Oh, and what did he say to that?'

'We're trying to work out a scheme by which library privileges can be extended to those who seriously want them, people like you and me and I suppose the good Mercer.'

'I forget for the moment what form you are in.'

'Modern Upper. Please don't think from that that I am a scientist. It's simply that in the Navy we had to drop Classics. My interests are entirely literary and political. And of course hedonistic.'

'Oh.'

'Hedonistic above all. By the way, I've been looking through the political and economic section. It's very quaintly chosen, with glaring lacunae. I've just filled three pages in the Suggestions Book. I thought perhaps you'd care to append your signature.'

'No thanks. It's not usual for people without library privileges to write in the Suggestions Book. Besides, I've no interest in economics.'

'I've also written a suggestion about extending the library privileges. Frank needs something to work on, that he can put before the committee.'

He brought the book to the Art bay; Charles read 'That since seniority is no indication of literary taste the system of library privileges be revised to provide facilities for those genuinely desirous of using them to advantage.'

'Neatly put, I think,' said Curtis-Dunne.

'You'll be thought frightfully above yourself, writing this.'

'It is already generally recognized that I *am* above myself, but I want other signatures.'

Charles hesitated. To gain time he said, 'I say, what on earth have you got on your feet? Aren't those house shoes?'

Curtis-Dunne pointed a toe shod in shabby, soft black leather; a laced shoe without a toecap, in surface like the cover of a well-worn Bible. 'Ah, you have observed my labour-saving device. I wear them night and morning. They are a constant perplexity to those in authority. When questioned, as happened two or three times a week during my first term, I say they are a naval pattern which my father, on account of extreme poverty, has asked me to wear out. That embarrasses them. But I am sure you do not share these middle-class prejudices. Dear boy, your name, please, to this subversive manifesto.'

Still Charles hesitated. The suggestion outraged Spierpoint taste in all particulars. Whatever intrigues, blandishments and self-advertisements were employed by the ambitious at Spierpoint were always elaborately disguised. Self-effacement and depreciation were the rule. To put oneself explicitly forward for preferment was literally not done. Moreover, the lead came from a boy who was not only in another house and immeasurably Charles's inferior, but also a notorious eccentric. A term back Charles would have rejected the proposal with horror, but today and all this term he was aware of a new voice in his inner counsels, a detached, critical Hyde who intruded his presence more and more often on the conventional, intolerant, subhuman, wholly respectable Dr Jekyll; a voice, as it were, from a more civilized age, as from the chimney corner in mid-Victorian times there used to break sometimes the sardonic laughter of grandmama, relic of Regency, a clear, outrageous, entirely self-assured disturber among the high and muddled thoughts of her whiskered descendants.

'Frank's all for the suggestion, you know,' said Curtis-

Dunne. 'He says the initiative must come from us. He can't go pushing reforms which he'll be told nobody really wants. He wants a concrete proposal to put before the library committee.'

That silenced Jekyll. Charles signed.

'Now,' said Curtis-Dunne, 'there should be little difficulty with the lad Mercer. He said he'd sign if you would.'

By lunch-time there were twenty-three signatories, including the prefect-in-charge.

'We have this day lit a candle,' said Curtis-Dunne.

There was some comment around Charles in Hall about his conduct in the library.

'I know he's awful,' said Charles, 'but he happens to amuse me.'

'They all think he's barmy in Brent's.'

'Frank doesn't. And anyway I call that a recommendation. As a matter of fact, he's one of the most intelligent men I ever met. If he'd come at the proper time he'd probably be senior to all of us.'

Support came unexpectedly from Wheatley. 'I happen to know the Head took him in as a special favour to his father. He's Sir Samson Curtis-Dunne's son, the Member for this division. They've got a big place near Steyning. I wouldn't at all mind having a day's shooting there next Veniam day.'

On Sunday afternoons, for two hours, the House Room was out of bounds to all except the Settle; in their black coats and with straw hats under their arms the school scattered over the countryside in groups, pairs and occasional disconsolate single figures, for 'walks'. All human habitations were barred; the choice lay between the open down behind Spierpoint Ring and the single country road to the isolated Norman church of St Botolph. Tamplin and Charles usually walked together.

'How I hate Sunday afternoons,' said Charles.

'We might get some blackberries.'

But at the door of the house they were stopped by Mr Graves.

'Hullo, you two,' he said, 'would you like to make yourselves useful? My press has arrived. I thought you might help put it together.' He led them into his room, where half-opened crates filled most of the floor. 'It was all in one piece when I bought it. All I've got to go on is this.' He showed them a woodcut in an old book. 'They didn't change much from Caxton's day until the steam presses came in. This one is about a hundred years old.'

'Damned sweat,' muttered Tamplin.

'And here, young Ryder, is the "movable type" you deplore so much.'

'What sort of type is it, sir?'

'We'll have to find out. I bought the whole thing in one lot from a village stationer.'

They took out letters at random, set them, and took an

impression by pressing them, inked, on a sheet of writing paper. Mr Graves had an album of typefaces.

'They all look the same to me,' said Tamplin.

In spite of his prejudice, Charles was interested. 'I've got it, I think, sir; Baskerville.'

'No. Look at the serifs. How about Caslon Old Style?'

At last it was identified. Then Charles found a box full of ornamental initials, menu headings of decanters and dessert, foxes' heads and running hounds for sporting announcements, ecclesiastical devices and monograms, crowns, Odd Fellows' arms, the wood-cut of a prize bull, decorative bands, the splendid jumble of a century of English job-printing.

'I say, sir, what fun. You could do all sorts of things with these.'

'We will, Charles.'

Tamplin looked at the amateurs with disgust. 'I say, sir, I've just remembered something I must do. Do you mind awfully if I don't stay?'

'Run along, old Tamplin.' When he had gone, Mr Graves said, 'I'm sorry Tamplin doesn't like me.'

'Why can he not let things pass?' thought Charles. 'Why does he always have to comment on everything?'

'You don't like me either, Charles. But you like the press.'

'Yes,' said Charles, 'I like the press.'

The type was tied up in little bags. They poured it out, each bagful into the tray provided for it in the worn oak tray.

'Now for the press. This looks like the base.'

It took them two hours to rebuild. When at last it was assembled, it looked small, far too small for the number and size of the cases in which it had travelled. The main cast-iron supports terminated in brass Corinthian capitals and the summit was embellished with a brass urn bearing the engraved date 1824. The common labour, the problems and discoveries, of erection had drawn the two together; now they surveyed its completion in common pride. Tamplin was forgotten.

'It's a lovely thing, sir. Could you print a book on it?'

'It would take time. Thank you very much for your help. And now,' Mr Graves looked at his watch, 'as, through some grave miscarriage of justice, you are not on the Settle, I expect you have no engagement for tea. See what you can find in the locker.'

The mention of the Settle disturbed their intimacy. Mr Graves repeated the mistake a few minutes later when they had boiled the kettle and were making toast on the gas-ring. 'So at this moment Desmond O'Malley is sitting down to his first Settle tea. I hope he's enjoying it. I don't think somehow he is enjoying this term very much so far.' Charles said nothing. 'Do you know, he came to me two days ago and asked to resign from it? He said that if I didn't let him he would do something that would make me degrade him. He's an odd boy, Desmond. It was an odd request.'

'I don't suppose he'd want me to know about it.'

'Of course he wouldn't. Do you know why I'm telling you? Do you?'

'No, sir.'

'I think you could make all the difference to him, whether his life is tolerable or not. I gather all you little beasts in the Upper Dormitory have been giving him hell.'

'If we have, it's because he asked for it.'

'I dare say, but don't you think it rather sad that in life there are so many different things different people are asking for, and the only people who get what they ask for are the Desmond O'Malleys?'

At that moment, beyond the box-room, the Settle tea had reached its second stage; surfeited with crumpets, five or six each, they were starting on the éclairs and cream-slices. There was still a warm, soggy pile of crumpets left uneaten and according to custom O'Malley, as junior man, was deputed to hand them round the House Room.

Wheatley was supercilious. 'What is that, O'Malley? Crumpets? How very kind of you, but I am afraid I never eat them. My digestion, you know.'

Tamplin was comic. 'My figure, you know,' he said.

Jorkins was rude. 'No, thanks. They look stale.'

There was loud laughter among the third-year men and some of their more precocious juniors. In strict order of seniority, O'Malley travelled from boy to boy, rebuffed, crimson.

All the Upper Dormitory refused. Only the fags watched, first in wonder that anyone should refuse crumpets on a cold afternoon, later with brightening expectancy as the full plate came nearer to them.

'I say, thanks awfully, O'Malley.' They soon went at the under-school table and O'Malley returned to his chair before the empty grate, where he sat until chapel silently eating confectionery.

'You see,' said Mr Graves, 'the beastlier you are to O'Malley, the beastlier he'll become. People are like that.'

IV

Sunday, Sept. 28th. Choral. Two or three faints otherwise uneventful. Tried to do the initial and border for 'The Bells of Heaven' but made a mess of it. Afterwards talked to Curtis-Dunne in the library. He intrigues me. With Frank's approval we are agitating for library privileges. I don't suppose anything will come of it except that everyone will say we are above ourselves. After luncheon Tamplin and I were going for a walk when Graves called us in and made us help put up his printing press. Tamplin escaped. Graves tried to get things out of me about ragging Dirty Desmond but without success. In the evening we had another rag. Tamplin, Wheatley, Jorkins and I hurried up to the dormitory as soon as the bell went and said our prayers before Dirty D. arrived. Then when he said,

'Say your dibs' we just sat on our beds. He looked frightfully bored and said 'Must I repeat my instructions?' As the other men were praying we said nothing. Then he said, 'I give you one more chance to say your dibs. If you don't I'll report you.' We said nothing so off Dirty D. went in his dressing-gown to Anderson who was with the other house-captains at hot-air with Graves. Up came Anderson. 'What's all this about your prayers?' 'We've said them already.' 'Why?' 'Because Tamplin got a late for taking too long so we thought we'd better start early.' 'I see. Well we'll talk about it tomorrow.' So far nothing has been said. Everyone thinks we shall get beaten but I don't see how we can be. We are entirely in our rights. Geoghegan has just been round to all four of us to say we are to stay behind after First Evening so I suppose we are going to be beaten.

After First Evening, when the House Room was clear of all save the four and the bell for Hall had died away and ceased, Geoghegan, the head of the house, came in carrying two canes, accompanied by Anderson.

'I am going to beat you for disobeying an order from the head of your dormitory. Have you anything to say?'

'Yes,' said Wheatley. 'We had already said our prayers.'

'It is a matter of indifference to me how often you pray. You have spent most of the day on your knees in chapel, praying all the time, I hope. All I am concerned about is that you obey the orders of the head of the dormitory. Anyone else anything to say? Then get the room ready.'

They pushed back the new men's table and laid a bench on its side across the front of the fireplace. The routine was familiar. They were beaten in the House Room twice a term, on the average.

'Who's senior? You, I think, Wheatley.'

Wheatley bent over the bench.

'Knees straight.' Geoghegan took his hips and arranged him to his liking, slightly oblique to the line of advance. From the corner he had three steps to the point of delivery. He skipped forward, struck and slowly turned back to the corner. They were given three strokes each; none of them moved. As they walked across the Hall, Charles felt the slight nausea turn to exhilaration.

'Was he tight?'

'Yes, he was, rather. And damned accurate too.'

After Hall, in the cloisters, O'Malley approached Charles.

'I say, Ryder, I'm frightfully sorry about tonight.'

'Oh, push off.'

'I had to do my duty, you know.'

'Well, go and do it, but don't come and bother me.'

'I'll do anything you like to make up. Anything outside the House, that is. I'll tell you what – I'll kick anyone else in another house, anyone you care to choose. Spratt, if you like.'

'The best thing you can do is to kick yourself, Dirty Desmond, right round the cloisters.'

SCOTT-KING'S MODERN EUROPE

MARIAE IMMACULATAE ANTONIAE
CONIUGIS PRUDENTIORIS
AUDACI CONIUGI

Scott-King's Modern Europe

I

In 1946 Scott-King had been classical master at Granchester for twenty-one years. He was himself a Granchesterian and had returned straight from the University after failing for a fellowship. There he had remained, growing slightly bald and slightly corpulent, known to generations of boys first as 'Scottie', then of late years, while barely middle-aged, as 'old Scottie'; a school 'institution', whose precise and slightly nasal lamentations of modern decadence were widely parodied.

Granchester is not the most illustrious of English public schools but it is, or, as Scott-King would maintain, was, entirely respectable; it plays an annual cricket match at Lord's; it numbers a dozen or so famous men among its old boys, who, in general, declare without apology: 'I was at Granchester' — unlike the sons of lesser places who are apt to say: 'As a matter of fact I was at a place called —. You see at the time my father . . .'

When Scott-King was a boy and when he first returned as a master, the school was almost equally divided into a

Classical and a Modern Side, with a group of negligible and neglected specialists called 'the Army Class'. Now the case was altered and out of 450 boys scarcely fifty read Greek. Scott-King had watched his classical colleagues fall away one by one, some to rural rectories, some to the British Council and the B.B.C., to be replaced by physicists and economists from the provincial universities, until now, instead of inhabiting solely the rare intellectual atmosphere of the Classical Sixth, he was obliged to descend for many periods a week to cram lower boys with Xenophon and Sallust. But Scott-King did not repine. On the contrary he found a peculiar relish in contemplating the victories of barbarism and positively rejoiced in his reduced station, for he was of a type, unknown in the New World but quite common in Europe, which is fascinated by obscurity and failure.

'Dim' is the epithet for Scott-King and it was a fellow-feeling, a blood-brotherhood in dimness, which first drew him to study the works of the poet Bellorius.

No one, except perhaps Scott-King himself, could be dimmer. When, poor and in some discredit, Bellorius died in 1646 in his native town of what was then a happy kingdom of the Hapsburg Empire and is now the turbulent modern state of Neutralia,* he left as his life's work a single folio

---

* The Republic of Neutralia is imaginary and composite and represents no existing state.

volume containing a poem of some 1500 lines of Latin hexameters. In his lifetime the only effect of the publication was to annoy the Court and cause his pension to be cancelled. After his death it was entirely forgotten until the middle of the last century when it was reprinted in Germany in a collection of late Renaissance texts. It was in this edition that Scott-King found it during a holiday on the Rhine, and at once his heart stirred with the recognition of kinship. The subject was irredeemably tedious – a visit to an imaginary island of the New World where in primitive simplicity, untainted by tyranny or dogma, there subsisted a virtuous, chaste and reasonable community. The lines were correct and melodious, enriched by many happy figures of speech; Scott-King read them on the deck of the river steamer as vine and turret, cliff and terrace and park, swept smoothly past. How they offended – by what intended or unintended jab of satire, blunted today; by what dangerous speculation – is not now apparent. That they should have been forgotten is readily intelligible to anyone acquainted with the history of Neutralia.

Something must be known of this history if we are to follow Scott-King with understanding. Let us eschew detail and observe that for three hundred years since Bellorius's death his country has suffered every conceivable ill the body politic is heir to. Dynastic wars, foreign invasion, disputed successions, revolting colonies, endemic syphilis, impoverished soil, masonic intrigues, revolutions, restorations, cabals, juntas, pronunciamentos, liberations, constitutions, *coups d'état*, dictatorships, assassinations, agrarian reforms, popular elections, foreign intervention, repudiation of loans, inflations of currency, trades unions, massacres, arson, atheism, secret societies – make the list full, slip in as many personal foibles as you will, you will find all these in the last three centuries of Neutralian history. Out of it emerged the present republic of Neutralia, a typical modern state, governed by a single party, acclaiming a dominant Marshal, supporting a vast ill-paid bureaucracy whose work is tempered and humanized by corruption. This you must know; also that the Neutralians being a clever Latin race are little given to hero-worship and make considerable fun of their Marshal behind his back. In one thing only did he earn their full-hearted esteem. He kept out of the Second World War. Neutralia sequestered herself and, from having been the cockpit of factious sympathies, became remote, unconsidered, dim; so that, as the face of Europe coarsened and the war, as it appeared in the common-room newspapers and the common-room wireless, cast its heroic and chivalrous disguise and became a sweaty tug-of-war between teams of indistinguishable louts, Scott-King, who had never set foot there, became Neutralian in his loyalty and as an act of homage resumed with fervour the task on which he had intermittently worked, the translation of Bellorius into Spenserian stanzas. The work was finished at the time of the

Normandy landings – translation, introduction, notes. He sent it to the Oxford University Press. It came back to him. He put it away in a drawer of the pitch-pine desk in his smoky gothic study above the Granchester quadrangle. He did not repine. It was his opus, his monument to dimness.

But still the shade of Bellorius stood at his elbow demanding placation. There was unfinished business between these two. You cannot keep close company with a man, even though he be dead three centuries, without incurring obligations. Therefore at the time of the peace celebrations Scott-King distilled his learning and wrote a little essay, 4,000 words long, entitled *The Last Latinist*, to commemorate the coming tercentenary of Bellorius's death. It appeared in a learned journal. Scott-King was paid twelve guineas for this fruit of fifteen years' devoted labour; six of them he paid in income tax; with six he purchased a large gunmetal watch which worked irregularly for a month or two and then finally failed. There the matter might well have ended.

These, then, in a general, distant view, are the circumstances – Scott-King's history; Bellorius; the history of Neutralia; the year of Grace 1946 – all quite credible, quite humdrum, which together produced the odd events of Scott-King's summer holiday. Let us now 'truck' the camera forward and see him 'close-up'. You have heard all about Scott-King but you have not yet met him.

Meet him, then, at breakfast on a bleak morning at the

beginning of the summer term. Unmarried assistant masters at Granchester enjoyed the use of a pair of collegiate rooms in the school buildings and took their meals in the common-room. Scott-King came from his class-room where he had been taking early school, with his gown flowing behind him and a sheaf of fluttering exercise papers in his numb fingers. There had been no remission of war-time privations at Granchester. The cold grate was used as ashtray and waste-paper basket and was rarely emptied. The breakfast-table was a litter of small pots, each labelled with a master's name, containing rations of sugar, margarine and a spurious marmalade. The breakfast dish was a slop of 'dried' eggs. Scott-King turned sadly from the sideboard. 'Anyone', he said, 'is welcome to my share in this triumph of modern science.'

'Letter for you, Scottie,' said one of his colleagues. "The Honourable Professor Scott-King Esquire." Congratulations.'

It was a large, stiff envelope, thus oddly addressed, emblazoned on the flap with a coat of arms. Inside were a card and a letter. The card read:

His Magnificence the Very Reverend the Rector of the University of Simona and the Committee of the Bellorius Tercentenary Celebration Association request the honour of Professor Scott-King's assistance at the public acts to be held at Simona on July 28th–August 5th, 1946. R.S.V.P. His Excellency Dr Bogdan Antonic, International Secretary of the Association, Simona University, Neutralia.

The letter was signed by the Neutralian Ambassador to the Court of St James's. It announced that a number of distinguished scholars were assembling from all over the world to do honour to the illustrious Neutralian political thinker Bellorius and delicately intimated that the trip would be without expense on the part of the guests.

Scott-King's first thought on reading the communication was that he was the victim of a hoax. He looked round the table expecting to surprise a glance of complicity between his colleagues, but they appeared to be busy with their own concerns. Second thoughts convinced him that this sumptuous embossing and engraving was beyond their resources. The thing was authentic, then; but Scott-King was not pleased. He felt, rather, that a long-standing private intimacy between himself and Bellorius was being rudely disturbed. He put the envelope into his pocket, ate his bread and margarine, and presently made ready for morning chapel. He stopped at the secretary's office to purchase a packet of crested school writing paper on which to inscribe 'Mr Scott-King regrets . . .'

For the strange thing is that Scott-King was definitely blasé. Something of the kind has been hinted before, yet, seeing him cross the quadrangle to the chapel steps, middle-aged, shabby, unhonoured and unknown, his round and learned face puckered against the wind, you would have said: 'There goes a man who has missed all the compensations of life – and knows it.' But that is because you do not yet know Scott-King; no voluptuary surfeited by conquest, no colossus of the drama bruised and rent by doting adolescents, not Alexander, nor Talleyrand, was more blasé than Scott-King. He was an adult, an intellectual, a classical scholar, almost a poet; he was travel-worn in the large periphery of his own mind, jaded with accumulated experience of his imagination. He was older, it might have been written, than the rocks on which he sat; older, anyway, than his stall in chapel; he had died many times, had Scott-King, had dived deep, had trafficked for strange webs with Eastern merchants. And all this had been but the sound of lyres and flutes to him. Thus musing, he left the chapel and went to his class-room, where for the first hours he had the lowest set.

They coughed and sneezed. One, more ingenious than the rest, attempted at length to draw him out as, it was known, he might sometimes be drawn: 'Please, sir, Mr Griggs says it's a pure waste of our time learning classics,' but Scott-King merely replied: 'It's a waste of time coming to me and *not* learning them.'

After Latin gerunds they stumbled through half a page of Thucydides. He said: 'These last episodes of the siege have been described as tolling like a great bell,' at which a chorus rose from the back bench – 'The bell? Did you say it was the bell, sir?' and books were noisily shut. 'There are another twenty minutes. I said the book tolled like a bell.'

'Please, sir, I don't quite get that, sir, how can a book be like a bell, sir?'

'If you wish to talk, Ambrose, you can start construing.'

'Please, sir, that's as far as I got, sir.'

'Has anyone done any more?' (Scott-King still attempted to import into the lower school the adult politeness of the Classical Sixth.) 'Very well, then, you can all spend the rest of the hour preparing the next twenty lines.'

Silence, of a sort, reigned. There was a low muttering from the back of the room, a perpetual shuffling and snuffling, but no one spoke directly to Scott-King. He gazed through the leaded panes to the leaden sky. He could hear through the wall behind him the strident tones of Griggs, the civics master, extolling the Tolpuddle martyrs. Scott-King put his hand in his coat-pocket and felt the crisp edges of the Neutralian invitation.

He had not been abroad since 1939. He had not tasted wine for a year, and he was filled, suddenly, with deep homesickness for the South. He had not often nor for long visited those enchanted lands; a dozen times perhaps, for a few weeks – for one year in total of his forty-three years of life – but his treasure and his heart lay buried there. Hot oil and garlic and spilled wine; luminous pinnacles above a dusky wall; fireworks at night, fountains at noonday; the impudent, inoffensive hawkers of lottery tickets moving from table to table on to the crowded pavement; the shepherd's pipe on the scented hillside – all that travel agent ever sought to put in a folder, fumed in Scott-King's mind that drab morning. He had left his coin in the waters of Trevi; he had wedded the Adriatic; he was a Mediterranean man.

In the mid-morning break, on the crested school paper, he wrote his acceptance of the Neutralian invitation. That evening, and on many subsequent evenings, the talk in the common-room was about plans for the holidays. All despaired of getting abroad; all save Griggs who was cock-a-hoop about an International Rally of Progressive Youth Leadership in Prague to which he had got himself appointed. Scott-King said nothing even when Neutralia was mentioned.

'I'd like to go somewhere I could get a decent meal,' said one of his colleagues. 'Ireland or Neutralia, or somewhere like that.'

'They'd never let you into Neutralia,' said Griggs. 'Far too much to hide. They've got teams of German physicists making atomic bombs.'

'Civil war raging.'

'Half the population in concentration camps.'

'No decent-minded man would go to Neutralia.'

'Or to Ireland for that matter,' said Griggs.

And Scott-King sat tight.

II

Some weeks later Scott-King sat in the aerodrome waiting-room. His overcoat lay across his knees, his hand luggage at his feet. A loudspeaker, set high out of harm's way in the dun concrete wall, discoursed dance music and official announcements. This room, like all the others to which he had been driven in the course of the morning, was sparsely furnished and indifferently clean; on its walls, sole concession to literary curiosity, hung commendations of government savings bonds and precautions against gas attack. Scott-King was hungry, weary and dispirited for he was new to the amenities of modern travel.

He had left his hotel in London at seven o'clock that morning; it was now past noon and he was still on English soil. He had not been ignored. He had been shepherded in and out of charabancs and offices like an idiot child; he had been weighed and measured like a load of merchandise; he had been searched like a criminal; he had been cross-questioned about his past and his future, the state of his health and of his finances, as though he were applying for permanent employment of a confidential nature. Scott-King had not been nurtured in luxury and privilege, but this was not how he used to travel. And he had eaten nothing except a piece of flaccid toast and margarine in his bedroom. The ultimate asylum where he now sat proclaimed itself on the door as 'For the use of V.I.P.s only'.

'V.I.P.?' he asked their conductress.

She was a neat, impersonal young woman, part midwife, part governess, part shop-walker, in manner. 'Very Important Persons,' she replied without evident embarrassment.

'But is it all right for me to be here?'

'It is essential. You are a V.I.P.'

I wonder, thought Scott-King, how they treat quite ordinary, unimportant people?

There were two fellow-travellers, male and female, similarly distinguished, both bound for Bellacita, capital city of Neutralia; both, it presently transpired, guests of the Bellorius Celebration Committee.

The man was a familiar type to Scott-King; his name Whitemaid, his calling academic, a dim man like himself, much of an age with him.

'Tell me,' said Whitemaid, 'tell me frankly' – and he looked furtive as men do when they employ that ambiguous expression – 'have you ever heard of the worthy Bellorius?'

'I know his work. I have seldom heard it discussed.'

'Ah, well, of course, he's not in my subject. I'm Roman Law,' said Whitemaid, with an accession of furtiveness that took all grandiosity from the claim. 'They asked the Professor of Poetry, you know, but he couldn't get away. Then they tried the Professor of Latin. He's red. Then they asked for anyone to represent the University. No one else was enthusiastic so I put myself forward. I find expeditions of this kind highly diverting. You are familiar with them?'

'No.'

'I went to Upsala last vacation and ate very passable caviare twice a day for a week. Neutralia is not known for delicate living, alas, but one may count on rude plenty – and, of course, wine.'

'It's all a racket, anyhow,' said the third Very Important Person.

This was a woman no longer very young. Her name, Scott-King and Whitemaid had learned through hearing it frequently called through the loudspeaker and seeing it chalked on blackboards, calling her to receive urgent messages at every stage of their journey, was Miss Bombaum. It was a name notorious to almost all the world except, as it happened, to Scott-King and Whitemaid. She was far from dim; once a roving, indeed a dashing, reporter who in the days before the war had popped up wherever there was unpleasantness – Danzig, the Alcazar, Shanghai, Wal-Wal; now a columnist whose weekly articles were syndicated in the popular press of four continents. Scott-King did not read such articles and he had wondered idly at frequent intervals during the morning what she could be. She did not look a lady; she did not even look quite respectable, but he could not reconcile her typewriter with the calling of actress or courtesan; nor for that matter the sharp little sexless face under the too feminine hat and the lavish style of hairdressing. He came near the truth in suspecting her of being, what he had often heard of but never seen in the life, a female novelist.

'It's all a racket,' said Miss Bombaum, 'of the Neutralian Propaganda Bureau. I reckon they feel kind of left out of things now the war's over and want to make some nice new friends among the United Nations. We're only part of it. They've got a religious pilgrimage and a Congress of Physical Culture and an International Philatelists' Convention and heaven knows what else. I reckon there's a story in it — in Neutralia, I mean; not in Bellorius, of course, he's been done.'

'Done?'

'Yes, I've a copy somewhere,' she said, rummaging in her bag. 'Thought it might come in useful for the speeches.'

'You don't think,' said Scott-King, 'that we are in danger of being required to make speeches?'

'I can't think what else we've been asked for,' said Miss Bombaum. 'Can you?'

'I made three long speeches at Upsala,' said Whitemaid. 'They were ecstatically received.'

'Oh, dear, and I have left all my papers at home.'

'Borrow this any time you like,' said Miss Bombaum, producing Mr Robert Graves's *Count Belisarius*. 'It's sad though. He ends up blind.'

The music suddenly ceased and a voice said: 'Passengers for Bellacita will now proceed to Exit D. Passengers for Bellacita will now proceed to Exit D,' while, simultaneously, the conductress appeared in the door-way and said: 'Follow me, please. Have your embarkation papers, medical cards, customs clearance slips, currency control vouchers, passports, tickets, identity dockets, travel orders, emigration certificates, baggage checks and security sheets ready for inspection at the barrier, please.'

The Very Important Persons followed her out, mingled with the less important persons who had been waiting in a nearby room, stepped into a dusty gale behind the four spinning screws of the aeroplane, mounted the step-ladder and were soon strapped into their seats as though waiting the attention of the dentist. A steward gave them brief instructions in the case of their being forced down over the sea and announced: 'We shall arrive at Bellacita at sixteen hours Neutralian time.'

'An appalling thought occurs to me,' said Whitemaid, 'can this mean we get no luncheon?'

'They eat very late in Neutralia, I believe.'

'Yes, but four o'clock!'

'I'm sure they will have arranged something for us.'

'I pray they have.'

Something had been arranged but not a luncheon. The Very Important Persons stepped out some hours later into the brilliant sunshine of Bellacita airport and at once found their hands shaken in swift succession by a deputation of their hosts. 'I bid you welcome to the land of Bellorius,' said their spokesman.

His name, he told them with a neat bow, was Arturo Fe; his rank Doctor of Bellacita University; but there was nothing academic in his appearance. Rather, Scott-King thought, he might be a slightly ageing film actor. He had thin, calligraphic moustaches, a hint of side-whisker, sparse but well-ordered hair, a gold-rimmed monocle, three gold teeth, and neat, dark clothes.

'Madam,' he said, 'gentlemen, your luggage will be cared for. The motor-cars await you. Come with me. Passports? Papers? Do not give them a thought. Everything is arranged. Come.'

At this stage Scott-King became aware of a young woman standing stolidly among them. He had taken notice of her in London where she had towered some six inches above the heads of the crowd.

'I come,' she said.

Dr Fe bowed. 'Fe,' he said.

'Sveningen,' she answered.

'You are one of us? Of the Bellorius Association?' asked Dr Fe.

'I speak not English well. I come.'

Dr Fe tried her in Neutralian, French, Italian and German.

She replied in her own remote Nordic tongue. Dr Fe raised hands and eyes in a pantomime of despair.

'You speak much English. I speak little English. So we speak English, yes? I come.'

'You come?' said Dr Fe.

'I come.'

'We are honoured,' said Dr Fe.

He led them between flowering oleanders and borders of camomile, past shaded café tables at which Whitemaid longingly looked, through the airport vestibule to the glass doors beyond.

Here there was a hitch. Two sentries, shabbily uniformed but armed for action, war-worn, it seemed, but tigers for duty, barred their passage. Dr Fe tried a high hand, he tried charm, he offered them cigarettes; suddenly a new side of his character was revealed; he fell into demoniac rage, he shook his fists, he bared his chryselephantine teeth, he narrowed his eyes to Mongol slits of hate; what he said was unintelligible to Scott-King but it was plainly designed to wound. The men stood firm.

Then, as suddenly as it had arisen, the squall passed. He turned to his guests. 'Excuse one moment,' he said. 'These stupid fellows do not understand their orders. It will be arranged by the officer.' He despatched an underling.

'We box the rude mens?' suggested Miss Sveningen, moving cat-like towards the soldiers.

'No. Forgive them I beg you. They think it their duty.'

'Such little men should be polite,' said the giantess.

The officer came; the doors flew open; the soldiers did something with their tommy-guns which passed as a salute. Scott-King raised his hat as the little party swept out into the blaze of sunshine to the waiting cars.

'This superb young creature,' said Scott-King, 'would you say she was a slightly incongruous figure?'

'I find her eminently, transcendently congruous,' said White-maid. 'I exult in her.'

Dr Fe gallantly took the ladies under his own charge. Scott-King and Whitemaid rode with an underling. They bowled along through the suburbs of Bellacita; tram-lines, half-finished villas, a rush of hot wind, a dazzle of white concrete. At first, when they were fresh from the upper air, the heat had been agreeable; now his skin began to prick and tickle and Scott-King realized that he was unsuitably dressed.

'Exactly ten hours and a half since I had anything to eat,' said Whitemaid.

The underling leaned towards them from the front seat and pointed out places of interest. 'Here,' he said, 'the anarchists shot General Cardenas. Here syndico-radicals shot the auxiliary bishop. Here the Agrarian League buried alive ten Teaching Brothers. Here the bimetallists committed unspeakable atrocities on the wife of Senator Mendoza.'

'Forgive me for interrupting you,' said Whitemaid, 'but could you tell us where we are going?'

'To the Ministry. They are all happy to meet you.'

'And we are happy to meet them. But just at the moment my friend and I are rather hungry.'

'Yes,' said the underling with compassion. 'We have heard of it in our papers. Your rations in England, your strikes. Here things are very expensive but there is plenty for all who pay, so our people do not strike but work hard to become rich. It is better so, no?'

'Perhaps. We must have a talk about it some time. But at the moment it is not so much the general economic question as a personal immediate need –'

'We arrive,' said the underling. 'Here is the Ministry.'

Like much modern Neutralian building the Ministry was unfinished, but it was conceived in severe one-party style. A portico of unembellished columns, a vast, blank door-way, a bas-relief symbolizing Revolution and Youth and Technical Progress and the National Genius. Inside, a staircase. On the staircase was a less predictable feature; ranged on either side like playing-cards, like a startling hand composed entirely of Kings and Knaves, stood ascending ranks of trumpeters aged from sixty to sixteen, dressed in the tabards of medieval heralds; more than this they wore blond bobbed wigs; more than this their cheeks were palpably rouged. As Scott-King and Whitemaid set foot on the lowest step these figures of fantasy raised their trumpets to their lips and sounded a flourish, while one who might from his extreme age have been father to them all, rattled in a feeble way on a little kettle-drum. 'Frankly,' said Whitemaid, 'I am not in good heart for this kind of thing.'

They mounted between the blaring ranks, were greeted on the piano nobile by a man in plain evening-dress, and led to the reception hall which with its pews and thrones had somewhat the air of a court of law and was in fact not infrequently used for condemning aspiring politicians to exile on one or other of the inhospitable islands that lay off the coast of the country.

Here they found an assembly. Under a canopy, on the central throne, sat the Minister of Rest and Culture, a saturnine young man who had lost most of his fingers while playing with a bomb during the last revolution. Scott-King and Whitemaid were presented to him by Dr Fe. He smiled rather horribly and extended a maimed hand. Half a dozen worthies stood round him. Dr Fe introduced them. Honorific titles, bows, smiles, shakes of the hand; then Scott-King and Whitemaid were led to their stalls amid their fellow-guests, now about twelve in number. In each place, on the red-plush seat, lay a little pile of printed matter. 'Not precisely esculent,' said Whitemaid. Trumpets and drum sounded without; another and final party arrived and was presented; then the proceedings began.

The Minister of Rest and Culture had a voice, never soft perhaps, now roughened by a career of street-corner harangues. He spoke at length and was succeeded by the venerable Rector of Bellacita University. Meanwhile Scott-King studied the books and leaflets provided for him, lavish productions of the Ministry of Popular Enlightenment — selected speeches by the Marshal, a monograph on Neutralian pre-History, an illustrated guide to the ski-ing resorts of the country, the annual report of the Corporation of Viticulture. Nothing seemed to have bearing upon the immediate situation except one, a polyglot programme of the coming celebrations. '17.00 hrs.,' he read. '*Inauguration of the Ceremonies by the Minister of Rest and Culture. 18.00 hrs. Reception of delegates at the University of Bellacita. Official dress. 19.30 hrs. Vin d'honneur offered to the delegates by the Municipality of Bellacita. 21.00 hrs. Banquet offered by the Committee of the Bellorius Tercentenary Committee. Music by Bellacita Philharmonic Youth Squadron. Evening dress. Delegates will spend the night at the Hôtel 22nd March.*'

'Look,' said Whitemaid, 'nothing to eat until nine o'clock and, mark my words, they will be late.'

'In Neutralia,' said Dr Arturo Fe, 'in Neutralia, when we are happy, we take no account of time. Today we are *very* happy.'

The Hôtel 22nd March was the name, derived from some forgotten event in the Marshal's rise to power, by which the chief hotel of the place was momentarily graced. It had had as many official names in its time as the square in which it stood – the Royal, the Reform, the October Revolution, the Empire, the President Coolidge, the Duchess of Windsor – according to the humours of local history, but Neutralians invariably spoke of it quite simply as the 'Ritz'. It rose amid sub-tropical vegetation, fountains and statuary, a solid structure, ornamented in the rococo style of fifty years ago. Neutralians of the upper class congregated there, sauntered about its ample corridors, sat in its comfortable foyer, used the concierge as a poste restante, borrowed small sums from its barmen, telephoned sometimes, gossiped always, now and then lightly dozed. They did not spend any money there. They could not afford to. The prices were fixed, and fixed high, by law; to them were added a series of baffling taxes – thirty per cent. for service, two per cent. for stamp duty, thirty per cent. for luxury tax, five per cent. for the winter relief fund, twelve per cent. for those mutilated in the revolution, four per cent. municipal dues, two per cent. federal tax, eight per cent. for living accommodation in excess of minimum requirements, and others of the same kind; they mounted up, they put the bedroom floors and the brilliant dining-rooms beyond the reach of all but foreigners.

There had been few in recent years; official hospitality alone flourished at the Ritz; but still the sombre circle of Neutralian male aristocracy – for, in spite of numberless revolutions and the gross dissemination of free-thought, Neutralian ladies still modestly kept the house – foregathered there; it was their club. They wore very dark suits and very stiff collars, black ties, black buttoned boots; they smoked their cigarettes in long tortoise-shell holders; their faces were brown and wizened; they spoke of money and women, dryly and distantly, for they had never enough of either.

On this afternoon of summer when the traditional Bellacita season was in its last week and they were all preparing to remove to the seaside or to their family estates, about twenty of these descendants of the crusaders sat in the cool of the Ritz lounge. They were rewarded first by the spectacle of the foreign professors' arrival from the Ministry of Rest and Culture. Already they seemed hot and weary; they had come to fetch their academic dress for the reception at the University. The last-comers – Scott-King, Whitemaid, Miss Sveningen and Miss Bombaum – had lost their luggage. Dr Arturo Fe was like a flame at the reception desk; he pleaded, he threatened, he telephoned. Some said the luggage was impounded at the customs, others that the taxi driver had stolen it. Presently it was discovered in a service lift abandoned on the top storey.

At last Dr Fe assembled his scholars, Scott-King in his M.A. gown and hood, Whitemaid, more flamboyantly, in the robes of his new doctorate of Upsala. Among the vestments of many seats of learning, some reminiscent of Daumier's law courts, some of Mr Will Hay of the music-hall stage, Miss Sveningen stood conspicuous in sports dress of zephyr and white shorts. Miss Bombaum refused to go. She had a story to file, she said.

The party trailed out through the swing doors into the dusty evening heat, leaving the noblemen to compare their impressions of Miss Sveningen's legs. The subject was not exhausted when they returned; indeed, had it risen earlier in the year it would have served as staple conversation for the whole Bellacita season.

The visit to the University had been severe, an hour of speeches followed by a detailed survey of the archives. 'Miss Sveningen, gentlemen,' said Dr Fe. 'We are a little behind. The Municipality is already awaiting us. I shall telephone them that we are delayed. Do not put yourselves out.'

The party dispersed to their rooms and reassembled in due time dressed in varying degrees of elegance. Dr Fe was splendid, tight white waistcoat, onyx buttons, a gardenia, half a dozen miniature medals, a kind of sash. Scott-King and Whitemaid seemed definitely seedy beside him. But the little brown marquesses and counts had no eye for these things. They were waiting for Miss Sveningen. If her academic dress had exposed such uncovenanted mercies, such superb, such unpredictable expanses and lengths of flesh, what would she not show them when gowned for the evening?

She came.

Chocolate-coloured silk enveloped her from collar-bone to humerus and hung to within a foot of the ground; low-heeled black satin shoes covered feet which seemed now unusually large. She had bound a tartan fillet in her hair. She wore a broad patent-leather belt. She had a handkerchief artfully attached to her wrist by her watch-strap. For perhaps a minute the inky, simian eyes regarded her aghast; then, one by one, with the languor born of centuries of hereditary disillusionment, the Knights of Malta rose from their places and sauntered with many nods to the bowing footmen towards the swing doors, towards the breathless square, towards the subdivided palaces where their wives awaited them.

'Come, lady and gentlemen,' said Dr Arturo Fe. 'The cars are here. We are eagerly expected at the Hotel de Ville.'

No paunch, no jowl, no ponderous dignity of the counting-house or of civic office, no hint indeed of pomp or affluence, marked the Lord Mayor of Bellacita. He was young, lean and plainly ill at ease; he was much scarred by his revolutionary exploits, wore a patch on one eye and supported himself on a crutch-stick. 'His Excellency, alas, does not speak English,' said Dr Fe as he presented Scott-King and Whitemaid.

They shook hands. The Lord Mayor scowled and muttered something in Dr Fe's ear.

'His Excellency says it is a great pleasure to welcome such

illustrious guests. In the phrase of our people he says his house is yours.'

The English stood aside and separated. Whitemaid had sighted a buffet at the far end of the tapestried hall. Scott-King stood diffidently alone; a footman brought him a glass of sweet effervescent wine. Dr Fe brought him someone to talk to.

'Allow me to present Engineer Garcia. He is an ardent lover of England.'

'Engineer Garcia,' said the newcomer.

'Scott-King,' said Scott-King.

'I have work seven years with the firm Green, Gorridge and Wright Limited at Salford. You know them well, no doubt?'

'I am afraid not.'

'They are a very well-known firm, I think. Do you go often to Salford?'

'I'm afraid I've never been there.'

'It is a very well-known town. What, please, is your town?'

'I suppose, Granchester.'

'I am not knowing Granchester. It is a bigger town than Salford?'

'No, much smaller.'

'Ah. In Salford is much industry.'

'So I believe.'

'How do you find our Neutralian champagne?'

'Excellent.'

'It is sweet, eh? That is because of our Neutralian sun. You prefer it to the champagne of France?'

'Well, it is quite different, isn't it?'

'I see you are a connoisseur. In France is no sun. Do you know the Duke of Westminster?'

'No.'

'I saw him once at Biarritz. A fine man. A man of great propriety.'

'Indeed?'

'Indeed. London is his propriety. Have you a propriety?'

'No.'

'My mother had a propriety but it is lost.'

The clamour in the hall was tremendous. Scott-King found himself the centre of an English-speaking group. Fresh faces, new voices crowded in on him. His glass was repeatedly filled; it was over-filled and boiled and cascaded on his cuff. Dr Fe passed and re-passed. 'Ah, you have soon made friends.' He brought reinforcements; he brought more wine. 'This is a special bottle,' he whispered. 'Special for you, Professor,' and refilled Scott-King's glass with the same sugary froth as before. The din swelled. The tapestried walls, the painted ceiling, the chandeliers, the gilded architrave, danced and dazzled before his eyes.

Scott-King became conscious that Engineer Garcia was seeking to draw him into a more confidential quarter.

'How do you find our country, Professor?'

'Very pleasant, I assure you.'

'Not how you expected it, eh? Your papers do not say it is pleasant. How is it allowed to scandalize our country? Your papers tell many lies about us.'

'They tell lies about everyone, you know.'

'Please?'

'They tell lies about everyone,' shouted Scott-King.

'Yes, lies. You see for yourself it is perfectly quiet.'

'Perfectly quiet.'

'How, please?'

'Quiet,' yelled Scott-King.

'You find it too quiet? It will become more gay soon. You are a writer?'

'No, merely a poor scholar.'

'How, poor? In England you are rich, no? Here we must work very hard for we are a poor country. In Neutralia for a scholar of the first class the salary is 500 ducats a month. The rent of his apartment is perhaps 450 ducats. His taxes are hundred. Oil is thirty ducats a litre. Meat is forty-five ducats a kilo. So you see, we work.

'Dr Fe is a scholar. He is also a lawyer, a judge of the Lower Court. He edits the *Historical Review*. He has a high position in the Ministry of Rest and Culture, also at the Foreign Office and the Bureau of Enlightenment and Tourism. He speaks often on the radio about the international situation. He owns one-third share in the Sporting Club. In all the New Neutralia

I do not think there is anyone works harder than Dr Fe, yet he is not rich as Mr Green, Mr Gorridge and Mr Wright were rich in Salford. And they scarcely worked at all. There are injustices in the world, Professor.'

'I think we must be quiet. The Lord Mayor wishes to make a speech.'

'He is a man of no cultivation. A politician. They say his mother . . .'

'Hush.'

'This speech will not be interesting, I believe.'

Something like silence fell on the central part of the hall. The Lord Mayor had his speech ready typed on a sheaf of papers. He squinnied at it with his single eye and began haltingly to read.

Scott-King slipped away. As though at a great distance he descried Whitemaid, alone at the buffet, and unsteadily made his way towards him.

'Are you drunk?' whispered Whitemaid.

'I don't think so — just giddy. Exhaustion and the noise.'

'I am drunk.'

'Yes. I can see you are.'

'How drunk would you say I was?'

'Just drunk.'

'My dear, my dear Scott-King, there if I may say so, you are wrong. In every degree and by every known standard I am very, very much more drunk than you give me credit for.'

'Very well. But let's not make a noise while the Mayor's speaking.'

'I do not profess to know very much Neutralian but it strikes me that the Mayor, as you call him, is talking the most consummate rot. What is more, I doubt very much that he is a mayor. Looks to me like a gangster.'

'Merely a politician, I believe.'

'That is worse.'

'The essential, the immediate need is somewhere to sit down.'

Though they were friends only of a day, Scott-King loved this man; they had suffered, were suffering, together; they spoke, pre-eminently, the same language; they were comrades in arms. He took Whitemaid by the arm and led him out of the hall to a cool and secluded landing where stood a little settee of gilt and plush, a thing not made for sitting on. Here they sat, the two dim men, while very faintly from behind them came the sound of oratory and applause.

'They were putting it in their pockets,' said Whitemaid.

'Who? What?'

'The servants. The food. In the pockets of those long braided coats they wear. They were taking it away for their families. I got four macaroons.' And then swiftly veering he remarked: 'She looks terrible.'

'Miss Sveningen?'

'That glorious creature. It was a terrible shock to see her

when she came down changed for the party. It killed something here,' he said, touching his heart.

'Don't cry.'

'I can't help crying. You've seen her brown dress? And the hair ribbon? And the handkerchief?'

'Yes, yes, I saw it all. And the belt.'

'The belt,' said Whitemaid, 'was more than flesh and blood could bear. Something snapped, here,' he said, touching his forehead. 'You must remember how she looked in shorts? A Valkyrie. Something from the heroic age. Like some god-like, some unimaginably strict school prefect, *a dormitory monitor*,' he said in a kind of ecstasy. 'Think of her striding between the beds, a pigtail, bare feet, in her hand a threatening hairbrush. Oh, Scott-King, do you think she rides a bicycle?'

'I'm sure of it.'

'In shorts?'

'Certainly in shorts.'

'I can imagine a whole life lived riding tandem behind her, through endless forests of conifers, and at midday sitting down among the pine needles to eat hard-boiled eggs. Think of those strong fingers peeling an egg, Scott-King, the brown of it, the white of it, the shine. Think of her *biting* it.'

'Yes, it would be a splendid spectacle.'

'And then think of her now, in there, in that brown dress.'

'There are things not to be thought of, Whitemaid.' And Scott-King, too, shed a few tears of sympathy, of common sorrow in the ineffable, the cosmic sadness of Miss Sveningen's party frock.

'What is this?' said Dr Fe, joining them some minutes later. 'Tears? You are not enjoying it?'

'It is only,' said Scott-King, 'Miss Sveningen's dress.'

'This is tragic, yes. But in Neutralia we take such things bravely, with a laugh. I came, not to intrude, simply to ask, Professor, you have your little speech ready for this evening? We count on you at the banquet to say a few words.'

For the banquet they returned to the Ritz. The foyer was empty save for Miss Bombaum who sat smoking a cigar with a man of repellent aspect. 'I have had my dinner. I'm going out after a story,' she explained.

It was half-past ten when they sat down at a table spread with arabesques of flower-heads, petals, moss, trailing racemes and sprays of foliage until it resembled a parterre by Le Nôtre. Scott-King counted six wineglasses of various shapes standing before him amid the vegetation. A menu of enormous length, printed in gold, lay on his plate beside a typewritten place-card '*Dr Scotch-Kink*'. Like many explorers before him, he found that prolonged absence from food destroyed the appetite. The waiters had already devoured the hors-d'oeuvre, but when at length the soup arrived, the first mouthful made him hiccup. This, too, he remembered, had befallen Captain Scott's doomed party in the Antarctic.

'Comment dit-on en français "hiccup"?' he asked his neighbour.

'Plaît-il, mon professeur?'

Scott-King hiccuped. 'Ça,' he said.

'Ça c'est le hoquet.'

'J'en ai affreusement.'

'Évidemment, mon professeur. Il faut du cognac.'

The waiters had drunk and were drinking profusely of brandy and there was a bottle at hand. Scott-King tossed off a glassful and his affliction was doubled. He hiccuped without intermission throughout the long dinner.

This neighbour, who had so ill-advised him, was, Scott-King saw from the card, Dr Bogdan Antonic, the International Secretary of the Association, a middle-aged, gentle man whose face was lined with settled distress and weariness. They conversed, as far as the hiccups permitted, in French.

'You are not Neutralian?'

'Not yet. I hope to be. Every week I make my application to the Foreign Office and always I am told it will be next week. It is not so much for myself I am anxious – though death is a fearful thing – as for my family. I have seven children, all born in Neutralia, all without nationality. If we are sent back to my unhappy country they would hang us all without doubt.'

'Jugo-Slavia?'

'I am a Croat, born under the Hapsburg Empire. That was

a true League of Nations. As a young man I studied in Zagreb, Budapest, Prague, Vienna — one was free, one moved where one would; one was a citizen of Europe. Then we were liberated and put under the Serbs. Now we are liberated again and put under the Russians. And always more police, more prisons, more hanging. My poor wife is Czech. Her nervous constitution is quite deranged by our troubles. She thinks all the time she is being watched.'

Scott-King essayed one of those little, inarticulate, non-committal grunts of sympathy which come easily to the embarrassed Englishman; to an Englishman, that is, who is not troubled by the hiccups. The sound which in the event issued from him might have been taken as derisive by a less sensitive man than Dr Antonic.

'I think so, too,' he said severely. 'There are spies everywhere. You saw that man, as we came in, sitting with the woman with the cigar. He is one of them. I have been here ten years and know them all. I was second secretary to our Legation. It was a great thing, you must believe, for a Croat to enter our diplomatic service. All the appointments went to Serbs. Now there is no Legation. My salary has not been paid since 1940. I have a few friends at the Foreign Office. They are sometimes kind and give me employment, as at the present occasion. But at any moment they may make a trade agreement with the Russians and hand us over.'

Scott-King attempted to reply.

'You must take some more brandy, Professor. It is the only thing. Often, I remember, in Ragusa I have had the hiccups from laughing. . . . Never again, I suppose.'

Though the company was smaller at the banquet than at the *vin d'honneur*, the noise was more oppressive. The private dining-room of the Ritz, spacious as it was, had been built in a more trumpery style than the Hôtel de Ville. There the lofty roof had seemed to draw the discordant voices upwards into the cerulean perspective with which it was painted, and disperse them there amid the floating deities; the Flemish hunting scenes on the walls seemed to envelop and muffle them in their million stitches. But here the din banged back from gilding and mirrors; above the clatter and chatter of the dinner-table and the altercations of the waiters, a mixed choir of young people sang folk-songs, calculated to depress the most jovial village festival. It was not thus, in his classroom at Granchester, that Scott-King had imagined himself dining.

'At my little house on the point at Lapad, we used to sit on the terrace laughing so loudly, sometimes, that the passing fishermen called up to us from their decks asking to share the joke. They sailed close inshore and one could follow their lights far out towards the islands. When we were silent, their laughter came to us across the water when they were out of sight.'

The neighbour on Scott-King's left did not speak until the

dessert, except to the waiters; to them he spoke loudly and often, sometimes blustering, sometimes cajoling, and by this means got two helpings of nearly every course. His napkin was tucked into his collar. He ate intently with his head bowed over his plate so that the morsels which frequently fell from his lips were not permanently lost to him. He swigged his wine with relish, sighing after each draught and tapping the glass with his knife to call the waiter's attention to the need of refilling it. Often he jammed glasses on his nose and studied the menu, not so much, it seemed, for fear of missing anything, as to fix in his memory the fleeting delights of the moment. It is not entirely easy to achieve a Bohemian appearance in evening-dress but this man did so with his shock of grizzled hair, the broad ribbon of his pincenez, and a three days' growth of beard and whisker.

With the arrival of the dessert, he raised his countenance, fixed on Scott-King his large and rather bloodshot eyes, belched mildly and then spoke. The words were English; the accent had been formed in many cities from Memphis (Mo.) to Smyrna. 'Shakespeare, Dickens, Byron, Galsworthy,' he seemed to say.

This late birth of a troublesome gestation took Scott-King by surprise; he hiccuped non-committally.

'They are all great English writers.'

'Well, yes.'

'Your favourite, please?'

'I suppose Shakespeare.'

'He is the more dramatic, the more poetic, no?'

'Yes.'

'But Galsworthy is the more modern.'

'Very true.'

'I am modern. You are a poet?'

'Hardly that. A few translations.'

'I am an original poet. I translate my poems myself into English prose. They have been published in the United States. Do you read the *New Destiny?*'

'I am afraid not.'

'It is the magazine which publishes my translations. Last year they sent me ten dollars.'

'No one has ever paid me for my translations.'

'You should send them to the *New Destiny*. It is not possible, I think,' continued the Poet, 'to render the poetry of one language into the poetry of another. Sometimes I translate English prose into Neutralian poetry. I have done a very beautiful rendering of some selected passages of your great Priestley. I hoped it would be used in the High Schools but it is not. There is jealousy and intrigue everywhere – even at the Ministry of Education.'

At this moment a splendid figure at the centre of the table rose to make the first speech. 'Now to work,' said his neighbour, produced a note-book and pencil and began busily writing in shorthand. 'In the new Neutralia we all work.'

The speech was long and provoked much applause. In the course of it a note came to Scott-King by the hand of a waiter: '*I shall call on you to reply to his Excellency. Fe*'.

Scott-King wrote in answer: '*Terribly sorry. Not tonight. Indisposed. Ask Whitemaid,*' stealthily left his place and, still hiccuping, passed behind the table to the dining-room door.

Outside the foyer was almost deserted; the great glass dome which throughout the years of war had blazed aloft nightly, a candle in a naughty world, rose darkly. Two night porters shared a cigar behind one of the pillars; a huge empty carpet, strewn with empty chairs, lay before Scott-King in the subdued light to which a parsimonious management had reduced the earlier blaze. It was not much past midnight but in the New Neutralia memories persisted of the revolutionary curfew, of police roundups, of firing squads in the public gardens; New Neutralians liked to get home early and bolt their doors.

As Scott-King stepped into this silent space, his hiccups mysteriously ceased. He went through the swing doors and breathed the air of the piazza where under the arc-lamps workmen were washing away with hoses the dust and refuse of the day; the last of the trams, which all day long rattled round the fountains, had long since returned to its shed. He breathed deeply, testing, as it were, the limits of his miraculous recovery, and knew it to be complete. Then he turned back, took his key and, barely conscious, ascended.

During the first tumultuous afternoon and evening in Bellacita there had been little opportunity for more than the barest acquaintance between Scott-King and his fellow-guests of the Bellorius Association. Indeed he had scarcely distinguished them from their hosts. They had bowed and shaken hands, they had exchanged nods among the University archives, they had apologized one to the other as they jostled and jogged elbows at the *vin d'honneur*, Scott-King had no share in whatever intimacies flourished after the banquet. He remembered an affable American and a Swiss of extreme hauteur and an Oriental whom on general principles he assumed to be Chinese. Now on the morning following he came cheerfully to join them in the Ritz foyer in accordance with the printed programme. They were to leave at 10.30 for Simona. His bags were packed; the sun, not yet oppressive, shone brilliantly through the glass dome. He was in the best of tempers.

He had awoken in this rare mood after a night of untroubled sleep. He had breakfasted on a tray of fruit, sitting on his verandah above the square, showering copious blessings on the palms and fountains and trams and patriotic statuary. He approached the group in the foyer with the intention of making himself peculiarly agreeable.

Of the festive Neutralians of the day before only Dr Fe and the Poet remained. The rest were at work elsewhere constructing the New Neutralia.

'Professor Scott-King, how are you this morning?'

There was more than politeness in Dr Fe's greeting; there was definite solicitude.

'Extremely well, thank you. Oh, of course, I had forgotten about last night's speech. I was very sorry to fail you; the truth was . . .'

'Professor Scott-King, say no more. Your friend Whitemaid I fear is not so well.'

'No?'

'No. He has sent word that he cannot join us.' Dr Fe raised exquisitely expressive eyebrows.

The Poet drew Scott-King momentarily aside. 'Do not be alarmed,' he said. 'Reassure your friend. Not a hint of last night's occurrences shall appear. I speak with the authority of the Ministry.'

'You know I'm completely in the dark.'

'So are the public. So they shall remain. You sometimes laugh at us in your democratic way for our little controls, but they have their uses, you see.'

'But I don't know what has happened.'

'So far as the press of Neutralia is concerned, nothing happened.'

The Poet had shaved that morning and shaved ruthlessly.

The face he thrust near Scott-King's was tufted with cotton-wool. Now he withdrew it and edged away. Scott-King joined the group of delegates.

'Well,' said Miss Bombaum, 'I seem to have missed a whole packet of fun last night.'

'I seem to have missed it too.'

'And how's the head this morning?' asked the American scholar.

'Seems like you had fun,' said Miss Bombaum.

'I went to bed early,' said Scott-King coldly. 'I was thoroughly over-tired.'

'Well, I've heard it called plenty of things in my time. I reckon that covers it too.'

Scott-King was an adult, an intellectual, a classical scholar, almost a poet; provident Nature who shields the slow tortoise and points the quills of the porcupine, has given to such tender spirits their appropriate armour. A shutter, an iron curtain, fell between Scott-King and these two jokers. He turned to the rest of the company and realized too late that jocularity was the least he had to fear. The Swiss had not been cordial the day before; this morning he was theatrical in his coldness; the Asiatic seemed to have spun himself a cocoon of silken aloofness. The assembled scholars did not positively cut Scott-King; in their several national fashions they signified that they were not unaware of Scott-King's presence amongst them. Further than this they did not go.

They too had their shutters, their iron curtains. Scott-King was in disgrace. Something unmentionable had happened in which he was vicariously but inextricably implicated; a gross, black, inexpungible blot had fallen on Scott-King overnight.

He did not wish to know more. He was an adult, an intellectual; he was all that has already been predicated of him. He was no chauvinist. Throughout six embattled years he had remained resolutely impartial. But now his hackles rose; quite literally he felt the roots of his sparse hairs prick and tingle. Like the immortal private of the Buffs he stood in Elgin's place; not untaught certainly, nor rude, nor abysmally low-born, but poor and, at the moment, reckless, bewildered and alone, a heart with English instinct fraught he yet could call his own.

'I may have to keep the party waiting a few minutes,' he said. 'I must go and call on my colleague Mr Whitemaid.'

He found him in bed looking strange rather than ill; almost exalted. He was still rather drunk. The windows stood wide open on to the balcony and on the balcony, modestly robed in bath towels, sat Miss Sveningen eating beefsteak.

'They tell me downstairs that you are not coming with us to Simona?'

'No. I'm not quite up to it this morning. I have things to attend to here. It is not easy for me to explain.' He nodded towards the giant carnivore on the balcony.

'You spent an agreeable evening?'

'A total blank, Scott-King. I remember being with you at some kind of civic reception. I remember a fracas with the police, but that was much later. Hours must have intervened.'

'The police?'

'Yes. At some kind of dancing place. Irma here was splendid — like something in a film. They went down like nine-pins. But for her I suppose I should be in a cell at this moment instead of happily consuming Bromo-Seltzer in your company.'

'You made a speech.'

'So I gather. You missed it? Then we shall never know what I said. Irma in her blunt way described it as long and impassioned but incomprehensible.'

'Was it about Bellorius?'

'I rather suppose not. Love was uppermost in my mind, I think. To tell you the truth I have lost my interest in Bellorius. It was never strong. It wilted and died this morning when I learned that Irma was not of us. She has come for the Physical Training Congress.'

'I shall miss you.'

'Stay with us for the gymnastics.'

For a second Scott-King hesitated. The future at Simona was obscure and rather threatening.

'There are to be five hundred female athletes. Contortionists perhaps from the Indies.'

'No,' said Scott-King at length firmly. 'I must keep faith with Bellorius.'

And he returned to the delegates who now sat impatiently in a charabanc at the doors of the Ritz.

III

The town of Simona stands within sight of the Mediterranean Sea on the foothills of the great massif which fills half the map of Neutralia. Groves of walnut and cork-oak, little orchards of almond and lemon, cover the surrounding country and grow to the foot of the walls which jut out among them in a series of sharp bastions, ingeniously contrived in the seventeenth century and never, in a long history of strife, put to the test of assault; for they enclose little of military significance. The medieval university, the baroque cathedral, twenty churches in whose delicate limestone belfries the storks build and multiply, a rococo square, two or three tiny shabby palaces, a market and a street of shops are all that can be found there and all that the heart of man can properly desire. The railway runs well clear of the town and betrays its presence only by rare puffs of white smoke among the tree-tops.

At the hour of the angelus Scott-King sat with Dr Bogdan Antonic at a café table on the ramparts.

'I suppose Bellorius must have looked out on almost precisely the same prospect as we see today.'

'Yes, the buildings at least do not change. There is still the illusion of peace while, as in Bellorius's time, the hills behind us are a nest of brigands.'

'He alludes to them, I remember, in the eighth canto, but surely today? . . .'

'It is still the same. Now they call them by different names – partisans, resistance groups, unreconcilables, what you will. The effect is the same. You need police escort to travel many of the roads.'

They fell silent. In the course of the circuitous journey to Simona, sympathy had sprung up between Scott-King and the International Secretary.

Bells deliciously chimed in the sunlit towers of twenty shadowy churches.

At length Scott-King said: 'You know I suspect that you and I are the only members of our party who have read Bellorius.'

'My own knowledge of him is slight. But Mr Fu has written of him very feelingly, I believe, in demotic Cantonese. Tell me, Professor, do you think the celebration is a success?'

'I'm not really a professor, you know.'

'No, but for the occasion all are professors. You are more professor than some who are here. I was obliged to cast my net rather wide to have all countries represented. Mr Jungman, for example, is simply a gynaecologist from The Hague, and Miss Bombaum is I do not know what. The Argentine and the Peruvian are mere students who happened to be in the country at this time. I tell you these things because I trust you and because I think you suspect them already. You have not perceived an element of deception?'

'Well, yes.'

'It is the wish of the Ministry. You see, I am their cultural adviser. They required a celebration this summer. I searched the records for an anniversary. I was in despair until by chance I hit on the name of Bellorius. They had not heard of him, of course, but then they would have been equally in the dark if he had been Dante or Goethe. I told them,' said Dr Antonic with a sad, sly, highly civilized little smile, 'that he was one of the greatest figures of European letters.'

'So he should be.'

'You really think so? You do not find the whole thing a masquerade? You think it is a success? I hope so, for you see my position at the Ministry is far from secure. There is jealousy everywhere. Imagine it, that anyone should be jealous of me. But in the New Neutralia all are so eager to work. They would snap up my little post greedily. Dr Arturo Fe would like it.'

'Surely not? He seems fully employed already.'

'That man collects government posts as in the old days churchmen collected benefices. He has a dozen already and he covets mine. That is why it is such a triumph to have brought him here. If the celebration is not a success, he will be implicated. Already, today, the Ministry have shown displeasure that the statue of Bellorius is not ready to be unveiled tomorrow. It is not our fault. It is the Office of Rest and Culture. It is the plot of an enemy named Engineer Garcia, who seeks to ruin Dr Fe and to succeed him in some of his posts. But Dr Fe will explain; he will improvise. He is of the country.'

Dr Fe improvised next day.

The party of savants were quartered in the main hotel of Simona, which that morning had the aspect of a war-time railway station owing to the arrival some time after midnight of fifty or sixty international philatelists for whom no accommodation had been arranged. They had slept in the lounge and hall; were, some of them, still sleeping when the Bellorius delegation assembled.

This was the day set down in the programme for the unveiling of the Bellorius statue. Hoarding and scaffolding in the town square marked the site of the proposed monument, but it was already well known among the delegates that the statue had not arrived. They had lived by rumour during the past three days for nothing in their exhilarating experiences had quite corresponded with the printed plan. 'They say the 'bus has gone back to Bellacita for new tyres.' – 'Have you heard we are to dine with the Lord Mayor?' – 'I heard Dr Fe say we should not leave till three o'clock.' 'I believe we ought all to be at the Chapter House' . . . and so on. This was the atmosphere of the tour, and in it the social barriers which had threatened to divide them at Bellacita had quickly broken down. Whitemaid was forgotten, Scott-King found himself once more befriended, made part of a fellowship of bewilderment. They were two days on the road sleeping at places far from their original route; they were wined and feasted at unexpected hours, disconcertingly greeted by brass bands and deputations, disconcertingly left stranded in deserted squares; once they crossed paths and for several frantic hours exchanged luggage with a party of religious pilgrims; once they had two dinners within an hour of each other; once they had none. But here they were in the end where they should be, at Simona. The only absentee was Bellorius.

Dr Fe improvised.

'Miss Bombaum, gentlemen, a little addition to our programme. Today we go to pay homage to the National Memorial.' Obediently they trooped out to the 'bus. Some philatelists were sleeping there and had to be dislodged. With them were embarked a dozen vast wreaths of laurel.

'What are these?'

'Those are our homage.'

Red ribbons across the foliage bore the names of the countries thus curiously represented.

They drove out of the town into the land of cork-oak and almond. After an hour they were stopped and an escort of armoured cars formed up before and behind them.

'A little token of our esteem,' said Dr Fe.

'It is for fear of the partisans,' whispered Dr Antonic.

Dust from the military enveloped the 'bus and hid the landscape. After two hours they halted. Here on a bare hillock stood the National Memorial. Like all modern state-architecture it was a loveless, unadorned object saved from insignificance only by its bulk; a great truncated pyramid of stone. A squad of soldiers were at work seeking lethargically to expunge a message daubed across the inscribed face in red paint: 'Death to the Marshal'.

Dr Fe ignored their activities and led his party to the further side which was innocent of any legend, patriotic or subversive. Here under a fierce sun they left their wreaths, Scott-King stepping forward, when called, to represent Great Britain. The poet-journalist crouched and snapped with his camera. The escort cheered. The fatigue-men came round with their mops to see what was going on. Dr Fe said a few words in Neutralian. The ceremony was over. They had luncheon in a neighbouring town at what seemed to be a kind of barrack-canteen, a bare room decorated only by a large photograph of the Marshal; a substantial but far from sumptuous meal eaten at narrow tables on thick earthenware plates. Scott-King drank several glasses of the heavy, purplish wine. The 'bus had stood long in the sun and was scorching hot. The wine and the thick stew induced sleep, and Scott-King lolled away the hours of the return journey unconscious of the jungle-whispering which prevailed around him in that tropic air.

Whispering, however, there was, and it found full voice when at length the party returned to Simona.

Scott-King awoke to it as he entered the hotel. 'We must call a meeting,' the American professor was saying. 'We must vote a resolution.'

'We want a show-down,' said Miss Bombaum. 'Not here,' she added, taking stock of the stamp-collectors who still squatted in the public rooms. 'Upstairs.'

It would be tedious in the extreme to recount all that was said in Miss Bombaum's bedroom after the expulsion of two philatelists who had taken refuge there. It was tedious to sit there, thought Scott-King, while the fountains were splashing in the square and the breeze stirring among the orange leaves on the city walls. Speeches were made, repeated, translated and mis-translated; there were calls for order and small private explosions of ill-temper. Not all the delegates were present. The Swiss Professor and the Chinese could not be found; the Peruvian and Argentine students refused to come, but there were six savants in the little bedroom besides Miss Bombaum, all of them, except Scott-King, very indignant about something.

The cause of offence emerged through many words and the haze of tobacco smoke. In brief it was this: the Bellorius Association had been made dupes of the politicians. But for Miss Bombaum's insatiable curiosity nothing need ever have been known of it. She had nosed out the grim truth like a truffle and the fact was plain. The National Monument was nothing more or less than a fetish of civil strife. It commemorated the massacre, execution, liquidation – what you will – ten years back on that sunny spot of some fifty leaders of the now dominant Neutralian party by those then dominant. The delegates of the Bellorius Association had been tricked into leaving wreaths there and, worse than this, had been photographed in the act. Miss Bombaum's picture was at that moment, she said, being rushed out to the newspapers of the world. More than this they had lunched at the party Headquarters at the very tables where the ruffians of the party were wont to refresh themselves after their orgies of terrorization. What was more, Miss Bombaum said, she had just learned from a book in her possession that Bellorius had never had any connection with Neutralia at all; he had been a Byzantine general.

Scott-King petulantly joined issue on this point. Strong words were used of him. 'Fascist beast.' – 'Reactionary cannibal.' – 'Bourgeois escapist.'

Scott-King withdrew from the meeting.

Dr Fe was in the passage. He took Scott-King's arm and silently led him downstairs and out into the arcaded street.

'They are not content,' said Dr Fe. 'It is a tragedy of the first magnitude.'

'You shouldn't have done it, you know,' said Scott-King.

'I should not have done it? My dear Professor, I wept when it was first suggested. I delayed our journey two days on the road precisely to avoid this. But would they listen? I said to the Minister of Popular Enlightenment: "Excellency, this is an international occasion. It is in the realm of pure scholarship. These great men have not come to Neutralia for political purposes." He replied coarsely: "They are eating and drinking at our expense. They should show their respect for the Régime. The Physical Training delegates have all saluted the Marshal in the Sports Stadium. The philatelists have been issued with the party badge and many of them wear it. The professors, too, must help the New Neutralia." What could I say? He is a person of no delicacy, of the lowest origins. It was he, I have no doubt, who induced the Ministry of Rest and Culture to delay sending the statue. Professor, you do not understand politics. I will be frank with you. It was all a plot.'

'So Miss Bombaum says.'

'A plot against me. For a long time now they have been plotting my downfall. I am not a party man. You think because I wear the badge and give the salute I am of the New Neutralia. Professor, I have six children, two of them girls of marriageable age. What can one do but seek one's fortune? And now I think I am ruined.'

'Is it as bad as that?'

'I cannot express how bad it is. Professor, you must go back to that room and persuade them to be calm. You are English. You have great influence. I have remarked during our journey together how they have all respected you.'

'They called me "a fascist beast".'

'Yes,' said Dr Fe simply, 'I heard it through the keyhole. They were very discontented.'

After Miss Bombaum's bedroom, the streets were cool and sweet; the touch of Dr Fe's fingers on Scott-King's sleeve was light as a moth. They walked on in silence. At a dewy flower-stall Dr Fe chose a buttonhole, haggled fiercely over the price, presented it with Arcadian grace to Scott-King and then resumed the sorrowful promenade.

'You will not go back?'

'It would do no good, you know.'

'An Englishman admits himself beaten,' said Dr Fe desperately.

'It amounts to that.'

'But you yourself will stay with us to the end?'

'Oh certainly.'

'Why, then, we have lost nothing of consequence. The celebrations can proceed.' He said it politely, gallantly, but he sighed as they parted.

Scott-King climbed the worn steps of the ramparts and sat alone under the orange trees watching the sun set.

The hotel was tranquil that evening. The philatelists had been collected and carted off; they left dumbly and glumly for an unknown destination like Displaced Persons swept up in the machinery of 'social engineering'. The six dissident delegates went with them, in default of other transport. The Swiss, the Chinese, the Peruvian and the Argentine alone remained. They dined together, silently, lacking a common tongue, but in good humour. Dr Fe, Dr Antonic and the Poet dined at another table, also silent, but sorrowful.

Next day the errant effigy arrived by lorry and the day following was fixed for the unveiling. Scott-King passed the time happily. He studied the daily papers, all of which, true to Miss Bombaum's forecast, displayed large photographs of the ceremony at the National Monument. He pieced together the sense of a leading article on the subject, he ate, he dozed, he visited the cool and glowing churches of the town, he composed the speech which, he was told, was expected of him on the morrow. Dr Fe, when they met, showed the reserve proper to a man of delicate feeling who had in emotion revealed too much of himself. It was a happy day for Scott-King.

Not so for his colleagues. Two disasters befell them severally, while he was pottering around. The Swiss Professor and the Chinese went for a little drive together in the hills. Their companionship was grounded on economy rather than mutual liking. An importunate guide; insensibility to the contemplative pleasures of Western architecture; a seemingly advantageous price; the promise of cool breezes, a wide panorama, a little restaurant; these undid them. When at evening they had not returned, their fate was certain.

'They should have consulted Dr Fe,' said Dr Antonic. 'He would have chosen a more suitable road and found them an escort.'

'What will become of them?'

'With the partisans you cannot say. Many of them are worthy, old-fashioned fellows who will treat them hospitably and wait for a ransom. But some are occupied with politics. If our friends have fallen among those, I am afraid they will certainly be murdered.'

'I did not like the Swiss.'

'Nor I. A Calvinist. But the Ministry will not be pleased that he is murdered.'

The fate of the South Americans was less romantic. The police took them off during luncheon.

'It seems they were not Argentine or Peruvian,' said Dr Antonic. 'Not even students.'

'What had they done?'

'I suppose they were informed against.'

'They certainly had a villainous appearance.'

'Oh yes, I suppose they were desperate fellows – spies, bimetallists, who can say? Nowadays it is not what you do that counts, but who informs against you. I think someone very high up must have informed against that pair. Otherwise Dr Fe could have had the business postponed until after our little ceremony. Or perhaps Dr Fe's influence is on the wane.'

So in the end, as was indeed most fitting, one voice only was raised to honour Bellorius.

The statue, when at last after many ineffective tugs at the controlling cord it was undraped and stood clear, stonily, insolently unabashed under the fierce Neutralian sun, while the populace huzzaed and, according to their custom, threw firecrackers under the feet of the notables, as the pigeons fluttered above in high alarm and the full weight of the band followed the opening trumpets – the statue was appalling.

There are no contemporary portraits of Bellorius still extant. In their absence some sharp business had been done in the Ministry of Rest and Culture. The figure now so frankly brought to view had lain long years in a mason's yard. It had been commissioned in an age of free enterprise for the tomb of a commercial magnate whose estate, on his death, had proved to be illusory. It was not Bellorius; it was not the fraudulent merchant prince; it was not even unambiguously male; it was scarcely human; it represented perhaps one of the virtues.

Scott-King stood aghast at the outrage he had unwittingly committed on that gracious square. But he had already spoken and his speech had been a success. He had spoken in Latin; he had spoken from the heart. He had said that a torn and embittered world was that day united in dedicating itself to the majestic concept of Bellorius, in rebuilding itself first in Neutralia, then among all the yearning peoples of the West, on the foundations Bellorius had so securely laid. He had said that they were lighting a candle that day which by the Grace of God should never be put out.

And after the oration came a prodigious luncheon at the University. And after the luncheon he was invested with a Doctorate of International Law. And after the investiture he was put into a 'bus and driven with Dr Fe, Dr Antonic and the Poet, back to Bellacita.

By the direct road the journey took barely five hours. It was not yet midnight when they drove down the brilliant boulevard of the capital city. Little had been said on the road. When they drew up at the Ministry, Dr Fe said: 'So our little expedition is over. I can only hope, Professor, that you have enjoyed it a particle as much as we.' He held out his hand and smiled under the arc-lamps. Dr Antonic and the Poet collected their modest luggage. 'Good night,' they said. 'Good night. We shall walk from here. The taxis are so expensive – the double fare operates after nine o'clock.'

They walked. Dr Fe ascended the steps of the Ministry.

'Back to work,' he said. 'I have had an urgent summons to report to my chief. We work late in the New Neutralia.'

There was nothing furtive about his ascent but it was swift. Scott-King caught him as he was about to enter a lift.

'But, I say, where am I to go?'

'Professor, our humble town is yours. Where would you like to go?'

'Well, I suppose I must go to an hotel. We were at the Ritz before.'

'I am sure you will be comfortable there. Tell the porter to get you a taxi and see he does not try to overcharge you. Double fare but not more.'

'But I shall see you tomorrow?'

'I hope *very* often.'

Dr Fe bowed and the doors of the lift shut upon his bow and his smile.

There was in his manner something more than the reserve proper to a man of delicate feeling who had in emotion revealed too much of himself.

IV

'Officially,' said Mr Horace Smudge, 'we don't even know you're here.'

He gazed at Scott-King through hexagonal spectacles

across the Pending Tray and twiddled a new-fangled fountain pen; a multiplicity of pencils protruding from his breast-pocket and his face seemed to suggest that he expected one of the telephones on his desk to ring at any moment with a message about something far more important than the matter under discussion; he was for all the world, Scott-King thought, like the clerk in the food office at Granchester.

Scott-King's life had been lived far from chanceries, but once, very many years ago at Stockholm, he had been asked to luncheon, by mistake for someone else, at the British Embassy. Sir Samson Courtenay had been *chargé d'affaires* at the time and Scott-King gratefully recalled the air of nonchalant benevolence with which he had received a callow undergraduate where he had expected a Cabinet Minister. Sir Samson had not gone far in his profession but for one man at least, for Scott-King, he remained the fixed type of English diplomat.

Smudge was not as Sir Samson; he was the child of sterner circumstances and a more recent theory of public service; no uncle had put in a bland word for Smudge in high places; honest toil, a clear head in the examination room, a genuine enthusiasm for Commercial Geography, had brought him to his present position as second secretary at Bellacita. 'You've no conception,' said Smudge, 'what a time we have with Priorities. I've had to put the Ambassadress off the plane twice, at the last moment, to make room for I.C.I. men. As it is I have four electrical engineers, two British Council lecturers and a trades unionist all wanting passages. Officially we have not heard of Bellorius. The Neutralians brought you here. It's their business to get you back.'

'I've been to them twice a day for three days. The man who organized everything, Dr Fe, seems to have left the Ministry.'

'You could always go by train, of course. It takes a little time but it would probably be quicker in the end. I presume you have all the necessary visas?'

'No. How long would they take to get?'

'Perhaps three weeks, perhaps longer. It's the Inter-Allied Zone Authority which holds things up.'

'But I can't afford to go on living here indefinitely. I was only allowed to bring £75 and the prices are terrible.'

'Yes, we had a case like that the other day. A man called Whitemaid. He'd run out of money and wanted to cash a cheque, but of course that is specifically contrary to the currency regulations. The consul took charge of him.'

'Did he get home?'

'I doubt it. They used to ship them by sea, you know, as Distressed British Subjects and hand them over to the police on arrival, but all that has been discontinued since the war. He was connected with your Bellorius celebration I think. It has caused a good deal of work to us one way and another. But it's worse for the Swiss. They've had a professor murdered and that always involves a special report on counsellor-level. I'm sorry I can't do more for you. I only deal with air priorities. You are the business of the consulate really. You had better let them know in a week or two how things turn out.'

The heat was scarcely endurable. In the ten days Scott-King had been in the country, the summer seemed to change temper and set its face angrily against him. The grass had turned brown in the square. Men still hosed the streets but the burning stone was dry again in an instant. The season was over; half the shops were shut and the little brown noblemen had left their chairs in the Ritz.

It was no great distance from the Embassy to the hotel, but Scott-King was stumbling with exhaustion before he reached the revolving doors. He went on foot for he was obsessed now by parsimony; he could no longer eat with pleasure, counting the price of each mouthful, calculating the charge for service, the stamp duty, the luxury taxes; groaning in that scorching summer under the weight of the Winter Relief Fund. He should leave the Ritz without delay, he resolved, and yet he hesitated; once ensconced in some modest pension, in some remote side street where no telephone ever rang and no one in passage from the outer world ever set foot, might he not be lost irretrievably, submerged, unrecognizable in his dimness, unremembered? Would he perhaps, years hence, exhibit a little discoloured card advertising lessons in English conversation, grow shabbier and greyer and plumper with the limp accretions of despair and destitution and die there at last nameless? He was an adult, an intellectual, a classical scholar, almost a poet, but he could not face that future without terror. So he clung to the Ritz, empty as it was, contemptuously as he felt himself regarded there, as the one place in Neutralia where salvation might still be found. If he left, he knew it would be for ever. He lacked the assurance of the native nobility who could sit there day by day, as though by right. Scott-King's only right lay in his travellers' cheques. He worked out his bill from hour to hour. At the moment he had nearly forty pounds in hand. When he was down to twenty, he decided, he would move. Meanwhile he looked anxiously round the dining-room before starting the daily calculation of how cheaply he could lunch.

And that day he was rewarded. His number turned up. Sitting not two tables away, alone, was Miss Bombaum. He rose to greet her. All the hard epithets with which they had parted were forgotten.

'May I sit here?'

She looked up, first without recognition, then with pleasure. Perhaps there was something in his forlorn appearance, in the diffidence of his appeal, which cleared him in Miss Bombaum's mind. This was no fascist beast that stood before her, no reactionary cannibal.

'Surely,' she said. 'The guy who invited me hasn't shown up.'

A ghastly fear, cold in that torrid room, struck Scott-King, that he would have to pay for Miss Bombaum's luncheon. She was eating a lobster, he noted, and drinking hock.

'When you've finished,' he said. 'Afterwards, with coffee perhaps in the lounge.'

'I've a date in twenty minutes,' she said. 'Sit down.'

He sat and at once, in answer to her casual enquiry, poured out the details of his predicament. He laid particular stress on his financial problems and, as pointedly as he could, ordered the humblest dish on the menu. 'It's a fallacy not to eat in hot weather,' said Miss Bombaum. 'You need to keep your resistance up.'

When he had finished the recital she said, 'Well, I reckon it shouldn't be hard to fix you up. Go by the Underground.'

Blacker despair in Scott-King's haunted face told Miss Bombaum that she had not made herself clear.

'You've surely heard of the Underground? It's –' she quoted from one of her recent articles on the subject – 'it's an alternative map of Europe, like a tracing overlying all the established frontiers and routes of communication. It's the new world taking shape below the surface of the old. It's the new ultra-national citizenship.'

'Well I'm blessed.'

'Look, I can't stop now. Be here this evening and I'll take you to see the key man.'

That afternoon, his last, as it turned out, in Bellacita, Scott-King received his first caller. He had gone to his room to sleep through the heat of the day, when his telephone rang and a voice announced Dr Antonic. He asked for him to be sent up.

The Croat entered and sat by his bed.

'So you have acquired the Neutralian custom of the *siesta*. I am too old. I cannot adapt myself to new customs. Everything in this country is as strange to me as when I first came here.

'I was at the Foreign Office this morning enquiring about my papers of naturalization and I heard by chance you were still here. So I came at once. I do not intrude? I thought you would have left by now. You have heard of our misfortunes? Poor Dr Fe is disgraced. All his offices taken from him. More than this there is trouble with his accounts. He spent more, it appears, on the Bellorius celebrations than the Treasury authorized. Since he is out of office he has no access to the books and cannot adjust them. They say he will be prosecuted, perhaps sent to the islands.'

'And you, Dr Antonic?'

'I am never fortunate. I relied on Dr Fe for my naturalization. Whom shall I turn to now? My wife thought that perhaps you could do something for us in England to make us British subjects.'

'There is nothing I can do.'

'No, I suppose not. Nor in America?'

'Still less there.'

'So I told my wife. But she is a Czech and so more hopeful. We Croats do not hope. It would be a great honour if you would come and explain these things to her. She will not believe me when I say there is no hope. I promised I would bring you.'

So Scott-King dressed and was led through the heat to a new quarter on the edge of the town, to a block of flats.

'We came here because of the elevator. My wife was so weary of Neutralian stairs. But alas the elevator no longer works.'

They trudged to the top floor, to a single sitting-room full of children, heavy with the smell of coffee and cigarette smoke.

'I am ashamed to receive you in a house without an elevator,' said Mme Antonic in French; then turning to the children, she addressed them in another tongue. They bowed, curtsied, and left the room. Mme Antonic prepared coffee and brought a plate of biscuits from the cupboard.

'I was sure you would come,' she said. 'My husband is too timid. You will take us with you to America.'

'Dear madam, I have never been there.'

'To England then. We must leave this country. We are not at our ease here.'

'I am finding the utmost difficulty in getting to England myself.'

'We are respectable people. My husband is a diplomat. My father had his own factory at Budweis. Do you know Mr Mackenzie?'

'No, I don't think so.'

'He was a *very* respectable Englishman. He would explain that we come of good people. He visited often to my father's factory. If you will find Mr Mackenzie he will help us.'

So the conversation wore on. 'If we could only find Mr Mackenzie,' Mme Antonic repeated, 'all our troubles would be at an end.' Presently the children returned.

'I will take them to the kitchen,' said Mme Antonic, 'and give them some jam. Then they will not be a nuisance.'

'You see,' said Dr Antonic, as the door closed, 'she is always hopeful. Now I do not hope. Do you think,' he asked, 'that in Neutralia Western Culture might be born again? That this country has been preserved by Destiny from the horrors of war so that it can become a beacon of hope for the world?'

'No,' said Scott-King.

'Do you not?' asked Dr Antonic anxiously. 'Do you not? Neither do I.'

That evening Miss Bombaum and Scott-King took a cab to the suburbs and left it at a café where they met a man who had sat with Miss Bombaum in the Ritz on her first evening. No names were exchanged.

'Who's this guy, Martha?'

'An English friend of mine I want you to help.'

'Going far?'

'England. Can he see the chief?'

'I go ask. He's on the level?'

'Surely.'

'Well, stick around while I ask.'

He went to telephone and returned saying, 'The chief'll see him. We can drop him off there, then have our talk.'

They took another cab and drove further from the city into a district of tanneries and slaughterhouses, recognizable by their smell in the hot darkness. Presently they stopped at a lightless villa.

'In there. Don't ring. Just push the door.'

'Hope you have a good trip,' said Miss Bombaum.

Scott-King was not a reader of popular novels and so was unfamiliar with the phrase 'It all happened so quickly that it was not until afterwards . . .' That, however, expressed his situation. The cab drove off as he was still stumbling up the garden path. He pushed the door, entered an empty and lightless hall, heard a voice from another room call 'Come in,' went in, and found himself in a shabby office confronting a Neutralian in the uniform of a major of police.

The man addressed him in English. 'You are Miss Bombaum's friend? Sit down. Do not be alarmed by my uniform. Some of our clients are *very* much alarmed. A silly boy tried to shoot me last week when he saw me like this. He suspected a trap. You want to go to England, I think. That is very difficult. Now if you had said Mexico or Brazil or Switzerland it would be easier. You have reasons which make England preferable?'

'I have reasons.'

'Curious. I spent many years there and found it a place of few attractions. The women had no modesty, the food upset my stomach. I have a little party on their way to Sicily. That would not do instead?'

'I am afraid not.'

'Well, we must see what can be done. You have a passport? This is lucky. English passports come very dear just now. I hope Miss Bombaum explained to you that mine is not a charitable organization. We exist to make profits and our expenses are high. I am constantly bothered by people who come to me supposing I work for the love of it. I do love my work, but love is not enough. The young man I spoke of just now, who tried to shoot me – he is buried just outside under the wall – he thought this was a political organization. We help people irrespective of class, race, party, creed or colour – for cash in advance. It is true, when I first took over, there were certain amateur associations that had sprung up during the World War – escaping prisoners, communist agents, Zionists, spies and so on. I soon put them out of business. That is where my position in the police is a help. Now I can say I have a virtual monopoly. Our work increases every day. It is extraordinary how many people without the requisite facilities seem anxious to cross frontiers today. I also have a valued connection with the Neutralian government. Troublesome fellows whom they want to dispose of pass through my hands in large numbers. How much have you got?'

'About forty pounds.'

'Show me.'

Scott-King handed him his book of travellers' cheques.

'But there are seventy pounds here.'

'Yes, but my hotel bill . . .'

'There will be no time for that.'

'I am sorry,' said Scott-King firmly. 'I could not possibly leave an hotel with my bill unpaid, especially in a foreign country. It may seem absurdly scrupulous to you but it is one of the things a Granchesterian simply cannot do.'

The Major was not a man to argue from first principles. He took men as they came and in his humane calling he dealt with many types.

'Well, I shan't pay it,' he said. 'Do you know anyone else in Bellacita?'

'No one.'

'Think.'

'There was a man called Smudge at our Embassy.'

'Smudge shall have your bill. These cheques want signing.'

Despite his high training Scott-King signed and the cheques were put away in the bureau drawer.

'My luggage?'

'We do not handle luggage. You will start this evening. I have a small party leaving for the coast. We have our main clearinghouse at Santa Maria. From there you will travel by steamer, perhaps not in the grand luxury, but what will you? No doubt as an Englishman you are a good sailor.'

He rang a bell on his desk and spoke to the answering secretary in rapid Neutralian.

'My man here will take charge of you and fit you out. You speak Neutralian? No? Perhaps it is as well. We do not encourage talk in my business, and I must warn you, the strictest discipline has to be observed. From now on you are under orders. Those who disobey never reach their destinations. Good-bye and a good journey.'

Some few hours later a large and antiquated saloon car was bumping towards the sea. In it sat in extreme discomfort seven men habited as Ursuline nuns. Scott-King was among them.

The little Mediterranean seaport of Santa Maria lay very near the heart of Europe. An Athenian colony had thrived there in the days of Pericles and built a shrine to Poseidon; Carthaginian slaves had built the breakwater and deepened the basin; Romans had brought fresh water from the mountain springs; Dominican friars had raised the great church which gave the place its present name; the Hapsburgs had laid out the elaborate little piazza; one of Napoleon's marshals had made it his base and left a classical garden there. The footprints of all these gentler conquerors were still plain to see but Scott-King saw nothing as, at dawn, he bowled over the cobbles to the water-front.

The Underground dispersal centre was a warehouse; three wide floors, unpartitioned, with boarded windows, joined by an iron staircase. There was one door near which the guardian had set her large brass bedstead. At most hours of the day she reclined there under a coverlet littered with various kinds of food, weapons, tobacco and a little bolster on which she sometimes made lace of an ecclesiastical pattern. She had the face of a *tricoteuse* of the Terror. 'Welcome to Modern Europe,' she said as the seven Ursulines entered.

The place was crowded. In the six days which he spent there Scott-King identified most of the groups who messed together by languages. There were a detachment of Slovene royalists, a few Algerian nationals, the remnants of a Syrian anarchist association, ten patient Turkish prostitutes, four French Petainist millionaires, a few Bulgarian terrorists, a half-dozen former Gestapo men, an Italian air-marshal and his suite, a Hungarian ballet, some Portuguese Trotskyites. The English-speaking group consisted chiefly of armed deserters from the American and British Armies of Liberation. They had huge sums of money distributed about the linings of their clothes, the reward of many months' traffic round the docks of the central sea.

Such activity as there was took place in the hour before dawn. Then the officer in charge, husband, it seemed, of the guardian hag, would appear with lists and a handful of passports; a roll would be called and a party despatched. During the day the soldiers played poker – a fifty-dollar ante and a hundred-dollar raise. Sometimes in the hours of darkness there were newcomers. The total number at the clearing station remained fairly constant.

At last on the sixth day there was a commotion. It began at midday with a call from the chief of police. He came with sword and epaulettes and he talked intently and crossly in Neutralian with the custodian.

One of the Americans, who had picked up more languages during his time in the Old World than most diplomats, explained: 'The guy with the fancy fixings says we got to get the hell out of here. Seems there's a new officer going to raid this joint.'

When the officer had gone, the custodian and his wife debated the question. 'The old girl says why don't he hand us over and get rewarded. The guy says Hell, the most likely reward they'd get would be hanging. Seems there's some stiffs planted round about.'

Presently a sea-captain appeared and talked Greek. All the Underground travellers sat stock still listening, picking up a word here and there. 'This guy's got a ship can take us off.'

'Where?'

'Aw, some place. Seems they're kinda more interested in finance than geography.'

A bargain was struck. The captain departed, and the Underground conductor explained to each language group in turn that there had been a slight dislocation of plan. 'Don't worry,' he said. 'Just go quiet. Everything's all right. We'll look after you. You'll all get where you want to in time. Just at the moment you got to move quick and quiet, that's all.'

So, unprotesting, at nightfall, the strangely assorted party was hustled on board a schooner. Noah's animals cannot have embarked with less sense of the object of their journey. The little ship was not built for such cargo. Down they went into a dark hold; hatches were battened down; the unmistakeable sound of moorings being cast off came to them in their timbered prison; an auxiliary Diesel engine started up; sails were hoisted; soon they were on the high seas in very nasty weather.

This is the story of a summer holiday; a light tale. It treats, at the worst, with solid discomfort and intellectual doubt. It would be inappropriate to speak here of those depths of the human spirit, the agony and despair, of the next few days of Scott-King's life. To even the Comic Muse, the gadabout, the adventurous one of those heavenly sisters, to whom so little that is human comes amiss, who can mix in almost any company and find a welcome at almost every door – even to her there are forbidden places. Let us leave Scott-King then on the high seas and meet him again as, sadly changed, he comes at length into harbour. The hatches are off, the August sun seems cool and breathless, Mediterranean air fresh and spring-like as at length he climbs on deck. There are soldiers; there is barbed wire; there is a waiting lorry; there is a drive through a sandy landscape, more soldiers, more wire. All the time Scott-King is in a daze. He is first fully conscious in a tent, sitting stark naked while a man in khaki drill taps his knee with a ruler.

'I say, Doc, I know this man.' He looks up into a vaguely familiar face. 'You *are* Mr Scott-King, aren't you? What on earth are you doing with this bunch, sir?'

'Lockwood! Good gracious, you used to be in my Greek set! Where am I?'

'No. 64 Jewish Illicit Immigrants' Camp, Palestine.'

Granchester reassembled in the third week of September. On the first evening of term, Scott-King sat in the masters' common-room and half heard Griggs telling of his trip abroad. 'It gives one a new angle to things, getting out of England for a bit. What did you do, Scottie?'

'Oh, nothing much. I met Lockwood. You remember him. Sad case, he was a sitter for the Balliol scholarship. Then he had to go into the army.'

'I thought he was still in it. How typical of old Scottie that all he has to tell us after eight weeks away is that he met a prize pupil! I shouldn't be surprised to hear you did some work, too, you old blackleg.'

'To tell you the truth I feel a little *désoeuvré*. I must look for a new subject.'

'You've come to the end of old Bellorius at last?'

'Quite to the end.'

Later the headmaster sent for Scott-King.

'You know,' he said, 'we are starting this year with fifteen fewer classical specialists than we had last term?'

'I thought that would be about the number.'

'As you know I'm an old Greats man myself. I deplore it as much as you do. But what are we to do? Parents are not interested in producing the "complete man" any more. They want to qualify their boys for jobs in the modern world. You can hardly blame them, can you?'

'Oh yes,' said Scott-King. 'I can and do.'

'I always say you are a much more important man here than I am. One couldn't conceive of Granchester without Scott-King. But has it ever occurred to you that a time may come when there will be no more classical boys at all?'

'Oh yes. Often.'

'What I was going to suggest was — I wonder if you will consider taking some other subject as well as the classics? History, for example, preferably economic history?'

'No, headmaster.'

'But, you know, there may be something of a crisis ahead.'

'Yes, headmaster.'

'Then what do you intend to do?'

'If you approve, headmaster, I will stay as I am here as long as any boy wants to read the classics. I think it would be very wicked indeed to do anything to fit a boy for the modern world.'

'It's a short-sighted view, Scott-King.'

'There, headmaster, with all respect, I differ from you profoundly. I think it the most long-sighted view it is possible to take.'

Tactical Exercise

John Verney married Elizabeth in 1938, but it was not until the winter of 1945 that he came to hate her steadily and fiercely. There had been countless brief gusts of hate before this, for it was a thing which came easily to him. He was not what is normally described as a bad-tempered man, rather the reverse; a look of fatigue and abstraction was the only visible sign of the passion which possessed him, as others are possessed by laughter or desire, several times a day.

During the war he passed among those he served with as a phlegmatic fellow. He did not have his good or his bad days; they were all uniformly good and bad; good, in that he did what had to be done, expeditiously without ever 'getting in a flap' or 'going off the deep end'; bad, from the intermittent, invisible sheet-lightning of hate which flashed and flickered deep inside him at every obstruction or reverse. In his orderly room when, as a company commander, he faced the morning procession of defaulters and malingerers; in the mess when the subalterns disturbed his reading by playing the wireless; at the Staff College when the 'syndicate' disagreed with his solution; at Brigade H.Q. when the staff-sergeant mislaid a file or the telephone orderly muddled a call; when the driver of his car missed a turning; later, in hospital, when the doctor seemed to look too cursorily at his wound and the nurses stood gossiping jauntily at the beds of more likeable patients instead of doing their duty to him – in all the annoyances of army life which others dismissed with an oath and a shrug, John Verney's eyelids drooped wearily, a tiny grenade of hate exploded and the fragments rang and ricocheted round the steel walls of his mind.

There had been less to annoy him before the war. He had some money and the hope of a career in politics. Before marriage he served his apprenticeship to the Liberal party in two hopeless by-elections. The Central Office then rewarded him with a constituency in outer London which offered a fair chance in the next General Election. In the eighteen months before the war he nursed this constituency from his flat in Belgravia and travelled frequently on the continent to study political conditions. These studies convinced him that war was inevitable; he denounced the Munich agreement pungently and secured a commission in the territorial army.

Into this peacetime life Elizabeth fitted unobtrusively. She was his cousin. In 1938 she had reached the age of twenty-six, four years his junior, without falling in love. She was a calm, handsome young woman, an only child, with some money of her own and more to come. As a girl, in her first season, an injudicious remark, let slip and overheard, got her the reputation of cleverness. Those who knew her best ruthlessly called her 'deep'.

Thus condemned to social failure, she languished in the ballrooms of Pont Street for another year and then settled down to a life of concert-going and shopping with her mother, until she surprised her small circle of friends by marrying John Verney. Courtship and consummation were tepid, cousinly, harmonious. They agreed, in face of the coming war, to remain childless. No one knew what Elizabeth felt or thought about anything. Her judgements were mainly negative, deep or dull as you cared to take them. She had none of the appearance of a woman likely to inflame great hate.

John Verney was discharged from the Army early in 1945 with an M.C. and one leg, for the future, two inches shorter than the other. He found Elizabeth living in Hampstead with her parents, his uncle and aunt. She had kept him informed by letter of the changes in her condition but, preoccupied, he had not clearly imagined them. Their flat had been requisitioned by a government office; their furniture and books sent to a repository and totally lost, partly burned by a bomb, partly pillaged by firemen. Elizabeth, who was a linguist, had gone to work in a clandestine branch of the Foreign Office.

Her parents' house had once been a substantial Georgian villa overlooking the Heath. John Verney arrived there early in the morning after a crowded night's journey from Liverpool.

The wrought-iron railings and gates had been rudely torn away by the salvage collectors, and in the front garden, once so neat, weeds and shrubs grew in a rank jungle trampled at night by courting soldiers. The back garden was a single, small bomb-crater; heaped clay, statuary and the bricks and glass of ruined greenhouses; dry stalks of willow-herb stood breast high over the mounds. All the windows were gone from the back of the house, replaced by shutters of card and board, which put the main rooms in perpetual darkness. 'Welcome to Chaos and Old Night,' said his uncle genially.

There were no servants; the old had fled, the young had been conscripted for service. Elizabeth made him some tea before leaving for her office.

Here he lived, lucky, Elizabeth told him, to have a home. Furniture was unprocurable, furnished flats commanded a price beyond their income, which was now taxed to a bare wage. They might have found something in the country, but Elizabeth, being childless, could not get release from her work. Moreover, he had his constituency.

This, too, was transformed. A factory, wired round like a prisoner-of-war camp, stood in the public gardens. The streets surrounding it, once the trim houses of potential Liberals, had been bombed, patched, confiscated and filled with an immigrant proletarian population. Every day he received a heap of complaining letters from constituents exiled in provincial boarding-houses. He had hoped that his decoration and his limp might earn him sympathy, but he found the new inhabitants indifferent to the fortunes of war. Instead they showed a sceptical curiosity about Social Security. 'They're nothing but a lot of reds,' said the Liberal agent.

'You mean I shan't get in?'

'Well, we'll give them a good fight. The Tories are putting up a Battle-of-Britain pilot. I'm afraid he'll get most of what's left of the middle-class vote.'

In the event John Verney came bottom of the poll, badly. A rancorous Jewish schoolteacher was elected. The Central Office paid his deposit, but the election had cost him dear. And when it was over there was absolutely nothing for John Verney to do.

He remained in Hampstead, helped his aunt make the beds after Elizabeth had gone to her office, limped to the greengrocer and fishmonger and stood, full of hate, in the queues; helped Elizabeth wash up at night. They ate in the kitchen, where his aunt cooked deliciously the scanty rations. His uncle went three days a week to help pack parcels for Java.

Elizabeth, the deep one, never spoke of her work, which, in fact, was concerned with setting up hostile and oppressive governments in Eastern Europe. One evening at a restaurant, a man came and spoke to her, a tall young man whose sallow, aquiline face was full of intellect and humour. 'That's the head of my department,' she said. 'He's so amusing.'

'Looks like a Jew.'

'I believe he is. He's a strong Conservative and hates the work,' she added hastily, for since his defeat in the election John had become fiercely anti-Semitic.

'There is absolutely no need to work for the State now,' he said. 'The war's over.'

'Our work is just beginning. They won't let any of us go. You must understand what conditions are in this country.'

It often fell to Elizabeth to explain 'conditions' to him. Strand by strand, knot by knot, through the coalless winter, she exposed the vast net of government control which had been woven in his absence. He had been reared in traditional Liberalism and the system revolted him. More than this, it had him caught, personally, tripped up, tied, tangled; wherever he wanted to go, whatever he wanted to do or have done, he found himself baffled and frustrated. And as Elizabeth explained she found herself defending. This regulation was necessary to avoid that ill; such a country was suffering, as Britain was not, for having neglected such a precaution; and so on, calmly and reasonably.

'I know it's maddening, John, but you must realize it's the same for everyone.'

'That's what all you bureaucrats want,' he said. 'Equality through slavery. The two-class state – proletarians and officials.'

Elizabeth was part and parcel of it. She worked for the State and the Jews. She was a collaborator with the new, alien, occupying power. And as the winter wore on and the gas burned feebly in the stove, and the rain blew in through the patched windows, as at length spring came and buds broke in the obscene wilderness round the house, Elizabeth in his mind became something more important. She became a symbol. For just as soldiers in far-distant camps think of their wives, with a tenderness they seldom felt at home, as the embodiment of all the good things they have left behind, wives who perhaps were scolds and drabs, but in the desert and jungle become transfigured until their trite air-letters become texts of hope, so Elizabeth grew in John Verney's despairing mind to more than human malevolence as the archpriestess and maenad of the century of the common man.

'You aren't looking well, John,' said his aunt. 'You and Elizabeth ought to get away for a bit. She is due for leave at Easter.'

'The State is granting her a supplementary ration of her husband's company, you mean. Are we sure she has filled in all the correct forms? Or are commissars of her rank above such things?'

Uncle and aunt laughed uneasily. John made his little jokes with such an air of weariness, with such a droop of the eyelids that they sometimes struck chill in that family circle. Elizabeth regarded him gravely and silently.

John was far from well. His leg was in constant pain so that he no longer stood in queues. He slept badly; as also, for the first time in her life, did Elizabeth. They shared a room now, for the winter rains had brought down ceilings in many parts of the shaken house and the upper rooms were thought to be unsafe. They had twin beds on the ground floor in what had once been her father's library.

In the first days of his homecoming John had been amorous. Now he never approached her. They lay night after night six feet apart in the darkness. Once when John had been awake for two hours he turned on the lamp that stood on the table between them. Elizabeth was lying with her eyes wide open staring at the ceiling.

'I'm sorry. Did I wake you?'

'I haven't been asleep.'

'I thought I'd read for a bit. Will it disturb you?'

'Not at all.'

She turned away. John read for an hour. He did not know whether she was awake or asleep when he turned off the light.

Often after that he longed to put on the light, but was afraid to find her awake and staring. Instead he lay, as others lie in a luxurious rapture of love, hating her.

It did not occur to him to leave her; or, rather, it did occur from time to time, but he hopelessly dismissed the thought. Her life was bound tight to his; her family was his family; their finances were intertangled and their expectations lay together in the same quarters. To leave her would be to start fresh, alone and naked in a strange world; and lame and weary at the age of thirty-eight, John Verney had not the heart to move.

He loved no one else. He had nowhere to go, nothing to do. Moreover he suspected, of late, that it would not hurt her if he went. And, above all, the single steadfast desire left to him was to do her ill. 'I wish she were dead,' he said to himself as he lay awake at night. 'I wish she were dead.'

Sometimes they went out together. As the winter passed, John took to dining once or twice a week at his club. He assumed that on these occasions she stayed at home, but one morning it transpired that she too had dined out the evening before. He did not ask with whom, but his aunt did, and Elizabeth replied, 'Just someone from the office.'

'The Jew?' John asked.

'As a matter of fact, it was.'

'I hope you enjoyed it.'

'Quite. A beastly dinner, of course, but he's very amusing.'

One night when he returned from his club, after a dismal little dinner and two crowded Tube journeys, he found Elizabeth in bed and deeply asleep. She did not stir when he entered. Unlike her normal habit, she was snoring. He stood for a minute, fascinated by this new and unlovely aspect of her, her head thrown back, her mouth open and slightly dribbling at the corner. Then he shook her. She muttered something, turned over and slept heavily and soundlessly.

Half an hour later, as he was striving to compose himself for sleep, she began to snore again. He turned on the light, looked at her more closely and noticed with surprise, which suddenly changed to joyous hope, that there was a tube of unfamiliar pills, half empty, beside her on the bed table.

He examined it. '24 *Comprimés narcotiques, hypnotiques,*' he read, and then in large, scarlet letters, 'NE PAS DEPASSER DEUX.' He counted those which were left. Eleven.

With tremulous butterfly wings Hope began to flutter in his heart, became a certainty. He felt a fire kindle and spread inside him until he was deliciously suffused in every limb and organ. He lay, listening to the snores, with the pure excitement of a child on Christmas Eve. 'I shall wake up tomorrow and find her dead,' he told himself, as once he had felt the flaccid stocking at the foot of his bed and told himself, 'Tomorrow I shall wake up and find it full.' Like a child, he longed to sleep to hasten the morning and, like a child, he was wildly, ecstatically sleepless. Presently he swallowed two of the pills himself and almost at once was unconscious.

Elizabeth always rose first to make breakfast for the family. She was at the dressing-table when sharply, without drowsiness, his memory stereoscopically clear about the incidents of the night before, John awoke. 'You've been snoring,' she said.

Disappointment was so intense that at first he could not speak. Then he said, 'You snored, too, last night.'

'It must be the sleeping-tablet I took. I must say it gave me a good night.'

'Only one?'

'Yes, two's the most that's safe.'

'Where did you get them?'

'A friend at the office – the one you called the Jew. He has them prescribed by a doctor for when he's working too hard. I told him I wasn't sleeping, so he gave me half a bottle.'

'Could he get me some?'

'I expect so. He can do most things like that.'

So he and Elizabeth began to drug themselves regularly and passed long, vacuous nights. But often John delayed, letting the beatific pill lie beside his glass of water, while, knowing the vigil was terminable at will, he postponed the joy of unconsciousness, heard Elizabeth's snores, and hated her sumptuously.

One evening while the plans for the holiday were still under discussion, John and Elizabeth went to the cinema. The film was a murder story of no great ingenuity but with showy scenery. A bride murdered her husband by throwing him out of a window, down a cliff. Things were made easy for her by his taking a lonely lighthouse for their honeymoon. He was very rich and she wanted his money. All she had to do was confide in the local doctor and a few neighbours that her husband frightened her by walking in his sleep; she doped his coffee, dragged him from the bed to the balcony — a feat of some strength — where she had already broken away a yard of balustrade, and rolled him over. Then she went back to bed, gave the alarm next morning, and wept over the mangled body which was presently discovered half awash on the rocks. Retribution overtook her later, but at the time the thing was a complete success.

'I wish it were as easy as that,' thought John, and in a few hours the whole tale had floated away in those lightless attics of the mind where films and dreams and funny stories lie spider-shrouded for a lifetime unless, as sometimes happens, an intruder brings them to light.

Such a thing happened a few weeks later when John and Elizabeth went for their holiday. Elizabeth found the place. It belonged to someone in her office. It was named Good Hope Fort, and stood on the Cornish coast. 'It's only just been derequisitioned,' she said: 'I expect we shall find it in pretty bad condition.'

'We're used to that,' said John. It did not occur to him that she should spend her leave anywhere but with him. She was as much part of him as his maimed and aching leg.

They arrived on a gusty April afternoon after a train journey of normal discomfort. A taxi drove them eight miles from the station, through deep Cornish lanes, past granite cottages and disused, archaic tin workings. They reached the village which gave the house its postal address, passed through it and out along a track which suddenly emerged from its high banks into open grazing land on the cliff's edge, high, swift clouds and sea-birds wheeling overhead, the turf at their feet alive with fluttering wild flowers, salt in the air, below them the roar of the Atlantic breaking on the rocks, a middle-distance of indigo and white tumbled waters and beyond it the serene arc of the horizon. Here was the house.

'Your father,' said John, 'would now say, "Your castle hath a pleasant seat."'

'Well, it has rather, hasn't it?'

It was a small stone building on the very edge of the cliff, built a century or so ago for defensive purposes, converted to a private house in the years of peace, taken again by the Navy during the war as a signal station, now once more reverting to gentler uses. Some coils of rusty wire, a mast, the concrete foundations of a hut, gave evidence of its former masters.

They carried their things into the house and paid the taxi.

'A woman comes up every morning from the village. I said we shouldn't want her this evening. I see she's left us some oil for the lamps. She's got a fire going, too, bless her, and plenty of wood. Oh, and look what I've got as a present from father. I promised not to tell you until we arrived. A bottle of whisky. Wasn't it sweet of him. He's been hoarding his ration for three months . . .' Elizabeth talked brightly as she began to arrange the luggage. 'There's a room for each of us. This is the only proper living-room, but there's a study in case you feel like doing any work. I believe we shall be quite comfortable . . .'

The living-room was built with two stout bays, each with a french window opening on a balcony which overhung the sea. John opened one and the sea-wind filled the room. He stepped out, breathed deeply, and then said suddenly: 'Hullo, this is dangerous.'

At one place, between the windows, the cast-iron balustrade had broken away and the stone ledge lay open over the cliff. He looked at the gap and at the foaming rocks below, momentarily puzzled. The irregular polyhedron of memory rolled uncertainly and came to rest.

He had been here before, a few weeks ago, on the gallery of the lighthouse in that swiftly forgotten film. He stood there, looking down. It was exactly thus that the waves had come swirling over the rocks, had broken and dropped back with the spray falling about them. This was the sound they had made; this was the broken ironwork and the sheer edge.

Elizabeth was still talking in the room, her voice drowned by wind and sea. John returned to the room, shut and fastened the door. In the quiet she was saying '. . . only got the furniture out of store last week. He left the woman from the village to arrange it. She's got some queer ideas, I must say. Just look where she put . . .'

'What did you say this house was called?'

'Good Hope.'

'A good name.'

That evening John drank a glass of his father-in-law's whisky, smoked a pipe and planned. He had been a good tactician. He made a leisurely, mental 'appreciation of the situation'. Object: murder.

When they rose to go to bed he asked: 'You packed the tablets?'

'Yes, a new tube. But I am sure I shan't want any tonight.'

'Neither shall I,' said John, 'the air is wonderful.'

During the following days he considered the tactical problem. It was entirely simple. He had the 'staff-solution' already. He considered it in the words and form he had used in the army. '... Courses open to the enemy ... achievement of surprise ... consolidation of success.' The staff-solution was exemplary. At the beginning of the first week, he began to put it into execution.

Already, by easy stages, he had made himself known in the village. Elizabeth was a friend of the owner; he the returned hero, still a little strange in civvy street. 'The first holiday my wife and I have had together for six years,' he told them in the golf club and, growing more confidential at the bar, hinted that they were thinking of making up for lost time and starting a family.

On another evening he spoke of war-strain, of how in this war the civilians had had a worse time of it than the services. His wife, for instance; stuck it all through the blitz; office work all day, bombs at night. She ought to get right away, alone somewhere for a long stretch; her nerves had suffered; nothing serious, but to tell the truth he wasn't quite happy about it. As a matter of fact, he had found her walking in her sleep once or twice in London.

His companions knew of similar cases; nothing to worry about, but it wanted watching; didn't want it to develop into anything worse. Had she seen a doctor?

Not yet, John said. In fact she didn't know she had been sleepwalking. He had got her back to bed without waking her. He hoped the sea air would do her good. In fact, she seemed much better already. If she showed any more signs of the trouble when they got home, he knew a very good man to take her to.

The golf club was full of sympathy. John asked if there were a good doctor in the neighbourhood. Yes, they said, old Mackenzie in the village, a first-class man, wasted in a little place like that; not at all a stick-in-the-mud. Read the latest books; psychology and all that. They couldn't think why Old Mack had never specialized and made a name for himself.

'I think I might go and talk to Old Mack about it,' said John.

'Do. You couldn't find a better fellow.'

Elizabeth had a fortnight's leave. There were still three days to go when John went off to the village to consult Dr Mackenzie. He found a grey-haired, genial bachelor in a consulting room that was more like a lawyer's office than a physician's, book-lined, dark, permeated by tobacco smoke.

Seated in the shabby leather armchair he developed in more precise language the story he had told in the golf club. Dr Mackenzie listened without comment.

'It's the first time I've run up against anything like this,' he concluded.

At length Dr Mackenzie said: 'You got pretty badly knocked about in the war, Mr Verney?'

'My knee. It still gives me trouble.'

'Bad time in hospital?'

'Three months. A beastly place outside Rome.'

'There's always a good deal of nervous shock in an injury of that kind. It often persists when the wound is healed.'

'Yes, but I don't quite understand . . .'

'My dear Mr Verney, your wife asked me to say nothing about it, but I think I must tell you that she has already been here to consult me on this matter.'

'About her sleepwalking? But she can't . . .' then John stopped.

'My dear fellow, I quite understand. She thought you didn't know. Twice lately you've been out of bed and she had to lead you back. She knows all about it.'

John could find nothing to say.

'It's not the first time,' Dr Mackenzie continued, 'that I've been consulted by patients who have told me their symptoms and said they had come on behalf of friends or relations. Usually it's girls who think they're in the family-way. It's an interesting feature of your case that you should want to ascribe the trouble to someone else, probably the decisive feature. I've given your wife the name of a man in London who I think will be able to help you. Meanwhile I can only advise plenty of exercise, light meals at night . . .'

John Verney limped back to Good Hope Fort in a state of consternation. Security had been compromised; the operation must be cancelled; initiative had been lost . . . all the phrases of the tactical school came to his mind, but he was still numb after this unexpected reverse. A vast and naked horror peeped at him and was thrust aside.

When he got back Elizabeth was laying the supper table. He stood on the balcony and stared at the gaping rails with eyes smarting with disappointment. It was dead calm that evening. The rising tide lapped and fell and mounted again silently among the rocks below. He stood gazing down, then he turned back into the room.

There was one large drink left in the whisky bottle. He poured it out and swallowed it. Elizabeth brought in the supper and they sat down. Gradually his mind grew a little calmer. They usually ate in silence. At last he said: 'Elizabeth, why did you tell the doctor I had been walking in my sleep?'

She quietly put down the plate she had been holding and

looked at him curiously. 'Why?' she said gently. 'Because I was worried, of course. I didn't think you knew about it.'

'But have I been?'

'Oh yes, several times – in London and here. I didn't think it mattered at first, but the night before last I found you on the balcony, quite near that dreadful hole in the rails. I was really frightened. But it's going to be all right now. Dr Mackenzie has given me the name . . .'

It was possible, thought John Verney; nothing was more likely. He had lived night and day for ten days thinking of that opening, of the sea and rock below, the ragged ironwork and the sharp edge of stone. He suddenly felt defeated, sick and stupid, as he had as he lay on the Italian hillside with his smashed knee. Then as now he had felt weariness even more than pain.

'Coffee, darling.'

Suddenly he roused himself. 'No,' he almost shouted. 'No, no, no.'

'Darling, what is the matter? Don't get excited. Are you feeling ill? Lie down on the sofa near the window.'

He did as he was told. He felt so weary that he could barely move from his chair.

'Do you think coffee would keep you awake, love? You look quite fit to drop already. There, lie down.'

He lay down and, like the tide slowly mounting among the rocks below, sleep rose and spread in his mind. He nodded and woke with a start.

'Shall I open the window, darling, and give you some air?'

'Elizabeth,' he said, 'I feel as if I have been drugged.' Like the rocks below the window – now awash, now emerging clear from falling water; now awash again, deeper; now barely visible, mere patches on the face of gently eddying foam – his brain was softly drowning. He roused himself, as children do in nightmare, still scared, still half asleep. 'I can't be drugged,' he said loudly, 'I never touched the coffee.'

'Drugs in the coffee?' said Elizabeth gently, like a nurse soothing a fractious child. 'Drugs in the *coffee*? What an absurd idea. That's the kind of thing that only happens on the films, darling.'

He did not hear her. He was fast asleep, snoring stertorously by the open window.

Compassion

I

The military organization into which Major Gordon drifted during the last stages of the war enjoyed several changes of name as its function became less secret. At first it was called 'Force X'; then 'Special Liaison Balkan Irregular Operations'; finally, 'Joint Allied Mission to the Jugo-Slav Army of Liberation'. Its work was to send observing officers and wireless operators to Tito's partisans.

Most of these appointments were dangerous and uncomfortable. The liaison parties parachuted into the forests and the mountains and lived like brigands. They were often hungry, always dirty, always on the alert, prepared to decamp at any move of the enemy's. The post to which Major Gordon was sent was one of the safest and softest. Begoy was the headquarters of a partisan corps in Northern Croatia. It lay in a large area, ten miles by twenty, of what was called 'Liberated Territory', well clear of the essential lines of communication. The Germans were pulling out of Greece and Dalmatia and were concerned only with main roads and supply points. They made no attempt now to administer or patrol the hinterland. There was a field near Begoy where aircraft could land unmolested. They did so nearly every week in the summer of 1944 coming from Bari with partisan officials and modest supplies of equipment. In this area congregated a number of men and women who called themselves the Praesidium of the Federal Republic of Croatia. There was even a Minister of Fine Arts. The peasants worked their land undisturbed except by requisitions for the support of the politicians. Besides the British Military Mission, there was a villa full of invisible Russians, half a dozen R. A. F. men who managed the landing ground and an inexplicable Australian doctor who had parachuted into the country a year before with orders to instruct the partisans in field hygiene and had wandered about with them ever since, rendering first aid. There were also one hundred and eight Jews.

Major Gordon met them on the third day of his residence. He had been given a small farmhouse half a mile outside the town and the services of an interpreter who had lived for some years in the United States and spoke English of a kind. This man, Bakic, was in the secret police. His duty was to keep Major Gordon under close attention and to report every evening at OZNA headquarters. Major Gordon's predecessor had warned him of this man's proclivities, but Major Gordon was sceptical for such things were beyond his experience.

Three Slav widows were also attached to the household. They slept in a loft and acted as willing and tireless servants.

After breakfast on the third day Bakic announced to Major Gordon: 'Dere's de Jews outside.'

'What Jews?'

'Dey been dere two hour, maybe more. I said to wait.'

'What do they want?'

'Dey're Jews. I reckon dey always want sometin. Dey want see de British major. I said to wait.'

'Well, ask them to come in.'

'Dey can't come in. Why, dere's more'n a hundred of dem.'

Major Gordon went out and found the farmyard and the lane beyond thronged. There were some children in the crowd, but most seemed old, too old to be the parents, for they were unnaturally aged by their condition. Everyone in Begoy except the peasant women was in rags, but the partisans kept regimental barbers and there was a kind of dignity about their tattered uniforms. The Jews were grotesque in their remnants of bourgeois civility. They showed little trace of racial kinship. There were Semites among them, but the majority were fair, snub-nosed, high-cheek-boned, the descendants of Slav tribes judaized long after the Dispersal. Few of them, probably, now worshipped the God of Israel in the manner of their ancestors.

A low chatter broke out as Major Gordon appeared. Then

three leaders came forward, a youngish woman of better appearance than the rest and two crumpled old men. The woman asked him if he spoke French, and when Major Gordon nodded introduced her companions — a grocer from Mostar, a lawyer from Zagreb — and herself — a Viennese, wife of a Hungarian engineer.

Here Bakic roughly interrupted in Serbo-Croat and the three fell humbly and hopelessly silent. He said to Major Gordon: 'I tell dese peoples dey better talk Slav. I will speak for dem.'

The woman said: 'I only speak German and French.'

Major Gordon said: 'We will speak French. I can't ask you all in. You three had better come and leave the others outside.'

Bakic scowled. A chatter broke out in the crowd. Then the three with timid little bows crossed the threshold, carefully wiping their dilapidated boots before treading the rough board floor of the interior.

'I shan't want you, Bakic.'

The spy went out to bully the crowd, hustling them out of the farmyard into the lane.

There were only two chairs in Major Gordon's living-room. He took one and invited the woman to use the other. The men huddled behind and then began to prompt her. They spoke to one another in a mixture of German and Serbo-Croat; the lawyer knew a little French; enough to make him listen anxiously to all the woman said, and to interrupt. The grocer gazed steadily at the floor and seemed to take no interest in the proceedings. He was there because he commanded respect and trust among the waiting crowd. He had been in a big way of business with branch stores throughout all the villages of Bosnia.

With a sudden vehemence the woman, Mme Kanyi, shook off her advisers and began her story. The people outside, she explained, were the survivors of an Italian concentration camp on the island of Rab. Most were Jugo-Slav nationals, but some, like herself, were refugees from Central Europe. She and her husband were on their way to Australia in 1939; their papers were in order; he had a job waiting for him in Brisbane. Then they had been caught by the war.

When the King fled, the Ustashi began massacring Jews. The Italians rounded them up and took them to the Adriatic. When Italy surrendered, the partisans for a few weeks held the coast. They brought the Jews to the mainland, conscripted all who seemed capable of useful work, and imprisoned the rest. Her husband had been attached to the army headquarters as electrician. Then the Germans moved in; the partisans fled, taking the Jews with them. And here they were, a hundred and eight of them, half starving in Begoy.

Major Gordon was not an imaginative man. He saw the complex historical situation in which he participated, quite simply in terms of friends and enemies and the paramount importance of the war-effort. He had nothing against Jews and nothing against communists. He wanted to defeat the Germans and go home. Here it seemed were a lot of tiresome civilians getting in the way of this object. He said cheerfully: 'Well, I congratulate you.'

Mme Kanyi looked up quickly to see if he were mocking her, found that he was not, and continued to regard him now with sad, blank wonder.

'After all,' he continued, 'you're among friends.'

'Yes,' she said, too doleful for irony, 'we heard that the British and Americans were friends of the partisans. It is true, then?'

'Of course it's true. Why do you suppose I am here?'

'It is not true that the British and Americans are coming to take over the country?'

'First I've heard of it.'

'But it is well known that Churchill is a friend of the Jews.'

'I'm sorry, madam, but I simply do not see what the Jews have got to do with it.'

'But we are Jews. One hundred and eight of us.'

'Well, what do you expect me to do about that?'

'We want to go to Italy. We have relations there, some of us. There is an organization at Bari. My husband and I had our papers to go to Brisbane. Only get us to Italy and we shall be no more trouble. We cannot live as we are here. When winter comes we shall all die. We hear aeroplanes almost every night. Three aeroplanes could take us all. We have no luggage left.'

'My dear madam, those aeroplanes are carrying essential war equipment, they are taking out wounded and officials. I'm very sorry you are having a hard time, but so are plenty of other people in this country. It won't last long now. We've got the Germans on the run. I hope by Christmas to be in Zagreb.'

'We must say nothing against the partisans?'

'Not to me. Look here, let me give you a cup of cocoa. Then I have work to do.'

He went to the window and called to Bakic for cocoa and biscuits. While it was coming the lawyer said in English: 'We were better in Rab.' Then suddenly all three broke into a chatter of polyglot complaint, about their house, about their property which had been stolen, about their rations. If Churchill knew he would have them sent to Italy. Major Gordon said: 'If it was not for the partisans you would now be in the hands of the Nazis,' but that word had no terror for them now. They shrugged hopelessly.

One of the widows brought in a tray of cups and a tin of biscuits. 'Help yourselves,' said Major Gordon.

'How many, please, may we take?'

'Oh, two or three.'

With tense self-control each took three biscuits, watching

the others to see they did not disgrace the meeting by greed. The grocer whispered to Mme Kanyi and she explained: 'He says will you excuse him if he keeps one for a friend?' The man had tears in his eyes as he snuffed his cocoa; once he had handled sacks of the stuff.

They rose to go. Mme Kanyi made a last attempt to attract his sympathy. 'Will you please come and see the place where they have put us?'

'I am sorry, madam, it simply is not my business. I am a military liaison officer, nothing more.'

They thanked him humbly and profusely for the cocoa and left the house. Major Gordon saw them in the farmyard disputing. The men seemed to think Mme Kanyi had mishandled the affair. Then Bakic hustled them out. Major Gordon saw the crowd close round them and then move off down the lane in a babel of explanation and reproach.

II

There were thermal springs at Begoy. The little town had come into being about them. Never a fashionable spa, it had attracted genuine invalids of modest means from all over the Hapsburg Empire. Serbian rule changed it very little. Until 1940 it retained its Austrian style; now the place was ravaged. Partisans and Ustashi had fought there, or, rather, each in turn had fired it and fled. Most houses were gutted and the occupants camped in basements or improvised shelters. Major Gordon's normal routine did not take him into the town, for the officials and military were in farmhouses like his own on the outskirts, but he daily frequented the little park and public gardens. These had been charmingly laid out sixty years before and were, surprisingly, still kept in order by two old gardeners who had stayed on quietly weeding and pruning while the streets were in flames and noisy with machine-gun fire. There were winding paths and specimen trees, statuary, a bandstand, a pond with carp and exotic ducks, and the ornamental cages of what had once been a little zoo. The gardeners kept rabbits in one of these, fowls in another, a red squirrel in a third. The partisans had shown a peculiar solicitude for these gardens; they had cut a bed in the centre of the principal lawn in the shape of the Soviet star and had shot a man whom they caught chopping a rustic seat for firewood. Above the gardens lay a slope wooded with chestnut and full of paths carefully graded for the convalescent with kiosks every kilometre, where once postcards and coffee and medicinal water had been on sale. Here for an hour a day in the soft autumn sunshine Major Gordon could forget the war. More than once on his walks there he met Mme Kanyi, saluted her, and smiled.

Then, after a week, he received a signal from his headquarters in Bari saying: *U.N.R.R.A. research team require particulars displaced persons Jugo-Slavia stop report any your district.* He replied: *one hundred and eight Jews.* Next day (there was wireless communication for only two hours daily): *expedite details Jews names nationality conditions.* So his duty took him away from the gardens into the streets where the lime trees still flourished between the stucco shells. He passed ragged, swaggering partisans, all young, some scarcely more than children; girls in battle dress, bandaged, bemedalled, girdled with grenades, squat, chaste, cheerful, sexless, barely human, who had grown up in mountain bivouacs, singing patriotic songs, arm-in-arm along the pavements where a few years earlier rheumatics had crept with parasols and light, romantic novels.

The Jews lived in a school near the ruined church. Bakic led him there. They found the house in half darkness for the glass had all gone from the windows and been replaced with bits of wood and tin collected from other ruins. There was no furniture. The inmates for the most part lay huddled in little nests of straw and rags. As Major Gordon and Bakic entered they roused themselves, got to their feet and retreated towards the walls and darker corners, some raising their fists in salute, others hugging bundles of small possessions. Bakic called one of them forward and questioned him roughly in Scrbo-Croat.

'He says de others gone for firewood. Dese ones sick. What you want me tell em?'

'Say that the Americans in Italy want to help them. I have come to make a report on what they need.'

The announcement brought them volubly to life. They crowded round, were joined by others from other parts of the house until Major Gordon stood surrounded by thirty or more all asking for things, asking frantically for whatever came first to mind – a needle, a lamp, butter, soap, a pillow; for remote dreams – a passage to Telaviv, an aeroplane to New York, news of a sister last seen in Bucharest, a bed in a hospital.

'You see dey all want somepin different, and dis is only a half of dem.'

For twenty minutes or so Major Gordon remained, overpowered, half-suffocated. Then he said: 'Well, I think we've seen enough. I shan't get much further in this crowd. Before we can do anything we've got to get them organized. They must make out their own list. I wish we could find that Hungarian woman who talked French. She made some sense.'

Bakic inquired and reported: 'She don't live here. Her husband works on the electric light so dey got a house to demselves in de park.'

'Well, let's get out of here and try to find her.'

They left the house and emerged into the fresh air and sunshine and the singing companies of young warriors. Major Gordon breathed gratefully. This was the world he understood, arms, an army, allies, an enemy, injuries given and taken honourably. Very high above them a huge force of minute shining bombers hummed across the sky in perfect formation on its daily route from Foggia to somewhere east of Vienna.

'There they go again,' he said. 'I wouldn't care to be underneath when they unload.'

It was one of his duties to impress the partisans with the might of their allies, with the great destruction and slaughter on distant fields which would one day, somehow, bring happiness here where they seemed forgotten. He delivered a little statistical lecture to Bakic about block-busters and pattern-bombing. But another part of his mind was all the time slowly being set in motion. He had seen something entirely new, which needed new eyes to see clearly: humanity in the depths, misery of quite another order from anything he had guessed before. He was as yet not conscious of terror or pity. His steady Scottish mind would take some time to assimilate the experience.

III

They found the Kanyis' house. It was a tool shed hidden by shrubs from the public park. A single room, an earth floor, a bed, a table, a dangling electric globe; compared with the schoolhouse, a place of delicious comfort and privacy. Major Gordon did not see the interior that afternoon for Mme Kanyi was hanging washing on a line outside, and she led him away from the hut, saying that her husband was asleep. 'He was up all night and did not come home until nearly midday. There was a breakdown at the plant.'

'Yes,' said Major Gordon, 'I had to go to bed in the dark at nine.'

'It is always breaking. It is quite worn out. He cannot get the proper fuel. And all the cables are rotten. The General does not understand and blames him for everything. Often he is out all night.'

Major Gordon dismissed Bakic and talked about U.N.R.R.A. Mme Kanyi did not react in the same way as the wretches in the schoolhouse; she was younger and better fed and therefore more hopeless. 'What can they do for us?' she asked. 'How can they? Why should they? We are of no importance. You told us so yourself. You must see the Commissar,' she said. 'Otherwise he will think there is some plot going on. We can do nothing, accept nothing, without the Commissar's permission. You will only make more trouble for us.'

'But at least you can produce the list they want in Bari.'

'Yes, if the Commissar says so. Already my husband has been questioned about why I have talked to you. He was very much upset. The General was beginning to trust him. Now they think he is connected with the British, and last night the lights failed when there was an important conference. It is better that you do nothing except through the Commissar. I know these people. My husband works with them.'

'You have rather a privileged position with them.'

'Do you believe that for that reason I do not want to help my people?'

Some such thoughts had passed through Major Gordon's mind. Now he paused, looked at Mme Kanyi and was ashamed. 'No,' he said.

'I suppose it would be natural to think so,' said Mme Kanyi gravely. 'It is not always true that suffering makes people unselfish. But sometimes it is.'

Major Gordon returned to his quarters in a reflective mood that was unusual to him.

IV

The partisans were nocturnal in their habits. They slept late in the mornings, idled about at midday smoking, ate in the early afternoon, and then towards sundown seemed to come alive. Most of their conferences took place after dark.

That evening Major Gordon was thinking of going to bed when he was summoned to the General. He and Bakic stumbled along cart tracks to the villa which housed the general staff. They found the General, his second-in-command, the Commissar, and the old lawyer who was called the Minister of the Interior.

Most meetings in this room were concerned with supplies. The General would submit a detailed, exorbitant list of immediate requirements – field artillery, boots, hospital equipment, wireless apparatus – and so forth. They worked on the principle of asking for everything and item by item reducing their demands to practicable size. In these tedious negotiations Major Gordon enjoyed the slight advantage of being the giver and the final judge of what was reasonable; all the partisans could do was dissipate any sense he might have of vicarious benefaction. He always left feeling a skinflint. Formal politeness was maintained and sometimes even a faint breath of cordiality.

Tonight, however, the atmosphere was entirely changed. The General and the Commissar had served together in Spain, the second-in-command was a professional officer from the Royal Jugo-Slav Army, the Minister of the Interior was a nonentity introduced to give solemnity to the occasion. They sat round the table. Bakic stood in the background. His place as interpreter was taken by a young communist of undefined position whom Major Gordon had met once or twice before at headquarters. He spoke excellent English.

'The General wishes to know why you went to visit the Jews today.'

'I was acting on orders from my headquarters.'

'The General does not understand how the Jews are the concern of the Military Mission.'

Major Gordon attempted an explanation of the aims and organization of U.N.R.R.A. He did not know a great deal about them and had no great respect for the members he had met, but he did his best. General and Commissar conferred. Then: 'The Commissar says if those measures will take place after the war, what are they doing now?'

Major Gordon described the need for planning. U.N.R.R.A. must know what quantities of seed corn, bridge-building materials, rolling stock and so on were needed to put ravaged countries on their feet.

'The Commissar does not understand how this concerns the Jews.'

Major Gordon spoke of the millions of displaced persons all over Europe who must be returned to their homes.

'The Commissar says that is an internal matter.'

'So is bridge-building.'

'The Commissar says bridge-building is a good thing.'

'So is helping displaced persons.'

Commissar and General conferred. 'The General says any questions of internal affairs should be addressed to the Minister of the Interior.'

'Tell him that I am very sorry if I have acted incorrectly. I merely wished to save everyone trouble. I was sent a question by my superiors. I did my best to answer it in the simplest way. May I now request the Minister of the Interior to furnish me with a list of the Jews?'

'The General is glad that you understand that you have acted incorrectly.'

'Will the Minister of the Interior be so kind as to make the list for me?'

'The General does not understand why a list is needed.'

And so it began again. They talked for an hour. At length Major Gordon lost patience and said: 'Very well. Am I to report that you refuse all co-operation with U.N.R.R.A.?'

'We will co-operate in all necessary matters.'

'But with regard to the Jews?'

'It must be decided by the Central Government whether that is a necessary matter.'

At length they parted. On the way home Bakic said: 'Dey mighty sore with you, Major. What for you make trouble with dese Jews?'

'Orders,' said Major Gordon, and before going to bed drafted a signal: *'Jews condition now gravely distressed will become desperate winter stop Local authorities unco-operative stop Only hope higher level.'*

A fortnight passed. Three aeroplanes landed, delivered their loads and took off. The R. A. F. officer said: 'There won't be many more of these trips. They usually get snow by the end of October.'

The partisans punctiliously checked all supplies and never failed to complain of their quantity or quality.

Major Gordon did not forget the Jews. Their plight oppressed him on his daily walks in the gardens, where the leaves were now falling fast and burning smokily in the misty air. The Jews were numbered, very specially, among his allies and the partisans lapsed from his friendship. He saw them now as a part of the thing he had set out hopefully to fight in the days when there had been a plain, unequivocal issue between right and wrong. Uppermost in his conscious mind was resentment against the General and Commissar for their reprimand. By such strange entrances does compassion sometimes slip, disguised, into the human heart.

At the end of the fortnight he was elated to receive the signal: *'Central Government approves in principle evacuation Jews stop Dispatch two repeat two next plane discuss problem with U.N.R.R.A.'*

Major Gordon went with this signal to the Minister of the Interior who was lying in bed drinking weak tea. Bakic explained, 'He's sick and don't know nothing. You better talk to de Commissar.'

The Commissar confirmed that he had received instructions.

'I suggest we send the Kanyis.'

'He say, why de Kanyis?'

'Because they make most sense.'

'Pardon me?'

'Because they seem the most responsible pair.'

'De Commissar says, responsible for what?'

'They are the best able to put their case sensibly.'

A long discussion followed between the Commissar and Bakic. 'He won't send de Kanyis.'

'Why not?'

'Kanyi got plenty work with de dynamo.'

So another pair was chosen and sent to Bari, the grocer and the lawyer who had first called on him. Major Gordon saw them off. They seemed stupefied and sat huddled among bundles and blankets on the airfield during the long wait. Only when the aeroplane was actually there, illumined by the long line of bonfires lit to guide it, did they both suddenly break into tears. When Major Gordon held out his hand to them, they bent and kissed it.

Two days later Bari signalled: *'Receive special flight four Dakotas 1130 hrs tonight stop dispatch all Jews.'* In a mood of real joy Major Gordon set about making the arrangements.

V

The landing-strip was eight miles from the town. Before dusk the procession started. Some had somehow contrived to hire peasant carts. Most went on foot, bowed and laden. At ten o'clock Major Gordon drove out and found them, a dark mass, on the embankment of what had once been a railway. Most were asleep. There was mist on the ground. He said to the Squadron Leader: 'Is this going to lift?'

'It's been getting thicker for the last hour.'

'Will they be able to land?'

'Not a chance.'

'We'd better get these people home.'

'Yes, I'm just sending the cancellation signal now.'

Major Gordon could not bear to wait. He drove back alone but could not rest; hours later, he went out and waited in the mist at the junction of lane and road until the weary people hobbled past into the town.

Twice in the next three weeks the grim scene was repeated. On the second occasion the fires were lit, the aeroplanes were overhead and could be heard circling, recirculing and at length heading west again. That evening, Major Gordon prayed: 'Please God make it all right. You've done things like that before. Just make the mist clear. Please God help these people.' But the sound of the engines dwindled and died away, and the hopeless Jews stirred themselves and set off again on the way they had come.

That week came the first heavy fall of snow. There would be no more landing until the spring.

Major Gordon despaired of doing anything for the Jews, but powerful forces were at work on their behalf in Bari. He soon received a signal: *'Expect special drop shortly relief supplies for*

Jews stop Explain partisan HQ these supplies only repeat only for distribution Jews.' He called on the General with this communication.

'What supplies?'

'I presume food and clothing and medicine.'

'For three months I have been asking for these things for my men. The Third Corps have no boots. In the hospital they are operating without anaesthetics. Last week we had to withdraw from two forward positions because there were no rations.'

'I know. I have signalled about it repeatedly.'

'Why is there food and clothes for the Jews and not for my men?'

'I cannot explain. All I have come to ask is whether you can guarantee distribution.'

'I will see.'

Major Gordon signalled: *'Respectfully submit most injudicious discriminate in favour of Jews stop Will endeavour secure proportionate share for them of general relief supplies,'* and received in answer: *'Three aircraft will drop Jewish supplies point C 1130 hrs twenty-first stop These supplies from private source not military stop Distribute according previous signal.'*

On the afternoon of the twenty-first the Squadron Leader came to see Major Gordon.

'What's the idea?' he said. 'I've just been having the hell of a schemozzle with the Air Liaison comrade about tonight's drop. He wants the stuff put in bond or something till he gets orders from higher up. He's a reasonable sort of chap usually. I've never seen him on such a high horse. Wanted everything checked in the presence of the Minister of the Interior and put under joint guard. Never heard such a lot of rot. I suppose someone at Bari has been playing at politics as usual.'

That night the air was full of parachutes and of 'free-drops' whistling down like bombs. The Anti-Fascist Youth retrieved them. They were loaded on carts, taken to a barn near the General's headquarters and formally impounded.

VI

The war in Jugo-Slavia took a new turn. The first stage of German withdrawal was complete; they stood now on a line across Croatia and Slovenia. Marshal Tito flew from Vis to join the Russian and Bulgarian columns in Belgrade. A process of reprisal began in the 'liberated' areas. The Germans remained twenty miles to the north of Begoy, but behind nothing except snow now closed the road to Dalmatia. Major Gordon took part in many Victory Celebrations. But he did not forget the Jews; nor did their friends at Bari. In mid-December Bakic one day announced: 'De Jews again', and going out into the yard Major Gordon found it full of his former visitors, but now transformed into a kind of farcical army. All of them, men and women, wore military greatcoats, Balaclava helmets and knitted woollen gloves. Orders had been received from Belgrade, and distribution of the stores had suddenly taken place, and here were the recipients to thank him. The spokesmen were different on this occasion. The grocer and lawyer had disappeared for ever. Madame Kanyi kept away for reasons of her own; an old man made a longish speech which Bakic rendered 'Dis guy say dey's all very happy.'

For the next few days a deplorable kind of ostentation seemed to possess the Jews. A curse seemed to have been lifted. They appeared everywhere, trailing the skirts of their greatcoats in the snow, stamping their huge new boots, gesticulating with their gloved hands. Their faces shone with soap, they were full of Spam and dehydrated fruits. They were a living psalm. And then, as suddenly, they disappeared.

'What has happened to them?'

'I guess dey been moved some other place,' said Bakic.

'Why?'

'People make trouble for them.'

'Who?'

'Partisan people dat hadn't got no coats and boots. Dey make trouble wid de Commissar so de Commissar move dem on last night.'

Major Gordon had business with the Commissar. The Anti-Fascist Theatre Group was organizing a Liberation Concert and had politely asked him to supply words and music of English anti-fascist songs, so that all the allies would be suitably represented. Major Gordon had to explain that his country had no anti-fascist songs and no patriotic songs that anyone cared to sing. The Commissar noted this further evidence of Western decadence with grim satisfaction. For once there was no need to elaborate. The Commissar understood. It was just as he had been told years before in Moscow. It had been the same thing in Spain. The Attlee Brigade would never sing.

When the business was over Major Gordon said: 'I see the Jews have moved.'

Bakic was left outside nowadays, and the intellectual young man acted as interpreter. Without consulting his chief he answered: 'Their house was required for the Ministry of Rural Economy. New quarters have been found for them a few miles away.'

The Commissar asked what was being said, grunted and rose. Major Gordon saluted and the interview was at an end. On the steps the young interpreter joined him.

'The question of the Jews, Major Gordon. It was necessary for them to go. Our people could not understand why they should have special treatment. We have partisan women who work all day and have no boots or overcoats. How are we to explain that these old people who are doing nothing for our cause, should have such things?'

'Perhaps by saying that they *are* old and *have* no cause. Their need is greater than a young enthusiast's.'

'Besides, Major Gordon, they were trying to make business. They were bartering the things they had been given. My parents are Jewish and I understand these people. They want always to make some trade.'

'Well, what's wrong with that?'

'War is not a time for trade.'

'Well, anyway, I hope they have decent quarters.'

'They have what is suitable.'

VII

The gardens in winter seemed smaller than they had done in full leaf. You could see right through them from fence to fence; snow obliterated lawns and beds; the paths were only traceable by boot-prints. Major Gordon daily took a handful of broken biscuits to the squirrel and fed him through the bars. One day while he was thus engaged, watching the little creature go through the motions of concealment, cautiously return, grasp the food, jump away and once more perform the mime of digging and covering, he saw Mme Kanyi approach down the path. She was carrying a load of brushwood, stooping under it, so that she did not see him until she was quite close.

Major Gordon was particularly despondent that day for he had just received a signal for recall. The force was being re-named and re-organized. He was to report as soon as feasible to Bari. Major Gordon was confident that word had come from Belgrade that he was no longer *persona grata*.

He greeted Mme Kanyi with warm pleasure. 'Let me carry that.'

'No, please. It is better not.'

'I insist.'

Mme Kanyi looked about her. No one was in sight. She let Major Gordon take the load and carry it towards her hut.

'You have not gone with the others?'

'No, my husband is needed.'

'And you don't wear your greatcoat.'

'Not out of doors. I wear it at night in the hut. The coats and boots make everyone hate us, even those who had been kind before.'

'But partisan discipline is so firm. Surely there was no danger of violence?'

'No, that was not the trouble. It was the peasants. The partisans are frightened of the peasants. They will settle with them later, but at present they are dependent on them for food. Our people began to exchange things with the peasants. They would give needles and thread, razors, things no one can get, for turkeys and apples. No one wants money.

COMPASSION

The peasants preferred bartering with our people to taking the partisans' bank-notes. That was what made the trouble.'

'Where have the others gone?'

She spoke a name which meant nothing to Major Gordon. 'You have not heard of that place? It is twenty miles away. It is where the Germans and Ustashi made a camp. They kept the Jews and gypsies and communists and royalists there, to work on the canal. Before they left they killed what were left of the prisoners – not many. Now the partisans have found new inhabitants for it.'

They had reached the hut and Major Gordon entered to place his load in a corner near the little stove. It was the first and last time he crossed the threshold. He had a brief impression of orderly poverty and then was outside in the snow. 'Listen, Mme Kanyi,' he said. 'Don't lose heart. I am being recalled to Bari. As soon as the road is clear I shall be leaving. When I get there I promise I'll raise Cain about this. You've plenty of friends there and I'll explain the whole situation to them. We'll get you all out, I promise.'

Major Gordon had one further transaction with Mme Kanyi before his departure. There fell from the heavens one night a huge parcel of assorted literature – the gift of one of the more preposterous organizations which abounded in Bari. This department aimed at re-educating the Balkans by distributing *Fortune, The Illustrated London News* and handbooks of popular, old-fashioned agnosticism. From time to time during Major Gordon's tour of duty bundles of this kind had arrived. He had hitherto deposited them in the empty office of the Director of Rest and Culture. On this last occasion, however, he thought of Mme Kanyi. She had a long, lonely winter ahead of her. She might find something amusing in the pile. So he despatched it to her by one of the widows, who finding her out, left it on the step in the snow. Then within a few days the road to the coast was declared open and Major Gordon laboriously made his way to Split and so to Bari.

VIII

Bari had much besides the bones of St Nicholas. Those who were quartered there complained but they constituted the Mont Parnasse of the Allied Armies. One met more queer old friends in its messes and clubs than anywhere else in the world at this last stage of the war, and to those on leave from the Balkans its modest amenities seemed the height of luxury. But Major Gordon, during his fortnight of 'reporting to headquarters' had deeper interests than on earlier leaves. He was determined to get the Jews out of Croatia and by dint of exploring the by-ways of semi-official life, of visiting committees and units with noncommittal designations in obscure offices, he was in fact able to quicken interest, supply detailed information and in the end set the official machine to work which eventually resulted in a convoy of new Ford trucks making the journey from the coast to Begoy and back for the sole and specific purpose of rescuing the Jews.

By the time that they arrived in Italy Major Gordon was back in Jugo-Slavia for a brief appointment as liaison with a camp of escaped prisoners of war, but he got news of the move and for the first time tasted the sweet and heady cup of victory. 'At least I've done something worthwhile in this bloody war,' he said.

When next he passed through Bari it was on his way home to England, for the military mission was being wound up and replaced by regular diplomatic and consular officials. He had not forgotten his Jews, however, and, having with difficulty located them, drove out to a camp near Lecce, in a flat country of olive and almond and white beehive huts. Here they rested, part of a collection of four or five hundred, all old and all baffled, all in army greatcoats and Balaclava helmets.

'I can't see the point of their being here,' said the Commandant. 'We feed them and doctor them and house them. That's all we can do. No one wants them. The Zionists are only interested in the young. I suppose they'll just sit here till they die.'

'Are they happy?'

'They complain the hell of a lot but then they've got quite a lot to complain about. It's a lousy place to be stuck in.'

'I'm particularly interested in a pair called Kanyi.'

The Commandant looked down his list. 'No trace of them here.'

'Good. That probably means they got off to Australia all right.'

'Not from here, old man. I've been here all along. No one has ever left.'

'Could you make sure? Anyone in the Begoy draft would know about them.'

The Commandant sent his interpreter to inquire while he took Major Gordon into the shed he called his mess, and gave him a drink. Presently the man returned. 'All correct, sir. The Kanyis never left Begoy. They got into some kind of trouble there and were jugged.'

'May I go with the interpreter and ask about it?'

'By all means, old man. But aren't you making rather heavy weather of it? What do two more or less matter?'

Major Gordon went into the compound with the interpreter. Some of the Jews recognized him and crowded round with complaints and petitions. All he could learn about the Kanyis was that they had been taken off the truck by the partisan police just as it was about to start.

He had one more day in Bari before his flight home. He spent it revisiting the offices where he had begun his work of liberation. But this time he received little sympathy. 'We don't really want to bother the Jugs any more. They really co-operated very well about the whole business. Besides the war's over now in that part. There's no particular point in moving people out. We're busy at the moment moving people in.' This man was in fact at that moment busy despatching royalist officers to certain execution.

The Jewish office showed no interest when they understood that he had not come to sell them illicit arms. 'We must first set up the State,' they said. 'Then it will be a refuge for all. First things first.'

So Major Gordon returned to England unsatisfied and he might never have heard any more of the matter, had he not a cousin in the newly reopened Ministry at Belgrade. Months later he heard from him: *'I've been to a lot of trouble and made myself quite unpopular in getting information about the couple you're interested in. The Jugs are very close but at last I got matey with the head of the police who wants us to return some refugees we've got in our zone in Austria. He dug out the file for me. Both were condemned by a Peoples' Court and executed. The man had committed sabotage on the electric light plant. The woman had been a spy for a "foreign power". Apparently she was the mistress of a foreign agent who frequented her house while the husband was busy destroying the dynamo. A lot of foreign propaganda publications were found in her house and produced as evidence. What very unsavoury friends you seem to have.'*

It so happened that this letter arrived on the day when the

Allies were celebrating the end of the war in Asia. Major Gordon was back with his regiment. He did not feel inclined to go out that evening and join in the rejoicing. The mess was empty save for the misanthropic second-in-command and the chaplain (although of Highland origin the regiment was full of Glasgow Irish and had a Benedictine monk attached to them).

The second-in-command spoke as he had spoken most evenings since the General Election . . . 'I don't know what they mean by "Victory". We start the bloody war for Poland. Well that's ceased to exist. We fight it in Burma and Egypt – and you can bet your boots we shall give them up in a few months to the very fellows who've been against us. We spent millions knocking Germany down and now we shall spend millions building it up again . . .'

'Don't you think, perhaps, people feel better than they did in 1938?' said the chaplain.

'No,' said the second-in-command.

'They haven't got rid of that unhealthy sense of guilt they had?'

'No,' said Major Gordon. 'I never had it before. Now I have.'

And he told the story of the Kanyis. 'Those are the real horrors of war – not just people having their legs blown off,' he concluded. 'How do you explain that, padre?'

There was no immediate answer until the second-in-command said: 'You did all you could. A darn sight more than most people would have done.'

'That's your answer,' said the chaplain. 'You mustn't judge actions by their apparent success. Everything you did was good in itself.'

'A fat lot of good it did the Kanyis.'

'No. But don't you think it just possible that *they* did *you* good? No suffering need ever be wasted. It is just as much part of Charity to receive cheerfully as to give.'

'Well, if you're going to start preaching a sermon, padre,' said the second-in-command, 'I'm off to bed.'

'I'd like you to tell me a bit more about that,' said Major Gordon.

LOVE AMONG THE RUINS

A ROMANCE OF THE NEAR FUTURE

BY

Evelyn Waugh

WITH DECORATIONS BY VARIOUS
EMINENT HANDS INCLUDING
THE AUTHOR'S

MCMLXII
CHAPMAN & HALL
LONDON

JOHANNI McDOUGALL

Amico

Qui Nostri Sedet in Loco Parentis

Love Among the Ruins

A Romance of the Near Future

I

Despite their promises at the last Election, the politicians had not yet changed the climate. The State Meteorological Institute had so far produced only an unseasonable fall of snow and two little thunderbolts no larger than apricots. The weather varied from day to day and from county to county as it had done of old, most anomalously.

This was a rich, old-fashioned Tennysonian night.

Strains of a string quartet floated out from the drawing-room windows and were lost amid the splash and murmur of the gardens. In the basin the folded lilies had left a brooding sweetness over the water. No gold fin winked in the porphyry font and any peacock which seemed to be milkily drooping in the moon-shadows was indeed a ghost, for the whole flock of them had been found mysteriously and rudely slaughtered a day or two ago in the first disturbing flush of this sudden summer.

Miles, sauntering among the sleeping flowers, was suffused with melancholy. He did not much care for music and this was his last evening at Mountjoy. Never again, perhaps, would he be free to roam these walks.

Mountjoy had been planned and planted in the years of which he knew nothing; generations of skilled and patient husbandmen had weeded and dunged and pruned; generations of dilettanti had watered it with cascades and jets; generations of collectors had lugged statuary here; all, it seemed, for his enjoyment this very night under this huge moon. Miles knew nothing of such periods and processes, but he felt an incomprehensible tidal pull towards the circumjacent splendours.

Eleven struck from the stables. The music ceased. Miles turned back and, as he reached the terrace, the shutters began to close and the great chandeliers were one by one extinguished. By the light of the sconces which still shone on their panels of faded satin and clouded gold, he joined the company dispersing to bed through the islands of old furniture.

His room was not one of the grand succession which lay along the garden front. Those were reserved for murderers. Nor was it on the floor above, tenanted mostly by sexual offenders. His was a humbler wing. Indeed he overlooked the luggage porch and the coal bunker. Only professional men visiting Mountjoy on professional business and very poor relations had been put here in the old days. But Miles was attached to this room, which was the first he had ever called his own in all his twenty years of Progress.

His next-door neighbour, a Mr Sweat, paused at his door to say good-night. It was only now after twenty months' proximity, when Miles's time was up, that this veteran had begun to unbend. He and a man named Soapy, survivals of another age, had kept themselves to themselves, talking wistfully of cribs they had cracked, of sparklers, of snug bar-parlours where they had met their favourite fences, of strenuous penal days at the Scrubs and on the Moor. They had small use for the younger generation; crime, calvinism and classical music were their interests. But at last Mr Sweat had taken to nodding, to grunting, and finally, too late for friendship, to speaking to Miles.

'What price the old strings tonight, chum?' he asked.

'I wasn't there, Mr Sweat.'

'You missed a treat. Of course nothing's ever good enough for old Soapy. Made me fair sick to hear Soapy going on all the time. The viola was scratchy, Soapy says. They played the Mozart just like it was Haydn. No feeling in the Debussy pizzicato, says Soapy.'

'Soapy knows too much.'

'Soapy knows a lot more than some I could mention, schooling or no schooling. Next time they're going to do the Grosse Fugue as the last movement of the B flat. That's something to look forward to, that is, though Soapy says no late Beethoven comes off. We'll see. Leastways, me and Soapy will; you won't. You're off tomorrow. Pleased?'

'Not particularly.'

'No, no more wouldn't I be. It's a funny thing but I've settled down here wonderful. Never thought I should. It all seemed a bit too posh at first. Not like the old Scrubs. But it's a real pretty place once you're used to it. Wouldn't mind settling here for a lifer if they'd let me. The trouble is there's no security in crime these days. Time was, you knew just what a job was worth, six months, three years; whatever it was, you knew where you were. Now what with prison commissioners and Preventative Custody and Corrective Treatment they can keep you in or push you out just as it suits them. It's not right.

'I'll tell you what it is, chum,' continued Mr Sweat. 'There's no understanding of crime these days like what there was. I remember when I was a nipper, the first time I came up before the beak, he spoke up straight: "My lad," he says, "you are embarking upon a course of life that can only lead to disaster and degradation in this world and everlasting damnation in the next." Now that's talking. It's plain sense and it shows a personal interest. But last time I was up, when they sent me here, they called me an "antisocial phenomenon", said I was "maladjusted". That's no way to speak of a man what was doing time before they was in long trousers, now is it?'

'They said something of the same kind to me.'

'Yes and now they're giving you the push, just like you hadn't no Rights. I tell you it's made a lot of the boys uncomfortable your going out all of a sudden like this. Who'll it be next time, that's what we're wondering?

'I tell you where you went wrong, chum. You didn't give enough trouble. You made it too easy for them to say you was cured. Soapy and me got wise to that. You remember them birds as got done in? That was Soapy and me. They took a lot of killing too; powerful great bastards. But we got the evidence all hid away tidy and if there's ever any talk of me and Soapy being "rehabilitated" we'll lay it out conspicuous.

'Well, so long, chum. Tomorrow's my morning for Remedial Repose so I daresay you'll be off before I get down. Come back soon.'

'I hope so,' said Miles and turned alone into his own room.

He stood briefly at the window and gazed his last on the cobbled yard. He made a good figure of a man, for he came of handsome parents and all his life had been carefully fed and doctored and exercised; well clothed too. He wore the drab serge dress that was the normal garb of the period — only certified homosexuals wore colours — but there were differences of fit and condition among these uniforms. Miles displayed the handiwork of tailor and valet. He belonged to a privileged class.

The State had made him.

No clean-living, God-fearing, Victorian gentleman, he; no complete man of the renaissance; no gentil knight nor dutiful pagan nor, even, noble savage. All that succession of past worthies had gone its way, content to play a prelude to Miles. He was the Modern Man.

His history, as it appeared in multuplet in the filing cabinets of numberless State departments, was typical of a thousand others. Before his birth the politicians had succeeded in bringing down his father and mother to penury; they, destitute, had thrown themselves into the simple diversions of the very poor and thus, between one war and the next, set in motion a chain-reaction of divorces which scattered them and their various associates in forlorn couples all over the Free World. The aunt on whom the infant Miles had been quartered was conscribed for work in a factory and shortly afterwards died of boredom at the conveyer-belt. The child was put to safety in an Orphanage.

Huge sums were thenceforward spent upon him; sums which, fifty years earlier, would have sent whole quiversful of boys to Winchester and New College and established them in the learned professions. In halls adorned with Picassos and Legers he yawned through long periods of Constructive Play. He never lacked the requisite cubic feet of air. His diet was balanced and on the first Friday of every month he was psychoanalysed. Every detail of his adolescence was recorded and microfilmed and filed, until at the appropriate age he was transferred to the Air Force.

There were no aeroplanes at the station to which he was posted. It was an institution to train instructors to train instructors to train instructors in Personal Recreation.

There for some weeks he tended a dish-washing machine and tended it, as his adjutant testified at his trial, in an exemplary fashion. The work in itself lacked glory, but it was the normal novitiate. Men from the Orphanages provided the hard core of the Forces, a caste apart which united the formidable qualities of Janissary and Junker. Miles had been picked early for high command. Dish-washing was only the beginning. The adjutant, an Orphan too, had himself washed both dishes and officers' underclothes, he testified, before rising to his present position.

Courts Martial had been abolished some years before this. The Forces handed their defaulters over to the civil arm for treatment. Miles came up at quarter sessions. It was plain from the start, when Arson, Wilful Damage, Manslaughter, Prejudicial Conduct and Treason were struck out of the Indictment and the whole reduced to a simple charge of Antisocial Activity, that the sympathies of the Court were with the prisoner.

The Station Psychologist gave his opinion that an element of incendiarism was inseparable from adolescence. Indeed, if checked, it might produce morbid neuroses. For his part he thought the prisoner had performed a perfectly normal act and, moreover, had shown more than normal intelligence in its execution.

At this point some widows, mothers and orphans of the incinerated airmen set up an outcry from the public gallery and were sharply reminded from the Bench that this was a Court of Welfare and not a meeting of the Housewives' Union.

The case developed into a concerted eulogy of the accused. An attempt by the prosecution to emphasize the extent of the damage was rebuked from the Bench.

'The jury,' he said, 'will expunge from their memories these sentimental details which have been most improperly introduced.'

'May be a detail to you,' said a voice from the gallery. 'He was a good husband to me.'

'Arrest that woman,' said the Judge.

Order was restored and the panegyrics continued.

At last the Bench summed up. He reminded the jury that it was a first principle of the New Law that no man could be held responsible for the consequences of his own acts. The jury must dismiss from their minds the consideration that much valuable property and many valuable lives had been lost and the cause of Personal Recreation gravely retarded. They had merely to decide whether in fact the prisoner had arranged inflammable material at various judiciously selected points in the Institution and had ignited them. If he had done so, and the evidence plainly indicated that he had, he contravened the Standing Orders of the Institution and was thereby liable to the appropriate penalties.

Thus directed the jury brought in a verdict of guilty coupled with a recommendation of mercy towards the various bereaved persons who from time to time in the course of the hearing had been committed for contempt. The Bench reprimanded the jury for presumption and impertinence in the matter of the prisoners held in contempt, and sentenced Miles to residence during the State's pleasure at Mountjoy Castle (the ancestral seat of a maimed V. C. of the Second World War, who had been sent to a Home for the Handicapped when the place was converted into a gaol).

The State was capricious in her pleasures. For nearly two years Miles enjoyed her particular favours. Every agreeable remedial device was applied to him and applied, it was now proclaimed, successfully. Then without warning a few days back, while he lay dozing under a mulberry tree, the unexpected blow had fallen; they had come to him, the Deputy-Chief Guide and the sub-Deputy, and told him bluntly and brutally that he was rehabilitated.

Now on this last night he knew he was to wake tomorrow on a harsh world. Nevertheless he slept and was gently awoken for the last time to the familiar scent of china tea on his bed table, the thin bread and butter, the curtains drawn above the luggage porch, the sunlit kitchen-yard and the stable clock just visible behind the cut-leaf copper beech.

He breakfasted late and alone. The rest of the household were already engaged in the first community-songs of the day. Presently he was called to the Guidance Office.

Since his first day at Mountjoy, when with other entrants Miles had been addressed at length by the Chief Guide on the Aims and Achievements of the New Penology, they had seldom met. The Chief Guide was almost always away addressing penological conferences.

The Guidance Office was the former house-keeper's room stripped now of its plush and patriotic pictures; sadly tricked out instead with standard civil-service equipment, class A.

It was full of people.

'This is Miles Plastic,' said the Chief Guide. 'Sit down, Miles. You can see from the presence of our visitors this morning what an important occasion this is.'

Miles took a chair and looked and saw seated beside the Chief Guide two elderly men whose faces were familiar from the television screen as prominent colleagues in the Coalition Government. They wore open flannel shirts, blazers with numerous pens and pencils protruding from the breast pocket, and baggy trousers. This was the dress of very high politicians.

'The Minister of Welfare and the Minister of Rest and Culture,' continued the Chief Guide. 'The stars to which we have hitched our waggon. Have the press got the hand-out?'

'Yes, Chief.'

'And the photographers are all ready?'

'Yes, Chief.'

'Then I can proceed.'

He proceeded as he had done at countless congresses, at countless spas and university cities. He concluded, as he always did: 'In the New Britain which we are building, there are no criminals. There are only the victims of inadequate social services.'

The Minister of Welfare, who had not reached his present eminence without the help of a certain sharpness in debate, remarked: 'But I understood that Plastic is from one of our own Orphanages . . .'

'Plastic is recognized as a Special Case,' said the Chief Guide.

The Minister of Rest and Culture, who in the old days had more than once done time himself, said: 'Well, Plastic, lad, from all they do say I reckon you've been uncommon smart.'

'Exactly,' said the Chief Guide. 'Miles is our first success, the vindication of the Method.'

'Of all the new prisons established in the first glorious wave of Reform, Mountjoy alone has produced a complete case of rehabilitation,' the Minister of Welfare said. 'You may

Coalition

or may not be aware that the Method has come in for a good deal of criticism both in Parliament, and outside. There are a lot of young hotheads who take their inspiration from our Great Neighbour in the East. You can quote the authorities to them till you're black in the face but they are always pressing for all latest gadgets of capital and corporal punishment, for chain gangs and solitary confinement, bread and water, the cat-o'-nine-tails, the rope and the block, and all manner of new-fangled nonsense. They think we're a lot of old fogeys. Thank goodness we've still got the solid sense of the people behind us, but we're on the defensive now. We have to show results. That's why we're here this morning. To show them results. You are our Result.'

These were solemn words and Miles in some measure responded to the occasion. He gazed before him blankly with an expression that might seem to be awe.

'You'd best watch your step now, lad,' said the Minister of Rest and Culture.

'Photographs,' said the Minister of Welfare. 'Yes, shake my hand. Turn towards the cameras. Try to smile.'

Bulbs flashed all over the dreary little room.

'State be with you,' said the Minister of Welfare.

'Give us a paw, lad,' said the Minister of Rest and Culture, taking Miles's hand in his turn. 'And no funny business, mind.'

Then the politicians departed.

'The Deputy-Chief will attend to all the practical matters,' said the Chief wearily. 'Go and see him now.'

Miles went.

'Well, Miles, from now on I must call you Mr Plastic,' said the Deputy-Chief. 'In less than a minute you become a Citizen. This little pile of papers is You. When I stamp them, Miles the Problem ceases to exist and Mr Plastic the Citizen is born. We are sending you to Satellite City, the nearest Population Centre, where you will be attached to the Ministry of Welfare as a sub-official. In view of your special training you are not being classified as a Worker. The immediate material rewards, of course, are not as great. But you are definitely in the Service. We have set your foot on the bottom rung of the non-competitive ladder.'

The Deputy-Chief Guide picked up the rubber stamp and proceeded to his work of creation. Flip-thump, flip-thump the papers were turned and stained.

'There you are, Mr Plastic,' said the Deputy-Chief handing Miles, as it were, the baby.

At last Miles spoke: 'What must I do to get back here?' he asked.

'Come, come, you're rehabilitated now, remember. It is your turn to give back to the State some of the service the State has given you. You will report this morning to the Area Progressive. Transport has been laid on. State be with you,

Mr Plastic. Be careful, that's your Certificate of Human Personality you've dropped – a *vital* document.'

II

Satellite City, one of a hundred such grand conceptions, was not yet in its teens but already the Dome of Security showed signs of wear. This was the name of the great municipal edifice about which the city was planned. The eponymous dome had looked well enough in the architect's model, shallow certainly but amply making up in girth what it lacked in height, the daring exercise of some new trick of construction. But to the surprise of all, when the building arose and was seen from the ground, the dome blandly vanished. It was hidden for ever among the roofs and butting shoulders of the ancillary wings and was never seen again from the outside except by airmen and steeplejacks. Only the name remained. On the day of its dedication, among massed politicians and People's Choirs the great lump of building materials had shone fine as a factory in all its brilliance of glass and new concrete. Since then, during one of the rather frequent week-ends of international panic, it had been camouflaged and its windows blackened. Cleaners were few and usually on strike. So the Dome of Security remained blotched and dingy, the sole permanent building of Satellite City. There were no workers' flats, no officials' garden suburb, no parks, no playgrounds yet. These were all on the drawing-boards in the surveyor's office, tattered at the edges, ringed by tea cups; their designer long since cremated and his ashes scattered among the docks and nettles. Thus the Dome of Security comprised, even more than had been intended, all the aspirations and amenities of the city.

The officials subsisted in perpetual twilight. Great sheets of glass, planned to 'trap' the sun, admitted few gleams from scratches in their coat of tar. At evening when the electric light came on, there was a faint glow, here and there. When, as often, the power-station was 'shedding its load' the officials stopped work early and groped their way back to their darkened huts where in the useless refrigerators their tiny rations were quietly putrefying. On working days the officials, male and female, trudged through cigarette ends round and round, up and down what had once been lift-shafts, in a silent, shabby, shadowy procession.

Among these pilgrims of the dusk, in the weeks that followed his discharge from Mountjoy, moved the exiled Miles Plastic.

He was in a key department.

Euthanasia had not been part of the original 1945 Health Service; it was a Tory measure designed to attract votes from the aged and the mortally sick. Under the Bevan–Eden

Coalition the service came into general use and won instant popularity. The Union of Teachers was pressing for its application to difficult children. Foreigners came in such numbers to take advantage of the service that immigration authorities now turned back the bearers of single tickets.

Miles recognized the importance of his appointment even before he began work. On his first evening in the hostel his fellow sub-officials gathered round to question him.

'Euthanasia? I say, you're in luck. They work you jolly hard, of course, but it's the one department that's expanding.'

'You'll get promoted before you know your way about.'

'Great State! You *must* have pull. Only the very bright boys get posted to Euthanasia.'

'I've been in Contraception for five years. It's a blind alley.'

'They say that in a year or two Euthanasia will have taken over Pensions.'

'You must be an Orphan.'

'Yes, I am.'

'That accounts for it. Orphans get all the plums. I had a Full Family Life, State help me.'

It was gratifying, of course, this respect and envy. It was well to have fine prospects; but for the time being Miles's duties were humble enough.

He was junior sub-official in a staff of half a dozen. The Director was an elderly man called Dr Beamish, a man whose character had been formed in the nervous 'thirties, now much embittered, like many of his contemporaries, by the fulfilment of his early hopes. He had signed manifestos in his hot youth, had raised his fist in Barcelona and had painted abstractedly for *Horizon*; he had stood beside Spender at great concourses of Youth, and written 'publicity' for the Last Viceroy. Now his reward had come to him. He held the most envied post in Satellite City and, sardonically, he was making the worst of it. Dr Beamish rejoiced in every attenuation of official difficulties.

Satellite City was said to be the worst served Euthanasia Centre in the State. Dr Beamish's patients were kept waiting so long that often they died natural deaths before he found it convenient to poison them.

His small staff respected Dr Beamish. They were all of the official class, for it was part of the grim little game which Dr Beamish played with the higher authorities to economize extravagantly. His department, he maintained, could not, on its present allotment, afford workers. Even the furnace-man and the girl who despatched unwanted false teeth to the Dental Redistribution Centre were sub-officials.

Sub-officials were cheap and plentiful. The Universities turned them out in thousands every year. Indeed, ever since the Incitement to Industry Act of 1955, which exempted workers from taxation – that great and popular measure of reform which had consolidated the now permanent Coalition Government – there had been a nefarious one-way traffic of expensively State-educated officials 'passing', as it was called, into the ranks of the workers.

Miles's duties required no special skill. Daily at ten the service opened its doors to welfare-weary citizens. Miles was the man who opened them, stemmed the too eager rush and admitted the first half-dozen; then he closed the doors on the waiting multitude until a Higher Official gave the signal for the admission of another batch.

Once inside they came briefly under his charge; he set them in order, saw that they did not press ahead of their turn, and adjusted the television-set for their amusement. A Higher Official interviewed them, checked their papers and arranged for the confiscation of their property. Miles never passed the door through which they were finally one by one conducted. A faint whiff of cyanide sometimes gave a hint of the mysteries beyond. Meanwhile he swept the waiting-room, emptied the waste-paper basket and brewed tea – a worker's job, for which the refinements of Mountjoy proved a too rich apprenticeship.

In his hostel the same reproductions of Léger and Picasso as had haunted his childhood still stared down on him. At the cinema, to which he could afford, at the best, a weekly visit, the same films as he had seen free at Orphanage, Air Force station and prison, flickered and drawled before him. He was a child of Welfare, strictly schooled to a life of boredom, but he had known better than this. He had

Exiles from Welfare

known the tranquil melancholy of the gardens at Mountjoy. He had known ecstasy when the Air Force Training School had whirled to the stars in a typhoon of flame. And as he moved sluggishly between Dome and hostel there rang in his ears the words of the old lag: 'You didn't give enough trouble.'

Then one day, in the least expected quarter, in his own drab department, hope appeared.

Miles later remembered every detail of that morning. It had started in the normal way; rather below normal indeed, for they were reopening after a week's enforced idleness. There had been a strike among the coal-miners and Euthanasia had been at a standstill. Now the necessary capitulations had been signed, the ovens glowed again, and the queue at the patients' entrance stretched half-way round the Dome. Dr Beamish squinted at the waiting crowd through the periscope and said with some satisfaction: 'It will take months to catch up on the waiting list now. We shall have to start making a charge for the service. It's the only way to keep down the demand.'

'The Ministry will never agree to that, surely, sir?'

'Damned sentimentalists. My father and mother hanged themselves in their own back-yard with their own clothes-line. Now no one will lift a finger to help himself. There's something wrong in the system, Plastic. There are still rivers to drown in, trains – every now and then – to put your head under; gas-fires in some of the huts. The country is full of the natural resources of death, but everyone has to come to us.'

It was not often he spoke so frankly before his subordinates. He had overspent during the week's holiday, drunk too much at his hostel with other unemployed colleagues. Always after a strike the senior officials returned to work in low spirits.

'Shall I let the first batch in, sir?'

'Not for the moment,' said Dr Beamish. 'There's a priority case to see first, sent over with a pink chit from Drama. She's in the private waiting-room now. Fetch her in.'

Miles went to the room reserved for patients of importance. All one wall was of glass. Pressed to it a girl was standing, turned away from him, looking out at the glum queue below. Miles stood, the light in his eyes, conscious only of a shadow which stirred at the sound of the latch and turned, still a shadow merely but of exquisite grace, to meet him. He stood at the door, momentarily struck silent at this blind glance of beauty. Then he said: 'We're quite ready for you now, miss.'

The girl came nearer. Miles's eyes adjusted themselves to the light. The shadow took form. The full vision was all that the first glance had hinted; more than all, for every slight movement revealed perfection. One feature only broke the canon of pure beauty; a long, silken, corn-gold beard.

She said, with a deep, sweet tone, all unlike the flat conventional accent of the age: 'Let it be quite understood that I don't want anything done to me. I consented to come here. The Director of Drama and the Director of Health were so pathetic about it all that I thought it was the least I could do. I said I was quite willing to hear about your service, but I do not want anything done.'

'Better tell him inside,' said Miles.

He led her to Dr Beamish's room.

'Great State!' said Dr Beamish, with eyes for the beard alone.

'Yes,' she said. 'It is a shock, isn't it? I've got used to it by now but I can understand how people feel seeing it for the first time.'

'Is it real?'

'Pull.'

'It is strong. Can't they do anything about it?'

'Oh they've tried everything.'

Dr Beamish was so deeply interested that he forgot Miles's presence. 'Klugmann's operation, I suppose?'

'Yes.'

'It does go wrong like that every now and then. They had two or three cases at Cambridge.'

'I never wanted it done. I never want anything done. It was the Head of the Ballet. He insists on all the girls being sterilized. Apparently you can never dance really well again after you've had a baby. And I did want to dance really well. Now this is what's happened.'

'Yes,' said Dr Beamish. 'Yes. They're far too slap-dash. They had to put down those girls at Cambridge, too. There was no cure. Well, we'll attend to you, young lady. Have you any arrangements to make or shall I take you straight away?'

'But I don't want to be put down. I told your assistant here, I've simply consented to come at all, because the Director of Drama cried so, and he's rather a darling. I've not the smallest intention of letting you kill me.'

While she spoke, Dr Beamish's geniality froze. He looked at her with hatred, not speaking. Then he picked up the pink form. 'Then this no longer applies?'

'No.'

'Then for State's sake,' said Dr Beamish, very angry, 'what are you wasting my time for? I've got more than a hundred urgent cases waiting outside and you come in here to tell me that the Director of Drama is a darling. I know the Director of Drama. We live side by side in the same ghastly hostel. He's a pest. And I'm going to write a report to the Ministry about this tomfoolery which will make him and the lunatic who thinks he can perform a Klugmann, come round to me begging for extermination. And then I'll put them at the bottom of the queue. Get her out of here, Plastic, and let some sane people in.'

Miles led her into the public waiting-room. 'What an old

beast,' she said. 'What a perfect beast. I've never been spoken to like that before even in the ballet-school. He seemed so nice at first.'

'It's his professional feeling,' said Miles. 'He was naturally put out at losing such an attractive patient.'

She smiled. Her beard was not so thick as quite to obscure her delicate ovoid of cheek and chin. She might have been peeping at him over ripe heads of barley.

Her smile started in her wide grey eyes. Her lips under her golden moustachios were unpainted, tactile. A line of pale down sprang below them and ran through the centre of the chin, spreading and thickening and growing richer in colour till it met the full flow of the whiskers, but leaving on either side, clear and tender, two symmetrical zones, naked and provocative. So might have smiled some carefree deacon in the colonnaded schools of fifth-century Alexandria and struck dumb the heresiarchs.

'I think your beard is beautiful.'

'Do you really? I can't help liking it too. I can't help liking anything about myself, can you?'

'Yes. Oh, yes.'

'That's not natural.'

Clamour at the outer door interrupted the talk. Like gulls round a lighthouse the impatient victims kept up an irregular flap and slap on the panels.

'We're all ready, Plastic,' said a senior official. 'What's going on this morning?'

What was going on? Miles could not answer. Turbulent sea birds seemed to be dashing themselves against the light in his own heart.

'Don't go,' he said to the girl. 'Please, I shan't be a minute.'

'Oh, I've nothing to take me away. My department all think I'm half dead by now.'

Miles opened the door and admitted an indignant half-dozen. He directed them to their chairs, to the registry. Then he went back to the girl who had turned away slightly from the crowd and drawn a scarf peasantwise round her head, hiding her beard.

'I still don't quite like people staring,' she said.

'Our patients are far too busy with their own affairs to notice anyone else,' said Miles. 'Besides you'd have been stared at all right if you'd stayed on in ballet.'

Miles adjusted the television but few eyes in the waiting-room glanced towards it; all were fixed on the registrar's table and the doors beyond.

'Think of them all coming here,' said the bearded girl.

'We give them the best service we can,' said Miles.

'Yes, of course, I know you do. Please don't think I was finding fault. I only meant, fancy wanting to die.'

'One or two have good reasons.'

'I suppose you would say that I had. Everyone has been trying to persuade me, since my operation. The medical officials were the worst. They're afraid they may get into trouble for doing it wrong. And then the ballet people were almost as bad. They are so keen on Art that they say: "You were the best of your class. You can never dance again. How can life be worth living?" What I try to explain is that it's just because I could dance that I *know* life is worth living. That's what Art means to me. Does that sound very silly?'

'It sounds unorthodox.'

'Ah, but you're not an artist.'

'Oh, I've danced all right. Twice a week all through my time at the Orphanage.'

'Therapeutic dancing?'

'That's what they called it.'

'But, you see, that's quite different from Art.'

'Why?'

'Oh,' she said with a sudden full intimacy, with fondness. 'Oh what a lot you don't know.'

The dancer's name was Clara.

III

Courtship was free and easy in this epoch but Miles was Clara's first lover. The strenuous exercises of her training, the austere standards of the corps-de-ballet and her devotion to her art had kept her body and soul unencumbered.

For Miles, child of the State, Sex had been part of the curriculum at every stage of his education; first in diagrams, then in demonstrations, then in application, he had mastered all the antics of procreation. Love was a word seldom used except by politicians and by them only in moments of pure fatuity. Nothing that he had been taught prepared him for Clara.

Once in drama, always in drama. Clara now spent her days mending ballet shoes and helping neophytes on the wall bars. She had a cubicle in a Nissen hut and it was there that she and Miles spent most of their evenings. It was unlike anyone else's quarters in Satellite City.

Two little paintings hung on the walls, unlike any paintings Miles had seen before, unlike anything approved by the Ministry of Art. One represented a goddess of antiquity, naked and rosy, fondling a peacock on a bank of flowers; the other a vast, tree-fringed lake and a party in spreading silken clothes embarking in a pleasure boat under a broken arch. The gilt frames were much chipped but what remained of them was elaborately foliated.

'They're French,' said Clara. 'More than two hundred years old. My mother left them to me.'

All her possessions had come from her mother, nearly enough of them to furnish the little room – a looking glass framed in porcelain flowers, a gilt, irregular clock. She and

Miles drank their sad, officially compounded coffee out of brilliant, riveted cups.

'It reminds me of prison,' said Miles when he was first admitted there.

It was the highest praise he knew.

On the first evening among this delicate bric-a-brac his lips found the bare twin spaces of her chin.

'I knew it would be a mistake to let the beastly doctor poison me,' said Clara complacently.

Full summer came. Another moon waxed over these rare lovers. Once they sought coolness and secrecy among the high cow-parsley and willow-herb of the waste building sites. Clara's beard was all silvered like a patriarch's in the midnight radiance.

'On such a night as this,' said Miles, supine, gazing into the face of the moon, 'on such a night as this I burned an Air Force Station and half its occupants.'

Clara sat up and began lazily smoothing her whiskers, then more vigorously tugged the comb through the thicker, tangled growth of her head, dragging it from her forehead; re-ordered the clothing which their embraces had loosed. She was full of womanly content and ready to go home. But Miles, all male, *post coitum tristis*, was struck by a chill sense of loss. No demonstration or exercise had prepared him for this strange new experience of the sudden loneliness that follows requited love.

Walking home they talked casually and rather crossly.

'You never go to the ballet now.'

'No.'

'Won't they give you seats?'

'I suppose they would.'

'Then why don't you go?'

'I don't think I should like it. I see them often rehearsing. I don't like it.'

'But you lived for it.'

'Other interests now.'

'Me?'

'Of course.'

'You love me more than the ballet?'

'I am very happy.'

'Happier than if you were dancing?'

'I can't tell, can I? You're all I've got now.'

'But if you could change?'

'I can't.'

'If?'

'There's no "if".'

'Damn.'

'Don't fret, darling. It's only the moon.'

And they parted in silence.

November came, a season of strikes; leisure for Miles, unsought and unvalued; lonely periods when the ballet school worked on and the death house stood cold and empty.

Clara began to complain of ill health. She was growing stout.

'Just contentment,' she said at first, but the change worried her. 'Can it be that beastly operation?' she asked. 'I heard the reason they put down one of the Cambridge girls was that she kept growing fatter and fatter.'

'She weighed nineteen stone,' said Miles. 'I know because Dr Beamish mentioned it. He has strong professional objections to the Klugmann operation.'

'I'm going to see the Director of Medicine. There's a new one now.'

When she returned from her appointment, Miles, still left idle by the strikers, was waiting for her among her pictures and china. She sat beside him on the bed.

'Let's have a drink,' she said.

They had taken to drinking wine together, very rarely because of the expense. The State chose and named the vintage. This month the issue was 'Progress Port'. Clara kept it in a crimson, white-cut, Bohemian flagon. The glasses were modern, unbreakable and unsightly.

'What did the doctor say?'

'He's very sweet.'

'Well?'

'Much cleverer than the one before.'

'Did he say it was anything to do with your operation?'

'Oh, yes. Everything to do with it.'

'Can he put you right?'

'Yes, he thinks so.'

'Good.'

They drank their wine.

'That first doctor did make a mess of the operation, didn't he?'

'Such a mess. The new doctor says I'm a unique case. You see, I'm pregnant.'

'*Clara.*'

'Yes, it is a surprise, isn't it?'

'This needs thinking about,' said Miles.

He thought.

He refilled their glasses.

He said: 'It's hard luck on the poor little beast not being an Orphan. Not much opportunity for it. If he's a boy we must try and get him registered as a worker. Of course it might be a girl. Then,' brightly, 'we could make her a dancer.'

'Oh, don't mention dancing,' cried Clara, and suddenly began weeping. 'Don't speak to me of dancing.'

Her tears fell fast. No tantrum this, but deep uncontrolled inconsolable sorrow.

And next day she disappeared.

IV

Santa-Claus-tide was near. Shops were full of shoddy little dolls. Children in the schools sang old ditties about peace and goodwill. Strikers went back to work in order to qualify for their seasonal bonus. Electric bulbs were hung in the conifers and the furnaces in the Dome of Security roared again. Miles had been promoted. He now sat beside the assistant registrar and helped stamp and file the documents of the dead. It was harder work than he was used to and Miles was hungry for Clara's company. The lights were going out in the Dome and on the Goodwill Tree in the car park. He walked the half-mile of hutments to Clara's quarters. Other girls were waiting for their consorts or setting out to find them in the Recreatorium, but Clara's door was locked. A note, pinned to it, read: *Miles, Going away for a bit. C.* Angry and puzzled he returned to his hostel.

Clara, unlike himself, had uncles and cousins scattered about the country. Since her operation she had been shy of visiting them. Now, Miles supposed, she was taking cover among them. It was the manner of her flight, so unlike her gentle ways, that tortured him. For a busy week he thought of nothing else. His reproaches sang in his head as the undertone to all the activities of the day and at night he lay sleepless, repeating in his mind every word spoken between them and every act of intimacy.

After a week the thought of her became spasmodic and regular. The subject bored him unendurably. He strove to keep it out of his mind as a man might strive to control an attack of hiccups, and as impotently. Spasmodically, mechanically, the thought of Clara returned. He timed it and found that it came every 7½ minutes. He went to sleep thinking of her, he woke up thinking of her. But between times he slept. He consulted the departmental psychiatrist who told him that he was burdened by the responsibility of parentage. But it was not Clara the mother who haunted him, but Clara the betrayer.

Next week he thought of her every twenty minutes. The week after that he thought of her irregularly, though often; only when something outside himself reminded him of her. He began to look at other girls and considered himself cured.

He looked hard at other girls as he passed them in the dim corridors of the Dome and they looked boldly back at him. Then one of them stopped him and said: 'I've seen you before with Clara', and at the mention of her name all interest in the other girl ceased in pain. 'I went to visit her yesterday.'

'Where?'

'In hospital, of course. Didn't you know?'

'What's the matter with her?'

'She won't say. Nor will anyone else at the hospital. She's top secret. If you ask me she's been in an accident and there's some politician involved. I can't think of any other reason for all the fuss. She's covered in bandages and gay as a lark.'

Next day, December twenty-fifth, was Santa Claus Day; no holiday in the department of Euthanasia, which was an

Tidings of Comfort and Joy

essential service. At dusk Miles walked to the hospital, one of the unfinished edifices, all concrete and steel and glass in front and a jumble of huts behind. The hall porter was engrossed in the television, which was performing an old obscure folk play which past generations had performed on Santa Claus Day, and was now revived and revised as a matter of historical interest.

It was of professional interest to the porter for it dealt with maternity services before the days of Welfare. He gave the number of Clara's room without glancing up from the strange spectacle of an ox and an ass, an old man with a lantern and a young mother. 'People here are always complaining,' he said. 'They ought to realize what things were like before Progress.'

The corridors were loud with relayed music. Miles found the hut he sought. It was marked 'Experimental Surgery. Health Officers Only'. He found the cubicle. He found Clara sleeping, the sheet pulled up to her eyes, her hair loose on the pillow. She had brought some of her property with her. An old shawl lay across the bed-table. A painted fan stood against the television-set. She awoke, her eyes full of frank welcome, and pulled the sheet higher, speaking through it.

'Darling, you shouldn't have come. I was keeping it for a surprise.'

Miles sat by the bed and thought of nothing to say except: 'How are you?'

'Wonderful. They've taken the bandages off today. They

won't let me have a looking glass yet but they say everything has been a tremendous success. I'm something very special, Miles — a new chapter in surgical progress.'

'But what has happened to you? Is it something to do with the baby?'

'Oh no. At least, it was. That was the first operation. But that's all over now.'

'You mean our child?'

'Yes, that had to go. I should never have been able to dance afterwards. I told you all about it. That was why I had the Klugmann operation, don't you remember?'

'But you gave up dancing.'

'That's where they've been so clever. Didn't I tell you about the sweet, clever new medical director? He's cured all that.'

'Your dear beard.'

'Quite gone. An operation the new director invented himself. It's going to be named after him or even perhaps after me. He's so unselfish he wants to call it the Clara operation. He's taken off all the skin and put on a wonderful new substance, a sort of synthetic rubber that takes grease-paint perfectly. He says the colour isn't perfect but that it will never show on the stage. Look, feel it.'

She sat up in bed, joyful and proud.

Her eyes and brow were all that was left of the loved face. Below it something quite inhuman, a tight, slippery mask, salmon pink.

Experimental Surgery

Miles stared. In the television screen by the bed further characters had appeared – Food Production Workers. They seemed to declare a sudden strike, left their sheep and ran off at the bidding of some kind of shop-steward in fantastic dress. The machine by the bedside broke into song, an old, forgotten ditty:

'O tidings of comfort and joy, comfort and joy, O tidings of comfort and joy.'

Miles retched unobtrusively. The ghastly face regarded him with fondness and pride. At length the right words came to him; the trite, the traditional sentence uttered by countless lips of generations of baffled and impassioned Englishmen: 'I think I shall go for a short walk.'

But first he walked only as far as his hostel. There he lay down until the moon moved to his window and fell across his sleepless face. Then he set out, walking far into the fields, out of sight of the Dome of Security, for two hours until the moon was near setting.

He had travelled at random but now the white rays fell on a signpost and he read: '*Mountjoy* ¾'. He strode on with only the stars to light his way till he came to the Castle gates.

They stood open as always, gracious symbol of the new penology. He followed the drive. The whole lightless face of the old house stared at him silently, without rebuke. He knew now what was needed. He carried in his pocket a cigarette lighter which often worked. It worked for him now.

No need for oil here. The dry old silk of the drawing-room curtains lit like paper. Paint and panelling, plaster and tapestry and gilding bowed to the embrace of the leaping flames. He stepped outside. Soon it was too hot on the terrace and he retreated further, to the marble temple at the end of the long walk. The murderers were leaping from the first-storey windows but the sexual offenders, trapped above, set up a wail of terror. He heard the chandeliers fall and saw the boiling lead cascading from the roof. This was something altogether finer than the strangulation of a few peacocks. He watched exultant as minute by minute the scene disclosed fresh wonders. Great timbers crashed within; outside the lily-pond hissed with falling brands; a vast ceiling of smoke shut out the stars and under it tongues of flame floated away into the tree-tops.

Two hours later when the first engine arrived, the force of the fiery storm was already spent. Miles rose from his marble throne and began the long walk home. But he was no longer at all fatigued. He strode out cheerfully with his shadow, cast by the dying blaze, stretching before him along the lane.

On the main road a motorist stopped him and asked: 'What's that over there? A house on fire?'

'It was,' said Miles. 'It's almost out now.'

'Looks like a big place. Only Government property, I suppose?'

'That's all,' said Miles.

'Well hop in if you want a lift.'

'Thanks,' said Miles, 'I'm walking for pleasure.'

V

Miles rose after two hours in bed. The hostel was alive with all the normal activity of morning. The wireless was playing; the sub-officials were coughing over their wash-basins; the reek of State sausages frying in State grease filled the asbestos cubicle. He was slightly stiff after his long walk and slightly footsore, but his mind was as calm and empty as the sleep from which he had awoken. The scorched-earth policy had succeeded. He had made a desert in his imagination which he might call peace. Once before he had burned his childhood. Now his brief adult life lay in ashes; the enchantments that surrounded Clara were one with the splendours of Mountjoy; her great golden beard, one with the tongues of flame that had leaped and expired among the stars; her fans and pictures and scraps of old embroidery, one with the gilded cornices and silk hangings, black, cold and sodden. He ate his sausage with keen appetite and went to work.

All was quiet too at the Department of Euthanasia.

The first announcement of the Mountjoy disaster had been on the early news. Its proximity to Satellite City gave it a special poignancy there.

'It is a significant phenomenon,' said Dr Beamish, 'that any bad news has an immediate effect on our service. You see it whenever there is an international crisis. Sometimes I think people only come to us when they have nothing to talk about. Have you looked at our queue today?'

Miles turned to the periscope. Only one man waited outside, old Parsnip, a poet of the 'thirties who came daily but was usually jostled to the back of the crowd. He was a comic character in the department, this veteran poet. Twice in Miles's short term he had succeeded in gaining admission but on both occasions had suddenly taken fright and bolted.

'It's a lucky day for Parsnip,' said Miles.

'Yes. He deserves some luck. I knew him well once, him and his friend Pimpernell. *New Writing*, the Left Book Club, they were all the rage. Pimpernell was one of my first patients. Hand Parsnip in and we'll finish him off.'

So old Parsnip was summoned and that day his nerve stood firm. He passed fairly calmly through the gas chamber on his way to rejoin Pimpernell.

'We might as well knock off for the day,' said Dr Beamish. 'We shall be busy again soon when the excitement dies down.'

But the politicians seemed determined to keep the excitement up. All the normal features of television were interrupted and curtailed to give place to Mountjoy. Survivors appeared on the screen, among them Soapy, who described how long

Parsnip ad Portas

practice as a cat burglar had enabled him to escape. Mr Sweat, he remarked with respect, had got clear away. The ruins were surveyed by the apparatus. A sexual maniac with broken legs gave audience from his hospital bed. The Minister of Welfare, it was announced, would make a special appearance that evening to comment on the disaster.

Miles dozed intermittently beside the hostel set and at dusk rose, still calm and free; so purged of emotion that he made his way once more to the hospital and called on Clara.

She had spent the afternoon with looking glass and make-up box. The new substance of her face fulfilled all the surgeon's promises. It took paint to perfection. Clara had given herself a full mask as though for the lights of the stage; an even creamy white with sudden high spots of crimson on the cheek bones, huge hard crimson lips, eyebrows extended and turned up catwise, the eyes shaded all round with ultramarine and dotted at the corners with crimson.

'You're the first to see me,' she said. 'I was half-afraid you wouldn't come. You seemed cross yesterday.'

'I wanted to see the television,' said Miles. 'It's so crowded at the hostel.'

'So dull today. Nothing except this prison that has been burned down.'

'I was there myself. Don't you remember? I often talked of it.' Parsnip ad Portas

'Did you, Miles? Perhaps so. I've such a bad memory for

things that don't concern me. Do you really want to hear the Minister? It would be much cosier to talk.'

'It's him I've come for.'

And presently the Minister appeared, open-necked as always but without his usual smile; grave to the verge of tears. He spoke for twenty minutes. '. . . The great experiment must go on . . . the martyrs of maladjustment shall not have died in vain . . . A greater, new Mountjoy shall rise from the ashes of the old . . .' Eventually tears came — real tears for he held an invisible onion — and trickled down his cheeks. So the speech ended.

'That's all I came for,' said Miles, and left Clara to her cocoa-butter and face-towel.

Next day all the organs of public information were still piping the theme of Mountjoy. Two or three patients, already bored with the entertainment, presented themselves for extermination and were happily despatched. Then a message came from the Regional Director, official-in-chief of Satellite City. He required the immediate presence of Miles in his office.

'I have a move order for you, Mr Plastic. You are to report to the Ministers of Welfare and Rest and Culture. You will be issued with a Grade A hat, umbrella and briefcase for the journey. My congratulations.'

Equipped with these insignia of sudden, dizzy promotion, Miles travelled to the capital leaving behind a domeful of sub-officials chattering with envy.

At the terminus an official met him. Together in an official car they drove to Whitehall.

'Let me carry your briefcase, Mr Plastic.'

'There's nothing in it.'

Miles's escort laughed obsequiously at this risqué joke.

At the Ministry the lifts were in working order. It was a new and alarming experience to enter the little cage and rise to the top of the great building.

'Do they always work here?'

'Not *always*, but very very often.'

Miles realized that he was indeed at the heart of things.

'Wait here. I will call you when the Ministers are ready.'

Miles looked from the waiting-room window at the slow streams of traffic. Just below him stood a strange, purposeless obstruction of stone. A very old man, walking by, removed his hat to it as though saluting an acquaintance. Why? Miles wondered. Then he was summoned to the politicians.

They were alone in their office save for a gruesome young woman. The Minister of Rest and Culture said: 'Ease your feet, lad' and indicated a large leatherette armchair.

'Not such a happy occasion, alas, as our last meeting,' said the Minister of Welfare.

'Oh, I don't know,' said Miles. He was enjoying the outing.

'The tragedy at Mountjoy Castle was a grievous loss to the cause of penology.'

'But the great work of Rehabilitation will continue,' said the gruesome young woman.

'A greater Mountjoy will arise from the ashes,' said the Minister.

'Those noble criminal lives have not been lost in vain.'

'Their memory will inspire us.'

'Yes,' said Miles. 'I heard the broadcast.'

'Exactly,' said the Minister. 'Precisely. Then you appreciate, perhaps, what a change the occurrence makes in your own position. From being, as we hoped, the first of a continuous series of successes, you are our only one. It would not be too much to say that the whole future of penology is in your hands. The destruction of Mountjoy Castle by itself was merely a set-back. A sad one, of course, but something which might be described as the growing pains of a great movement. But there is a darker side. I told you, I think, that our great experiment had been made only against considerable opposition. Now – I speak confidentially – that opposition has become vocal and unscrupulous. There is, in fact, a whispering campaign that the fire was no accident but the act of one of the very men whom we were seeking to serve. That campaign must be scotched.'

'They can't do us down as easy as they think,' said the Minister of Rest and Culture. 'Us old dogs know a trick or two.'

'Exactly. Counter-propaganda. You are our Exhibit A. The irrefutable evidence of the triumph of our system. We are going to send you up and down the country to lecture. My colleagues have already written your speech. You will be accompanied by Miss Flower here, who will show and explain the model of the new Mountjoy. Perhaps you will care to see it yourself. Miss Flower, the model please.'

All the time they were speaking Miles had been aware of a bulky, sheeted object on a table in the window. Miss Flower now unveiled it. Miles gazed in awe.

The object displayed was a familiar, standard packing-case, set on end.

'A rush job,' said the Minister of Welfare. 'You will be provided with something more elaborate for your tour.'

Miles gazed at the box.

It fitted. It fell into place precisely in the void of his mind, satisfying all the needs for which his education had prepared him. The conditioned personality recognized its proper pre-ordained environment. All else was insubstantial; the gardens of Mountjoy, Clara's cracked Crown Derby and her enveloping beard were trophies of a fading dream.

The Modern Man was home.

'There is one further point,' continued the Minister of Welfare. 'A domestic one but not as irrelevant as it may seem. Have you by any chance formed an attachment in Satellite City? Your dossier suggests that you have.'

'Any woman trouble?' explained the Minister of Rest and Culture.

'Oh, yes,' said Miles. 'Great trouble. But that is over.'

'You see, perfect rehabilitation, complete citizenship should include marriage.'

'It has not,' said Miles.

'That should be rectified.'

'Folks like a bloke to be spliced,' said the Minister of Rest and Culture. 'With a couple of kids.'

'There is hardly time for *them*,' said the Minister of Welfare. 'But we think that psychologically you will have more appeal if you have a wife by your side. Miss Flower here has every qualification.'

'Looks are only skin deep, lad,' said the Minister of Rest and Culture.

'So if you have no preferable alternative to offer . . . ?'

'None,' said Miles.

'Spoken like an Orphan. I see a splendid career ahead of the pair of you.'

'When can we get divorced?'

'Come, come, Plastic. You mustn't look too far ahead. First things first. You have already obtained the necessary leave from your Director, Miss Flower?'

'Yes, Minister.'

'Then off you both go. And State be with you.'

In perfect peace of heart Miles followed Miss Flower to the Registrar's office.

Then the mood veered.

Miles felt ill at ease during the ceremony and fidgeted with something small and hard which he found in his pocket. It proved to be his cigarette-lighter, a most uncertain apparatus. He pressed the catch and instantly, surprisingly, there burst out a tiny flame – gemlike, hymeneal, auspicious.

BASIL SEAL RIDES AGAIN
OR
THE RAKE'S REGRESS

TO MRS IAN FLEMING

Dear Ann

*In this senile attempt to recapture the manner of my youth
I have resurrected characters from earlier stories which, if you
ever read them, you will have forgotten.*

Basil Seal was the hero of Black Mischief (1932) *and*
Put Out More Flags (1942). *Through my ineptitude the
colour of his eyes changed during the intervening decade. At the
end of the latter book he considered marriage with the newly
widowed, very rich Angela Lyne who had long been his mistress.
Ambrose Silk, an aesthete, also appeared in that book. Peter, Lord
Pastmaster, first appeared as Peter Beste-Chetwynde in* Decline
and Fall (1928). *His mother, later Lady Metroland, appeared
there and in* Vile Bodies (1930). *Alastair Digby-Vane-
Trumpington was Lady Metroland's lover in 1928 and Sonia's
husband in 1942.*

*Albright is new: an attempt to extract something from the
rum modern world of which you afford me occasional glimpses
in your hospitable house.*

I should have liked to drop the title in favour of what I have here used as subtitle, but it was suggested that this might smack of sharp practice to readers who saw the story in the Sunday Telegraph and Esquire and might be led to expect something new.

       Ever your affec. coz.

Combe Florey. December 1962   E. W.

Basil Seal Rides Again
or
The Rake's Regress

I

'Yes.'

'What d'you mean: "Yes"?'

'I didn't hear what you said.'

'I said he made off with all my shirts.'

'It's not that I'm the least deaf. It's simply that I can't concentrate when a lot of fellows are making a row.'

'There's a row now.'

'Some sort of speech.'

'And a lot of fellows saying: "Shush".'

'Exactly. I can't concentrate. What did you say?'

'This fellow made off with all my shirts.'

'Fellow making the speech?'

'No, no. Quite another fellow – called Albright.'

'I don't think so. I heard he was dead.'

'This one isn't. You can't say he stole them exactly. My daughter gave them to him.'

'All?'

'Practically all. I had a few in London and there were a few at the wash. Couldn't believe it when my man told me. Went through all the drawers myself. Nothing there.'

'Bloody thing to happen. My daughter wouldn't do a thing like that.'

Protests from neighbouring diners rose in volume.

'They can't want to hear this speech. It's the most awful rot.'

'We seem to be getting unpopular.'

'Don't know who all these fellows are. Never saw anyone before except old Ambrose. Thought I ought to turn out and support him.'

Peter Pastmaster and Basil Seal seldom attended public banquets. They sat at the end of a long table under chandeliers and pier-glasses, looking, for all the traditional brightness of the hotel, too bright and too private for their surroundings. Peter was a year or two the younger but he, like Basil, had scorned to order his life with a view of longevity or spurious youth. They were two stout, rubicund, richly dressed old buffers who might have passed as exact contemporaries.

The frowning faces that were turned towards them were of all ages from those of a moribund Celtic bard to the cross adolescent critic's for whose dinner Mr Bentley, the organizer, was paying. Mr Bentley had, as he expressed it, cast his net wide. There were politicians and publicists there, dons and cultural attachés, Fulbright scholars, representatives of the Pen Club, editors; Mr Bentley, home-sick for the *belle époque* of the American slump, when in England the worlds of art and fashion and action harmoniously mingled, had solicited the attendance of a few of the early friends of the guest of honour, and Peter and Basil, meeting casually a few weeks before, had decided to go together. They were celebrating the almost coincident events of Ambrose Silk's sixtieth birthday and his investiture with the Order of Merit.

Ambrose, white-haired, pallid, emaciated, sat between Dr Parsnip, Professor of Dramatic Poetry at Minneapolis, and Dr Pimpernell, Professor of Poetic Drama at St Paul. These distinguished expatriates had flown to London for the occasion. It was not the sort of party at which decorations are worn but as Ambrose delicately inclined in deprecation of the honeyed words that dripped around him, no one could doubt his effortless distinction. It was Parsnip who was now on his feet attempting to make himself heard.

'I hear the cry of "silence",' he said with sharp spontaneity. His voice had assumed something of the accent of his place of exile but his diction was orthodox – august even; he had quite discarded the patiently acquired proletarian colloquialisms of thirty years earlier. 'It is apt, for, surely?, the object of our homage tonight is epitomized in that golden word. The voice which once clearly spoke the message of what I for one, and many of us here, will always regard as the most glorious decade of English letters, the nineteen-thirties' (growls of dissent from the youthful critic), 'that voice tardily perhaps, but at long last so illustriously honoured by official recognition, has been silent for a quarter of a century. Silent in Ireland, silent in Tangier, in Telaviv and Ischia and Portugal, now silent in his native London, our guest of honour has stood for us as a stern rebuke, a recall to artistic reticence and integrity. The books roll out from the presses, none by Ambrose Silk. Not for Ambrose Silk the rostrum, the television screen; for him the enigmatic and monumental silence of genius . . .'

'I've got to pee,' said Basil.

'I always want to nowadays.'

'Come on then.'

Slowly and stiffly they left the hotel dining-room.

As they stood side by side in the lavatory Basil said: 'I'm glad Ambrose has got a gong. D'you think the fellow making the speech was pulling his leg?'

'Must have been. Stands to reason.'

'You were going to tell me something about some shirts.'

'I did tell you.'

'What was the name of the chap who got them?'

'Albright.'

'Yes, I remember; a fellow called Clarence Albright. Rather an awful chap. Got himself killed in the war.'

'No one that I knew got killed in the war except Alastair Trumpington.'

'And Cedric Lyne.'

'Yes, there was Cedric.'

'And Freddy Sothill.'

'I never really considered I knew him,' said Basil.

'This Albright married someone – Molly Meadows, perhaps?'

'I married Molly Meadows.'

'So you did. I was there. Well, someone like that. One of those girls who were going round at the time – John Flintshire's sister, Sally perhaps. I expect your Albright is her son.'

'He doesn't look like anyone's son.'

'People always are,' said Basil, 'sons or daughters of people.'

This truism had a secondary, antiquated and, to Peter, an obvious meaning, which was significant of the extent by which Basil had changed from *enfant terrible* to 'old Pobble', the name by which he was known to his daughter's friends.

The change had been rapid. In 1939 Basil's mother, his sister, Barbara Sothill, and his mistress, Angela Lyne, had seen the war as the opportunity for his redemption. His embattled country, they supposed, would find honourable use for those deplorable energies which had so often brought him almost into the shadows of prison. At the worst he would fill a soldier's grave; at the best he would emerge as a second Lawrence of Arabia. His fate was otherwise.

Early in his military career, he lamed himself, blowing away the toes of one foot while demonstrating to his commando section a method of his own device for demolishing railway bridges, and was discharged from the army. From this disaster was derived at a later date the sobriquet 'Pobble'. Then, hobbling from his hospital bed to the registry office, he married the widowed Angela Lyne. Hers was one of those few, huge, astutely dispersed fortunes which neither international calamities nor local experiments with socialism could seriously diminish. Basil accepted wealth as he accepted the loss of his toes. He forgot he had ever walked without a stick and a limp, had ever been lean and active, had ever been put to desperate shifts for quite small sums. If he ever recalled that decade of adventure it was as something remote and unrelated to man's estate, like an end-of-term shortness of pocket money at school.

For the rest of the war and for the first drab years of peace he had appeared on the national register as 'farmer'; that is to say, he lived in the country in ease and plenty. Two dead men, Freddy Sothill and Cedric Lyne, had left ample cellars. Basil drained them. He had once expressed the wish to become one of the 'hard-faced men who had done well out of the war'. Basil's face, once very hard, softened and rounded. His scar became almost invisible in rosy suffusion. None of his few clothes, he found, now buttoned comfortably and when, in that time of European scarcity, he and Angela went to New York, where such things could then still be procured by the well-informed, he bought suits and shirts and shoes by the dozen and a whole treasury of watches, tie-pins, cufflinks and chains so that on his return, having scrupulously declared them and paid full duty at the customs – a thing he had never in his life done before – he remarked of his elder brother, who, after a tediously successful diplomatic career spent in gold-lace or starched linen allowed himself in retirement (and reduced circumstances) some laxity in dress: 'Poor Tony goes about looking like a scarecrow.'

Life in the country palled when food rationing ceased. Angela made over the house they had called 'Cedric's Folly' and its grottoes to her son Nigel on his twenty-first birthday, and took a large, unobtrusive house in Hill Street. She had other places to live, a panelled seventeenth-century apartment in Paris, a villa on Cap Ferrat, a beach and bungalow quite lately acquired in Bermuda, a little palace in Venice which she had once bought for Cedric Lyne but never visited in his lifetime – and among them they moved with their daughter Barbara. Basil settled into the orderly round of the rich. He became a creature of habit and of set opinions. In London finding Bratt's and Bellamy's disturbingly raffish, he joined that sombre club in Pall Mall that had been the scene of so many painful interviews with his self-appointed guardian, Sir Joseph Mannering, and there often sat in the chair which had belonged prescriptively to Sir Joseph and, as Sir Joseph had done, pronounced his verdict on the day's news to any who would listen.

*

Basil turned, crossed to the looking glasses and straightened his tie. He brushed up the copious grey hair. He looked at himself with the blue eyes which had seen so much and now saw only the round, rosy face in which they were set, the fine clothes of English make which had replaced the American improvisations, the starched shirt which he was almost alone in wearing, the black pearl studs, the buttonhole.

A week or two ago he had had a disconcerting experience in this very hotel. It was a place he had frequented all his life, particularly in the latter years, and he was on cordial terms with the man who took the men's hats in a den by the Piccadilly entrance. Basil was never given a numbered ticket and assumed he was known by name. Then a day came when he sat longer than usual over luncheon and found the man off duty. Lifting the counter he had penetrated to the rows of pegs and retrieved his bowler and umbrella. In the ribbon of the hat he found a label, put there for identification. It bore the single pencilled word 'Florid'. He had told his daughter, Barbara, who said: 'I wouldn't have you any different. Don't for heaven's sake go taking one of those cures. You'd go mad.'

Basil was not a vain man; neither in rags nor in riches had he cared much about the impression he made. But the epithet recurred to him now as he surveyed himself in the glass.

'Would you say Ambrose was "florid", Peter?'

'Not a word I use.'

'It simply means flowery.'

'Well, I suppose he is.'

'Not fat and red?'

'Not Ambrose.'

'Exactly.'

'I've been called "florid".'

'You're fat and red.'

'So are you.'

'Yes, why not? Almost everyone is.'

'Except Ambrose.'

'Well, he's a pansy. I expect he takes trouble.'

'We don't.'

'Why the hell should we?'

'We don't.'

'Exactly.'

The two old friends had exhausted the subject.

Basil said: 'About those shirts. How did your girl ever meet a fellow like that?'

'At Oxford. She insisted on going up to read History. She picked up some awfully rum friends.'

'I suppose there were girls there in my time. We never met them.'

'Nor in mine.'

'Stands to reason the sort of fellow who takes up with undergraduettes has something wrong with him.'

'Albright certainly has.'

'What does he look like?'

'I've never set an eye. My daughter asked him to King's Thursday when I was abroad. She found he had no shirts and she gave him mine.'

'Was he hard up?'

'So she said.'

'Clarence Albright never had any money. Sally can't have brought him much.'

'There may be no connection.'

'Must be. Two fellows without money both called Albright. Stands to reason they're the same fellow.'

Peter looked at his watch.

'Half past eleven. I don't feel like going back to hear those speeches. We showed up. Ambrose must have been pleased.'

'He was. But he can't expect us to listen to all that rot.'

'What did he mean about Ambrose's "silence"? Never knew a fellow who talked so much.'

'All a lot of rot. Where to now?'

'Come to think of it, my mother lives upstairs. We might see if she's at home.'

They rose to the floor where Margot Metroland had lived ever since the destruction of Pastmaster House. The door on the corridor was not locked. As they stood in the little vestibule, loud, low-bred voices came to them.

'She seems to have a party.'

Peter opened the door of the sitting-room. It was in darkness save for the ghastly light of a television set. Margot crouched over it, her old taut face livid in the reflection.

'Can we come in?'

'Who are you? What d'you want? I can't see you.'

Peter turned on the light at the door.

'Don't do that. Oh, it's you Peter. And Basil.'

'We've been dining downstairs.'

'Well, I'm sorry; I'm busy, as you can see. Turn the light out and come and sit down if you want to, but don't disturb me.'

'We'd better go.'

'Yes. Come and see me when I'm not so busy.'

Outside Peter said: 'She's always looking at that thing nowadays. It's a great pleasure to her.'

'Where to now?'

'I thought of dropping in at Bellamy's.'

'I'll go home. I left Angela on her own. Barbara's at a party of Robin Trumpington's.'

'Well, good-night.'

'I say, those places where they starve you, – you know what I mean – do they do any good?'

'Molly swears by one.'

'She's not fat and red.'

'No. She goes to those starving places.'

'Well, good-night.'

Peter turned east, Basil north, into the mild, misty October night. The streets at this hour were empty. Basil stumped across Piccadilly and up through Mayfair, where Angela's house was almost the sole survivor of the private houses of his youth. How many doors had been closed against him then that were now open to all comers as shops and offices!

The lights were on. He left his hat and coat on a marble table and began the ascent to the drawing-room floor, pausing on the half-landing to recuperate.

'Oh, Pobble, you toeless wonder. You always turn up just when you're wanted.'

Florid he might be, but there were compensations. It was not thus that Basil had often been greeted in limber youth. Two arms embraced his neck and drew him down, an agile figure inclined over the protuberance of his starched shirt, a cheek was pressed to his and teeth tenderly nibbled the lobe of his ear.

'Babs, I thought you were at a party. Why on earth are you dressed like that?'

His daughter wore very tight, very short trousers, slippers and a thin jersey. He disengaged himself and slapped her loudly on the behind.

'Sadist. It's that sort of party. It's a "happening".'

'You speak in riddles child.'

'It's a new sort of party the Americans have invented. Nothing is arranged beforehand. Things just happen. To-night they cut off a girl's clothes with nail scissors and then painted her green. She had a mask on so I don't know who it was. She might just be someone hired. Then what happened was Robin ran out of drink so we've all gone scouring for it. Mummy's in bed and doesn't know where old Nudge keeps the key and we can't wake him up.'

'You and your mother have been into Nudge's bedroom?'

'Me and Charles. He's the chap I'm scouring with. He's downstairs now trying to pick the lock. I think Nudge must be sedated, he just rolled over snoring when we shook him.'

At the foot of the staircase a door led to the servants' quarters. It opened and someone very strange appeared with an armful of bottles. Basil saw below him a slender youth, perhaps a man of twenty-one, who had a mop of dishevelled black hair and a meagre black fringe of beard and whiskers; formidable, contemptuous blue eyes above grey pouches; a proud, rather childish mouth. He wore a pleated white silk shirt, open at the neck, flannel trousers, a green cummerbund and sandals. The appearance, though grotesque, was not specifically plebeian and when he spoke his tone was pure and true without a taint of accent.

'The lock was easy,' he said, 'but I can't find anything except wine. Where d'you keep the whisky?'

'Heavens, I don't know,' said Barbara.

'Good evening,' said Basil.

'Oh, good evening. Where do you keep the whisky?'

'Is it a fancy dress party?' Basil asked.

'Not particularly,' said the young man.

'What have you got there?'

'Champagne of some kind. I didn't notice the label.'

'He's got the Cliquot rosé,' said Basil.

'How clever of him,' said Barbara.

'It will probably do,' said the young man. 'Though most people prefer whisky.'

Basil attempted to speak but found no words.

Barbara quoted:

'"His Aunt Jobiska made him drink

Lavender water tinged with pink,

For the world in general knows

There's nothing so good for a Pobble's toes."

Come along, Charles, I think we've got all we're going to get here. I sense a grudging hospitality.'

She skipped downstairs, waved from the hall and was out of the front door, while Basil still stood dumbfounded.

At length, even more laboriously than he was wont, he continued upward. Angela was in bed reading.

'You're home early.'

'Peter was there. No one else I knew except old Ambrose. Some booby made a speech. So I came away.'

'Very wise.'

Basil stood before Angela's long looking glass. He could see her behind him. She put on her spectacles and picked up her book.

'Angela, I don't drink much nowadays, do I?'

'Not as much as you used.'

'Or eat?'

'More.'

'But you'd say I led a temperate life?'

'Yes, on the whole.'

'It's just age,' said Basil. 'And dammit, I'm not sixty yet.'

'What's worrying you, darling?'

'It's when I meet young men. A choking feeling – as if I was going to have an apoplectic seizure. I once saw a fellow in a seizure, must have been about the age I am now – the Lieutenant-Colonel of the Bombardiers. It was a most unpleasant spectacle. I've been feeling lately something like that might strike me any day. I believe I ought to take a cure.'

'I'll come too.'

'Will you really, Angela? You are a saint.'

'Might as well be there as anywhere. They're supposed to be good for insomnia too. The servants would like a holiday. They've been wearing awfully overworked expressions lately.'

'No sense taking Babs. We could send her to Malfrey.'

'Yes.'

'Angela, I saw the most awful-looking fellow tonight with a sort of beard – here, in the house, a friend of Babs. She called him "Charles".'

'Yes, he's someone new.'

'What's his name?'

'I did hear. It sounded like a pack of fox hounds I once went out with. I know – Albrighton.'

'Albright,' cried Basil, the invisible noose tightening. 'Albright, by God.'

Angela looked at him with real concern. 'You know,' she said, 'you really do look rather rum. I think we'd better go to one of those starving places at once.'

And then what had seemed a death-rattle turned into a laugh.

'It was one of Peter's shirts,' he said, unintelligibly to Angela.

II

It may one day occur to a pioneer of therapeutics that most of those who are willing to pay fifty pounds a week to be deprived of food and wine, seek only suffering and that they could be cheaply accommodated in rat-ridden dungeons. At present the profits of the many thriving institutions which cater for the ascetic are depleted by the maintenance of neat lawns and shrubberies and, inside, of the furniture of a private house and apparatus resembling that of a hospital.

Basil and Angela could not immediately secure rooms at the sanatorium recommended by Molly Pastmaster. There was a waiting list of people suffering from every variety of infirmity. Finally they frankly outbid rival sufferers. A man whose obesity threatened the collapse of his ankles, and a woman raging with hallucinations were informed that their bookings were defective, and on a warm afternoon Basil and Angela drove down to take possession of their rooms.

There was a resident physician at this most accommodating house. He interviewed each patient on arrival and ostensibly considered individual needs.

He saw Angela first. Basil sat stolidly in an outer room, his hands on the head of his cane, gazing blankly before him.

When at length he was admitted, he stated his needs. The doctor did not attempt any physical investigation. It was a plain case.

'To refrain from technical language you complain of speechlessness, a sense of heat and strangulation, dizziness and subsequent trembling?' said this man of science.

'I feel I'm going to burst,' said Basil.

'Exactly. And these symptoms only occur when you meet young men?'

'Hairy young men especially.'

'Ah.'

'Young puppies.'

'And with puppies too? That is very significant. How do you react to kittens?'

'I mean the young men are puppies.'

'Ah. And are you fond of puppies, Mr Seal?'

'Reasonably.'

'Ah.' The man of science studied the paper on his desk. 'Have you always been conscious of this preference for your own sex?'

'I'm not conscious of it now.'

'You are fifty-eight years and ten months. That is often a crucial age, one of change, when repressed and unsuspected inclinations emerge and take control. I should strongly recommend your putting yourself under a psychoanalyst. We do not give treatment of that kind here.'

'I just want to be cured of feeling I'm going to burst.'

'I've no doubt our regime will relieve the symptoms. You will not find many young men here to disturb you. Our patients are mostly mature women. There is a markedly virile young physical training instructor. His hair is quite short but you had better keep away from the gym. Ah, I see from your paper that you are handicapped by war-wounds. I will take out all physical exercise from your timetable and substitute extra periods of manipulation by one of the female staff. Here is your diet sheet. You will notice that for the first forty-eight hours you are restricted to turnip juice. At the end of that period you embark on the carrots. At the end of the fortnight, if all goes well, we will have you on raw eggs and barley. Don't hesitate to come and see me again if you have any problem to discuss.'

*

The sleeping quarters of male and female inmates were separated by the length of the house. Basil found Angela in the drawing-room. They compared their diet sheets.

'Rum that it should be exactly the same treatment for insomnia and apoplexy.'

'That booby thought I was a pansy.'

'It takes a medical man to find out a thing like that. All these years and I never knew. They're always right, you know. So that's why you're always going to that odd club.'

'This is no time for humour. This is going to be a very grim fortnight.'

'Not for me,' said Angela. 'I came well provisioned. I'm only here to keep you company. And there's a Mrs Somebody next door to me who I used to know. She's got a private cache of all the sleeping-pills in the world. I've made great friends with her already. I shall be all right.'

On the third day of his ordeal, the worst according to *habitués* of the establishment, there came a telephone call from Barbara.

'Pobble, I want to go back to London. I'm bored.'

'Bored with Aunt Barbara?'

'Not with *her*, with *here*.'

'You stay where you're put, chattel.'

'No. *Please*, I want to go home.'

'Your home is where I am. You can't come here.'

'No. I want to go to London.'

'You can't. I sent the servants away for a fortnight.'

'Most of my friends live without servants.'

'You've sunk into a very low world, Babs.'

'Don't be such an ass. Sonia Trumpington hasn't any servants.'

'Well, she won't want you.'

'Pobble, you sound awfully feeble.'

'Who wouldn't who's only had one carrot in the last three days.'

'Oh, you are brave.'

'Yes.'

'How's mummy?'

'Your mother is not keeping the regime as strictly as I am.'

'I bet she isn't. Anyway, please, can I go back to London?'

'No.'

'You mean "No"?'

'Yes.'

'Fiend.'

Basil had gone hungry before. From time to time in his varied youth, in desert, tundra, glacier and jungle, in garrets and cellars, he had briefly endured extremities of privation. Now in the periods of repose and solitude, after the steam bath and the smarting deluge of the showers, after the long thumping and twisting by the huge masseuse, when the chintz curtains were drawn in his bedroom and he lay towel-wrapped and supine gazing at the pattern of the ceiling paper, familiar, forgotten pangs spoke to him of his past achievements.

He defined his condition to Angela after the first week of the regime. 'I'm not rejuvenated or invigorated. I'm etherealized.'

'You look like a ghost.'

'Exactly. I've lost sixteen pounds three ounces.'

'You're overdoing it. No one else keeps these absurd rules. We aren't expected to. It's like the "*rien ne va plus*" at roulette. Mrs What's-her-name has found a black market in the gym kept by the sergeant-instructor. We ate a grouse pie this morning.'

They were in the well-kept grounds. A chime of bells announced that the brief recreation was over. Basil tottered back to his masseuse.

Later, light-headed and limp, he lay down and stared once more at the ceiling paper.

As a convicted felon might in long vigils search his history for the first trespass that had brought him to his present state, Basil examined his conscience. Fasting, he knew, was in all religious systems the introduction to self-knowledge. Where had he first played false to his destiny? After the conception of Barbara; after her birth. She, in some way, was at the root of it. Though he had not begun to dote on her until she was eight years old, he had from the first been aware of his own paternity. In 1947, when she was a year old, he and Angela had gone to New York and California. That enterprise, in those days, was nefarious. Elaborate laws restricted the use of foreign currencies and these they had defied, drawing freely on undisclosed assets. But on his return he had made a full declaration to the customs. It was no immediate business of theirs to inquire into the sources of his laden trunks. In a mood of arrogance he had displayed everything and paid without demur. There lay the fount and origin of the deviation into rectitude that had disfigured him in recent years. As though waking after a night's drunkenness – an experience common enough in his youth – and confusedly articulating the disjointed memories of outrage and absurdity, he ruefully contemplated the change he had wrought in himself. His voice was not the same instrument as of old. He had first assumed it as a conscious imposture; it had become habitual to him; the antiquated, wordly wise moralities which, using that voice, he had found himself obliged to utter, had become his settled opinions. It had begun as nursery clowning for the diversion of Barbara; a parody of Sir Joseph Mannering; darling, crusty old Pobble performing the part expected of him; and now the parody had become the *persona*.

His meditation was interrupted by the telephone. 'Will you take a call from Mrs Sothill?'

'Babs.'

'Basil. I just wondered how you were getting on.'

'They're very pleased with me.'

'Thin?'

'Skinny. And concerned with my soul.'

'Chump. Listen. I'm concerned with Barbara's soul.'

'What's she been up to?'

'I think she's in love.'

'Rot.'

'Well, she's moping.'

'I expect she misses me.'

'When she isn't moping she's telephoning or writing letters.'

'Not to me.'

'Exactly. There's someone in London.'

'Robin Trumpington?'

'She doesn't confide.'

'Can't you listen in on the telephone?'

'I've tried that, of course. It's certainly a man she's talking to. I can't really understand their language but it sounds very affectionate. You won't like it awfully if she runs off, will you?'

'She'd never think of such a thing. Don't put ideas into the child's head, for God's sake. Give her a dose of castor oil.'

'I don't mind, if *you* don't. I just thought I should warn.'

'Tell her I'll soon be back.'

'She knows that.'

'Well, keep her under lock and key until I get out.'

Basil reported the conversation to Angela. 'Barbara says Barbara's in love.'

'Which Barbara?'

'Mine. Ours.'

'Well, it's quite normal at her age. Who with?'

'Robin Trumpington, I suppose.'

'He'd be quite suitable.'

'For heaven's sake, Angie, she's only a child.'

'I fell in love at her age.'

'And a nice mess that turned out. It's someone after my money.'

'My money.'

'I've always regarded it as mine. I shan't let her have a penny. Not till I'm dead anyway.'

'You look half dead now.'

'I've never felt better. You simply haven't got used to my new appearance.'

'You're very shaky.'

'"Disembodied" is the word. Perhaps I need a drink. In fact I know I do. This whole business of Babs has come as a shock – at a most unsuitable time. I might go and see the booby doctor.'

And, later, he set off along the corridor which led to the administrative office. He set off but had hardly hobbled six short paces when his newly sharpened conscience stabbed him. Was this the etherealized, the reborn, Basil slinking off like a schoolboy to seek the permission of a booby doctor for a simple adult indulgence? He turned aside and made for the gym.

There he found two large ladies in bathing-dresses sitting astride a low horse. They swallowed hastily and brushed crumbs from their lips. A rubbery young man in vest and shorts addressed him sternly: 'One moment, sir. You can't come in here without an appointment.'

'My visit is unprofessional,' said Basil. 'I want a word with you.'

The young man looked doubtful. Basil drew his note case from his pocket and tapped it on the knob of his cane.

'Well, ladies, I think that finishes the work-out for this morning. We're getting along very nicely. We mustn't expect immediate results you know. Same routine tomorrow.' He replaced the lid on a small enamelled bin. The ladies looked hungrily at it but went in peace.

'Whisky,' said Basil.

'Whisky? Why, I couldn't give you such a thing even if I had it. It would be as much as my job's worth.'

'I should think it is precisely what your job is worth.'

'I don't quite follow, sir.'

'My wife had grouse pie this morning.'

He was a cheeky young man much admired in his own milieu for his bounce. He was not abashed. A horrible smirk of complicity passed over his face. 'It wasn't really grouse,' he said. 'Just a stale liver pâté the grocer had. They get so famished here they don't care what they're eating, the poor creatures.'

'Don't talk about my wife in those terms,' said Basil, adding: 'I shall know what I'm drinking, at a pound a snort.'

'I haven't any whisky, honest. There may be a drop of brandy in the first-aid cupboard.'

'Let's look at it.'

It was of a reputable brand. Basil took two snorts. He gasped. Tears came to his eyes. He felt for support on the wall-bars beside him. For a moment he feared nausea. Then a great warmth and elation were kindled inside him. This was youth indeed; childhood no less. Thus he had been exalted in his first furtive swigging in his father's pantry. He had drunk as much brandy as this twice a day, most days of his adult life, after a variety of preliminary potations, and had felt merely a slight heaviness. Now in his etherealized condition he was, as it were, raised from the earth, held aloft and then lightly deposited; a mystical experience as though on Ganges bank or a spur of the Himalayas.

There was a mat near his feet, thick, padded, bed-like. Here he subsided and lay in ecstasy; quite outside his body, high and happy, his spirit soared; he shut his eyes.

'You can't stay here, sir. I've got to lock up.'

'Don't worry,' said Basil. 'I'm not here.'

The gymnast was very strong; it was a light task to hoist Basil on one of the trollies which in various sizes were part of the equipment of the sanatorium, and thus recumbent, dazed but not totally insensible, smoothly propelled up the main corridor, he was met by the presiding doctor.

'What have you there, sergeant?'

'Couldn't say at all. Never saw the gentleman before.'

'It looks like Mr Seal. Where did you find him?'

'He just walked into the gym, sir, looking rather queer and suddenly he passed out.'

'Gave you a queer look? Yes.'

'He rolls through the air with the greatest of ease, that darling young man on the flying trapeze,' Basil chanted with some faint semblance of tune in his voice.

'Been overdoing it a bit, sir, I wouldn't wonder.'

'You might be right, sergeant. You had better leave him now. The female staff can take over. Ah, Sister Gamage, Mr Seal needs help in getting to his room. I think the regime has proved too strenuous for him. You may administer an ounce of brandy. I will come and examine him later.'

But when he repaired to Basil's room he found his patient deeply sleeping.

He stood by the bed, gazing at his patient. There was an expression of peculiar innocence on the shrunken face. But the physician knew better.

'I will see him in the morning,' he said and then went to

instruct his secretary to inform the previous applicants that two vacancies had unexpectedly occurred.

III

'The sack, the push, the boot. I've got to be out of the place in an hour.'

'Oh Basil, that *is* like old times, isn't it?'

'Only deep psychoanalysis can help me, he says, and in my present condition I am a danger to his institution.'

'Where shall we go? Hill Street's locked up. There won't be anyone there until Monday.'

'The odd thing is I have no hangover.'

'Still ethereal?'

'Precisely. I suppose it means an hotel.'

'You might telephone to Barbara and tell her to join us. She said she was keen to leave.'

But when Angela telephoned to her sister-in-law, she heard: 'But isn't Barbara with you in London? She told me yesterday you'd sent for her. She went up by the afternoon train.'

'D'you think she can have gone to that young man?'

'I bet she has.'

'Ought I to tell Basil?'

'Keep it quiet.'

'I consider it very selfish of her. Basil isn't at all in good shape. He'll have a fit if he finds out. He had a sort of fit yesterday.'

'Poor Basil. He may never know.'

Basil and Angela settled their enormous bill. Their car was brought round to the front. The chauffeur drove. Angela sat beside Basil who huddled beside her occasionally crooning ill-remembered snatches of 'the daring young man on the flying trapeze'. As they approached London they met all the outgoing Friday traffic. Their own way was clear. At the hotel Basil went straight to bed – 'I don't feel I shall ever want another bath as long as I live,' he said – and Angela ordered a light meal for him of oysters and stout. By dusk he had rallied enough to smoke a cigar.

Next morning he was up early and spoke of going to his club.

'That dingy one?'

'Heavens no, Bellamy's. But I don't suppose there'll be many chaps there on a Saturday morning.'

There was no one. The barman shook him up an egg with port and brandy. Then, with the intention of collecting some books, he took a taxi to Hill Street. It was not yet eleven o'clock. He let himself into what should have been the empty and silent house. Music came from the room on the ground floor where small parties congregated before luncheon and dinner. It was a dark room, hung with tapestry and furnished with Bühl. There he found his daughter, dressed in pyjamas and one of her mother's fur coats, seated on the floor with her face caressing a transistor radio. Behind her in the fireplace large lumps of coal lay on the ashes of the sticks and paper which had failed to kindle them.

'Darling Pobble, never more welcome. I didn't expect you till Monday and I should have been dead by then. I can't make out how the central heating works. I thought the whole point of it was it just turned on and didn't need a man. Can't get the fire to burn. And don't start: "Babs, what are you doing here?" I'm freezing, that's what.'

'Turn that damn thing off.'

In the silence Barbara regarded her father more intently. 'Darling, what have they been doing to you? You aren't yourself at all. You're tottering. Not my fine stout Pobble at all. Sit down at once. Poor Pobble, all shrunk like a mummy. Beasts!'

Basil sat and Barbara wriggled round until her chin rested on his knees. 'Famine baby,' she said. Star-sapphire eyes in the child-like face under black touselled hair gazed deep into star-sapphire eyes sunk in empty pouches. 'Belsen atrocity,' she added fondly. 'Wraith. Skeleton-man. Dear dug-up corpse.'

'Enough of this flattery. Explain yourself.'

'I told you I was bored. You know what Malfrey's like as well as I do. Oh the hell of the National Trust. It's not so bad in the summer with the charabancs. Now it's only French art experts – half a dozen a week, and all the rooms still full of oilcloth promenades and rope barriers and Aunt Barbara in the flat over the stables and those ridiculous Sothills in the bachelors' wing and the height of excitement a pheasant shoot with lunch in the hut and then nothing to eat except pheasant and . . . Well, I registered a formal complaint, didn't I?, but you were too busy starving to pay any attention, and if your only, adored daughter's happiness doesn't count for more than senile vanity . . .' she paused, exhausted.

'There's more to it than that.'

'There is *something* else.'

'What?'

'Now, Pobble, you have to take this calmly. For your own good, not for mine. I'm used to violence, God knows. If you had been poor the police would have been after you for the way you've knocked me about all these years. I can take it; but you, Pobble, you are at an age when it might be dangerous. So keep quite calm and I'll tell you. I'm engaged to be married.'

It was not a shock; it was not a surprise. It was what Basil had expected. 'Rot,' he said.

'I happen to be in love. You must know what that means. You must have been in love once – with mummy or someone.'

'Rot. And dammit, Babs, don't blub. If you think you're old enough to be in love, you're old enough not to blub.'

'That's a silly thing to say. It's being in love makes me blub. You don't realize. Apart from being perfect and frightfully funny he's an artistic genius and everyone's after him and I'm jolly lucky to have got him and you'll love him too once you know him if only you won't be stuck-up and we got engaged on the telephone so I came up and he was out so for all I know someone else *has* got him and I almost died of cold and now you come in looking more like a vampire than a papa and start saying "rot".'

She pressed her face on his thigh and wept.

After a time Basil said: 'What makes you think Robin paints?'

'Robin? Robin Trumpington? You don't imagine I'm engaged to *Robin*, do you? He's got a girl of his own he's mad about. You don't know much about what goes on, do you, Pobble? If it's only Robin you object to, everything's all right.'

'Well, who the hell do you think you are engaged to?'

'Charles of course.'

'Charles à Court. Never heard of him.'

'Don't pretend to be deaf. You know perfectly well who I mean. You met him here the other evening only I don't think you really took him in.'

'*Albright*,' said Basil. It was evidence of the beneficial effect of the sanatorium that he did not turn purple in the face, did not gobble. He merely asked quietly: 'Have you been to bed with this man?'

'Not to *bed*.'

'Have you slept with him?'

'Oh, no *sleep*.'

'You know what I mean. Have you had sexual intercourse with him?'

'Well, perhaps; not in bed; on the floor and wide awake you *might* call it intercourse, I suppose.'

'Come clean, Babs. Are you a virgin?'

'It's not a thing any girl likes having said about her, but I think I am.'

'*Think?*'

'Well, I suppose so. Yes, really. But we can soon change all that. Charles is set on marriage, bless him. He says it's easier to get married to girls if they're virgins. I can't think why. I don't mean a big wedding. Charles is very unsocial and he's an orphan, no father, no mother, and his relations don't like him, so we'll just be married quietly in a day or two and then I thought if you and mummy don't want it we might go to the house in Bermuda. We shan't be any trouble to you at all, really. If you want to go to Bermuda, we'll settle for Venice, but Charles says that's a bit square and getting cold in November, so Bermuda will really be better.'

'Has it occurred to either of you that you need my permission to marry?'

'Now don't get legal, Pobble. You know I love you far too much ever to do anything you wouldn't like.'

'You'd better get dressed and go round to your mother at Claridges.'

'Can't get dressed. No hot water.'

'Have a bath there. I had better see this young man.'

'He's coming here at twelve.'

'I'll wait for him.'

'You'll freeze.'

'Get up and get out.'

There followed one of those scuffles that persisted between father and daughter even in her eighteenth year which ended in her propulsion, yelping.

Basil sat and waited. The bell could not be heard in the ante-room. He sat in the window and watched the doorstep, saw a taxi draw up and Barbara enter it, still in pyjamas and fur coat, carrying a small case. Later he saw his enemy strolling confidently from Berkeley Square. Basil opened the door.

'You did not expect to see me?'

'No, but I'm very glad to. We've a lot to discuss.'

They went together to the ante-room. The young man was less bizarre in costume than on their previous meeting but his hair was as copious and his beard proclaimed his chosen, deleterious status. They surveyed one another in silence. Then Basil said: 'Lord Pastmaster's shirts are too big for you.'

It was a weak opening

'It's not a thing I should have brought up if you hadn't,' said Albright, 'but *all* your clothes look too big for *you*.'

Basil covered his defeat by lighting a cigar.

'Barbara tells me you've been to that sanatorium in Kent,' continued the young man easily; 'there's a new place, you know, much better, in Sussex.'

Basil was conscious of quickening recognition. Some faint, odious inkling of kinship; had he not once, in years far gone by, known someone who had spoken in this way to his elders? He drew deeply on his cigar and studied Albright. The eyes, the whole face seemed remotely familiar; the reflection of a reflection seen long ago in shaving-mirrors.

'Barbara tells me you have proposed marriage to her.'

'Well, *she* actually popped the question. I was glad to accept.'

'You are Clarence Albright's son?'

'Yes, did you know him? I barely did. I hear he was rather awful. If you want to be genealogical, I have an uncle who is a duke. But I barely know him either.'

'And you are a painter?'

'Did Barbara tell you that?'

'She said you were an artistic genius.'

'She's a loyal little thing. She must mean my music.'

'You compose?'

'I improvise sometimes. I play the guitar.'

'Professionally?'

'Sometimes – in coffee bars, you know.'

'I do not know, I'm afraid. And you make a living by it?'

'Not what *you* would call a living.'

'May I ask, then, how you propose to support my daughter?'

'Oh that doesn't come into it. It's the other way round. I'm doing what you did, marrying money. Now I know what's in your mind. "Buy him off," you think. I assure you that won't work. Barbara is infatuated with me and, if it's not egotistical to mention it, I am with her. I'm sure you won't want one of those "Gretna Green Romances" and press photographers following you about. Besides, Barbara doesn't want to be a nuisance to you. She's a loyal girl, as we've already remarked. The whole thing can be settled calmly. Think of the taxes your wife will save by a good solid marriage settlement. It will make no appreciable difference to your own allowance.'

And still Basil sat steady, unmoved by any tremor of that volcanic senility which a fortnight ago would have exploded in scalding, blinding showers. He was doing badly in this first encounter which he had too lightly provoked. He must take thought and plan. He was not at the height of his powers. He had been prostrate yesterday. Today he was finding his strength. Tomorrow experience would conquer. This was a worthy antagonist and he felt something of the exultation which a brave of the sixteenth century might have felt when in a brawl he suddenly recognized in the clash of blades a worthy swordsman.

'Barbara's mother has the best financial advice,' he said.

'By the way, where is Barbara? She arranged to meet me here.'

'She's having a bath in Claridges.'

'I ought to go over and see her. I'm taking her out to lunch. You couldn't lend me a fiver, could you?'

'Yes,' said Basil. 'Certainly.'

If Albright had known him better he would have taken alarm at this urbanity. All he thought was: 'Old crusty's a much softer job than anyone told me.' And Basil thought: 'I hope he spends it all on luncheon. That bank-note is all he will ever get. He deserved better.'

IV

Sonia Trumpington had never remarried. She shared a flat with her son Robin but saw little of him. Mostly she spent her day alone with her needlework and in correspondence connected with one or two charitable organizations with which, in age, she had become involved. She was sewing when Basil sought her out after luncheon (oysters again, two dozen this time with a pint of champagne – his strength waxed hourly) and she continued to stitch at the framed grospoint while he confided his problem to her.

'Yes, I've met Charles Albright. He's rather a friend of Robin's.'

'Then perhaps you can tell me what Barbara sees in him.'

'Why, *you*, of course,' said Sonia. 'Haven't you noticed? He's the dead spit – looks, character, manner, everything.'

'Looks? Character? Manner? Sonia you're raving.'

'Oh, not as you are now, not even after your cure. Don't you remember at all what you were like at his age?'

'But he's a monster.'

'So were you, darling. Have you quite forgotten? It's all as clear as clear to me. You Seals are so incestuous. Why do you suppose you got keen on Barbara? Because she's just like Barbara Sothill. Why is Barbara keen on Charles? Because he's *you*.'

Basil considered this proposition with his newly resharpened wits.

'That beard.'

'I've seen you with a beard.'

'That was after I came back from the Arctic and I never played the guitar in my life,' he said.

'Does Charles play the guitar? First I've heard of it. He does all sorts of things – just as you did.'

'I wish you wouldn't keep bringing me into it.'

'Have you quite forgotten what you were like? Have a look at some of my old albums.'

Like most of her generation Sonia had in youth filled large volumes with press-cuttings and photographs of herself and her friends. They lay now in a shabby heap in a corner of the room.

'That's Peter's twenty-firster at King's Thursday. First time I met you, I think. Certainly the first time I met Alastair. He was Margot's boy-friend then, remember? She was jolly glad to be rid of him . . . That's my marriage. I bet you were there.' She turned the pages from the posed groups of bride, bridegroom and bridesmaids to the snapshots taken at the gates of St Margaret's. 'Yes, here you are.'

'No beard. Perfectly properly dressed.'

'Yes, there are more incriminating ones later. Look at that . . . and that.'

They opened successive volumes. Basil appeared often.

'I don't think any of them very good likenesses,' said Basil stiffly. 'I'd just come back from the Spanish front there – of course I look a bit untidy.'

'It's not clothes we're talking about. Look at your expression.'

'Light in my eyes,' said Basil.

'1937. That's another party at King's Thursday.'

'What a ghastly thing facetious photographs are. What on earth am I doing with that girl?'

'Throwing her in the lake. I remember the incident now. I took the photograph.'

'Who?'

'I've no idea. Perhaps it says on the back. Just "Basil and Betty". She must have been much younger than us, not our kind at all. I've got an idea she was the daughter of some duke or other. The Stayles – that's who she was.'

Basil studied the picture and shuddered. 'What can have induced me to behave like that?'

'Youthful high spirits.'

'I was thirty-four, God help me. She's very plain.'

'I'll tell you who she is – was. Charles Albright's mother. That's an odd coincidence if you like. Let's look her up and make sure.'

She found a *Peerage* and read: 'Here we are. Fifth daughter of the late duke. Elizabeth Ermyntrude Alexandra, for whom H. R. H. The Duke of Connaught stood sponsor. Born 1920. Married 1940 Clarence Albright, killed in action 1943. Leaving issue. Died 1956. I remember hearing about it – cancer, very young. That's Charles, that issue.'

Basil gazed long at the photograph. The girl was plump and, it seemed, wriggling; annoyed rather than amused by the horseplay. 'How one forgets. I suppose she was quite a friend of mine once.'

'No, no. She was just someone Margot produced for Peter.'

Basil's imagination, once so fertile of mischief, lately so dormant, began now, in his hour of need, to quicken and stir.

'That photograph has given me an idea.'

'Basil, you've got that old villainous look. What are you up to?'

'Just an idea.'

'You're not going to throw Barbara into the Serpentine.'

'Something not unlike it,' he said.

'Let us go and sit by the Serpentine,' said Basil to his daughter that afternoon.

'Won't it be rather cold?'

'It will be quiet. Wrap up well. I have to talk to you seriously.'

'Good temper?'

'Never better.'

'Why not talk here?'

'Your mother may come in. What I have to say doesn't concern her.'

'It's about me and Charles, I bet.'

'Certainly.'

'Not a scolding?'

'Far from it. Warm fatherly sympathy.'

'It's worth being frozen for that.'

They did not speak in the car. Basil sent it away, saying they would find their own way back. At that chilly tea-time, with the leaves dry and falling, there was no difficulty in finding an empty seat. The light was soft; it was one of the days when London seems like Dublin.

'Charles said he'd talked to you. He wasn't sure you loved him.'

'I love him.'

'Oh, *Pobble*.'

'He did not play the guitar but I recognized his genius.'

'Oh, Pobble, what are you up to?'

'Just what Sonia asked.' Basil leaned his chin on the knob of his cane. 'You know, Babs, that all I want is your happiness.'

'This doesn't sound at all like you. You've got some sly scheme.'

'Far from it. You must never tell him or your mother what I am about to say. Charles's parents are dead so they are not affected. I knew his mother very well; perhaps he doesn't know how well. People often wondered why she married Albright. It was a blitz marriage, you know, while he was on leave and there were air raids every night. It was when I was first out of hospital, before I married your mother.'

'Darling Pobble, it's very cold here and I don't quite see what all this past history has to do with me and Charles.'

'It began,' said Basil inexorably, 'when – what was her name? – Betty was younger than you are now. I threw her into the lake at King's Thursday.'

'What began?'

'Betty's passion for me. Funny what excites a young girl – with you a guitar, with Betty a ducking.'

'Well, I think that's rather romantic. It sort of brings you and Charles closer.'

'Very close indeed. It was more than romantic. She was too young at the beginning – just a girlish crush. I thought she would get over it. Then, when I was wounded, she took to visiting me every day in hospital and the first day I came out – you won't be able to understand the sort of exhilaration a man feels at a time like that, or the appeal lameness has for some women, or the sense of general irresponsibility we all had during the blitz – I'm not trying to excuse myself. I was not the first man. She had grown up since the splash in the lake. It only lasted a week. Strictly perhaps I should have married her, but I was less strict in those days. I married your mother instead. You can't complain about that. If I hadn't, you wouldn't exist. Betty had to look elsewhere and fortunately that ass Albright turned up in the nick. Yes, Charles is your brother, so how could I help loving him?'

Soundlessly Barbara rose from the seat and sped through the twilight, stumbled on her stiletto heels across the sand of the Row, disappeared behind the statuary through Edinburgh Gate. Basil at his own pace followed. He stopped a taxi, kept it waiting at the kerb while he searched Bellamy's vainly for a friendly face, drank another egg-nog at the bar, went on towards Claridges.

'What on earth's happened to Barbara?' Angela asked. 'She

came in with a face of tragedy, didn't speak and now she's locked herself in your bedroom.'

'I think she's had a row with that fellow she was keen on. What was his name? Albright. A good thing really, a likeable fellow but not at all suitable. I daresay Babs needs a change of scene. Angie, if it suits you, I think we might all three of us go to Bermuda tomorrow.'

'Can we get tickets?'

'I have them already. I stopped at the travel office on my way from Sonia's. I don't imagine Babs will want much dinner tonight. She's best left alone at the moment. I feel I could manage a square meal. We might have it downstairs.'

Details of First Publication

'Work Suspended: Two Chapters of an Unfinished Novel', Chapman & Hall, London, 1943. This is a revised version of the text; the original version appeared in 1942.

'Charles Ryder's Schooldays', *The Times Literary Supplement*, 5 March 1982, with an introduction by Micheal Sissons.

'Scott-King's Modern Europe' (abridged version), *Cornhill*, summer 1947, and as 'A Sojourn in Neutralia', *Heart's International* combined with *Cosmopolitan*, November 1947.

'Tactical Exercise', *Strand*, March 1947, and as 'The Wish', *Good Housekeeping*, New York, March 1947.

'Compassion', *The Month*, August 1949. First appearing as 'The Major Intervenes', *The Atlantic*, July 1949. ('Compassion' is an expansion of this text.)

'Love Among the Ruins: A Romance of the Near Future', Chapman & Hall, London, 1953.

'Basil Seal Rides Again or The Rake's Regress', Chapman & Hall, London, 1963.